By Jenny Colgan

Mure

The Summer Seaside Kitchen
A Very Distant Shore (*novella*)
The Endless Beach
An Island Christmas
Christmas at the Island Hotel

Kirrinfief

The Bookshop on the Corner
(was *The Little Shop of Happy
Ever After*)
The Bookshop on the Shore
Five Hundred Miles from You

Little Beach Street Bakery

Little Beach Street Bakery
Summer at Little Beach
Street Bakery
Christmas at Little Beach
Street Bakery

Sweetshop of Dreams

Welcome to Rosie Hopkins'
Sweetshop of Dreams
Christmas at Rosie
Hopkins' Sweetshop
The Christmas Surprise

Cupcake Café

Meet Me at the Cupcake Café
Christmas at the Cupcake Café

The Little School by the Sea

Class
Rules
Lessons

Other Fiction

West End Girls
Operation Sunshine
Diamonds Are a Girl's
Best Friend
The Good, the Bad and
the Dumped
The Loveliest Chocolate
Shop in Paris
Amanda's Wedding
Talking to Addison
Looking for Andrew McCarthy
Working Wonders
Do You Remember the
First Time?
Where Have All the
Boys Gone?

By Jenny T. Colgan

Resistance Is Futile
Spandex and the City

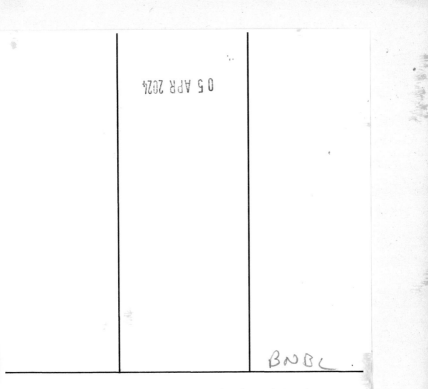

0 5 APR 2024

BNBC

Please return/renew this item by the last date shown
on this label, or on your self-service receipt.

To renew this item, visit **www.librarieswest.org.uk**
or contact your library

Your borrower number and PIN are required.

Libraries**West**

Praise for Jenny Colgan

'This funny, sweet story is Jenny
Colgan at her absolute best'
Heat

'She is very, very funny'
Express

'A delicious comedy'
Red

'Fast-paced, funny, poignant and well observed'
Daily Mail

'Sweeter than a bag of jelly beans ...
had us eating up every page'
Cosmopolitan

'Will make you feel warm inside – it
makes a fab Mother's Day gift'
Closer

'Chick-lit with an ethical kick'
Mirror

Jenny Colgan is the author of numerous *Sunday Times* bestselling novels and has won various awards for her writing, including the Melissa Nathan Award for Comedy Romance, the RNA Romantic Novel of the Year Award and the RNA Romantic Comedy Novel of the Year Award. Her books have sold more than five million copies worldwide and in 2015 she was inducted into the Love Stories Hall of Fame. Jenny is married with three children and lives in Scotland.

For more about Jenny, visit her website and her Facebook page, or follow her on Twitter and Instagram.
Twitter: @jennycolgan
Facebook: jennycolganbooks
Instagram: jennycolganbooks

JENNY COLGAN

five hundred miles from you

sphere

SPHERE

First published in Great Britain in 2020 by Sphere
This paperback edition published by Sphere in 2021

1 3 5 7 9 10 8 6 4 2

Copyright © 2020 by Jenny Colgan

The moral right of the author has been asserted.

'I'm Gonna Be (500 Miles)': Words and music by Craig Morris Reid and
Charles Stobo Reid, Zoo Music Ltd (PRS) by kind permission.
All rights administered by Warner Chappell Music Ltd.

'Sunshine on Leith': Words and music by Charles Stobo Reid and
Craig Morris Reid, Zoo Music Ltd (PRS) by kind permission.
All rights administered by Warner Chappell Music Ltd.

A CIP catalogue record for this book is available from the British Library.

ISBN 978-0-7515-7202-5

Typeset in Caslon by M Rules
Printed and bound in Great Britain by Clays Ltd, Elcograf S.p.A.

Papers used by Sphere are from well-managed forests
and other responsible sources.

Sphere
An imprint of
Little, Brown Book Group
Carmelite House
50 Victoria Embankment
London EC4Y 0DZ

An Hachette UK Company
www.hachette.co.uk

www.littlebrown.co.uk

To everyone who has their organ donor card

There are two teachers in the school,
One has a gentle voice and low,
And smiles upon her scholars, as
She softly passes to and fro.
Her name is Love; 'tis very plain
She shuns the sharper teacher, Pain.

Or so I sometimes think; and then,
At other times, they meet and kiss,
And look so strangely like, that I
Am puzzled to tell how this is,
Or whence the change which makes it vain
To guess if it be – Love or Pain

Susan Coolidge, from 'In School', *What Katy Did*

PART ONE

Chapter One

It should have started with ominous dark crows; great murmurations and flutterings; bad omens taking to the sky; great storm clouds rolling in; clocks striking thirteen.

In fact, it started with an extremely undignified argument with an old lady over a bar of chocolate.

'But you have a bar of Dairy Milk right there in your hand!'

Mrs Marks looked up at her, heavy and glowering, from the cracked brown leather sofa.

'I do not!'

'Behind your back!'

Like a tiny child, Mrs Marks refused to remove her hand, just shook her head mutinously.

Lissa Westcott put down the medical equipment she'd been packing away and strode back into the centre of the room, exasperated.

'You thought I'd gone! You thought I was leaving the room and you were making a grab for a hidden Dairy Milk!'

Mrs Marks fixed her with beady eyes.

'What the bleedin' hell are you then, the chocolate police?'

'No. Yes!' said Lissa rather desperately. She held out her hand.

Mrs Marks finally handed the chocolate over. It was, in fact, a bar of Bournville.

'Ha!' said Mrs Marks.

Lissa looked at her.

Old Mrs Marks lived on the fourteenth floor of a South London tower block where the lifts were often broken. Her foot was gradually giving in to diabetes, and Lissa was trying her absolute hardest to save it. She glanced out from the dingy, fussy room with its dusty fake flowers everywhere, towards the beautiful views over the river to the north: the great towers of the City were glinting in the light, bright and beautiful, clean and full of money, like a vast array of glittering palaces, completely out of reach, less than two miles away.

'We've just been talking about your diet for twenty minutes!' she said to the poor woman, who was practically a shut-in, with only her daughter to visit her. Watching *EastEnders* with family bars of choccie was one of the few pleasures she had left, but it wasn't doing her any good.

'I don't want to have to be coming up here one day and finding you in a coma,' said Lissa as severely as she dared. Mrs Marks just laughed at her.

'Oh, don't you worry about me, duck. Whatever will be will be.'

'That's not how health care works!' said Lissa, glancing at her watch. She was due in Peckham in twenty minutes. Driving in London was an absolute fool's errand but she didn't have any choice; she couldn't carry drugs on the tube.

Lissa was an NPL: a nurse practitioner liaison. She followed up on hospital discharges who had trouble attending outpatients departments in the hope that they wouldn't become readmissions. Or, she said in her more cynical moments, she did half of what community nurses used to when they still had the budget, and half of what GPs used to do when they could still be arsed to leave the office. Originally trained as an A&E nurse, she loved her job – which involved rather fewer drunks spewing up on her than casualty did – particularly the bits of it when she got chocolate.

Her hopes, though, in Mrs Marks's case, were not at their highest.

'You're not exactly a sylph yourself,' said Mrs Marks.

'You sound like my mum,' complained Lissa, who had inherited her curvy frame from her mother, to said parent's alternately vocal or silent disappointment.

'You take it then,' said Mrs Marks grudgingly. Lissa made a face.

'I hate dark chocolate,' she said. But she took it anyway.

'Please,' she said again. 'Please. I'd hate them to admit you again. Next time you might lose your foot. Seriously.'

In response, Mrs Marks sighed and indicated the entire old brown three-piece suite. Lissa put her hands down the back of the cushions and found chocolate bars behind every single one.

'I'm donating them to a food bank,' she said. 'Do you want me to buy them off you?'

Mrs Marks waved her away.

'No,' she said. 'But if I do end up back in that place again, I'll blame you.'

'Deal,' said Lissa.

➤ ➤

It was chilly for early March as Lissa left the tall building, but the sun was shining behind a faint cloud of smog, and she could sense spring coming, somewhere on the horizon. She prayed, as she always did, that nobody would have seen the medical personnel sticker on her car and attempted to break into it in case she'd left any drugs in there. She also contemplated the new Korean barbecue place she was due to meet some friends in later. It looked good on Instagram, but this wasn't necessarily a good thing – sometimes quite the opposite if it was just full of people photographing cold food.

She noticed boys loitering in the stairwell, which was nothing unusual. It was hard to tell with some teenage boys whether they should be at school or not; they were so big these days. The best thing to do was keep her head down, hide her ringletty hair in a tight braid or a scarf and just keep moving past them. She remained profoundly glad of the unflattering green trousers she wore as part of her uniform that rendered her practically invisible.

These boys, however, weren't interested in her; they were arguing with one another. Just the normal teenage beefs, showing off, puffing out their chests with peacocks; a mix of races, tiny little wispy beards and moustaches, lanky legs and elbows too pointy, a strong smell of Lynx Africa and massive trainers the size of boats. It was slightly endearing in its way, watching them try to pretend they knew how to be men. But intimidating too, and she was about to give them a wide berth when she realised she recognised one of them. The fact made her wince. It was one of Ezra's cousins. Ezra, beautiful Ezra, whose graceful body and lovely face made him irresistible whenever he messaged her. Unfortunately, Ezra was well aware of this, which was why he felt obliged to spread himself pretty thinly all around South London. Every time he ghosted her, Lissa swore blind she'd never fall for it again. She was not much better at keeping that promise than she was about not eating Mrs Marks's leftover chocolate.

But she'd met Kai – by accident; Ezra had never introduced her to the rest of his family – down Brixton Market one morning when they were grabbing breakfast supplies. He was a bright, mouthy fifteen-year-old and should, Lissa thought with a sigh, really be in school. She wouldn't mention that.

'Kai!' She raised her hand.

Just as she did so, he turned to face her, his open mouth already starting to grin as he recognised her, and then, out of the blue on a chilly spring day, there was a sudden horrifying tear of an engine braking, a screech of brakes, a sudden glint in the sky as something was thrown, crashed down, and an intake of breath, and a sickening roar.

Chapter Two

Five hundred-odd miles north by north-west, in the small village of Kirrinfief, on the shores of Loch Ness, a cool March wind was blowing off the water, rippling the white tops of the little waves; and the clouds were hanging heavy off the tops of the purple mountains.

Cormac MacPherson, the town's NPL, glanced at his watch. Joan, the GP, had been over the other side of the moor tending to a hiatal hernia. In a human, Cormac assumed, although with Joan it could be hard to tell. She rarely travelled anywhere without being surrounded by a dust-cloud of wire fox terriers. So Jake, the local ambulance man, had corralled him in to help with a DNR on a very old lady. Jake knew Cormac could never say no to someone in distress and took wide advantage of his soft nature. They had sat with the family, made sure Edie was made as comfortable as possible to the end, in the little cottage and the bed she'd been born in ninety years before. As these things went, it had not been bad.

Now they were heading out for a well-deserved pint.

'Not a bad way to go,' said Jake philosophically as they headed down the cobbles, the air cool on their faces.

'Mmm,' said Cormac, glancing at his phone.

'Emer on you again?' Jake glanced over.

'Aw crap, she came over to make me a surprise dinner.'

'That's terrifying.'

'It's not terrifying,' protested Cormac weakly. 'It's sweet.'

'She must know you're out on calls all the time.'

'I said I was off duty.'

'Yeah, well,' said Jake, not looking remotely embarrassed. 'Might as well have a pint now though.'

Cormac glanced at his watch and shook his head just as a door opened from the little row of terraced houses (the sitting rooms came straight on to the street) they were passing.

'Jake! Cormac!' came a soft voice. 'I didnae want tae—'

'—bother the doctor,' finished Jake for them. 'Yup, we know.'

Chapter Three

A glint of something in the air. An incredible cacophony of sound.

She had only caught it briefly out of the corner of her eye while she had been watching the boys, gauging with that innate city sense whether or not they were dangerous or whether it was likely to escalate – Lissa had a good antenna for trouble, having mopped up the effects of so much of it – when she heard what sounded like a car speeding.

At first, she'd ignored it, but then she realised that rather than slowing down as it had rounded the corner into the estate, it had sped up. She had turned instinctively to where her own car was to make sure it didn't crash into it, and by the time she turned back, there was a huge howling screech from the engine as the vehicle mounted the kerb – deliberately mounted the kerb – and she saw … the only thing she saw was the glint of a phone, bouncing up in the air, spinning, catching the light, almost lovely, so slow …

And then everything happened so fast and there was a twist and a turn of a hideous shape; a thumping noise, horrible, wet and loud, reverberating around her head; something unthinkable following the phone, and the car's wheels, still moving, still revving, and the even harder, cracking noise as the huge, unthinkable shape hit the ground, lay there, twisted and misshapen. Lissa couldn't actually believe what she was looking at – it could not, absolutely could not be Kai – and she lifted up her eyes and found herself staring straight into the face of the driver, who was revving his engine while his mouth was drawn back in a snarl, or a leer, or something – something, thought Lissa, that through her incomprehension, through her panic she couldn't figure out, not at all, as there was screaming, something about 'staying out of Leaf Field' – and then the car sped on.

～ ⌒

There was a moment's silence, then the yelling started – disbelief, fury – and suddenly Lissa found herself clicking into action; found her training propping her up, propelling her forwards.

'I'm a nurse. Move away please – I can help.'

She expected to have to clear a path, but the other youths started yelling as they bounced upwards, shouting their heads off and dashing in screaming pursuit of the car.

'Dial 999!' Lissa shouted as she knelt down to examine Kai, pulling her phone out of her pocket. She had no idea if the lads could catch a car, and she was terrified they'd get hit again as there was only one way out of the estate – it would have to double back at some point – but she had to prioritise.

She looked down at the figure on the pavement, his head sideways on the stone, cigarette ends strewn in the gutter.

～ ⌒

'Can you hear me? Can you hear me, sweetheart?'

He was beautiful; so young. Lissa couldn't get over it. Not that that mattered; of course it didn't. It had absolutely nothing to do with it. But as she bent over him, desperately trying to save him while she finally, finally, heard the sirens she'd been waiting for, she couldn't get over the sheer heart-stopping beauty of the young soft skin, the curve of the neck, the dark hair. He was a child. She couldn't bear to think of how the family was going to take it. She cursed herself; her best friend had deleted Ezra's number from her phone, for her own good, so she couldn't even call him.

Even when the paramedics arrived, she didn't stop CPR. She carried on compressing, using the heels of her hands as they joined her, monitoring the oxygen, grabbing the adrenaline to shoot into his heart. She knew the paramedics; they trusted her and brought her along to hospital, Ashkan working with her, Kerry driving like a fiend as the blue lights screamed over the traffic. The overwhelmingly crowded London roads were completely clogged up, too stuffed full with lorries, vans, taxis and motorbikes, everything jammed up so tight they could barely find room to pull over to let an ambulance through.

The body suddenly contorted, bouncing in the air as Ashkan shouted 'Clear', and Lissa had jumped back instinctively, watching it twitch, wondering at the back of her mind if the policewoman back at the crime scene had started the weary business of figuring out who he was, had started the unbearable process of contacting his family.

Lissa let her training take over completely so she wouldn't let herself think any more about that, automatically putting the oxygen mask back on the boy's lips, still blue, injecting another shot of adrenaline and loading another pint of blood above his arm. All of them were desperately hoping he could hold on just until they got there. None of them spoke apart from the basic terms used in the attempt to resuscitate him, and while trying to get more blood into him than was leaving him.

Attempts to resuscitate are, even with the most extraordinarily advanced equipment in the world, much more unsuccessful than not. People see miracle returns from the dead on TV all the time so they don't see blood pumping out as fast as it could be pumped in, the lack of response in the pupils every time they're checked, the artificial twitching and stimulation of the young body, the barked commands and steady listening for independent breath and the hot chaos of it all. The ambulance swerved and howled through the thick London rush hour, only one of many screaming sirens, helicopters, despatches; pain and blood.

'The doctors are going to call it,' predicted Ashkan, glancing at his watch.

'You can't,' said Lissa.

Ashkan swore. The pointlessness of it. A hit and run that looked deliberate. On a child. He turned away and tuned into the police radio for a bit, then even half smiled.

'They got him,' he said grimly. 'The rest of the lads jumped on the car, wouldn't let it leave. Smashed in his windows. It must have felt like a zombie attack.'

It didn't register with Lissa at all.

'Carry on,' said Lissa fiercely, and redoubled her efforts, hissing into the boy's ear, 'More blood! Now! Come *on*, Kai! Wake up! WAKE UP!'

They arrived at Guy's Hospital where the ambulance doors were hurled open without ceremony and two porters and an A&E doctor jumped aboard.

'Move,' said the young doctor, who looked about nine.

'I'm not finished here,' said Lissa strongly as she continued to work the oxygen mask, shining light in Kai's eyes, checking for vitals.

'Yes, you are,' said the doctor. 'Let me look at him.'

'I can do it!' said Lissa. His face. His beautiful face. He was a child, a child asleep; still warm – or was that their efforts? – still sleeping, dreaming, losing his homework, wishing he was a footballer or a rock star.

'Stand back!'

'I CAN DO IT!'

Lissa didn't realise she had screamed; didn't realise everyone

12

had stopped to look at her, as Ashkan pulled her back gently, his face a mask of concern. The junior was already moving in, ignoring her.

'Step back.'

'I just ...'

It was unheard of for a nurse to defy a doctor in this way, even if this particular doctor looked like he'd drawn his moustache on with a biro that morning.

'Step back!'

But she couldn't. She could only stand as if she had absolutely no idea where she was, her arms reaching out uselessly, muttering 'Kai ... Kai ...' into thin air, still believing fervently, even as the doctor looked at his watch and shook his head, even as the blood was no longer dripping on the floor but was getting ready to pool, to congeal. The only thread to life was her.

'I can just ... try one more time ...'

'Get her out of here,' the young doctor was muttering as the porters tried to move the body onto the trolley. Several other medics appeared; Lissa recognised them despite her state of shock.

'Is next of kin here?' yelled one of them, and Lissa watched in horror at the tense, impersonal work of the transplant team.

'He's not even dead, you *vultures*,' she found herself screaming, and Ashkan really did move then, bodily removing her from inside the ambulance as she swore and pulled away. 'He's not even ...'

'I'm calling it,' said the doctor. 'Take him to the HDU.'

This was where they held transplant patients in a twilight world between life and death, just holding on for long enough to get the necessary signatures; to beg and plead that a life taken in vain would not be entirely in vain.

'15.38,' the doctor said. 'Can we move it fast?'

And his voice sounded so very, very weary.

'Hit and run incoming.'

Lissa collapsed onto the wet pavement and burst into tears, deep racking sobs. She was a professional; had been doing this

13

for four years, had seen road accidents, murders, every kind of horrible thing it was possible to see.

But it was a boy she knew, whose name was Kai who broke her, at just gone six-thirty, on a totally normal Tuesday.

Chapter Four

Ashkan tried to move her again.

'Mate,' he hissed under his breath. 'Mate, you have to move. They're going to haul you into the nutter room.'

There were no gentle words among the London Ambulance Service when it came to occupational health and the therapy unit. As far as paramedics were concerned, they were a gang of outlaws; pirates, screaming through the streets on a mission to save. Once you started wobbling the lip about it, like every other bugger would, well then. What was the point of you? Someone had to scrape people off the ground; someone had to hold the line. If you started crying and needing therapy and basket weaving, well, then you were no use. Nobody denied that it was a tough gig. That was the point of it. Paramedic teams relied on each other like little else.

Lissa was finding it impossible even to get up, even as the rain – when did that start? – was creeping down the collar of her heavy green jacket.

'Everything okay?' said Dev, the station controller, coming over, his kind face concerned, his glasses up around his bald head – they were always dangling around his neck, in his pockets or wherever he wouldn't be able to find them as soon as he needed them.

'Fine!' said Ashkan breezily. Lissa was aware they were there, that they were around, but somehow she couldn't concentrate, couldn't really focus on what they were asking of her or why she was sitting on a wet pavement. It was like her body didn't belong to her at all, that she was somewhere else and everything was going on without her, and the person sitting on the wet pavement didn't belong to her.

Dev looked concerned.

'Lissa? Were you on the hit and run?'

'She knew the lad,' said Ashkan. 'Bad bloody luck. Bit of a shock.'

Lissa couldn't even nod her head to respond. The police took her away for a statement which she gave, blindly. Ashkan waited for her, even though his shift had ended.

'Come on,' he said gently. 'Let's fill you up with tea.'

He frogmarched her towards the canteen, and Lissa let him, as if her legs were moving without any input from her at all, as if it was someone else.

The ground-floor canteen was quiet at this time of night. There were on-duty doctors keeping an eye on their bleeps and phones; one poor soul was fast asleep by a pot plant, his head looking uncomfortable on a wicker divider. There was also a clutch of porters playing cards and a few nervous-looking family members, as if they were not sure they were in the right place. The catering staff was gone for the day; it was just vending machines and hideous coffee in plastic cups with plastic stirrers. Ashkan brought back two teas and gave both of them to Lissa, pulling out his own flask of vegetable juice he'd squeezed himself. He took his health extremely seriously and usually headed straight for the gym at the end of his shift. Lissa had always teased him about how vain he was – he spent longer on his black shiny quiff than she did on her spirally curls, which were liable to turn into frizz in the wet, so she just got them out of the way in a tight ponytail. Plus, the fewer things that stood out about her physically, the less abuse she normally had to take from people not quite in their right minds by the time they showed up at A&E.

Lissa took the tea, feeling it burn her fingers through the thin plastic – Ashkan was fiercely opposed to single-use plastic, so his doing this was a clear sign of how concerned he was. She understood all of this – kind of – from a long, long way away. She could sense how worried he was. But somehow, she just didn't care. About anything. Because that boy was dead, and nothing mattered, and she felt half-dead herself.

The harsh strip lights felt purgatorial; the rain-spattered windows showed nothing but them reflected back to them. Lissa wondered, for a second, if they had all died in that ambulance. Her eye was drawn to the door as a bent-over woman entered, her face anxiously scanning everybody in the room. When she saw Lissa, she blinked. She couldn't have been much older than Lissa; was surely only in her thirties. But the expression on her face as she approached them was that of someone who'd lived a million lives.

Chapter Five

The woman was pulling her cardigan round herself, shuddering in the cold wind, the rain spattering from the south.

'Och, hello there, Cormac.'

'Hello there yourself, Mrs Coudrie.'

There was a pause.

'Could you just ...? I really don't want to bother the doctor.'

Cormac turned to Jake.

'Off you go,' he said. 'I can get myself home.'

Jake grimaced.

'Is it wee Islay?'

The woman nodded.

'Aye, aye, I'll come along,' said Jake with the resigned voice of a man who knows that their dream of a lovely foaming pint and possibly a quick flirt with Ginty McGhie has almost certainly just vanished for ever.

Chapter Six

Lissa lifted her eyes to the strange woman's. The lady's face was drawn with pain.

'Excuse me,' she said.

It was as if someone was speaking from far away. Lissa managed to blink.

'Yes?'

'I'm . . . I'm Kai Mitchell's mother?'

She said it so quaveringly, as if she wasn't completely sure whether she was or not, or whether she could still describe herself as such. Perhaps, Lissa found herself thinking. Perhaps she wasn't a mother any more. She must be Ezra's auntie.

Ashkan jumped up and offered her a chair.

'No,' she said gravely. 'No, thank you. I don't want to sit.'

She looked around the clinical chilly cafeteria.

'I'm not staying.'

Ashkan leant over.

'I am so, so sorry for your loss.'

She held up her hand.

'I'm not. I'm furious.'

Lissa nodded, something stirring within her.

'Me too,' she said. Ashkan shot her a warning glance that she ignored. Instead, she stood up.

'I'm furious too.'

'I just wanted to know,' said the woman. Behind her, at the door, stood a cluster of frightened, upset people; friends and family. Outside, Lissa knew, would be cameras, journalists; the media, desperate to spin another narrative of death.

In here, in this now silent room, was just a desolate mother.

'You have people helping you?' said Ashkan, looking over. 'You won't be alone?'

'Yes, I will,' said the woman. 'Were you with him?'

Ashkan indicated Lissa. 'She was with him the most. She did the most.'

'I didn't do enough,' said Lissa dully. If she'd been braver . . . If she'd realised the car was going too fast and shouted a warning . . . If she'd paid more attention . . .

'You need to know,' said Ashkan, for they couldn't be too careful these days, with lawyers hanging around like carrion crows. 'We did everything we could. We tried . . .'

But the woman wasn't listening to him. She had stepped forward and was taking Lissa's cold hands.

'You held his hand?'

Lissa nodded.

'This hand held his hand?'

'We tried,' said Lissa. And suddenly the two women were weeping in each other's arms, clinging on to one another. Ashkan was very unhappy. This wasn't appropriate, not at all. He wasn't sure what to do.

'I'm so sorry,' Lissa sobbed.

'Did he say anything?'

Lissa desperately wanted to say he had asked for her or said to tell her that he loved her. But she couldn't.

'He was . . . he was already so unwell,' she said. The woman nodded.

'Oh well,' she said. 'I'm glad . . . I'm glad someone was with him.'

Lissa nodded, wishing she could do more.

20

'All those people shouting at me,' said the woman, looking confused. 'You know, they want to chop him up! They were shouting at me! To chop him up! To cut up the body of my son! Before he's even cold! To cut bits off him!'

Ashkan winced. The transplant people were so desperate, so determined, and if Kai had good organs, oh, what a difference they would make to people.

Lissa seemed to snap out of herself a little then, and she straightened up.

'What did you say?' she asked.

Chapter Seven

The cottage was nearly identical to the one they'd just left, but furnished in a neutral, modern style, with a wood-burning stove and large prints of the children in black and white on the walls.

'Hello there, Islay,' Cormac said cheerily. 'Why aren't you asleep then?'

The tweenager was lying on the bed, blue and breathing heavily. Nonetheless, she attempted a grin for Cormac and a slightly flirtatious look for Jake, who was generally a hit with the ladies.

'Ach, you've looked better,' said Cormac, understating the case. The child had severe cardiomyopathy, and absolutely nothing seemed to be helping. The pacemaker was just the latest line in therapies that were failing her.

'I was thinking about maybe taking her in,' said her mother. They were extremely familiar with the hospital in Inverness.

'Well, let's have a listen,' said Cormac, pulling out his stethoscope. 'Those beta blockers not working on you, Islay?'

Trying to be helpful, the child shook her head just a fraction. How used to and how tired she was of the constant invasion, the constant questions. She looked so weary. Cormac felt his own heart sink. He'd left the Army to get away from the endless trauma cases, but this, in its own way, was just as difficult. Jake took her blood pressure and frowned.

'Well?' said Mrs Coudrie.

'I'll talk to Joan,' said Jake. 'This ...' He wrote down the number on a piece of paper, but Elspeth Coudrie already knew it by heart. ' ... is when we'd blue light. But I think we'll see what Joan has in her armoury.'

Cormac patted Islay on the hand. 'I know you want to stay up all night watching Mr Drake on the television.'

Islay rolled her eyes.

'It's Drake,' she wheezed. 'Not Mr Drake. And I don't like him anyway.'

'That's good,' said Cormac. 'He's too old for you.'

Islay tried to smile.

'But the best thing you could do is get some sleep,' said Cormac.

This wasn't true. The best – and rapidly turning into the only – thing she could do was to get a heart transplant. If only it were that simple.

'Imagine,' said Mrs Coudrie as Islay tried to settle into bed. 'Imagine waiting for someone else's child to die. Imagine hoping that they will.'

➤ ❮

'I don't know!' said Kai's mother, her voice hysterical. 'They were all yelling. And I just wanted to see my boy. He's my boy! And they wanted to chop him up.'

Lissa took the woman's hands.

'Did you say no?' she said softly.

'I didn't know what I was saying!' said the woman, looking up at her. 'Yes. I think I said no.'

'Do you know,' said Lissa very softly and quietly, as if trying to soothe a child. 'Do you know what would be the most wonderful thing you could do for Kai, and Kai could do for the world?'

'But they want to chop him up! My boy! My beautiful boy!'

'He'd be giving his life for others,' Lissa said. 'That . . . that is very beautiful.'

The woman gently touched a small crucifix around her neck.

'He could save a life,' repeated Lissa.

'But my beautiful boy . . .'

'Would be a hero. A hero beyond heroes. For ever.'

The tears didn't stop falling. Mrs Mitchell stood back.

'Is it too late to say yes?'

Lissa shook her head, even though she wasn't sure; even though it might be.

'Come, please,' she said. 'Please. Can you come with me? Quickly?'

And together they ran back through the long corridors, the devil at their heels, Lissa terrified they would be too late, that they would have unplugged their machines, gone on their way, their tragic work unsuccessful.

They clattered into the HDU, panting and terrified. Thank God, thank God, thank God for all the cuts, was the only thing she could think. The staff had taken a break; the shift who would come on and remove the tubes and make up the body had not yet been called in – and there he still was, still connected.

They both froze. Kai's mother made a sound, an animal noise, as if it was all happening over again.

'You can do this,' said Lissa. 'You can do this.'

The officious young transplant woman was summoned with a beep, and she came clattering down the corridor, the fussiness in her face transformed, suddenly, into something like hope.

'Mrs Mitchell?'

The woman nodded blankly. She sat by his bed again, stroking the beautiful, still-warm skin.

'She made me come back.'

'I didn't!' said Lissa. And looking at the boy, so close to sleeping – so close she could totally understand the instinctive horror at cutting him up, parcelling him out and using him for parts.

'Give me the thing to sign,' said Mrs Mitchell. 'Quickly please. I don't want to change my mind again.'

The nurse brought the paperwork over.

'You have to understand—'

'That it's binding, yes, yes, I know that. Quick, I said!'

'No,' said the transplant nurse, straightening up. 'I just really want you to understand. What you are doing is the bravest, the most wonderful thing you can do.'

Mrs Mitchell stared at her, her mouth hanging open.

'You sound,' she said, 'like you want me to be *pleased*.'

Chapter Eight

Kim-Ange was up and waiting for Lissa. She helped her friend pull off her clothes, take out her contacts, put on her thick black-rimmed glasses and get into her tracksuit bottoms. Lissa couldn't deny being pleased to see her. Living in the nurses' home was hardly the lap of luxury – it was a grimy old sixties block near the hospital – but it was still much cheaper than trying to rent privately in London, or even getting the train in every day from where her parents lived in Hertfordshire, and it had the added benefit, even if it was noisy and the showers were peeling and the kitchens got very grim, of there always being someone to talk to if you'd had a bad day. A really, really, really bad day.

Kim-Ange had her hands up.

'I know,' she said, her face a mask of sadness. She was holding up a bottle of something. That was the good thing and bad thing about nurses' homes; word got around.

'It was Ezra's . . .'

'I know that too.' Kim-Ange swallowed. 'He's been seeing Yasmin.'

'Ah,' said Lissa, even in her exhaustion and misery registering that Ezra had been spreading himself round the exact same place she actually lived.

She felt utterly hollow inside.

Kim-Ange waved a bottle of some mysterious plum-coloured substance.

'Come try this.'

Ever since she'd found an old cocktail cabinet in a skip which she'd hoiked home single-handedly, Kim-Ange had been on a mission to invent something new, which meant experimenting with a lot of things that were disgusting. Lissa didn't care that evening though.

'So how bad are you feeling about it?' said Kim-Ange, eyeing her shrewdly. 'Tracksuit bottoms bad? I mean, you know other people can see you?'

Kim-Ange had extremely high sartorial standards. She herself was wearing a long pink and red nightdress, matching robe, marabou slippers and a full face of make-up.

'Yes,' said Lissa. 'It was a hit and run. Possibly deliberate. Fifteen years old.'

'The way they talked about it on the news,' said Kim-Ange. 'As if, you know, what do you expect.' She sighed.

Lissa sighed. 'Give me the purple elixir of joy and/or misery then,' she said, holding out her tooth mug for Kim-Ange to fill up.

'Oh my God, that's revolting,' said Lissa, collapsing onto her bed. Then she took another sip. 'Still bad.'

There was a pause and she tried again.

'Okay, now it's not so bad.'

'There we are,' said Kim-Ange, pleased. 'A three-sipper. One of my best yet!' and she started absent-mindedly folding Lissa's clothes.

'They're going to call me in too,' said Lissa after a while. 'Disciplinary, I think. I didn't get out of the way of the doctors. I messed up with the transplant protocol.'

'You stopped a transplant?!'

'No, I made one happen.'

'Oh, that is terrible.' Kim-Ange snorted sarcastically. 'And don't tell me, did you have a baby doctor who didn't know his arse from his elbow and couldn't tap a vein in either of them?'

'No, I crossed the line,' said Lissa.

'Thank God there's such a plethora of highly trained paramedical staff they could fill your job from,' said Kim-Ange, looking mischievous. Lissa half smiled.

'How short are they at the moment?'

'Four grade eights,' said Lissa.

'Haha,' said Kim-Ange. 'They'll never get rid of you. I mean, seriously. What else did you do? Did you have full sex in the ambulance?'

'KIM-ANGE!'

'I'll take that as a maybe.'

'No!'

'Did you steal the car afterwards?'

Lissa bit her lip.

'Stop it.'

'No, seriously, I am trying to work out ways they'd actually let you go. Did you make the ambulance stop at the KFC drive-through on the way to the hospital?'

'No.'

'There you go then. It'll be a telling-off.'

'I hate those too.'

Kim-Ange rolled her eyes. 'That's right, terrifying NHS management sitting on their fat arses ticking boxes all day. They are pretty tough and scary, right enough. I heard they don't even cry when they get a papercut.'

'Tell me about your day,' said Lissa, changing the subject. 'Hang on, didn't you have a date tonight?'

Kim-Ange approached Tinder with more or less as much tenacity as her job in cardiology.

'Hmm . . .' said Kim-Ange.

'Oh no!'

Lissa scrolled down her phone.

'But look at you on Insta! You look amazing!'

'I do,' said Kim-Ange.

Lissa looked at her, then back at the picture, then up at Kim-Ange again. 'Stop doing that!'

'What?' said Kim-Ange innocently.

'Giving yourself a waist. It looks really weird.'

'Beautiful weird?'

'I'm taking Facetune off your phone. You have gone *too far*. You look like a shark has bitten a chunk out of you.'

'Piss off!'

'You're beautiful as you are,' said Lissa, and Kim-Ange sighed.

'So, don't tell me. He was a shark-bite fetishist and then you turned up *without* a chunk out of you?'

'No,' said Kim-Ange. 'He just kept going on and on about kimchee.'

'Oh, you're kidding,' said Lissa. 'Did you tell him you're from Margate?'

'Yup. That's when he started telling me I really ought to get to know my own culture.'

Lissa laughed and rolled over on the bed, stuffing her pillow on her face. 'NOOOOO! "Know your culture" bro strikes again! Nooooo!'

Kim-Ange checked her waist in the mirror and breathed in, quite hard.

'What else did he say?' said Lissa from behind the pillow.

'Oh! He went to Cambodia on his gap year.'

'So?' Lissa removed the pillow.

'So! Obviously, I would want to hear *all about that*!'

Lissa screwed up her face, then pulled up her phone.

'Oh well. Let's see what everyone else is up to.'

'You mean, let's see where everyone else is face-tuning themselves?'

'And Lip Filler Watch.'

'On it,' said Kim-Ange, and she refilled their glasses with the filthy purple alcohol and they sat down and scrolled through the absurdly over-filtered pictures of everyone they'd ever known, and then for good measure made their own ridiculously over-filtered, face-tuned pic that turned them both into busty size sixes with vast fish lips, stuck their figures onto a background of a golden beach and posted them. Immediately the likes started pouring in.

'Oh, for *God's* sake,' said Lissa, rolling her eyes.

'Now everyone's going to ask me how Hawaii was,' said Kim-Ange, getting up to go to bed.

'Tell them you got sponsored by a luxury holiday company to go for free for the 'Gram,' suggested Lissa.

'I will, I will.' And Kim-Ange kissed Lissa on the cheek and she went to bed, feeling slightly better, or at least a little drunk.

Chapter Nine

Cormac wasn't entirely disappointed to notice that Emer had gone by the time he got home. There was a text on his phone he didn't read the whole of, but it definitely included the phrase 'you're like a really shit "Batman"'. He was pondering this when, for the third time that evening, Jake rang. Cormac hurried out to meet his friend.

'That was quick,' said Jake suspiciously. 'I take it she left.'

'Don't you start,' said Cormac.

'Ah,' said Jake. 'The thing about lady problems is . . .'

'Don't start,' said Cormac. 'And, for the third time, I'm *not even on call.*'

'I know,' said Jake as he tried and failed to suppress a smile.

Cormac gave him a sideways look. It wasn't like any job was great fun. Unless, in Jake's case, a supermodel had got herself stuck in the bath or something ridiculous like that.

'What?'

'I thought you might like this one.'

'*What?*'

'It's your young Islay.'

Cormac's heart started beating extremely quickly.

'What about her?'

'It's only come up. Ten minutes ago.'

'You are *kidding*,' said Cormac.

Jake shook his head. 'Nope. Some poor kid down south.'

'The right age?'

'Fifteen.'

'Oh God,' said Cormac. Then: 'Oh God.'

'I know.'

Jake whistled through his teeth. 'I never thought we'd get there.'

Heart and lung transplants were so rare and the chances of success were so slim that normally only the heart was transplanted into patients who really needed it.

'It's the right size: he was tiny. Couple more years' growing, and they can do it together.'

Cormac had watched the clock run down on patients before and had been fully expecting it to happen again.

'Chuffing hell,' he said. 'That is absolutely *brilliant* news.'

'Want to come with me to get her?' said Jake.

Cormac did.

And he clasped his hand on Jake's shoulder as they climbed into the van, Tim the Silent Driver pulling away.

Lissa couldn't sleep.

Outside the nursing block, with its single-glazed windows, was the ongoing sound of London, rumbling away. Normally Lissa didn't mind it. In fact, she quite liked the steady reassuring noise of lorries delivering goods, glasses being recycled from pubs, bin pick-ups, sirens, shouting, as well as the omnipresent scent of dope smoke drifting up on summer evenings. It was the city she'd been born in, the city she'd always known. It was her lullaby.

But tonight, it was getting right on her nerves, as she lay there, eyes dry and wide, wondering how many other Kais were out there, how many other boys wouldn't make it home to their mothers.

Normally in her job she followed people into their homes. Alive people, who got better hopefully, or at least reached a stage of acceptance and learned to deal with whatever hand of cards they'd been dealt.

This had happened the wrong way round and all she could see was a dripping pool of blood and wide staring eyes and someone who could have been her brother; could have been anyone she'd been at school with …

Every lorry stopping on the road sounded like danger; a car's screeching brakes made her stiffen. She could feel the adrenaline shoot through her without warning, feel it spurting through her system even as one bit of her was chanting 'must rest must rest' and her phone glowed on the table, counting down the minutes until she had to get up, even as she could see the sky lightening through her cheap thin standard issue curtains. She groaned, turned over in bed and stuffed her head under the pillow, feeling simultaneously grimly alert and as if all her limbs were pinned down by stones, and the night ground on.

Chapter Ten

Joan had arrived by the time the boys got back to Islay's house. All the lights were on in the quiet village street, blazing away. Mrs Murray, who ran the village shop, lived next door and had got up to see what all the fuss was about, just in case she missed any vitally important gossip. She didn't consider what she did to be gossip, but instead an intensely important life force to the surrounding area and in fact a moral source for good, practically heroic. And so she was standing in her eiderdown dressing gown on her (spotless) front step at one o'clock in the morning. Plus, poor wee Islay, everyone had known her from a bairn, knew it wisnae fair, the poor lass. When all the other kids were running themselves ragged down at Tara's nursery, she'd had to be kept home like a china doll sat on a shelf, never moving, jumping, running – everything children wanted to do – as if she was made of porcelain and couldn't be let out. It was a real hardship to live somewhere as beautiful as Kirrinfief, which had the loch close by, the mountains and as much freedom and space to play in as a child could dream of, and be stuck indoors all the time watching TV or playing with her iPad.

And here was all the medical folk of the town: Joan and Cormac and Jake as well – my goodness, a full house. But they were smiling and chatting and everyone was excited, and the next minute out came Islay herself, being wheeled on a stretcher, sitting up, a tube in her nose to keep her blood supplied with oxygen.

'I can't believe it,' Islay's mother was saying, clutching her hands to her chest. Gregor, her dad, was blinking hard, trying to shush her, saying that it was very early days, that these things weren't always a definite, that there were false alarms.

'Wheels up!' shouted Jake from his walkie-talkie, face beaming.

'Och, listen to you,' said Cormac, helping him wheel the bed. 'With your fancy language! What are you, on Air Force One?'

'They're sending a plane with the heart in it.'

'Who is?'

'British Airways! They volunteered!'

'They volunteered to fly here?'

'I think they have to move a plane,' said Jake. 'Anyway. They're rushing it.'

Cormac shook his head. 'That's amazing. That's just amazing.'

He patted Islay on the shoulder.

'Can you believe this? They're rolling the red carpet right out for you.'

They hopped in the ambulance, Jake in the front, Cormac and Islay's parents in the back. Even though Islay was thirteen, she was still clinging to an old raggedy toy seal she must have had since she was a baby.

Jake had every new gadget on his phone and pulled up an app that identified planes as they flew overhead. They ignored him at first, then gathered round in amazement, watching as the only flight in the air at that time. – a BA one, noted as 'special cargo' – blipped its way up the country from London. They fell into silence. Jake gave the phone to Islay to hold and started up the ambulance.

The trip through the pitch-black countryside seemed to take for ever. Creatures stirred in the road. Jake had the headlights on full beam, given the unlikeliness of bumping into anyone else on the roads – at least until 4.30 a.m., when the farmers started getting up – and every hedgerow seemed to contain a pair of suddenly glowing eyes, or hooting owls, or a shiver of starlings taking off from a tree, a quick, past-before-you-knew-it rustle in the gorse or the high grass as they rumbled through. Cormac imagined them as the only little pool of light in the whole world, as they shot past distant darkened farmhouses and vast fields of sleeping cows, one occasionally stirring herself sleepily to watch as the precious cargo sped by. The creatures of the Highlands, it felt to Cormac – ridiculously, of course – standing respectfully to let them through, nothing stopping in their way, as a girl sat on a bed, tracing a plane through the night skies.

Chapter Eleven

The sun rose at six a.m., approaching the March equinox, and Cormac was there to see it, partly because he'd been caught up in making sure the operation went all right, and partly because he had to wait for Tim, who needed to sleep an acceptable amount of time before he was allowed to drive the ambulance back again.

He didn't mind. He'd sat with the parents for a while. Then, as Joan was still back in Kirrinfief, he took the calls from the hospital office in London, after explaining who he was. He was a little intimidated talking to the world-class teaching hospital – it felt a bit like taking an exam – but he explained as much of Islay's back story and state of mind as he could, and felt they were more or less doing all right.

The plane had landed at shortly after one and another ambulance was despatched and greenlighted, screaming through the streets with absolutely no cares who it woke in the process. Cormac had watched as they'd jumped out of the back, running. The icebox was so small, so inconsequential-looking, like nothing, even though it contained the whole world.

How amazing. And also, the sheer luck: the tissue matched with astonishing exactness. He watched as they dashed in, said a wee prayer. Wondered, briefly, about the person who had sacrificed his life to give it. To think how very, very lucky they were here! Or should be.

~ ~

Lissa gave up at six a.m. It was light. She closed her heavy, crusty eyes, opened them again and thought at least she could get first in the shower, wash it all away. That was one good thing about the nurses' accommodation: it was triumphantly overheated, which meant almost limitless amounts of hot water, as long as you didn't mind the low water pressure that made it dribble.

She stood under the shower, hair tied up, for as long as she could. She should probably turn it to cold to wake herself up, but she couldn't bear it. Her whole body hung down. She was weary and grotty and grimy to her bones, even as she stood in the shower, and absolutely dreading the case meeting, whatever Kim-Ange said.

Chapter Twelve

The next few weeks were awful for Lissa. She received a written warning but more than that, she could see people pointing and talking about her. The young doctor had apparently been furious.

She tried to bury herself in her work, and by going out with friends. But she couldn't sleep. Not at all. Every time she lay down, she saw that young boy's beautiful face bleeding out. She heard herself screaming at him, saw the ambulance lights flash against the wet pavement. She called Ezra, but he wasn't answering anyone. She couldn't blame him.

During her years in A&E, she'd become steeled to practically anything. But when it was someone you knew, that was different. She got crankier and more careless, so exhausted she was in tears half the time. Not even Kim-Ange could cheer her up, even when she dated a man who liked to go to conventions dressed as a rhinoceros and wanted to know whether she, Kim-Ange, had ever considered doing the same and whether or not she would like to.

Kai's funeral was exactly what Lissa had feared: a massive community outburst of misery and sadness and rage. His entire school was there as well as his church. The whole of his estate, it seemed, turned up to pay their respects, singing and crying, spilling out of the large church and onto the street. It was a paroxysm of agony and grief, though his mother tried to stay dignified and the pastor tried to calm the anger at the terrible waste which was obvious in the crowd. Ezra didn't even look at her.

Lissa felt sick but that was nothing new these days. She wasn't sleeping well at all, and felt her heart race at the smallest thing. She wasn't doing well at work either; she could tell. Her regulars had all noticed and remarked upon it, missing her normal cheery demeanour.

But the spark had gone out of her. She was terrified of everything now: loud noises, even the ambulance sirens she heard every five minutes going in and out of hospitals, sudden movements. It felt like her heart was bursting out of her chest every five minutes. Whenever she tried to get some rest, she was bolt upright again, in agony. She tried sleeping pills but they made her feel worse than ever – foggy and disconnected – and she was scared they were going to make her drive the car.

At the church, she linked arms with Kim-Ange, whose large presence was always a comfort. Today Kim-Ange's hair was bright burgundy but thankfully she was wearing black rather than the orange and purple she favoured. Okay, it was a fuzzy-wuzzy coat that made her look like an enormous bear, but Lissa found it comforting nevertheless and leaned in as they approached the incredibly busy church. You could hear it a mile away. Traffic had stopped. People were standing crying in the street.

They found a tiny spot on a pew. Nobody ever liked to budge up to Kim-Ange. This bothered Kim-Ange not a bit, and she scooshed her sizeable bottom along the pew as far as she could and patted the seat beside her.

'Come on, darling.'

Lissa sat down. She was trembling, and patted her pocket with the tissues in, just to make sure it was all right. She got through many tissues these days.

There was a lot of noise and hustle and bustle; it seemed half the world was there. But suddenly there was a hush as the doors at the back of the church suddenly opened. It was like a wedding, Lissa thought, her heart racing. Only of course, so very wrong.

The choir stood to the side, their numbers absolutely packed out too. Very softly and sweetly, they began to sing 'Swing low, sweet chariot' gently and the pallbearers began a slow, long march down the aisle, carrying a pure white coffin.

Lissa collapsed. She was sobbing so hard she couldn't breathe. This wasn't her boy, wasn't her tragedy. She was drawing attention to herself. This was awful, completely inappropriate. People were looking at her crossly, and she didn't know what to do, even as she sounded louder than the choir. Someone tutted. Righteous and noisy grief was expected from contemporaries, and family, and young people. Not from a thirty-year-old young professional who didn't even know the family.

Kim-Ange looked at her, made a decision and half dragged, half hauled her outside. She set her down quite roughly on a park bench. There were still mourners trying to get in, who watched them with interest.

'Breathe,' said Kim-Ange, and when Lissa didn't respond, she pushed her head between her knees.

'Breathe!'

The brusque tone, oddly, was just what Lissa needed. Being told what to do without having to think about it. The panic attack was intense, but gradually her heart rate slowed, the blood returned to her head and she started to feel ever so slightly better.

'Sister,' said Kim-Ange, rubbing her back, as she finally came back to herself, 'this cannot go on. This really cannot go on. Also, the walls in our rooms are really thin and I can hear you getting up and pacing about half the night and it's extremely annoying. But I am mostly thinking about you. Although also when you have a shower at 5 a.m. you make a lot of noise. But also. For you. This cannot go on.'

Chapter Thirteen

Lissa liked the HR director Valerie Mnotse, always had done, had found her to be a friend and mentor, supportive of her career choices when working in the community was often seen as second-best. Valerie got it. She understood the importance of connecting the hospital with the people that used it, and how the better the care they got at home, the less likely they were to boomerang straight back to the hospital, clogging up A&E because they were so endlessly confused with a labyrinthine system, feeling bad but couldn't get a GP appointment. But this morning, Valerie looked grave.

'Health care in London is always difficult,' she started carefully.

Lissa was about to fire back that she wasn't burnt out, she was fine, she was a good nurse, she knew she was ... but she found, suddenly, that she couldn't get the words out – couldn't get any words out – because she was going to cry again.

No. She couldn't. She couldn't cry in front of Valerie, the most immaculate, punctilious woman she knew. She had to be strong. She'd defied her family to go to nursing school and get her university qualifications. She'd done it by herself, and worked in some of the toughest, most deprived wards in the entire country – the whole of Europe, in fact. She could do it. She could ...

'It's all right to cry,' said Valerie, pushing over a box of tissues.

Lissa felt the tears leak down her face and was furious with herself. If she showed weakness, they were going to move her, she knew it.

Lissa nodded slowly as Valerie picked up her phone.

'Could you send Juan in? Thanks.'

A slight man Lissa had seen around came in, looking neutral and nodding to her. She was terrified suddenly.

'What's happening? Am I getting fired?'

'No, you're not getting fired,' said Valerie. 'If we had the resources, we'd sign you off. But we don't.'

'I don't need to be signed off! I'm fine!'

'We think,' said Juan softly, 'that you might need to recalibrate.'

'That I might need to what?'

'We want you to see someone,' said Juan. 'We've assigned you a counsellor from occupational health. And—'

'We think maybe a quieter beat,' said Valerie. 'Just for three months. Just to give you a chance to breathe, to have another look at your approach.'

'We really feel this programme works well,' said Juan. 'We're desperately trying not to lose you. You must see that.'

He handed her a leaflet with pictures of lovely rolling green fields on it, the sun going down over some cows.

'What's this?' said Lissa sullenly.

'Just . . . about your options. We do swaps with rural practitioners who want to broaden their skills. Like a student exchange.'

'I'm not a student!'

'We've found the programme mutually beneficial,' said Juan.

'Lissa,' said Valerie quite firmly. 'I'd highly recommend you give it some very serious thought.'

Chapter Fourteen

Islay's recovery was going well, and Cormac called the London hospital to update them. Transplants happened in total secrecy and Cormac knew better than to ask. But what accident involving a fifteen-year-old could be anything other than a dreadful tragedy? Instead he conveyed as soberly as possible that Patient B had come through the operation and was currently in intensive care, that the prognosis was good, possibly even extremely good, and that everything was proceeding as usefully as possible.

The voice at the other end of the phone paused.

'And you're the NPL?' he said, looking something up on his computer.

'Uh-huh,' said Cormac warily.

'Cormac MacPherson?'

'Aye.'

'Because I'm looking at your HR form here.'

'Are you now?' said Cormac, instantly wary.

'You haven't always been an NPL, have you?'

There was a long pause. Cormac hadn't been expecting this at all.

'No. I was an Army medic. Why?'

'Have you heard of the exchange programme?'

'The what?'

'The three-month exchange programme. You could move up a grade. We have a place opening up here.'

'I'm no' moving to London!'

'The idea is to bolster the skills of people in different areas. So if you've always worked in a rural district, you might benefit from some more acute specialisation, that kind of thing. And vice versa.'

'You mean you're looking for somewhere to dump your burnouts,' said Cormac tartly. He might live in a village, but he wasn't its idiot. There was a wry chuckle at the other end of the line.

'I think you'd be good down here,' came the voice. 'Let me send you the brochure.'

'Aye, whatever,' said Cormac, who then hung up and thought no more about it.

He headed home and had a long shower. He found himself missing having someone to talk to, remembering the black-humoured camaraderie of the Army. He wondered if the London frontlines were like that. Probably.

He went out into the village to pick up some of the good local butter they did up at Lennox's farm. Lennox wasn't much of a talker, but the farm produce was spot on. He picked some local bacon too. It would make quite the sandwich.

➶ ➷

Kirrinfief is a village arranged around a central cobbled square, with a war memorial in the middle, Wullie's pub on the corner, Mrs Murray's general store, a hunting and fishing shop, three antiques/bits and bobbery stores, a bakery and, most days, a little book bus that stops to sell books. It is nestled in the hills, hidden away near Loch Ness but not on the main tourist routes. Any tourists who do stumble upon it, though, are generally taken by its atmosphere; it has an air of timelessness, a Brigadoon, which won't last long as soon as you hear old Alasdair and Wullie shouting at you from outside the pub, although they mean well really.

The sleeper train from London to Fort William runs close by; otherwise, it is a haven of peace and tranquillity, and that is just how people like it. Well. Mostly.

Cormac stalked across the square. It was a cold but sunny day; a few ambitious crocuses were pushing their way up in between the cobbles. He got three steps before an old lady stopped him. 'Oooh, Cormac, what was all that kerfuffle with young Islay?'

He smiled politely.

'Och, you know I cannae talk about that, Mrs Norrie.'

'Yes, well, everybody already knows,' she said rather sniffily.

'Well then.'

Mrs Murray in the shop was even more direct.

'Why did I see that young Emer in here earlier sniffing and buying three bars of Dairy Milk?' she said. 'That's not like her, young slim thing that she is. Three! Were they for you?'

'No,' said Cormac.

'Well then,' said Mrs Murray, as if that proved something. 'How's your ma?'

'She's good,' said Cormac slowly. He hadn't seen her in a fortnight, which was a lot round here. Rawdon had been commended for something and she'd wanted to talk about that in a rather emphatic way.

'Still fussing you about your job?'

'I'll just take this cheese,' said Cormac, smiling heartily. The shop was so overstuffed with things, he had to lean over the counter away from the newspapers. 'Thanks, Mrs Murray.'

'Oh well,' said Mrs Murray – who took rather a lot quite personally – as Cormac escaped.

He got home to an email from London. The brochure had a picture of bright high skyscrapers. 'Secondments in a fast-moving environment!' he read. 'Update your skills. Experience a high-paced community in central London and sharpen your clinical skills!'

Cormac had been to central London with a girlfriend long ago. They'd been to the Imperial War Museum, eaten at a steak house

46

where they'd had to sit in the window and get gawped at by other tourists and the food was absolutely awful, then gone to see a West End show about a lady murderer which had made him fall asleep fifteen minutes in. That relationship hadn't lasted longer either.

Chapter Fifteen

Valerie had sent Lissa home for the day – which was anxiety-creating enough in itself – and Lissa found the crowds on Tottenham Court Road rather overwhelming. She crossed and stumbled over the vast, honking, polluted Euston Road, and escaped into the relative quiet of Regent's Park. It was too warm for this early in the spring. It should feel good, the sunshine, but it wasn't: it felt ominous and scary; the world shifting and changing beneath her feet. Every teenage boy she passed, every laugh they gave or when they were shoving around with their mates, crowding her off the pavement, playing their music too loud, every single one made her flinch, made her want to grab them, hard, shout at them in their faces to be safe, to keep safe, to stay indoors, not to draw attention to themselves.

But they were teenage boys. It was part of their make-up to yell, to beef, to get into each other's faces. They felt invincible. Indeed, with their towering sizes and their massive trainers, they *looked* invincible.

But they were as fragile as day-old lambs. Lissa hurried on.

She could feel her breathing speeding up again, her heart pounding in her chest, and tried to calm herself down. She sat down near a bright wave of daffodils and concentrated on breathing in through her nose and out through her mouth as much as she could, in and out, slowly and not rushing, trying to get her equilibrium back, even as she wanted to scream, to scream to everyone that the world wasn't safe. It wasn't safe.

She swallowed hard. Maybe Valerie and Juan were right. She couldn't work like this; couldn't think like this. But it would pass, wouldn't it? Would it?

She opened up the leaflet they had given her. With its soothing view of rolling hills, it looked more like a funeral planning leaflet. Oh God. She couldn't bear it. If she felt bad, what on earth was life like now for his mother? How did you go on? How could anybody go on?

Nevertheless, she started to read.

Chapter Sixteen

Jake and Cormac were having a pint in the pub, nodding hello to Philip and Wullie, and petting Alasdair, the cheerful sheepdog who lived there and appeared in perfect and glossy health despite living on a major dietary supplement of beer, nuts and pickled onion crisps. It was a chilly evening, but the sun had come down purple in the sky, which was a pretty sight to render anyone more or less cheerful about the world. They'd even persuaded their friend Lennox in for half an hour, although it would literally be half an hour, and he'd be glancing at his watch for most of it. He had a wee lad at home and wouldn't miss bathtime for the world.

Jake was staring at Cormac, aghast.

'Run this past me again,' he said. 'They're offering you cheap accommodation in the middle of London, for three months, *and* a London bonus on your pay packet, to hang out in London, work a bit and do whatever the hell you want, without every old lady you meet in the street asking if you wouldn't mind looking up her bum?'

Cormac frowned.

'They don't do that.'

'Mrs MacGonnagall does that!'

'She does, aye.'

Cormac drained his pint.

'Seriously, you're so lucky. They should do that scheme with ambulance drivers!'

'Ha, that'd be a lot of use.'

'What do you mean?'

'"Hello, welcome to London, off you go to Oxford Street ..." "Och aye, sorry, where would that be now?"'

Jake sighed.

'Oh. Aye. Even more reason why you'd be absolutely mad not to go. The women in London, oh my God.'

'How do you know?'

Jake shrugged. 'In the papers, aye?'

Cormac looked at him suspiciously, but Jake was refusing to look his way.

'Have you been reading *Grazia* again?'

Jake sniffed.

'This is the chance of a lifetime, man. Kirrinfief, it's all right.'

In the corner, Alasdair's dog let out a massive fart right next to the fire, then looked around with an innocent expression as if it couldn't possibly have been him.

'Uh-huh.'

'But *London*! On cheap rent! Hot summers and amazing women and everything going on and famous people and stuff off the telly and that!'

'Well, I'll be working.'

'Yeah. Looking after hot models with toe injuries from wearing really, really high heels,' said Jake sadly, who had clearly given this quite an astonishing amount of thought. 'Seriously, mate. You're insane. You'll be back in three months. What's going to change for you in three months?'

Cormac stared out of the window. The clouds were hanging low today. Rain was threatened. Being somewhere sunny with models in it suddenly seemed rather exciting.

'Plus, you know, since you got back ...'

Cormac gave him a sharp look.

'What are you saying?'

'Nothing,' said Jake hastily. You didn't talk about Cormac leaving the Army. You just didn't. 'I just mean, it's quiet.'

Cormac looked at Lennox, who as usual wasn't saying much.

'What do you think?'

That was a pretty stupid question. Lennox had been to agricultural college, then come straight back to the farm he'd been born on. The most surprising thing Lennox had ever done was get together with the clever, nerdy English girl who ran the local bookshop, and even then she'd been renting one of his farm buildings. Literally all he'd had to do was fall across the road.

Lennox shrugged.

'No' for me,' he said to absolutely nobody's surprise. Above the cracking fire, the old clock ticked mournfully on. 'But you're just a bairn. You've no ties, nothing holding you back. Why wouldn't you?'

He stood up. 'And send me back some lads, will you? Brexit's put a bloody big hole in my harvesting teams, I'll tell you that for nothing.'

And with that he put down his glass, smiled and went home to his lovely Nina and their perfect darling baby boy, deeply happy in his soul that as far as he was concerned he never need decide to go anywhere other than home ever again.

PART TWO

PART TWO

Chapter One

There are few places lonelier than a crowded station platform five hundred miles away from home, where you know nobody but a lot of people are trying to get past you, or get you out of the way.

Cormac had taken the sleeper train down. He had thought that he wouldn't sleep, given he had so much to think about, but the comfortable bed and the rocking motion of the carriage as well as the nip of whisky he'd bought from the onboard bar had all combined to send him off into a surprisingly deep sleep, punctuated by dreams that had him swimming or riding a horse or anything involving motion.

Euston at 7.30 in the morning was absolutely heaving; grimy with dirt and full of smartly dressed people moving – why did they all have to walk so fast?

He looked around, standing under a huge four-faced clock, feeling ridiculously out of place. He must have stood out a mile to anyone, with his freckled complexion, messy sandy brown hair and cords. Perhaps he would have to rethink the cords. His mum had bought them for him, telling him that's what everyone wore in Edinburgh. Why she thought Edinburgh was the height of fashion sophistication he wasn't entirely sure. Nobody here was wearing cords. She was happy he had gone though. It wasn't easy, bearing the weight of his mother's disappointment. Another good reason to take some time away.

Anyway, everyone here was wearing expensive suits and skinny jeans and baggy pants and all sorts of weird and wonderful colours you didn't see much of in Kirrinfief. And Jake hadn't, it turned out, been lying about the women; some of them did, indeed look like models, all made up, with bright blonde or pink or blue hair, strange eyebrows (Cormac was not the expert on eyebrows) and incredibly outlandish clothes. The whole thing was bewildering. How did all these people know where they were going? Why didn't they all bang into each other? Why were they all holding canisters with green drinks in them?

Slowly, lumbering rather with his heavy rucksack, Cormac scratched his chin and went over in search of a London Underground map, narrowly missing clouting a tiny girl clip-clopping her way round him, who let out a sigh louder and more pointed than he would have expected from such a small woman.

꙳ ꙳

Kim-Ange had given her a big kiss as Lissa set off, looking sadly round the little room she was leaving behind.

'Into exile,' she'd moaned.

'Don't be stupid,' said Kim-Ange, bundling cake into Lissa's bag. 'It's not for long! It'll be an adventure.'

'I'm being suspended,' said Lissa. 'They never want me back.'

'Of course they do,' said Kim-Ange. 'You're definitely the second-best nurse on this floor.'

Lissa rolled her eyes.

'Oh God,' she said. 'I've never lived in the countryside. What's it going to be like?'

'Think of it this way,' said Kim-Ange. 'When anyone you don't want to phones you, you can just tell them your reception is cutting out.'

Lissa nodded.

'I suppose.'

Kim-Ange hugged her. 'Honestly. It'll be great. Peace and quiet. Get some sleep. Read some books. Build a massive Instagram brand of you looking at misty moors. Think of it as a holiday. And come back and be fabulous with me please. And think of me. I'm the one that's going to get some wittering country idiot being Scotch next to me!'

Lissa managed a wan smile.

'I'm sure he'll be perfectly nice.'

'Oh, you're sure. You're sure, are you? I don't even want a boy on this floor.'

She sniffed noisily, and Lissa gave her a hug.

'Thanks, Kim-Ange,' she said.

'The sacrifices I make! You'll miss me every day!'

'I will miss you every day,' promised Lissa, and meant it.

Chapter Two

Lissa looked at the paperwork again, carefully, anxiously, so terrified she'd get something wrong. She was taking on the caseload of one Cormac MacPherson, who was also lending her his apartment.

They each had a secure NHS.org log-in that they could exchange patient data on, only with one another, so they could achieve continuity of care, and they would be expected to debrief every day, for three months. They also had to write a weekly report for HR – effectively, Lissa discovered, they were guinea pigs for the entire scheme. At the bottom, Juan had added:

Good luck, Lissa – I think this will be a wonderful experience.

Lissa was not thinking this. Not at all. She felt banished; pied off; reduced to being put out of sight out of mind as if she'd gone crazy and needed to be out of the way. She loved London; it was the air she breathed. The idea of being stuck out in the country was ridiculous.

She'd googled Cormac MacPherson, but his Facebook page was locked and gave absolutely nothing away. He didn't seem to be on the internet much which was strange enough in this day and age. She'd spent more time looking at Kirrinfief on Google Earth. It was tiny!

She'd never really been in the country; London was all she'd ever known. She'd never been to Scotland at all.

But Lissa needed – absolutely desperately needed – the insomnia to stop, along with the nightmares when she finally drifted off into a shallow tainted half-life, and the grit she felt under her eyelids, plus the way she could not control her breath when she saw a bunch of lads on the street, or heard a shout or, worst of all, a car backfiring or accelerating. If going to this godforsaken place would help her get over that, then it was worth a shot. She would have vastly preferred to be at her Granny's in Antigua, but that wasn't an option the NHS was notably keen on offering her. So the wild north it was.

Chapter Three

Cormac was, he rapidly realised, somehow just too big for London. He'd played rugby for the Army, and it had never really left him. It wasn't just that he was tall, but he was also broad – and he really was – as there were plenty of other big-looking people; aye, there were plenty of people full stop. More people, he thought, than were surely strictly necessary or even viable. More people than you could figure out had crammed into these hot sticky streets that smelled of food and smoke and choking exhaust fumes. Didn't they notice how revolting the air was? Maybe not. London clung to you, put sticky fingerprints all over you.

The nurses' home was a tall, peeling eight-storey building situated outside a tube station by a roundabout in what Cormac would learn to call South London.

There didn't appear to be any automatically obvious way to get through the roundabout which was, on closer examination, actually two roundabouts, each with four lanes of traffic. The air was a haze. Cormac thought back to what he had slightly imagined when he pictured staying in central London for a month. It had definitely involved lots of parks with swans in them. And also Buckingham Palace.

He sighed and tried several times to reach the block through subway passages lined with people asleep on flattened cardboard boxes in filthy sleeping bags, and made it to Florence Nightingale House finally. The glass was security protected. He rang the bell and a large man saw him from inside and buzzed him in.

'Hi,' said Cormac nervously. 'I'm the secondment for . . .'

For a split-second he forgot her name.

'Alyssa Westcott? I'm taking over her room?'

The man stared at him, unperturbed, then ran his finger down a grubby list of printed names.

'Neh,' he said.

Cormac looked to the side, then tried again.

'I'm not Alyssa,' he said. 'I'm Cormac MacPherson?'

There was another very long pause.

'Yeh,' said the man, lifting a heavy finger from the page and sighing deeply.

'So, youse having a good day?' said Cormac cheerily.

The man looked at him, harrumphing with a loud noise as he had to get out of his chair – which creaked alarmingly – and stretched up to a long line of keys.

'I just got down on the sleeper. Didn't think I'd sleep much, but actually it was great . . .'

Cormac left space at the end of his sentence but the man wasn't responding. This was very odd.

In Kirrinfief, if you went up to Inverness for the afternoon, that would provoke a fairly long conversation in the grocer's about what you'd seen and who you'd met and whether you'd been to the big cinema which had something called a Nando's. Going on the sleeper was a next level adventure; it would have involved the input and discussion of anyone in the shop. The train had narrowly avoided a crash about three years ago and people still talked about it.

By contrast, this man didn't respond at all. As if Cormac wasn't there, or hadn't said anything.

'So, anyway. It's . . . well, this place looks interesting . . .'

Cormac was stuttering on, but in an increasingly confused

fashion. He felt like a dog wagging his tail and getting roundly ignored. He was just making conversation, that was all; it was what people did. What was this guy's problem?

The man grunted and put down a set of keys and gave him a bunch of forms to fill in, all the while avoiding eye contact. Perhaps, Cormac thought, perhaps there was something wrong with him. Yes. That had to be it.

He handed over his passport for photocopying and paid the deposit over, worrying again whether he'd left the cottage clean and tidy enough for the girl who was moving in there.

Lined with old random chairs, the lobby was the kind of place that smelled of smoke even though nobody had been allowed to smoke in there for years. Cormac leafed through an old copy of *Nursing Times* while the man, still ignoring him rather than making conversation like a human being, shifted his bulk around photocopying and laboriously noting down all of Cormac's details. It couldn't be pleasant, Cormac decided, being trapped inside that booth all day.

Meanwhile, the bell buzzed and nurses came and went. Cormac was used to being surrounded by women doing this job but this was a lot by even his standards. They were loud, confident, laughing and shouting; he felt slightly intimidated. Where he'd done his training, everyone had been local, more or less, and he'd known a couple of people from school and everyone was friendly ... This looked like a glamorous menagerie of colourful women, bold with great barking accents, saying 'yeah awight' and sounding like they were on *EastEnders*, along with a mix of accents and voices from across the world. He tried not to stare. It was more different types of people than he'd ever seen.

A few people gave him a glance as they passed but most of them assumed he was someone's boyfriend, a visitor waiting for someone. He wondered who he'd be living next to.

Finally, the man behind the glass box grunted and pushed his paperwork back towards him.

'Which room?' asked Cormac, figuring that surely this was the one question that would need an actual, spoken answer, but the man only put a burly finger on the cheap plastic tag next to the Yale key – 238.

'Brilliant,' said Cormac, who was not normally a sarcastic person. 'Thanks so much! For everything!'

But the man hadn't heard, or wouldn't hear, because this was London, and Cormac picked up his rucksack again and headed for the old creaking lift.

There were twelve rooms either side of the central lift, with a large, rather grotty kitchen at each end and two sets of bathrooms. The facility was obviously old, but the windows were big, looking out across the roundabout and into North London over the river itself. Cormac fiddled with the lock and entered the little student room.

He didn't know what he'd expected, but the room was almost completely bare. There was a north-facing window, a single bed, a sink with a mirror above it, harsh brown carpet and a cheap wardrobe with a few hangers inside it. He worried then, if he should have cleared everything out of the cottage – he'd left the books, and the pictures and the rugs. Was that not right? But it was only for three months, so he wasn't clearing out his entire life.

This person had though. There was nothing here at all.

Chapter Four

Lissa stood where the bus had dropped her off. After such a long journey, she was pretty sure she'd gone too far and round in circles. She could distantly appreciate the hills, dotted with lambs, and the deep blue of the loch, and the shadows cast by the crags on the fields, plus the farmers out ploughing new seed – she understood in the abstract that these things were nice, but looking through the dirty bus window was a bit like watching it on television, as if she was seeing it from a distance.

And then she was worried she'd miss her stop and she would have put any money on Uber not working out here, and everyone had been looking at her funny (she was convinced) and this bus driver was trying to chat her up, and this was all just awful and doing her anxiety no good at all.

Finally, after about half an hour during which she was simply sitting on her hands, trying to breathe, trying not to let everything get on top of her, the bus driver, who'd been trying to engage her in conversation for the last forty minutes and didn't understand why she didn't understand why making conversation with the bus driver was very much the least you could do on a bus, stopped in Kirrinfief square, where he normally liked to take a short break and buy a book, and smiled at his last passenger, the pretty girl with the curly hair, who was looking terrified.

'Come on the noo, lass, you've made it!' he said encouragingly. Lissa stared at him; she didn't understand a word. The driver nodded towards the door and Lissa jumped up and sidled past him. Was this it? She lugged her heavy bag and climbed down the steps, ignoring the driver offering to take her case, and not remembering to thank him either, which didn't change his idea of English people one iota, frankly.

But Lissa was too nervous to care. She tried to shake herself up. She never used to be like this! She'd travelled in South America one summer when she'd been a nursing student; travelled through strange countries, danced in strange bars, drunk tequila in beach bars in strange neighbourhoods. What had happened to that girl? In one terrible moment it had gone. In the scheme of things, of course, she was the lucky one. She felt guilty that she even felt bad when she had lost nothing and others had lost everything.

But still. She missed that girl. Here she was in a little village in a perfectly safe environment and the hand gripping her pull-along suitcase was shaking.

Lissa made it to the park bench. The sun was out, but the wind felt incredibly cold. You never really noticed the wind in London, except when you crossed the Thames. The Millennium Bridge, a short walk from the nurses' quarters, was always breezy.

Here on Kirrinfief's pretty open cobbled square, she could feel the full force of its chill, and pulled her new puffa jacket closer round her. The houses were higgledy-piggledy, in grey stone, with doors right out onto the pavement; there wasn't a straight roof to be found. Smoke puffed out of several chimneys. There was a cosy old pub on the corner, with hanging baskets outside, and a bright red painted grocer's with mops and brushes propped up against the window. A pale blue van was parked in the corner, selling books.

Lissa tried to imagine sitting and reading a book again. It seemed incredibly unlikely: managing to slow her brain down; managing to concentrate for long enough without breaking the spell. And she couldn't read anything triggering or upsetting ... Something else lost.

She looked at her watch. The local GP was supposed to be meeting her, talking her through the job. Bit of a jack of all trades, by the sounds of things, provision was so patchy and far apart. In London, it sometimes felt like there was a hospital every hundred yards. It didn't seem like that was the case here.

She looked around again, up the hill, where long streets of narrow terraced houses weaved their way upwards, backed against the deep green of the mountains. To her left, she could catch the sun glinting off Loch Ness. That was a bit mad. She wondered if it was rude to ask about the monster. She could see it was a pretty spot. But what did people *do* here? What on earth ...? How did you pass your days without restaurants and theatres and nightclubs and shopping and exhibitions and cocktail bars?

Suddenly, the oldest, dirtiest car Lissa had ever seen charged round the square at top speed. It was a vast old Volvo estate in a very unappetising shade of brown, and the back of it appeared to be full of straw and dogs. It screeched to a halt before her and a tall, imposing-looking woman stepped out, wearing a tweed skirt and a dark green polo neck. She had fine features but no make-up and her skin was weather-beaten; her hair grey and cut into a bob, more or less. Lissa had the oddest sense when looking at her that she hadn't changed her style since her first day at primary school. As premonitions go, she was spot on. The dogs, meanwhile, were going berserk.

'HELLO!' barked Dr Joan Davenport. Lissa frowned slightly, and felt her heart rate jump up and her nerves pile in.

'Um ...' said Lissa.

'Are you Alyssa Westcott?'

'Um, Lissa?'

Joan looked like she couldn't care less about that.

'Well. You're my charge, it appears. I did ask for a boy.'

Lissa was confused.

'Just my little joke! Never mind! Nobody reads, I get it, I get it.'

'Are you the GP?' said Lissa as Joan started striding towards her.

'Huh? Well, of course. Did Cormac not explain?'

Lissa didn't know how to tell Joan that she'd been too anxious and full of worry to contact Cormac to ask the questions she needed to know; she'd barely replied to his email at all, as if ignoring what was coming would somehow make it go away.

She shook her head, and Joan looked at her keenly. Her bluff manner wasn't put on – that was just who she was – but it didn't mean she wasn't perceptive.

'You've had a tough time,' she observed. Lissa fiddled with her bag and stared at the ground.

'I'm fine,' she said. 'I'm perfectly fit to work.'

Joan glanced at her again.

'Well, we'll try and keep your workload light. I'm sure they'll keep Cormac busy!'

Joan opened the back door of her ancient car and three scruffy terriers jumped out.

'Yesss!' she said, her tone instantly changing from brusque welcome to motherly concern.

'There we are, Montgomery, my angel! Jasper! Jasper! Come here, my lovely boy! Pepper! Pepper! Come here!'

But it was too late. All three dogs were immediately leaping up, covering Lissa with their mucky paws. She was frozen in fear. She had learned on her rounds to be very wary of dogs; many in London were bred to be guard dogs and righteously defended their property whenever she walked up the path. And these hairy beasts seemed completely uncontrollable. As she tried to make them go down, she saw Joan looking at her, the stern face completely gone.

'Aren't they wonderful?' she said. 'You're lucky. They like you.'

Lissa did not feel in the least bit lucky as she attempted to gingerly pat one on its fuzzy head.

'You'd better get used to dogs if you're going to work a country beat,' observed Joan.

And, almost completely surrounded by panting dogs – a state Joan appeared to consider entirely desirable – Lissa followed Joan up behind the square to a whitewashed stone house, separate from the others, with a brass plate on the wall announcing the GP surgery.

'Is it just you?' said Lissa, worried. 'Do you take the dogs in?'

'No,' said Joan. 'Bloody health and safety.'

She whistled, surprisingly loudly, and the dogs left Lissa alone and slunk around the back of the house. Lissa peered after them and saw a medium-sized, rather pretty garden and three dog kennels. The idea of a GP surgery having a garden rather tickled her.

'And it's just you?'

Joan nodded.

'Yes. Small population in the village, plus hamlets and homesteads. I spend a lot of time in the car, and so will you.'

'Oh yes,' said Lissa. 'They said there'd be a car . . .'

She pondered Joan's terrible brown estate for a second. How bad was her car going to be? In fact, as Joan showed her behind the surgery, it was a perfectly nice little Ford.

'Of course, you'll want to cycle most places,' said Joan. 'Lot easier than getting the cars up the road.'

'*Cycle?*' said Lissa. 'What about the drug box?'

'Try not to leave it by the post box,' said Joan drily, 'and I'm pretty sure you'll be fine.'

She started rifling through her daily files, then looked up as she remembered something.

'Are you going to need time off for therapy? How are they even doing that?'

Lissa winced even to hear the word. She wanted to shout, wanted to tell everyone: this wasn't the real her! She existed in the world! She was fun and carefree! The real her was cool, not some traumatised wreck! Not, she realised, a patient. She looked after patients. The idea that she needed looking after . . . she couldn't bear it.

'I'm to see someone over Skype,' she admitted grudgingly.

Joan sniffed loudly. 'Of course, London would be full of therapists. Lots of crazy English. You know what you really need?'

Lots of people had told Lissa what they thought she needed, and she hadn't enjoyed any of that either. A love affair, to get drunk, to go on holiday, to fall in love, to travel the world. She weighed up what she thought Joan's response would be.

'Is it "a dog"?' she said.

Joan smiled.

'Well, that and a bit of fresh air, I would say. Lots of walks, lots of being out in the countryside. That's a cure for just about anything.'

Lissa looked out of the window where it had clouded over ominously.

'Doesn't it rain all the time here?' she said.

'So what?' said Joan, stumped at the question. She went back to her files and pulled some out. 'Cormac will send you his case notes. These are just the current ones dished out.'

'So what kind of thing do you see round here then?' said Lissa.

'Oh, the usual. Some diabetes care. Bit of stoma work. Vaccinations. The elderly. Farming accidents.'

'What?' said Lissa.

'People lose bits to tractors. More often than you'd think. That kind of thing.'

'What kind of bits?'

'Sticky out bits,' said Joan ominously, walking from the waiting room into the unlocked clinic. Lissa twirled around.

'You leave your *door* open?'

'Well, they're very welcome to the *House & Garden* back issues and a broken toy garage.'

Lissa stepped through in wonder. The old front room of the house was the waiting room, and it was thankfully rather cleaner than Joan's car, although she faintly suspected that the dogs still did indeed get in here from time to time. There were toys, posters warning against smoking and drinking; nothing notably different, except that every other inch of the walls was covered in pictures of dogs and horses, and there was a stag's head on one wall and a stuffed greyhound in a glass case in the corner.

Lissa started when she saw it.

'Ah yes. Cosmo,' sighed Joan. 'Wonderful, wonderful animal. Could never let him go.'

'Doesn't it scare the children?'

'Don't be ridiculous! They love him!'

Lissa stared at the glassy eyes.

'Are you sure?'

Joan snorted. 'Here,' she said, indicating a whitewashed room, thankfully free of taxidermised pets. 'This is Cormac's office.'

'He gets an office to himself?'

'Aye. He's got one up at the hospital too.'

'You're kidding!'

Lissa normally did all her notes back in her room and if she was lucky she got to squeeze into a staff room at one of the bigger practices every now and again.

Joan blinked.

'There's six rooms upstairs we don't use at all.'

'Cor,' said Lissa. 'In London this would be worth, like, millions.'

'Yes,' sniffed Joan in a tone of utter disdain. 'But it would be *in London*.'

Chapter Five

Cormac looked round at the tiny room. There was not a piece of green to be seen anywhere out of the window, just concrete and cars and more concrete and the occasional spindly, sickly-looking bare tree, roped off from the pavement. His room was more of a cell than a room really: long, narrow and cheerless. How did people live like this? Where did they go when they needed to stretch their legs? He watched the people below him streaming across the round-about when the lights went green, taking big steps and little ones, as the endless circling traffic and lines of buses and cabs stopped and started and belched fuel and stopped again. It was dizzying. How did people stop? How did they calm down and take a deep breath? He opened the window. The air was harsh with exhaust fumes and the noise was incredible. He quickly shut the window again and poured himself a glass of water from the sink. Then he poured it away. It was lukewarm and chalky and hard and absolutely revolting. Perhaps it was just the pipes, he thought. Maybe it was just old pipes.

He looked at his watch. It was only ten in the morning and he didn't report for work until the following day. There were seven million people in the city, and he didn't know a single one of them.

He'd never been surrounded by so many people in his entire life, and he'd never felt so lonely.

There was a loud knock on the door.

Joan gave Lissa the list of appointments for the next day and the keys to the cottage.

'I have surgery,' she said. 'You'll be all right getting on, won't you?'

Lissa wasn't sure about this, but nodded her head.

'Are you always this quiet?' said Joan. 'You're like that other English girl.'

'There's another English girl?'

'Oh, we're infested with them.'

'You're English! Well, you sound English.'

Joan fixed her with a horrified glance.

'I'm from Edinburgh! This is how we talk.'

Lissa couldn't see why it could possibly matter whether you had an English accent or not and whether saying something like that wasn't rather ... racist ... but she tried to smile politely and listen to Joan's directions, even as they vanished from her brain as soon as she found herself outside the white surgery.

Cormac wouldn't have been entirely surprised if his mum and her friends from the church community Zumba group had appeared there with nine boxes of Tunnock's Teacakes, but in fact the apparition that greeted him was even less expected.

The most extraordinary person Cormac had ever seen was standing in the door frame. Was larger than the door frame, Cormac realised. At least six foot, with big burly shoulders, a huge swathe of beautiful shiny long black hair braided round their head, a fully made-up face including pink and yellow eyeshadow and vast amounts of pink sticky lipgloss, all balanced over an extremely roomy pair of blue scrubs, down to a pair of pink glittery trainers.

'HELLO!' said the voice with a broad Estuary accent. 'OOH! She didn't say you were a fittie!'

Cormac considered himself a fairly easy-going character on the whole but he wasn't the least bit sure where to look.

'I'm Kim-Ange,' continued the creature, entering the room. 'She didn't tell you about me? I thought you guys were emailing each other?'

'I've ... sent her one email,' said Cormac.

'I'm not surprised she wanted to keep you to herself!' said Kim-Ange. 'We tried to look you up. You know your Facebook profile is absolute crap.'

'Aye ... I don't really do Facebook.'

'You don't do Instagram either! And why not?'

Kim-Ange sat down on the bed in a familiar fashion; as it creaked beneath her weight.

'Um ... well, I see most of the people I want to see. And I don't really see the point of it otherwise unless you want to show off and that.'

'That,' said Kim-Ange, 'is annoyingly sensible. And misses out the joy of showing off.'

Cormac shook his head.

'But you've heard of the internet? They have the internet in Scotland?'

'As long as we've positioned the ram's horns in the right direction. So ... you're a nurse?'

'No, I just love the fabulous outfit,' said Kim-Ange, looking down at her dull scrubs in distaste.

'Which specialty?'

'Cardiology.'

'Oh, I bet you're useful. Lot of ...'

Cormac had been about to say that there was a lot of heaving heavy people about, which there was, but he realised just in time that this would not be the right thing to say as Kim-Ange gave him a look.

'Because of my warm and empathetic manner?'

'Um, yes,' said Cormac, blushing bright red to the roots of his sandy hair.

It was just a glance. But Kim-Ange caught it. She was absolutely attuned to being able to figure out whether people were allies or not. Abuse from strangers she could handle – had to, every single day of her life – but sometimes it was nice just to make a friend. She had come in to invite him to a nurse's' drinks party. Now she changed her mind.

Cormac had never met anyone like her before. He'd never given anything much thought beyond what he knew. His stuttered hesitation then hastily constructed excuse about being tired were simply confusion on his part, but taken for something rather worse by Kim-Ange. She turned on her surprisingly dainty feet with a quick tight smile and left the room, leaving Cormac with the horrible certainty that he'd been there five minutes and he'd already done something very, very wrong.

Chapter Six

If Kirrinfief had been a tiny bit bigger, Lissa would have immediately got lost, but not understanding Joan's directions had given her a chance to wander a little.

There was a small stream at the village's edge that fed into the loch, and down there she found a low building that formed the nursery (well, she assumed it was the nursery: a clutch of children were screaming their heads off in the garden and chasing each other with sticks, so either it was the nursery or something she really didn't want to get involved in at this stage) as well as a tiny redbrick school that looked incredibly cute and, a little further along the road, out of the village altogether on a grassy verge, stood the cottage.

Okay. She knew what her job paid. Cormac got paid less than her because she got central London weighting. But even with that, and even living in subsidised accommodation, even with all those things, she could never, ever afford a place of her own, certainly not one as beautiful as this.

It wasn't flashy, or incredible, or like something you'd see in an interiors magazine – nothing like that.

It was a cottage, roughly whitewashed again in the same style as the bigger house containing the GP's surgery. It had a roof that had obviously once been thatch, but was now slate, with two dormer windows in it, and there was a red wooden front door leading to a protruding porch that had a shoe rack, presumably for wellingtons, and an umbrella box with two walking sticks leaning out of it in a friendly way. There were two windows on either side of the door, giving it the friendly visage of a house a child might draw, and a stone step straight onto the pavement.

Behind the house was a small, tidy little garden with a vegetable patch planted neatly. Imagine, thought Lissa. Imagine having time to tend a vegetable patch. She had never met anyone in her life – not her family, always busy, nor her fellow nurses, some of whom worked two jobs to get through nursing college and the university courses that were required these days, nor her school friends – who had a garden, not to mention a vegetable patch. She had assumed this nurse guy was . . . well, she hadn't really thought about him at all after they'd failed to find him on Facebook. This was something that was happening to her, after all; he was inconsequential. However, she really, really hoped he didn't expect her to keep his vegetable patch alive. Because she really didn't have a scooby doo.

She added it to her worry stack, and went back round the front and turned the rusty key in the old lock, both nervous and rather excited.

The door creaked open straight onto a cosy sitting room – no hallway or corridor at all.

A wood-burning stove sat in the middle of the side wall, with an old fireplace surround; a leather sofa and a floral sofa bunched companionably around it. On the other side was a dinner table that looked under-utilised, and through the back was a small, functional kitchen in a wobbly-built extension with several glass windows overlooking the back garden. Behind the house was the stream, cutting through the bottom of the garden, and then – nothing.

Beyond were fields leading across the water to woods straight ahead, and the mountains loomed behind them. If there hadn't been an electricity pylon in the distance, Lissa could have been in any time from the past three centuries. It was really rather extraordinary.

She turned back and went upstairs. She was slightly worried about entering a strange man's bedroom as she mounted the small staircase. She needn't have worried. There were two tiny rooms underneath the eaves, with a tongue and groove bathroom in between them, and she was obviously expected to sleep in the spare, which suited her fine. The whole place was spotlessly clean. She wondered about him again. Gay? Some male nurses were but that didn't mean anything. Jack the Lad? She couldn't imagine many Jack the Lads would choose to live in a cottage in the middle of nowhere though.

Lissa hauled her bag up the narrow stairs and considered unpacking. The house was freezing and she couldn't find out where the central heating was. It then occurred to her that it might not have heating. Hang on. How was that going to work?

Back downstairs, she found a folder full of instructions for anything and everything, such as the hot water heater and the fact that she had to light the log burner and that would heat everything else. There were no instructions on how to light the log burner. This was obviously something they assumed everybody knew how to do. She opened the back door and glanced outside and sure enough, just next to the kitchen extension was a huge pile of chopped up logs that gave off a warm aromatic smell. In the kitchen was a small packet of firelighters and a box of matches. She stared at them for a long time, feeling as if civilisation had ended, and she was going to have to get on with life as the last person on earth. She felt the now familiar feelings of panic creep up on her.

Then there was a knock at the door.

Chapter Seven

Cormac figured he should probably go out and look at a bit of London. He took the tube up to Leicester Square, walked into M&M's World while wondering what on earth the point of that was, considered going to see a film until he saw the cost of a ticket, and ended up having a very poor meal in the window of a steak house, exactly as he had the last time. He didn't feel it was going very well.

'How's it going?' Jake texted him. 'Met any supermodels yet?'

Cormac rolled his eyes.

'I think I managed to insult someone already,' he replied. 'I'm not sure how I'm going to get on here.'

'Aye well, everyone in London's a weirdo,' typed Jake, man of the world. 'Was it a woman?'

'Think so,' typed Cormac tentatively.

'Did you apologise?'

'No.'

'Well, do that then!'

'I'm not sure what I'm apologising for.'

'That NEVER MATTERS with women.'

So Cormac set out to find the local supermarket next to his digs, quite pleased to have an errand.

He found it extremely confusing – there was no square sausage, the crisps were different, they didn't stock Irn Bru and in general it was not entirely unlike the time he'd been to Spain and wasn't sure what to ask for whenever he was hungry and once he'd asked for some toast with butter and everyone had laughed at him because he'd asked for toast with a donkey on it.

Anyway. He had made a mistake on his very first day and thought he'd take Kim-Ange a small minding. The shop didn't sell tablet or Tunnock's Teacakes or Edinburgh rock or Soor Plooms or Oddfellows so he was slightly puzzled as to what she might like but eventually he went for a box of Dairy Milk Celebrations, and knocked on her door.

Kim-Ange opened it up, looking magnificent in her Japanese robe.

'Och.'

Cormac pushed his hair out of his face, trying to look sorry.

'I thought ... I thought we maybe got off on the wrong foot,' he added.

Kim-Ange sniffed, folded her arms and raised a black eyebrow all at the same time.

'I'm ... from a very small village.'

'That had never heard of the internet or the outside world. We established that.'

Cormac looked down at the chocolates.

'Well, I'll just leave these here,' he said. English people were, he had concluded, very, very confusing.

'I'm lactose-intolerant,' said Kim-Ange.

'I'll throw them in the bin then,' said Cormac, picking them up and retreating.

Kim-Ange stuck her arm out of the doorway and snatched the box.

'Well,' she said quickly. 'It comes and goes.'

And she shut the door, making sure she didn't betray even a hint of a smile.

Chapter Eight

As soon as he'd knocked on the door of Cormac's cottage, Jake realised that turning up unannounced to greet a strange woman who'd just arrived in town might be seen as a bit ... well ... odd.

But on the other hand, he told himself, he was going to have to work with her after all. Might as well be friendly. Yeah. Friendly. Just checking in.

The sun was going down behind the meadow as Jake looked round. Ach, come on, surely she was going to like it here all right. It was gorgeous. And with someone like him to show her the sights ...

Of course, that wouldn't be appropriate. At all. But Jake liked playing the odds. Sure enough, Ginty McGhie still had her eye on him. But no harm in checking to see if there was any competition ...

'Yeah?'

A loud English voice shouted at him from the other side of the door instead of just yelling 'come in'. This was unheard of. Jake considered opening the door and just walking in as he'd have done if Cormac was home, but (thankfully) discarded that idea (Lissa would have hit him with a lamp she'd already eyed up).

'Hi ... uh, it's Jake Inglis? I'm the paramedic? Did Cormac no' mention me?'

Lissa cursed. This was the second time she was in trouble for not following the most basic of Cormac's instructions and actually reading the stuff he'd so thoughtfully typed up for her. She hadn't left him anything, just assumed that her entire world was pretty obvious. Was that what anxiety did to you? she thought. Made you so focused on the tumult inside you couldn't focus on anyone else, not properly?

Tentatively, she opened the door a crack. It wasn't locked, she realised. Presumably if he was going to murder her, he'd just have walked in.

Jake, perceiving what she was thinking, stepped back.

'Just me,' he said. 'Except of course, you don't know me, so saying "just me" isn't much use. Ha. Aye. And also I'm not in my uniform, so . . .'

Get it together, he thought to himself. This wasn't like him at all. But he hadn't expected . . . he hadn't thought of what to expect, truly. Not this pretty, curvy girl with ringlets coming out from her head at all angles, beautiful big freckles dotting her cheeks and tired dark eyes.

She was wearing old jeans and looked a bit cross. He wondered immediately what she'd look like with a bit of effort, and maybe a smile.

He tried one himself.

'Hello again,' he said. 'Jake Inglis.'

'Yeah, you said that,' said the girl, frowning. 'Sorry. I thought I didn't start till tomorrow.'

'Oh, you don't,' said Jake. 'I thought it would be polite to come and introduce myself . . .' Suddenly it didn't feel particularly polite to either of them, with twilight falling and the occasional owl hooting in the woods. ' . . .but I suppose I'll see you about.'

'Okay, thanks,' said Lissa. Inside, she was thinking how weird, how rude and stand-offish she was being. But she just couldn't . . . What was she supposed to do, make jolly conversation with a stranger? Nobody in London would do this in a million years.

'Well, let me know if you need anything – I promised Cormac I'd look out for the house if you need anything.'

'Okay, thanks – that's kind,' said Lissa, feeling her heart beat completely impractically. He was just being kind! she tried to tell herself. Nothing bad was going to happen! This was normal.

She found herself, anyway, closing the door on his face.

Oh well, thought Jake. You win some, you lose some.

Just as he was pulling out in his silver SUV, he heard her voice behind him.

'Sorry,' she said, and she did sound genuinely sorry; anguished almost. She was, Jake concluded, extremely odd.

'Aye, nae bother,' he said, stopping the car.

'No, I mean ... could you possibly ... ?'

She pulled at her curly hair. It really was quite something.

'Could you ...? Do you know how to light a fire?'

Jake slapped at his forehead.

'Did he no' leave you instructions? For God's sake, what a bampot.'

He jumped out of the car again.

'I mean, there's lots of wood ... but ...'

'But that's the only way to heat the house,' said Jake.

Lissa sighed.

'I was afraid of that.'

'And the water.' He looked at her. 'Were you just going to sit in the cold all night?'

Lissa tried to smile and looked rather rueful.

'Um. I don't ... I hadn't really thought about it.'

'Because it's going to be below zero tonight.' He grinned cheerfully. 'Just as well I turned up then.'

Lissa bit her lip, nerves returning.

'Suppose.'

Jake disappeared and came back with an armful of the neatly chopped logs.

'He's left you well-prepared. Good stuff too.'

He handed her one and she stared at him blankly.

'Smell it!' he said, and she took a tentative sniff. It had a deep, oaky aroma she couldn't quite place.

'Whisky barrel,' he said. 'When they don't use them any more. They burn like stink, and smell delicious. Right, watch this.'

And he showed her how to open the wood-burner and pile the logs up like Jenga to create a chimney inside the fireplace itself. Then he lit a firelighter, popped it down the middle of the logs, pushed open the flues and clunked shut the door. The entire thing was blazing merrily in ninety seconds flat.

'You may have to write that down for me,' said Lissa.

'Yeah, best thing is not to let it go out,' he said, showing her the basket of peat to the side with which she could damp the fire down through the night like a blanket, and let it smoulder. 'Then you'll be cosy all the time. Works all right this place. Once it's up and running.'

And he gave her a quick, charming smile and, before she even had the chance to get nervous – or offer him a cup of tea (if she had had any tea, which she didn't) – he'd bid her good night.

It turned that he was right: the cottage did heat up surprisingly quickly. There weren't any lamps, just a bright overhead light which reminded Lissa of the hospital, so she just sat as the evening grew pitch-dark, staring alternately listlessly at her phone and into the flickering flames. Then she opened her phone and looked for Deliveroo choices.

Blinking in amazement, she took in the terrible, terrible news. There were none.

Chapter Nine

Cormac gave himself an hour to get to the hospital the next morning, not understanding the layout of London at all, and was surprised to find himself there thirty-five minutes later. It was the oddest thing; he'd found, just by habit, when he got on to the packed tube train, that he looked around for a face he recognised like he would anywhere at home. Did you get over this? Not knowing a soul any place you walked? Everyone, regardless of colour or how they were dressed, had the same expression on their faces: a sort of studied disconnectedness; a completely inability to meet everyone else's eyes. Even the schoolchildren had it. It must be an animal's self-protection mechanism, he reckoned. Like dogs. Don't make eye contact, because you don't know anyone; you don't know how they'll react to you. What a strange way to live. Cormac couldn't really remember an existence where he didn't know most people nor they him. How did people cope? Wasn't everyone incredibly lonely all the time?

He liked Juan from HR at once, the diminutive form in a suit, phone going off constantly. Juan had smiled apologetically, said that it was great he was here, could he fill in a weekly questionnaire that someone would almost definitely not read, and by the way if there were another seventy or eighty full-time non-agency NPL staff available just like him up in the Highlands, would he mind terribly bringing them with him next time as they were a bit short-staffed? Oh, and one hundred and forty-seven midwives.

Cormac had smiled, realising what Juan was really saying: please, please get on with things and don't bother me. Which suited him just fine if Alyssa Westcott would just get in touch with him. He knew Jake was going round to see she was all right and, even if he hadn't known that, he'd have guessed it because that was pre-cisely the kind of thing Jake would do but, rather to his surprise, he hadn't contacted him. That wasn't like Jake at all. Normally he had a score out of ten for anyone between the ages of eighteen and about sixty-five, more if you included Helen Mirren. Maybe this Alyssa was just awful.

He opened up the case notes the hospital had sent him – the kind Alyssa was meant to be annotating for him – and thanked goodness for the GPS system.

$$\rightthreetimes \quad \rightthreetimes$$

Driving in London, however, he was not remotely prepared for. Cormac had been driving on his mates' farms since he was fifteen years old, like most Kirrinfief boys, and he could drive a tractor and had had a go on a baler.

But once he'd hit the open road, particularly for work, it was long hills of empty roads; single-track lanes when visiting farms; vistas of dappled mountain shadows so stunning that sometimes he would simply stop in a layby, push open the door of the little car, breathe in the sweet and bracing air and eat his cheese and pickle sandwiches staring out at the unpeopled view, feeling very pleased with his lot.

None of this was the least preparation for the crazed London traffic, with furious cabbies and delivery vans on insane sched-ules and huge Chelsea tractors doing the school run and red buses swaying everywhere; tourists stepping straight out into the middle of the road while keeping their eyes fast on the opposite way, expecting the traffic to come from the left; cyclists, darting through every gap in the road like birds. The exhaust fumes, the confusing lane systems, the vast roundabouts, the endless honking, the stop-starting – it was terrifying. And there was nowhere to stop, no quiet laybys, but red markings on the roadside which meant you couldn't stop at all, just try and rotate your head 360 degrees at all times to try and clock who was coming at you and from where.

Eventually, Cormac pulled into a large supermarket car park and took a deep breath. This was going to have to be got used to. These roads were insane. He took another deep breath and checked his satnav. Okay. There was an estate, not far from here, called Rosebud, and all the names of the buildings were flowers. He needed to be in Flat 19, Daffodil House.

➤ ↰

Daffodil House was the least likely thing to remind Cormac of daffodils he could imagine. It was a vastly high tower block, one of seven on the estate, cutting great bruised scars across the sky. As a child, he'd wondered what it would be like to live up high rather than their little terraced house. It sounded very exciting and glamorous.

Daffodil House was not like that at all.

There was deprivation in the Highlands, of course. Cormac had known houses without indoor plumbing. There were places that relied entirely on foraged wood to keep warm, and the usual ravages of all economies: drink; horse-racing; family breakdown.

But there were always the hills, the mountains, lochs and trees. There was work, even if it wasn't always the best paid. The schools still had plenty of outdoor space to play. You could still cycle your bike into the village and feel most people knew who you were, or walk into your local bakery and get a hello and a French cake for seventy-five pence and, rich or poor, that was one of the best things Cormac knew.

Whereas here ... There was an unpleasantly dark and dirty little convenience store with heavy bars on the windows and the grilles halfway down. A vast dog was chained up outside and it barked at him, setting off another few dogs around the place. Everything was grimy; nothing seemed friendly. Cormac was good at dogs – they didn't put that on the job description, though should have – but even he didn't feel like extending his hand to be sniffed by this fearsome-looking beast, who was baring his teeth at him.

'Good dog,' he muttered, heading on.

The lobby smelled absolutely dreadful, a concentrated mixture of hash and urine that made Cormac's eyes sting. He'd been buzzed in, but the trundling old lift took a very long time to come. There was graffiti everywhere. As he waited, an old lady came in pulling a shopping trolley on wheels.

'Morning!' said Cormac, standing back to let her go ahead.

'Fuck off,' she said instantly, and they had to stand for what to Cormac felt like another five years before the lift finally arrived, smelling, if anything, worse than the lobby. Two men got out, obviously in the middle of a fight about something, or so it sounded to Cormac.

'Yeah, roight, fing is, you cahnnnnt ...' trailed behind them as they swaggered past, all aftershave and wide knees. They glanced at Cormac as he went into the lift, though he kept staring straight ahead.

On the sixteenth floor, the scent of dope was still pretty strong, but was now mingled with food and cooking smells, some of which were good, some less so. Cormac paced up the hallway, which was covered in dirty linoleum. Most of the lights were broken and there was no natural light at all. Cormac didn't want to admit it but he was nervous. His admiration for his counterpart was rising in leaps and bounds.

He could hear music playing behind the door of number sixteen and knocked gingerly, then louder when it became obvious nobody could hear him. Eventually he rapped loud enough that the noise was turned down inside and a tumble of voices answered the door. He glanced down at his notes as a burly man pulled the door open, surrounded by children.

'Mergim Kavaja?' said Cormac, as best he could. The man frowned at him.

'Mer*gim* Ka*va*ja?'

Cormac tried again, with the emphasis on a different place. The man frowned at him suspiciously as a loud stream of questioning conversation from a voice took place behind him. He shouted back noisily, and Cormac simply showed him the name printed on the file at which he sniffed before pushing open the door.

The tiny flat, with its thin walls and cheap doors, was clean but full. Undeniably full. Through open doors, Cormac saw mattresses on the floors of each room and in the sitting room, bedding was piled beside two ancient worsted sofas. Men and boys sat around the living room and, where there wasn't space, they sat with their heads pressed against the wall. There was a smell of cooking as well as a lot of drying clothes, sweat and deodorant. The shower was running, and so was the washing machine.

'*Këtu eshtë infermierja, Mergim!*' said the man, somehow making it sound totally different to Cormac had, and in the corner a man raised his hand. They spoke to one another in an unintelligible string, then the man turned to Cormac.

'*Doktor,*' he said, pointing at him.

'Actually, I'm a nurse,' said Cormac, but everyone ignored him as he approached the man, who was sitting in the only armchair and had his leg up, his cheap tracksuit bottoms turned up to reveal a white skinny leg thick with black hair.

What Cormac saw was an absolute mess. He looked at it, blinking for a minute. He had stitches to take out, but the wound itself was a total mystery; it wavered up and around like a whirlpool, or a drunk.

'What did you do to yourself?' he asked, undeniably interested. He'd never seen anything like it.

The man – he was twenty-four according to Cormac's file – didn't say anything, but looked enquiring out into the throng. Eventually, a slender man with glasses who had been sitting on the side reading a comic in English got up, sighing. He hissed something at the man – presumably along the lines of 'speak English!' Cormac guessed – and then reluctantly came over.

'Hello,' he said. 'I Zlobdan. I speak English. Everyone else is . . .' He shot them a look. 'Very lazy men. Idiots.'

'Aye,' said Cormac. They didn't look lazy to him. They looked knackered and dusty from building sites, presumably on and off shift work, sharing beds even, if the amount of trainers was anything to go by.

'So what happened?'

'He have accident. With drill on site.'

'Okay,' said Cormac, taking a closer look at the wound. There were stitches all over the place; gaping holes that had puckered, then healed like that. It was fortunate he was young. In an old person, the skin wouldn't have been strong enough and would have stayed that way.

'He get stitched up here by . . .'

He indicated one of the men who blushed and went red.

'Is he a doctor?'

'No! He idiot!'

'Why didn't he go to hospital?'

'Because they are lazy idiots and didn't realise health is free here.'

'You're European though, right?'

'Yes! Albanian!'

'And you didn't know that?'

'I know that! Not lazy idiots know that!'

He gave the pair a look of withering scorn and the poor man stared at the floor.

'I sent him to hospital. After *all the screaming*.'

Cormac's lips almost twitched, contemplating how difficult it must be to share a tiny house with at least a dozen other men with whom you had nothing in common.

'We pay tax!' said the man fiercely.

'I know,' said Cormac, holding up his hands. 'It's okay; I'm just here to take the stitches out.'

He opened his box and took out his disinfectant wipes. Everyone was eyeing him up intensely; it was rather disconcerting. He wondered if there wasn't much to watch on Albanian TV. He snapped on the rubber gloves, then fingered the wound. It was a shame: it was a great creeping mess that almost certainly wouldn't have had to have been so if they'd cleaned it out properly and got a professional in. He looked at the man, who had now gone white.

'It's okay,' he said. 'I'm just going to take them out.'

'Drugs?' said the man who spoke English.

'There's no need,' said Cormac slightly sadly. The nerve endings would have been killed in the botch job, unfortunately. It would all be scar tissue from now on in.

'*Shiko nga dritarja, idiot i madh!*' said Zlobdan to the man, who looked as if he were starting to cry. The vast bear-like man stepped forward and drew out a plain bottle filled with what smelled to Cormac like white spirit. He passed it to the man in the chair, who took a huge swig, wincing as it went down. The bear-like man took it back, took a large swig himself, then put it back down.

'Um,' said Cormac, taking out the scissors. 'Honestly, you really don't have to worry.'

He took out a small pair of forceps, gripped the end of the metal stitch in his right hand, and gently started to unlace it.

There was a huge bang. One of the big bearded lads at the back had fainted out cold. There was a lot of conversation and chat about it until, sighing wearily, the big man took his bottle of spirits again and went over to revive him.

'Okay!' said Cormac, after he went over and attended to the

other man, including giving him a stitch in the back of his head while the others watched over him with interest, debating what he was doing in their own language.

'Everyone out!' he said as he tried to get back to his original patient. The men were nudging the big chap who'd done the original stitching, obviously admonishing him to watch and learn. He realised as he'd ordered everybody to leave that there was nowhere else to go in the minuscule apartment. The men crammed themselves politely into the hallway and stood, tense as if they were watching a football match.

'Tell him to look out of the window,' said Cormac, not wanting another fainting on his hands. Zlobdan promptly did so, and started shaking. Cormac leaned his arm on his patient's leg to keep it still and deftly pulled the metal stitches cleanly through the currently nerve-dead flesh. There was a little threading in and out, but the entire process was finished in less than a minute.

When Cormac announced to the room that he was finished, there was a pause – and then a huge burst of applause. Zlobdan burst into tears as the rest flooded in. Cormac found himself picked up and hugged. The bottle was offered to him, and it was quite difficult to refuse. He told Zlobdan to explain that he had to drive a car and Zlobdan thought that worrying about drinking before driving a car was the funniest thing he'd ever heard. One of the men produced a drawing of a huge angry spider in a web which Zlobdan explained the man was going to have as a tattoo and Cormac, affixing the bandage, explained that he couldn't have a tattoo for another three months and, when Zlobdan lifted an eyebrow, he added, 'Tell him if he does we'll have to take the leg off,' which was, hypothetically, potentially true even if it was profoundly unlikely, and when Zlobdan had explained to them once more that they didn't have to pay, the big man came out of the kitchen and handed Cormac a heavy plum cake.

And he left to the man tearfully shaking his head over and over while his friends cheered, as if he'd performed a miracle, and he felt both acutely ridiculous given the tiny job he'd done and rather pleased with himself, hearing the music start up again as he let himself back into the stinky lift with an exhausted-looking young women pushing a filthy double buggy and coping with a whining toddler who was covered in snot and in a T-shirt too cold for the brisk spring day.

He opened the door for her on the way out.

'Can I give you a hand with the buggy?' he asked, seeing her struggle.

'Fuck off, social work,' she barked him, and the day went on.

Chapter Ten

It was the silence, she considered, as she had sat down the previous evening on the deep, comfortable little sleigh bed in the sloping-roofed spare room, with its grey-washed floorboards and faded blue and yellow rug. Well, no, it wasn't silent, in fact: there were rustles outside and she could hear the wind moving through the trees, and the distant squawk of what, a bird? An animal? She didn't know.

Lissa prepared herself for not being able to sleep. She was in a strange bed, a very long way from home, cast into exile. She had a million new things to do tomorrow, a new case list to take on and a new set of worries as well as the ongoing ones, everything circling around in her brain. She was never going to be able to sleep – it was all so odd: the sweet-smelling air, the comforting crackle of the whisky-smoked wood in the fire and the faint tinkling of the stream in the bottom of the garden . . .

When she woke up nine and a half hours later, she hadn't even taken her contact lenses out.

In her surprise, Lissa was too late to make breakfast or do anything other than jump into the shower and, in her haste, use some of the old shampoo already there. It smelled of almonds.

She put on her glasses, tied up her damp hair and threw on her uniform. Of course, there wouldn't be any food; she was an idiot for not having planned all of this yesterday. Automatically, she went to open the fridge door anyway, then stopped as her hand didn't find the handle. That was odd. She tried it again, then smiled to herself. The door opened on the other side. It was a left-handed fridge. She supposed it wasn't that strange in the scheme of things but even though she was left-handed too, she had always considered such a thing the height of luxury. If he had a left-handed fridge, he would have left-handed scissors too! And tin openers! It was oddly thrilling. She glanced around but there wasn't a picture of him – or anyone or anything, in fact – up anywhere in the cosy little sitting room. Typical man, she thought. She had to email him. She glanced at her watch. Nope. No time. Damn it, and he'd have had Zlobdan's mob this morning, whom she'd come up against before. Could always do with a bit of prior warning. She glanced at her phone; there was a long message from him telling her what she should be doing.

Finding a half-empty box of cornflakes at the back of the cupboard, she grabbed a handful and looked at the message crossly. Well, wasn't *he* organised. Show-off. There was quite a lot of it. She'd look at it later.

✨

Lissa squinted at the address through the pouring rain but it wasn't making much more sense than it did before. She was parked on a narrow single-lane track, having a fight with the GPS as she had lost her phone connection which meant she couldn't download the attachment Cormac had sent her which presumably explained exactly what to do and where she was meant to be going to meet this patient. Oddly, this was making her cross with Cormac rather than, for example, herself.

94

She got out of the car and was struck once more by just how incredibly quiet everything was. She could see in the distance figures up and about on the hills – farmers, she supposed. Or shepherds. Where shepherds still a thing? She supposed they were. She looked closer. The white shapes on the hillsides had smaller white shapes prancing along beside them. She supposed they were lambs. It all looked like something out of a children's story book; an old orange farmhouse that she'd passed as she came in, set back from the road, with its red barn, would have appeared in something you'd read to a very small person.

Lissa had never in her life given her food a second thought beyond checking it was organic, sometimes, when she felt flush enough. She never cooked at all; why would you in London? Her mother hadn't cooked, had said it would put her in a domestic servitude role, whereas her job was to break out of feminine stereotypes. Which was why the nursing had never really gone down too well.

Anyway. Lissa wasn't going to think about that right now. Instead she drove back into the centre of the village, parking right in front of the bakery, to her utter amazement. There were no yellow lines or anything. She took a photograph to send to Kim-Ange, but she couldn't make it send.

Nothing seemed to have a street name, or at least nothing she recognised. There was something called The Binns, something else that looked like Lamb's Entry which she didn't like the look of in the slightest. Why they didn't put a farm name on when there were no signposts to farms, and they didn't show up on Google Maps, was unhelpful to say the least.

She looked in the window of the bakery. There were lots of things she hadn't seen before, including signs advertising PUDDLEDUB! and LORNE! Neither of which meant much to her, but she went in nonetheless. It was incredibly cosy and warm inside, and a cheery-looking woman looked up.

'Hello,' she said, taking in Lissa's uniform. 'Och!' she continued happily. 'You're yon lass that's up here doing Cormac's job for three months! Amazing, welcome, it's lovely to see you. Now listen, do you want me to put you down for a regular ginger delivery? And also the provost says could you join the Highland games committee but he says that to anyone who turns up so you don't have to say yes just to be polite, okay, dinnae mind it.'

Lissa had understood about one word in six of this and was seriously unnerved by why this woman was jabbering away to her, and how on earth she knew so much.

'So listen, if you join the Kirrinfief Facebook you can find out everything that's going on. There's a barn dance coming up if you're no' married – are you married? Cormac didn't think so, said there was only one person coming, and then Mrs Ochil said, well, maybe she's just trying to take a break from her man for a wee bit, you know men, can hardly blame her, and maybe he's got one of them big jobs down in London or you know, I know you're from London and it's all lesbians there too, I suppose ... Can I still call them lesbians? My son says I get it wrong all the time ...'

Her face looked worried as Lissa stood like a stone, completely unresponsive.

' ... Um,' said the woman, running out of steam. She met a lot of tourists in the summertime, but they were usually more than happy to chat, asking about walking trails and Highland coos and buying bags of shortbread and tablet and big sandwiches overspilling with coleslaw. She wasn't used to this. London, she supposed gloomily. She'd been once on a coach trip with her friend Agnes and neither of them had thought very much of it, and that was her settled opinion.

Lissa was trying not to panic. The woman was only trying to be friendly – she wasn't some spy sent to track her down – so she tried to tell the stupid voice in her head to shut up.

'Um ...' Lissa stared, bright red at the food behind the counter. A young labourer, unshaven and ready for the day in heavy work boots, came in with a cheery grin, shouted 'Hi, Deirds!' and ordered five steak bridies, two macaroni pies and four cheese scones, and Deirds asked him did he lose a bet and he replied yes indeed he did, but it could have been worse and it being the last thing he had asked for. When Deirdre's attention turned to Lissa again, she nervously asked for a cheese scone and was there the possibility of a coffee and Deirdre said of course and simply made her a Nescafé rather than asking her which of ninety-five different varieties she'd like to try, and charged her eighty pence for the privilege and handed her over a scorching plastic cup, and Lissa muttered her thanks and got out of there as soon as possible.

'That's the new girl?' said the labourer, Teddy. 'She's pretty.'

'Pretty rude,' sniffed Deirdre. 'Honestly. Why English people can't give you the time of day is beyond me.'

'It's because they're evil oppressors,' said Teddy, who had grown up in a staunchly independent family and was very clear as to what he thought of the visiting influx, which was why he kept working the land rather than somewhere nice and cosy inside a tourist operation.

'Aye, she's just never been made welcome afore,' said Deirdre. 'When Agnes and I were in yon London ...'

Teddy was only twenty-two but he was no stranger to Deirdre's conversations about how much she disliked yon London and although never minded to go there himself – Evil Oppressor Central – he knew he'd better get out to the lower field before Lennox gave him a kick up the arse. He was a great boss, Lennox, didn't interfere as long as the work was done, but you'd do no good getting on his wrong side during lambing season, anyone knew that, so Teddy bade Deirdre good morning and headed on his way, observing the strange English girl sitting in her car, looking as miserable as someone attempting to eat a warm cheese scone fresh out of the oven could possibly look, as word was already spreading about the village about her snotty ways, and if she hadn't been an Evil Oppressor, Teddy would have felt sorry for her.

➤ ➤

Lissa finally figured out which was Collin's Farm by asking another passer-by who, madly, also immediately knew who she was and was eager to engage her in conversation, asking if she wanted to join the village choir. She was pretty sure that wasn't in Cormac MacPherson's notes; he hadn't mentioned that she'd be expected to have a full personal conversation with literally everybody she met, and not much about how to get around. The fact was that it simply wouldn't have occurred to Cormac that she wouldn't have got all the necessary relevant information about how to get around by cheerfully talking to everyone she met; how else did people live?

The farm was small, a few cows and chickens mostly, the farmyard a churn of mud with the track, full of potholes, leading up to it single route. It did, however, crest a vast hill, and she suddenly caught a glimpse of the valley of the village down below beneath the shadows of the crags, with a straight train line on one side and the great expanse of Loch Ness on the other. She stared at it for a long while. It must be so strange to grow up here. All this space; all this fresh air. Did they like it? She supposed they must. How strange.

Blinking, she stepped out of the car, up to her ankles in mud.

'Hello?' she shouted out. The farmhouse itself was quiet, with old grey stone and empty-looking windows. It was perched high up in the hills and the cold wind whistled through her, as she was completely unprotected above the low stone walls, but suddenly she felt that the view was utterly breathtaking. She felt as if she was in the middle of a living, breathing painting in a million shades of green.

For the first time in a while, she wasn't constantly aware of whether her heart was jumping in her chest, or worried about loud noises or someone creeping up on her. She stopped to look at this vast canvas spread in front of her, with birds rising from scattered seed and tiny bounding spots of fluff on distant hillsides, mirroring the little clouds scudding quickly past in the cold sky. Lissa shut her eyes and took a deep breath.

So it was ironic, really, that the very next second she jumped out of her skin.

Chapter Eleven

The traffic wasn't getting any less frightening, Cormac noticed. He thought there was meant to be something called a rush hour, but it didn't seem to exist here. It was like that all the time.

The next address was a tower block too, but a very different one.

Right on the south bank of the river on a street called, mysteriously, Shad Thames, stood a high warehouse building and at the very top of it, as if it had been plonked on the top, was a white-panelled house in the shape of a lighthouse with a weathercock on the top of it. The warehouse was surrounded by terraces over-looking the Tower of London as well as looking up and down the sparkling river.

Inside, it was the most extraordinary place Cormac had ever seen. It was immaculate; beautifully furnished in a minimalis-tic way. Vast, expensive-looking paintings lined the walls, even though from the mirrors on three sides of the room the view was reward enough. It was a beautiful day in London, warm enough that Cormac's hi-vis jacket was an encumbrance, but the apartment was perfectly climate-controlled. Fresh flowers were lined up on every available surface. There weren't many drugs in Kirrinfief but Cormac had dealt with a few overdoses as a student on placement.

This was odd though, if the notes were correct. He'd never, ever met a junkie who kept flowers in a vase.

Barnabas Collier leaned against an island in the enormous kitchen, having buzzed Cormac up. At first, Cormac couldn't imagine what on earth he was doing there. His patient was standing with a glass of something he'd just taken from a huge American fridge. He was incredibly handsome: slim and fit-looking, he had floppy hair over the high planes of his face, with green eyes. It felt like a set-up, or a strange blind date gone a bit wrong.

'Hello,' said Barnabas warmly, shaking his hand. He was wearing lots of what was clearly an extremely expensive cologne. 'Coffee? Water? Wine?'

'I'm fine, thanks,' said Cormac, then he frowned and glanced at his hospital notes. Why couldn't Lissa have filled him in? There was nothing but the basics here. 'Sorry, it says here we have a wound treatment?'

'Yah,' said Barnabas, yawning ostentatiously and pouring himself a large glass of Chablis from the fridge. 'Sorry, don't mind if I do? Rather a hair of the dog – I was at a Serpentine party last night, and goodness, you know how they are.'

Cormac very much did not, and smiled awkwardly.

'So,' said Barnabas, leading him through to the seating area. It had floor-to-ceiling windows, two balconies, a vast grey modular sofa and a huge flat-screen television on the wall. Cormac didn't know many junkies who had those either.

'You're a very rugged young man. One of our Celtic cousins?'

'Scottish,' said Cormac shortly.

'Ooh lovely. Although I do miss busy Lissa . . . is she well?'

Cormac shrugged. 'Never met her.'

'Oh, that is *such* a shame. Seriously, my tastes are . . .' He gave Cormac a long-lashed look. '. . . very broad, but she is sweet as a peach.'

He sighed and sat down. Cormac frowned. This man didn't seem terribly ill at all.

'Sorry but . . . why isn't this being handled by your GP?'

Barnabas sighed.

'Oh yes ... we had a little bit of a rumpus ...' He smiled at the memory. 'Goodness me, she was quite the ... well. Mustn't be disrespectful.'

'Did you get struck off the list?' said Cormac, amazed.

'Oh darling, we both got struck off,' said Barnabas, smiling cruelly. 'Ho hum. *And* I'm banned from BUPA. Hence the riff-raff like you, darling.' He lifted up his glass. 'Are you *sure* you don't want a little glass of this? Just emptying Daddy's cellar ... It's quite tremendous.'

'No, thank you,' said Cormac. 'In fact, I've got lots of—'

'Yes, yes, more patients, I know.'

Barnabas stood up and unbuckled his trousers. He was wearing Calvin Klein underpants and, although too thin, was in beautiful shape: a narrow waist, long legs and a broad back. He looked like a statue, and gave an 'I just can't help being so gorgeous' look directly at Cormac as he did so.

'Aye, aye,' said Cormac. His attention focused on a small lump on the side of Barnabas's underpants, and he put on gloves to take a look at it. He had a good idea what it was, but he was utterly horrified when he finally unwrapped the bandage. Suddenly it became clear why Barnabas needed so much aftershave.

What was revealed wasn't merely a wound.

It was a hole, directly into his groin. Even Cormac, who had seen a few things – a man gored by a stag, for starters; a tankful of soldiers picked off by snipers – had never seen anything quite like this.

'I know,' said Barnabas, continuing to drawl. 'A *little* dramatic. Although it's quite the party piece.'

The thing was vicious; infected, oozing and incredibly deep.

'Why aren't you in hospital?'

Barnabas rolled his eyes. 'They won't give me the good stuff and they time everything.'

'You need a skin graft!'

'Yeeess ...' said Barnabas, staring out the window and gulping at his wine, and suddenly the full horror of what was actually happening struck Cormac forcibly.

Barnabas wasn't getting help because he didn't want it. A direct route into his body was actually fairly useful to feed his habit. The two men looked at each other, Cormac trying his best to hide his horror and disgust.

'And they still want to fuck me, can you believe it?' said Barnabas languidly.

The pain of it, Cormac thought. The amount of drugs he must need.

'I'll need to clean it out,' he said, gulping.

'Yes, please,' said Barnabas. 'I do pretty well, but it tends to make me faint.'

He slurped more of his wine, and Cormac got to work, trying not to stare out of the floor-to-ceiling windows or be distracted by the beautiful telescope and the great hanging works of art, or the Thames in full flow with dredgers, commuting boats, sightseeing boats and vast tugs full of slurry commuting up and down the great expanse underneath the bridges. It was a profound and extraordinary sight; the city laid at your feet, yours for the taking; everything you could possibly want. And what this beautiful, dissipated young man had wanted was to stuff himself so full of drugs that he had created an entire hole in his body. But he needed to focus on the job at hand.

Cormac hadn't really come up against money before – even the local laird was more or less skint, or certainly dressed as though he was. This hushed, thick-carpeted world was new to him.

He didn't like it at all.

He refilled Barnabas's glass at his request. Barnabas slugged it as if it were water. Then Cormac anaesthetised the area – Barnabas laughed at the idea of that doing him any good at all – and cleaned and swabbed it before filling it with packing and taping it together as best he could. It was nothing like enough.

'You need to be in hospital,' he said urgently. 'If you get sepsis, it could kill you.'

'Certainly not,' said Barnabas. 'I'm having far too good a time.'

He waved his arm around. 'You should join us tonight; there's a Shoreditch restaurant opening. Some filthy fusion thing, but the champagne should be good.'

'Thanks,' said Cormac, who thought it was perfectly natural to be asked to go somewhere on the spur of the moment. 'But I'd better skip to work.'

'Aw,' pouted Barnabas. 'It'll be adorable! You'll be like my pet nurse.'

He winced as Cormac spread the disinfectant further.

'Ooh,' he said. 'Yes – my private nurse! I can pay you. Better than what you're on, wouldn't be hard. Look after me. Keep it clean. You wouldn't even have to sleep with me!'

Cormac frowned.

'Don't talk to me like that. Don't talk to anyone like that.'

Barnabas pouted.

'Most people want to sleep with me.'

Cormac blinked.

'Where's your mum and dad?' he said quietly. Barnabas shrugged. 'Oh, Mummy's in Monaco, of course. She gets her drugs through plastic surgery. We both pretend we never notice. Daddy has two other families now. I can never remember the order; so very dreary.'

Cormac looked at him.

'I don't even want to try stitching it up.'

'No,' said Barnabas.

'But could you ... could you consider re-admitting yourself? Otherwise you're going to find yourself on the floor of A&E again.'

Barnabas waved his hand at Cormac. 'Oh, I will, I will. When I'm not so *busy*.'

He picked up his phone again and scrolled through Instagram, wincing at many different shots of his own beautiful face. Cormac stood up.

'Well, if you're sure you must go, darling ...'

'Please, please check yourself in.'

'Oh yes, darling,' said Barnabas. 'I'll add it to the therapists, the

103

rehab people, the psychiatrist, the art therapist and the yoga guru list Mummy sent over.'

He waved his hand towards a pile of invitations and thick gilt-edged cards. Cormac was still anxious about him.

'Are you in pain?'

'Why, what do you have?' said Barnabas.

'Not like that. I mean. Inside.'

Barnabas blinked.

'No,' he said finally. 'Everything's fabulous!' And he heaved himself to his feet. 'Come look.'

He grabbed Cormac by the shoulder, pulled him to the window.

'Look out there,' he said. 'Look at everything down there. Look at it. Look at that old tower . . .'

He indicated the vast sprawl of the Tower of London, dotted with bright red Beefeaters talking to cagouled tourists.

'See down there? That's layers of living history. Right in front of you. There's Traitors' Gate. That's where they rowed in Anne Boleyn for the last time. You can stand there, feel what went through her mind. Look at that bridge.'

Cormac gasped. He hadn't even realised Tower Bridge did still open up. But there it was, the cars and bright red buses lined up either side of its bright blue sides as incredibly slowly, the road itself, markings and all, began to move. It was hypnotic, particularly as a tall ship, sails furled, masts high, was carefully and elegantly sailing straight towards it. On the banks of the river, all sorts of people gathered to watch: parents pointing to children; well-fed businessmen at up-market Shad Thames restaurants, their expense account lunches forgotten, standing up to get a better look. The sun was gleaming off the water and the polished teak of the boat's hull as she glided through, as if impudently unaware of asking an entire city to stop just for her beauty.

'Wow,' he said.

'The city is yours for the taking,' said Barnabas. 'I don't want any more of it.'

'But you said tonight would be fun.'

'For you,' he said. 'Not for me.' He collapsed back onto the sofa. He looked very wasted now.

'Do not,' he said, 'let it use you up and spit you out. But do not waste it. And do not miss its magic.'

The bridge was slowly lowering again; the taxis were getting impatient, and the children pulling at their mother's skirts. Cormac let himself out and down the luxurious elevator, back to the new mysterious streets so far below.

Chapter Twelve

Aonghas Collins didn't mean to be frightening; he just had absolutely no idea why someone he assumed was Cormac from the uniform was hanging about his farmyard when they both had plenty to be getting on with, so he lumbered over carefully.

'Aye, whit are you doing, you lazy big Jessie?' he said, his brain, not being of the quickest sort, not quite getting into gear before he'd hit the fluorescent medical jacket squarely on the back with his good arm, knocking the figure forward and eliciting, to his horror, a loud scream.

The person turned round, black curls bouncing, hand up, ready to slap him in the face, true terror and panic in her eyes.

'Ah,' said Aonghas, jumping back in alarm. 'Ach, now.'

'What the hell?' yelled Lissa, red and furious. She realised her arm was up and slowly brought it down. 'What the hell are you doing?'

'Well, aye, well, this is my farm,' said Aonghas, muttering and looking around carefully just in case it might, for whatever reason, not actually be his farm.

Lissa was panting.

'Why did you *hit* me?'

'Aye, well, I thought you were Cormac,' said Aonghas, screwing up his eyes apologetically.

'Do I *look* like Cormac?'

'Aye, no, well, no, no you don't, no.'

'Why did you hit Cormac?'

Aonghas didn't really like being told off in his own farmyard.

'Didn't he tell you I was taking his place?'

It was entirely possible, Aonghas had to concede. Truth was, his mind wandered a little bit from time to time when people were talking too much, to wondering how his cows were getting on. He hadn't done well in school. But it hadn't mattered much. Although he supposed, indirectly, it had led to this – a strange woman shouting at him in his own farmyard ... His gaze wavered over to the high field, where he'd turned the cows out. The grass was so green it was practically fluorescent.

'Excuse me, are you listening?'

Aonghas looked at the girl again. She sounded bossy.

'Just ... don't sneak up on people ...' she said, as if she'd slightly run out of steam.

He blinked.

'But you're in my farmyard,' said Aonghas again, stubborn as his own cows when it came to sticking to a point.

They seemed to be at something of an impasse. Lissa, who had been shocked to the point of tears, then furious with both herself and this man at the realisation that of course she wasn't any better yet, how could she be, tried to shake herself out of it and glanced down at her notes.

'A-oooo,' she started, then gave up. 'Are you Mr Collins?'

'Aye,' said Aonghas, who was thinking it must be lunchtime.

'I'm standing in for Cormac. I'm here to look at your back.'

Aonghas didn't want this bossy person – a woman no less – to have anything to do with his wound but he didn't quite have the courage to say so in case she yelled at him again.

'Aye,' he said.

He looked in pretty good health from what Lissa could see but she followed him into the farmhouse.

Inside the low building was a nearly bare kitchen, with a long low table. One cup, plate and knife were neatly washed up on a draining board. Minimal supplies – porridge, flour, a small bowl of apples – were on the surfaces of the old kitchen; a fire was dying down in the corner. Aonghas paced over the flagstones, scowling. He didn't have people in the house very often, and he was never there himself during the day. He led Lissa to the table and sat on one of the ancient wooden chairs.

'Okay,' said Lissa. 'Can I have a look?'

Aonghas took off his heavy Shetland jumper and unbuttoned his ancient frayed check shirt until he was sitting in his vest – the air in the dark house was chill, but he didn't seem to notice. Lissa gasped when she took off the blood-soaked bandage. A great curl of skin had come off his back and the top of his right shoulder. It was all superficial but it was a horrible thing to see, like he'd been sandpapered. It must have hurt like hell.

'Are you all right? Doesn't it hurt?'

Aonghas shrugged.

'What happened? It looks like a burn.'

'Aye, Maisie got right shirty with me.'

Lissa rummaged in her bag for the disinfectant and Sudocrem and looked at him. Was that his wife? Girlfriend? Was she going to have to hand out one of her domestic violence leaflets?

'Oh yes,' she said, keeping her voice neutral as she always did in these situations. 'Did you have a bit of an argument? Had you been drinking?'

Aonghas snorted.

'Naw! She just kicked me.'

'You know,' said Lissa, inspecting it. It didn't smell, which was a good sign; it wasn't suppurating. She remembered suddenly that Barnabas had been on her list today. Oh crap. She really would have to warn Cormac about him.

'I'm going to clean it out,' she warned him. 'It might hurt a bit.'

'Aye,' said Aonghas, as if this didn't bother him, which indeed it didn't. He sat down as she ran a bowl with very hot water.

'So,' she said, launching into the spiel. 'Relationships can be tricky, can't they?'

Aonghas wouldn't know about that, as he had a special lady friend in Inverness whom he saw strictly on market days and the rest of the time got along just fine, thank you very much.

'Do you find you fight a lot?'

Lissa was abrading a small piece of flesh; Aonghas didn't even wince. Amazing.

'Sorry about this,' she said. 'So, about the fighting . . . I mean, it's hard, sometimes. To live together.'

Aonghas was looking out of the window thinking about whether he should sow some more buttercup seed in the big meadow. It was a waste of money, but they loved them, and it did look pretty in the sunshine.

'Does she kick you often? Because you know, there are organisations that can help out there. People tend to think that they're just for women, but they aren't; it's a common misconception. Everyone suffers from violence and there is help available. I can get you a leaflet . . .'

Aonghas turned round.

'Whit are you talking aboot?' he said, narrowing his eyes.

'I'm just saying,' said Lissa, 'abuse is nothing to be ashamed of. There are people out there who can help. Who care.'

'That my cow kicked me halfway to kingdom come because I had cold hands?'

There was a pause.

'Oh,' said Lissa. 'Oh!'

Her hand flew to her mouth.

'Sorry,' she said. 'I thought . . .'

'You thought what?'

'I thought Maisie was your wife.'

'*Maisie?*'

Aonghas couldn't suppress a laugh.

'I tell you, lass, if I had to marry one of my cows it wouldn't be that grumpy aul bitch!'

Lissa suddenly found herself bursting out laughing.

'Oh, thank goodness,' she said. 'Sorry. It's a horrible part of my job.'

'Aye,' said Aonghas reflectively, as Lissa disinfected the wound area without him even wincing. 'Must be.'

'Want a bit of lunch?' he said as she finished up with cream and rewrapping the bandage. Normally Lissa would have said no, but she was so unutterably starving hungry. Plus somehow being around the farmyard and out in the open air had done something to her appetite.

Aonghas got up and stoked the fire, then brought over an ancient stained tea-pot with fresh tea, a cup of foaming milk, a vast loaf of fresh white bread, a glass jar full of unidentifiable objects and a hunk of cheese. He handed Lissa a long thin metal prong which she had never seen before in her life. She took it and followed his lead as he sawed off a huge rough slice of the bread, poked his toasting fork through it and held it out just above the flames. Then he did the same with the lump of cheese until it was melting on the outside, just turning brown around the edges and starting to drip into the grate, whereupon he roughly spread it on the doorstep of bread, opening the glass jar and taking out a home-pickled onion, which he took bites of as if it were an apple.

Living in London, Lissa had taken advantages of the many amazing and varied cuisines the capital had to offer. She'd tried kangaroo; she'd eaten vegetarian mango curries with her fingers; she'd watched people throw things in the air at Benihana and lift up glass bowls of smoke and told to breathe in straw fumes. Kim-Ange had even once gone to a restaurant where everyone had to eat in the dark, and had a very happy evening confusing the other patrons and waiting staff.

But this was one of the strangest dining experiences she'd ever had. And yet the thick nutty bread, slightly charred around the edges, the strong melting cheese and the tartness of the sour onion ll taken together when you were absolutely starving, and washed down with the foamy milk, was one of the most delicious and satisfying meals she'd ever tasted. She sat back in front of the fire with a smile, the sun now streaming into the bare room, the silence total except for the ticking of an ancient clock on the mantelpiece.

'Thank you,' she said eventually. 'That was very kind.'

'You're welcome,' said Aonghas. 'I'll be sure to pass on your regards to Maisie.'

Lissa grinned.

'Okay. Listen, don't get it wet, try to sleep on your front and I think you can take the bandage off yourself in a week. Otherwise call the service and they'll make you another appointment.'

Aonghas smiled.

'Ach, lass, I think I can manage that.'

'I think you can too,' said Lissa. 'Good luck with Maisie.'

'She's an aul bitch,' said Aonghas.

And as Lissa drove away from the farm, she stopped by the side of the field where a clutch of extremely contented-looking peanut-butter-brown and white cows peacefully grazed in the cold sunshine on a field that glowed with buttercups, and they all looked beautiful.

Chapter Thirteen

After several more house calls and both of them getting lost countless times – with a near-miss when Cormac and a cyclist who called Cormac several names Cormac hadn't heard before and didn't feel he entirely deserved, and Lissa realising that, off-puttingly, people knew more and more about her as she did the rounds so that by the time she got to the last house someone was sending good wishes to her mother – each collapsed at home, equally exhausted. Lissa wasn't at all sure this placement was quite as restful as HR had thought it was, although she had rather enjoyed the twenty minutes she'd had to sit stationary in the car while a flock of sheep were herded up the road. She must take a book with her for next time, she found herself thinking, then realised what a long time it had been since she'd even felt unstressed enough to consider reading a book. Interesting.

Cormac, by contrast, was feeling antsy and oddly full of nervous energy for someone who was normally a pretty laid-back person. It was as if London had this static electricity that buzzed through it, making you wriggly. Maybe that was why so many people here were so skinny.

Also, Lissa thought, she had to log on to her Skype session with her therapist next and she was looking forward to that about as much as a plate of snake spaghetti, so she might as well get the emails over with first.

It was a very odd experience, sitting in someone's front room, with their telly and their Xbox and their sofa and their cups and plates, and introducing yourself to them. Biting her lip slightly, Lissa picked up her laptop and began.

> Hi, this is Alyssa Westcott. Thanks for the notes; they were really helpful

She lied. She would definitely read them later.

> The house is cool.

She didn't mention how the idea of having an entire house to yourself, with a garden and a spare bedroom and a stove and a stream, was insane. She was sitting in about five million quids' worth of real estate, if it could only be shifted 583 miles south.

> Here's what to look out for tomorrow. I don't know much about dogs, but I've learned this: James Felixton's dog will try and eat you, but Lee Cheung's is fine. James's is a little dog and Lee's is a big dog. Please don't try and talk too much at the Pooles; they have form for reporting people. And park in the home car park on the Effinch Estate but pay for street parking at the Widdings Estate as they're buggers.

Cormac looked at it. Well, that was a bit more useful. She didn't seem very friendly though. Which was pretty much what he'd heard from the villagers, who always had a lot to pass on about this kind of thing. Bit English and stand-offish and distracted was the general sense. He really hoped Kirrinfief wasn't going to turn out more stressful than London for her. Also, she hadn't asked him whether he was enjoying London. Probably assumed that he'd

113

absolutely have to love London; who wouldn't? He felt a little bristly about this.

> Hi Alyssa, thanks for all of that. Let me know if you need me to draw you any maps – I know some places are hard to find. Also I like drawing. 🙂 How are you settling in? Are you liking it?

But Lissa had already moved on to the next thing she had to do – the appointment she was dreading – and didn't reply. Well, so much for you, thought Cormac, leaving his phone and moving to the window, trying to open it to circulate the stale, trapped area of the heavily populated building.

Chapter Fourteen

Lissa made herself a huge cup of tea. Anything to postpone the inevitable. She knew lots of people had therapists. She didn't see any stigma in it, but she'd never felt the need for one herself. But that was before. And now it was 6.30. It was time.

The figure on the other side took a few moments for the pixels to rearrange themselves, but finally settled down on a woman of about fifty, but well put together, with a humorous tinge around her mouth and a level gaze visible even through the camera lens and the poor reception. She also appeared to be eating something from a bowl.

'Alyssa Westcott?' she said briskly and rather indistinctly.

'Uh-huh,' said Lissa, finding she was sitting cross-legged with her arms around her chest on the floor in front of the laptop.

The woman put her spoon down and squinted.

'Sorry,' she said. 'All I can see is knee. Do you mind?'

Lissa changed position but suddenly wasn't sure what to do. She moved the laptop onto a coffee table, then found herself awkwardly kneeling in front of it like she was in church, which she didn't like either. She tried sitting up and looking down into the screen, but in the little self-image, all she could see was her face looming over from above which wasn't a great concept. She was also increasingly aware of the fact that the more time it took her to make a decision about how she ought to be and sit, the more that would probably mean to the psychiatrist on the other end of the line, sitting waiting patiently, which made her start to blush and feel uncomfortable.

'Sorry!' she said, her voice sounding high and completely unlike herself, rather like some posh English woman asking if she was on the right train. 'I'm not quite sure where to sit!'

'It doesn't matter,' said the woman calmly which of course convinced Lissa that it did, very much, matter a lot, and she twisted round in a panic. She ended up back on the floor again, her legs tucked under her like a little girl.

Anita the psychiatrist was still smiling calmly at her, even with a quick glance at the upper right-hand quadrant of the screen which Lissa interpreted, correctly, as a glance at the clock on her computer.

'Um, ha! Hello! Sorry about that!'

'Don't spill your tea,' said Anita.

'No! Ha, it's not tea – it's vodka!'

Lissa had absolutely no idea why she just said that. Anita smiled politely, as if it didn't matter to her if it was tea or vodka.

'I'm only kidding! Look!'

Lissa tilted the cup towards the camera with predictable results, which lost more precious seconds in finding a tea towel and reconnecting the computer.

Anita continued to smile calmly and Lissa was just about to apologise and suggest they start over when a voice suddenly screamed, 'Mummmyyy!'

Anita's calm face winced, just a little.

'Mummy's busy, darling,' she hissed out of the side of her mouth. 'SAMOSA DONE FALL IN THE TOILET.'

Lissa and Anita both froze.

'Um, do you want to go sort that out?' said Lissa.

'No, no, I'm sure it's fine,' said Anita, doing her best to look

116

unflustered. 'Now, where were we? What we're going to do is carefully go through everything that happened that day, look carefully at the details . . .'

'I JUST EATING IT.'

There was another long pause.

'Just go,' said Lissa, even as Anita jumped up, knocking over a tall pile of notes and case files spilling onto the floor in view of the camera as she went. Lissa glanced at them as she heard a lot of yelling and negotiation taking place off screen. 'PTSD' was written on hers: she could make it out, bold as brass. She stared at it. Was that her? Was that who she was? Some crazy person? With a label and a title and a padded cell and . . .

Anita came back, her smooth dark hair ruffled, noisy crying still happening offscreen.

'So,' she said. She started clearing up the papers, spilling her coffee cup in the process. She screwed up her face.

'Sorry,' she said. 'Some days . . .'

'I know,' said Lissa. 'You work for the NHS. I know what it's like.'

But inside she was burning up with her diagnosis.

'So I have PTSD?' she found herself saying abruptly.

'What?'

Anita's phone was ringing. She glanced at it, hung it up. It started ringing again.

'That's . . . that's what you think I have?'

'I think it's a . . . sorry, I just have to get this.' She grabbed the phone. 'Where are you?'

There was a long pause.

'Well, where's your bus pass? But if you don't take your bus pass how can you expect . . .? I'm working here! . . . Well, you'll just have to wait. Where are you? Well what can you see?'

She made an apologetic face at Lissa who was beginning to wonder whether this was, in fact, the therapy, designed to make her feel better about being all by herself in the middle of nowhere.

By the time Anita had untangled herself from the complexities of the phone call and was nervously eyeing something Lissa couldn't see but could only assume was almost certainly her car keys, their time was almost up.

'Whether it is or whether it isn't PTSD,' said Anita eventually, 'we've found the standard treatment protocol helpful.'

'I know the standard treatment protocol,' said Lissa a little snappily. 'You want me to go over it all again.'

Anita nodded sympathetically.

'It's certainly something we'd want you to try.'

Her eyes meandered sideways again. Lissa saw red suddenly.

'But I do. I go ... I go through it in my head. Every day. All day. Every time I close my eyes. Every time I see a teenage boy, or hear a yell or a shout.'

'I realise that,' said Anita as patiently as she could. 'That's why you have to start from the beginning and go through every inch of it. So it loses its power. So. Tell me about that day.'

'That actual day?' The knot in Lissa's stomach tightened. She took a very deep breath.

'Uh-huh.'

'Right now?'

Anita nodded again.

➤ ➤

It was painstaking, painful. Every detail. The sun on the window frame. The saying goodbye to old Mrs Marks. The noise of the car revving up ... its speed, faster and faster, the gleam of the phone in the air ...

'I was looking at the boys shouting at each other ...'

Lissa dissolved into sobs.

'I can't,' she said. 'I can't.'

'You can,' said Anita softly. 'You can, Lissa. You were looking at the boys shouting at each other ...' she repeated. 'You were watching them. What did you notice?'

Lissa shook her face, creased with tears. Then she took another breath and opened her mouth.

'Mummy!'

A tiny, sweet face appeared, marched up to the screen, seemed to stare directly at Lissa, and then, to the surprise of everyone, slammed the computer shut.

❧ ❧

Lissa felt completely stranded. The tears still falling down her face, she re-opened the computer but the connection was gone and she couldn't call Anita back; that was how these consultations worked.

She went defeatedly upstairs and turned on the taps to the bath. The pounding of the hot water and the fizzing over of the bubbles gradually overtook her tears. But the fear remained. There was something wrong with her. That's why she'd been sent away.

She grabbed her book, retrieved her tea and sank slowly into the bubble bath. Every time her thoughts spun towards the trauma, she forced her attention back to her book and took another slug of tea. As her mind quieted, she listened to what was outside, to the wind whistling through the trees and the calls of distant owls, and instead of finding it threatening, she found it calming instead.

She knew, even in the brief time they'd managed to discuss it, that on one level Anita was absolutely right. She would have to think about it, would have to be able to work it through in her head to stop the panic attacks and the anxiety.

But right here, in a warm bath with a book, even if she still couldn't really concentrate on it, it still felt nice to feel the weight in her hands, almond-scented bubbles, a cup of tea and the sound of the wind through the trees instead of traffic and sirens and helicopters . . . well. She wasn't going to think about it. Not right now.

Chapter Fifteen

And Lissa did feel better when she'd woken up after another surprisingly long night's sleep. It had to be the fresh air; every breath felt like she'd never properly opened up her lungs before. It was very early, the light creeping through, and suddenly the fear had returned. She looked out of the window at the waving daffodils in the garden, trying to calm herself, then gave up and scrolled through Instagram until it was a decent time to get up.

Her first appointment wasn't until later so she popped to the little grocer's and picked up some amazingly cheap eggs (though she didn't know they were cheap as she'd never bought eggs) direct from Lennox's farm, some local butter and milk and some sliced bread from the baker, and she had time to make herself some scrambled eggs on toast. The sun had risen by now; there was a chill wind, but she discovered, out of the back of the cottage, the small patio next to the wall was an almost perfect sun trap, warm enough to sit out in regardless of the wind.

She tried to block out what had happened with the psychiatrist the evening before. Just to change the mental subject, she checked in with Kim-Ange, whose Instagram was full of her dressing up and wearing different hats in what looked suspiciously like the millinery department at Peter Jones, where they tended to take rather a dim view of that sort of thing. She missed her suddenly; missed her old life completely. It was practically the weekend. They would have been up to all sorts. Then she looked at her file casing for the day and her heart skipped a beat.

She knew she wasn't supposed to know. But seriously, you couldn't avoid it. Young, female, heart transplant, and the dates matched. They hadn't pulled this placement out of thin air. Not at all.

Cormac's notes were very straightforward: he'd typed 'BRILLIANT' at the top. Lissa did not think it was at all brilliant; she thought he was being unusually tactless.

She stood up and washed her dishes, then found herself making up a packed lunch – a packed lunch! Who was she?! But then it wasn't her fault there wasn't a Prêt for two hundred miles. She took a picture of it and sent it to Kim-Ange to make her smile: a cheese sandwich, augmented with something she found in Cormac's cupboards that she very much hoped was home-made pickle. No tofu. No beansprouts. No cronuts and no bento boxes. She added a couple of russets and contemplated buying a flask and smiled, just a little, wondering again who she was.

⤙ ⤚

It was truly a lovely morning, and Lissa decided to walk in – she was going to the centre of the village so she could put her medical bag in a rucksack on her shoulders, and it wasn't likely that she was going to be mugged or leave it on a tube.

And it really was a glorious day. She stopped for a full five minutes once she'd crossed the road, watching a field of brand-new lambs hop and skip. They were hilarious, tumbling, jumping over puddles, then every so often making bleating noises and skeetering back to the comfort and safety of their mothers, who placidly ignored them as they rang rings around them, and reached their little pink mouths up to suckle. They were entirely enchanting in the sunshine, and hard to watch without your spirits rising, at least a little.

Lissa focused on her breathing as she approached the little terraced house. Annoyance leapt in her once again as she wished her psychiatrist hadn't been so brusque or, if she was being truly honest, had tried to call her back. Stupid NHS cutbacks, she told herself. Throwing her in at the deep end like that. And now this.

The door was flung open almost before she had finished ringing it. The woman there though looked confused to see her.

'Och no!' she said. 'Where's Cormac?'

'Um, he's on secondment,' said Lissa. 'It's me instead. Sorry.'

'Aye!' said the woman beaming. 'Oh, I heard all about you!'

'Yes, I'm beginning to realise that,' said Lissa, trying to sound as friendly as the locals rather than slightly sarcastic.

'Och, I miss young Cormac,' said the woman, shaking her head. 'How's he getting on? Is he eating all right? Is he enjoying it?'

'How would I know?' said Lissa, genuinely confused.

The woman looked at her. 'But he's doing your job?'

'Yes.'

'But you've no' chatted about it?'

Lissa shrugged.

'Not really,' she said. 'How's . . .?'

She had trouble pronouncing the name, but the woman's face lit up.

'Oh well. You didn't see her before. You had to see her before. That's why I wish Cormac was here.'

'Well, he's isn't . . .'

'I know. But I wanted him to see this.'

Lissa followed, feeling very second best, into the tidy little sitting room.

Sitting in front of *Pitch Perfect* was a very thin pale little girl with black circles beneath her eyes. The fact that she was sitting up was somewhat lost on Lissa.

'Hello,' Lissa said softly.

The girl's face screwed up.

'Where's Cormac?'

Lissa smiled thinly. 'Oh well, he's in London. I'm standing in for him for a bit. Think of me as Other Cormac.'

There was a pause while Lissa wondered if she was going to meet a hostile reception. Then the girl's face brightened.

'Will you tell him? Will you tell him you saw me? Will you tell him everything?'

'Um, of course.'

'Will you take a photo?'

'No, that's not allowed.'

Islay frowned, but her mother relaxed and went through to put the kettle on.

'Take a picture!' insisted the girl bossily, and put on a vast grin and a ta-da with her hands.

'Do it!'

Lissa tried to smile patiently.

'I'd lose my job,' she said. The girl looked suspicious.

'And so would Cormac.'

But already the mother was bustling back in, smiling expectantly.

'Och, he'll be wanting a picture,' she said. Islay smiled triumphantly and posed again, and Lissa reluctantly snapped her.

The girl's blood pressure, heart rate, healing scar were all fine, totally normal. The parents both lingered at the doorway, fearfully watching her every move in a way that made the back of Lissa's neck prickle. She didn't understand why they were so smug and triumphant about it all. Didn't they realise? Didn't they know that an innocent boy's blood had trickled out on the pavement for this?

Um, hi. The Coudrie family asked me to write to you directly and send you a picture.
Oh, and thanks for the house and everything. I took the spare room by the way. Oh, and I picked some daffodils; I hope that was okay. Hope everything is okay with you.
Anyway, Islay seems fine, all vitals normal, I'm not sure I even

needed to be there. Scar fine and healing fast, patient well in herself, talkative, seems perfectly normal situation. Don't know if follow-up visits will be required as long as immuno-suppression initiation continues as normal, but they were very adamant I let you know and send you a picture. Please don't share it. I know I shouldn't send it but she was quite persuasive.

Yours sincerely,

Alyssa Westcott

It wasn't until later that night when she got the email back from Cormac that she realised what she had missed.

Cormac had had a trying day. He had mixed up the dogs, and was slightly perturbed that when discussing the dogs, Lissa had completely failed to mention that James had a boa-constrictor in the house. He hadn't been terrified exactly; it would just have been nice to have had a bit of forewarning.

On the plus side, he'd only got lost three times and been shouted at by two cyclists, once for reasons that almost weren't his fault. He'd gone for a pint after work and been charged seven pounds and, while he didn't think of himself as a stingy man and certainly didn't want to live up to any kind of Scottish cliché, internally he couldn't help wincing. And it wasn't like Wullie's pub, where anyone – hill walkers, tourists, locals, long-lost American cousins searching for their roots – would strike up a conversation with you; where the pub was a convivial meeting place full of dogs and farmers and weather and general hospitableness after a long day. Here there was nowhere to sit and there were large groups of aggressive young men and everyone was ignoring everyone else and there was a slight atmosphere of menace and the beer tasted like fizz and nothing else. Cormac had always thought of himself as a man of fairly simple tastes but he wasn't sure he fitted in here at all.

The streets were completely astonishing to him. There was a tramp, Dorcan, in Kirrinfief. He'd been there longer than anyone could remember, and nobody even knew if that was his real name. He came and went, slept in the churchyard, accepted soup and meals left out for him, spoke to no one and sat on his bench, then went on his way again to who knew where. Judith the friendly vicar, whose garden he was effectively sleeping in, left the vestry open for him, but he never used it, even on the wettest of nights.

But here, there were just people lying about everywhere. In underpasses and shop doorways and over vents and under bridges. And nobody batted an eyelid. It seemed completely fine. Cormac was completely baffled by the whole thing, but followed what other people did, buying the *Big Issue* when he saw it, blinking in puzzlement. Wasn't everyone here rich? Walking about the city he'd seen a gold car parked in Covent Garden; he'd seen restaurants where everything cost thirty pounds; shops that smelled of money, with fantastical window displays; jeweller's with watches that cost more than he made in a year.

He knew he didn't understand politics – he'd spent enough time sitting in a desert for reasons he didn't quite understand to pretend to know anything about anything. But it was so very odd that everyone had just learned to live with loads of people lying on the ground.

Lissa's email changed his mood in an instant. He pulled out his laptop in the pub and typed back:

> Hello, thank you for the dog warning, but if you feel like adding snake warnings at any point, that would also be appreciated!
> I bet Islay was persuasive! That's brilliant! That's just so fantastic! I can't believe she's sitting up! And talking of her own accord! Christ, they must be over the moon – thank you, thank you for doing the house call and reporting back. I've been worried sick. Amazing. Sometimes this job is really fricking amazing, don't you think? You should have seen her before.

And he attached a picture of Islay he had taken for her mother, when they thought it might be the very last time they saw her alive: a blue bag of skeletal bones, connected to every lead in the ICU department; a wraith; a frail whisper of an angel death had already clapped its scaly wings around.

Comparing the two pictures side by side and reading again Cormac's heartfelt joy, happiness and relief, Lissa considered the sickly girl she'd just met, back from the very foot of the grave, watching *Pitch Perfect*, eating ginger crunch biscuits, sitting up in her living room and being cheeky. And she understood, as she stared at the picture for a long time, and felt a little spark inside her.

She meant to put the file away. Then she found herself, on impulse, emailing back:

What's wrong with a lovely boa-constrictor?

To her total surprise, after a few moments she got back not an email but a text showing a photograph of a drawing, and she smiled.

Is that you?

Did you mean: oh, look at you, you poor thing being strangled by a boa-constrictor?

That's a terrible picture!

I'll have you know that's exactly what I look like.

You're definitely more scary than the snake.

Thanks very much.

And, shaking her head at the odd message, and hoping he hadn't scared James's pride and joy too much, she went to bed.

Chapter Sixteen

The week continued, even as they both started to get into the swing of things. Cormac peeled a layer of clothes off every day to stop being so hot, and Lissa added a layer every day to stop being so freezing.

Lissa didn't realise how much people were gossiping furiously about her and thought she was stand-offish because she generally considered not making eye contact the most polite way of dealing with strangers. Oblivious, she managed to cover the vast majority of her calls – there was diabetes management, as everywhere, and some quite complex psychiatric treatment she called the hospital to talk her through step by step, as well as other commonplace call-outs. Joan seemed, if not exactly over the moon with her, particularly when it turned out she had absolutely no opinion on the horse racing, not entirely displeased.

At 6.30 p.m. four days later though, Lissa was back staring at the laptop.

'Before we start, I meant to tell you, turn off your social,' said Anita, who was speaking fast and eating with chopsticks. Lissa watched her hands, fascinated.

'*What?*' said Lissa. 'What's that got to do with PTSD?'

'What have anxiety-creating engines designed to distract, enervate and worry you got to do with your mental health?'

Lissa frowned. There was a cough on the other side of the computer screen.

'I know,' said Anita, but not to Lissa. The forlorn cough came again.

'Sorry,' said Anita quickly. 'I had to keep her home from school.'

'I'm sorry about that,' said Lissa.

'IZ FINE,' came a small voice, followed by another racking cough.

'She's not fine. She just wants to watch *Frozen* again.'

'Maybe you'll start telling your clients to build a snowman,' said Lissa, and the two women smiled briefly at one another.

'Have you had a trial date yet?' asked Anita.

'No. It'll be ages away.'

'It probably won't,' said Anita. 'They fast-track these things, particularly with young lads.'

Lissa sighed.

'So you're going to have to be ready,' said Anita unnecessarily. 'If you can't stand up and tell your story, there might be a mistrial. They might be freed. There might be no justice.'

Lissa's heart sank again.

'Why does that mean I have to give up my social media?'

'Are you on it a lot?'

Lissa glanced at her phone. Kim-Ange appeared to be wearing a bowl of fruit on her head.

'That depends how you define a lot.'

'It's going to really impact your recovery,' said Anita, slurping. The coughing began again.

'How?'

'It's making you ill. It's making everyone ill with jealousy and self-doubt and you are particularly vulnerable and in danger from it.'

Lissa looked at Anita. She had a large splodge of curry sauce on her cheek, but her expression was serious.

'But I'm out here all alone, and then I'll be even more alone.'

'Good,' said Anita. 'Use your inner resources. Stop trying to distract yourself with tiny pictures and other people's lives. You're distracting yourself from things you ought to be owning up to.'

Lissa was biting her lip.

'Feel,' said Anita. 'You have to feel what you need to feel. Not to distract yourself every five seconds. Not to be constantly waiting for pinging and swipes and likes and making yourself anxious. Trust me, Lissa. You are already anxious. You need to get ready to tell this story and you only have four more sessions. Embrace the way you— Oh!'

'What?' said Lissa, but there was no need. Loud and painful sounds of vomiting were coming from off-screen.

'Not . . . not on the files!' Anita yelled as she jumped up.

Lissa waited for quite a while, but Anita did not return. Lissa knew she had six sessions of therapy and six only. That was two down already and they didn't quite seem to have got started yet. And the news that the trial would be soon, when she had assumed it would be months and months, was very worrying. She checked Google, and sure enough the mayor's office was trying to clamp down on youth crime in London by fast-tracking everything through the courts.

She sighed. That was very bad news indeed.

➤ ➤

But Lissa did that one thing. She muted her Facebook and Instagram accounts, leaving cheery messages to stop anyone worrying about her, and removed herself from the conversation. She thought she would be lonely and miserable. In fact, instead – and with the occasional WhatsApp check-in from her good friends – she found it oddly freeing.

Without really noticing it, she started talking more to the locals, simply because she had no choice, including Deirdre in the bakery and Mrs Murray in the general store. She also met another English girl called Nina who ran the book van, and who made her up a care package, to her delight, of books she might enjoy to cheer herself up, which worked beautifully – *Cold Comfort Farm* made her laugh out loud; she had never read Jeeves and Wooster before and found it incredibly daft and funny; and, oddly, *The Worst Journey in the World*, which Nina pressed on her – a story of Scott's journey to the South Pole – ended up being extremely cheering too. Things are, Lissa thought, never that bad if you're not stuck at the South Pole in minus forty degrees with no food, your tent blown away and a storm closing in.

It was odd advice. But good advice.

And every day she'd swap patient notes with Cormac, mostly brisk, but sometimes funny, or offbeat. Irritatingly, he'd normally heard about anything that happened to her: getting the car stuck up the dyke road, because apparently *everybody* knew you didn't drive up the dyke road after a heavy rainstorm, but nobody had thought to mention it to her, and it had taken half of Lennox's lads to pull her out again. He'd also caught her up with how Mrs Marks had switched to Turkish Delight, believing it to be okay.

> Seriously? Did you confiscate it like I told you?

Lissa had not hidden how appalled she was when she wrote back.

> Yes!

> What did you do with it?

> Nothing!

And then in the next email:

Lissa responded:

I am amazed that you had to become an NPL instead of a professional artist.

Me too. An endless and disappointing loss to the art world.

What do people do on the weekend round here? Have you got anything to do?

In fact, he did. There were people from Kirrinfief in London – not many, and it was his mother's idea to make contact with them, which rarely boded well as she didn't speak to him that much. But it was either that or literally nothing at all, sitting in one small room breathing bad air, so he'd said yes.

That's very unfair. You have a ready-made social life in the greatest city in the world.

So do you. Just go down the pub.

And make friends with Alasdair?

Well, that sounds like you already have.

Lissa signed off, and Cormac made a mental note that as put off as Jake had been before when he had visited her, it might be worth suggesting another shot. Meanwhile, he had the ordeal of a big London night to prepare for. He popped another piece of Turkish Delight into his mouth and chewed thoughtfully.

Chapter Seventeen

The night out wouldn't have happened if it hadn't been for Cormac's mum who did the Rotary Club with Larissa's aunt, although Cormac's mum just helped out and the very posh Larissa's aunt Tabitha was the local grandee in charge, who handed out the prizes at the local pet show and chaired the ball committee. Bridie hadn't forgiven her youngest son for ducking out of the Army and taking a local job, but she wasn't going to tell Tabitha this. In fact, she made quite the point of him going to London and hobnobbing with the hoi polloi, and wasn't Tabitha's niece there, and perhaps she could show him around, and Tabitha, who was a decent sort underneath it all and terrified of appearing a snob just because her brother was the Duke of Argyll, agreed and passed on the details.

And, in fact, she caught her niece at just the right moment. Larissa was still in an absolutely furious mood after being rejected the previous year by the local laird, Ramsay Urquart, who had, in fact, headed off with some guttersnipe nanny who'd inveigled her way sneakily into his pathetic affections – '*Such* a cliché,' she'd moaned to her friends, who'd all agreed with her completely and said he couldn't handle a strong woman with her own mind and poured more fizz and complained yet again about how shit all the men were those days and they'd all very much agreed with her, which was comforting.

Larissa hadn't seen a picture of Cormac. He wasn't on Tinder, not that she'd been looking at it or swiping at all and anyway Tinder was for absolute losers. It was kind of ridiculous, but they wouldn't let her on Raya – a disgrace, all her friends agreed, which was also comforting. Anyway, Tabitha said Cormac had looked after her knee when she'd had it replaced and was quite the totty, but Tabitha still thought Peter Bowles was the height of totty, whoever he was, so she wasn't going to take Tabitha's word for it.

And it rather appealed to her to see someone from Kirrinfief. Let that get back to Ramsay, see how much she absolutely did not care and was *not* a snob or only after him for his title – as *if*. Who wanted that stupid crumbling house of his when here she was dating a nurse or something? So. Pleasing her aunt, of whom she was fond, annoying her ex, bringing a (hopefully) hot new man into her circle *and* initiating some Scottish rube into what proper London sophistication actually looked like sounded entirely up her street, so she booked a table at her swanky London club and brought lots of her girlfriends on board and got the fizz in and was in general in excellent spirits.

Cormac, meanwhile, by the time Friday night came round was absolutely exhausted from the driving and from the myriad of different cases he now had on. He'd never treated sickle cell disease in his life before, for example, and was studying up and fast as he could. However, he got ready in a pair of twill trousers he had bought by mistake online once and never worn out in the village because everyone would laugh at them (they were a little tight, particularly down on the ankle) and a green-grey shirt Emer had bought him that she said exactly matched his eyes, which made him feel a bit of a prick when he wore it in case anyone thought that he had bought it for himself because it matched his eyes because he thought he was terribly good-looking.

Kim-Ange found him ironing in the laundry. She narrowed her eyes.

'Where are you going?'

'I don't know. Some house?'

'Somebody's house?'

'No,' said Cormac, wrinkling his face. 'It's called a house but it's not a house. But I don't know what it is. I have to give my name at the door.'

'Soho House?'

'No. But like that.'

'Stockton House?'

'Yes!'

'Oh my God!' said Kim-Ange. 'That's, like, a totally cool private members' club. You can't just walk in there.'

'Why not?' said Cormac. 'Is everything free?'

Kim-Ange snorted. 'No! Very expensive.'

'So why?'

'Exclusive, darling. For the glamorous people!'

They both looked down at the shirt he was ironing.

'No,' said Kim Ange. 'You want to stand out.'

'I really, really don't,' said Cormac.

'This is London, not Buttington McFuckington! You're not going to a sheepdog-shagger trial!'

Cormac gave her a look.

'You're being quite rude.'

'Come with me,' she ordered.

❧ ❧

Kim-Ange's room was as different from Lissa's as could be, despite being the identical size and shape. Somehow, she'd squeezed a double mattress in there, which took over the entire corner of the room next to the window. Purple and red cloths with tiny mirrors were draped over the walls and the ceiling, and there were large red shaded lamps that gave the room a pink glow.

'More flattering,' said Kim-Ange. Purple scatter cushions were everywhere, and scented candles cluttered up the surfaces, their scent lingering even though they weren't lit. Fairy lights lined the old faded curtain rails.

'Welcome to my boudoir!' she said, and Cormac had to admit, it was undeniably a boudoir.

'Now...' said Kim-Ange. She disappeared into the cupboard, rummaging among tightly stacked boxes as Cormac looked at a collection of fabulously high-heeled shoes.

Eventually, Kim-Ange brought out an old cardboard box. She smiled at it ruefully.

'Sentimental reasons,' she said.

She opened up the box. It was full of wrapped-in-tissue, carefully saved and beautifully folded men's clothes. Designer labels, high-end stuff, all of it. Some was garish; bright colours and the occasional rhinestone. Plenty of it was just perfectly normal, but beautifully cut and made.

Cormac blinked as she pulled out a snowy white shirt made of heavy, billowing material, then shook her head and expertly folded it up again.

'Was this ... was this yours?' he asked tentatively. Kim-Ange looked at him to check he wasn't being facetious, but he was clearly just interested.

'Yeah,' she said. 'It's like keeping an old photo album.'

She grabbed an exquisite cashmere black jumper.

'Oof,' she said. 'Dries Van Noten. I bought it in Antwerp.' She smiled to herself. 'What a weekend that was.'

She offered it to him.

'It would fit you,' she said. 'He cuts Dutch.'

Cormac didn't know what that meant, but there was no denying it was a beautiful piece of clothing, even to him, he who had only stopped letting his mum buy his M&S undies when he joined the Army.

'Wow!' he said.

'Have it,' said Kim-Ange. 'Seriously. It's of no use to me.'

She was wearing a lemon-yellow half scarf, half top with a pink gilet fringed in fake fur over it. Her hair was festooned with pink clasps.

'I'll . . . I'll bring it straight back.'

Kim-Ange waved her hand as Cormac pulled it over his head. It fitted in a way most people would have said was perfect, and Cormac found extremely tight.

'Oh yes,' said Kim-Ange. 'Have you got a white T-shirt? Brand-new, nothing faded or grungy in the wash.'

He had a pack of three vests, in fact, and Kim-Ange announced that as absolutely fine. The trousers were still a horror story, but there wasn't much to be done about that, and his black desert boots were passable, if disappointing.

She sent him off for a shower and shave, and demanded to see him afterwards.

'I'm just going to do your eyebrows,' she said. 'Sit down.'

'You're going to do my *what*?'

'Just remove the spare hairs. Tidy you up, nothing dramatic.'

'My *eyebrows*? What's wrong with my eyebrows?'

'You just have to be . . . a little groomed, that's all.'

Kim-Ange's own eyebrows looked like they'd been painted on with Dulux. She caught him staring.

'No, I promise. Just a quick shaping. Let me!'

She didn't say 'let me' in a way that sounded like a choice, and he allowed himself to sit down at her chair.

It hurt like absolute buggery and it was all he could do to stop himself from swearing aloud. She smiled at this.

'Oh, so much for the big tough farm boy!'

'Ow!'

And then an indignant scream.

'What the *hell* are you doing?'

'If you don't want that to hurt, don't let hair grow out of your nose,' was Kim-Ange's pert response. She took out a pair of scissors

138

and trimmed Cormac's eyebrows slightly straighter and neater across the top.

'There you are,' she said. 'Isn't that better?'

And as Cormac looked in the mirror at his reflection, in his expensive jumper, with his fresh shave and tidy, new-look eyebrows, he had to admit that, well, it was different. Jake would laugh at him, but it certainly wasn't worse, and the jumper did set off the tinge of green in his eyes and his curly brown hair.

'Thank you,' he said.

'That's all right,' Kim-Ange said, then added with a slight twinge of regret: 'And if you meet any of those pretty boy actors . . . do bring one home for me.'

➤ ⌒

Larissa got slightly more nervous about the situation as she waited for Cormac to turn up. What if he was an absolute lout, who drank crisps straight from the packet and was monosyllabic and/or drunk? Perhaps she could write it off as a joke. She told her friends Coco and Zafs et al that it was something she was doing as a favour to the old Scottish side of the family and he was some kind of village idiot so they'd forgive her if it all went tits up. But they saw Scottish as something slightly quaint and even exotic so they'd forgive him if he sounded like a country bumpkin cousin and was completely incomprehensible.

In fact, the large, open-faced man with brown curly hair and a few freckles sprinkled on his cheeks who she found lingering rather awkwardly in the lobby of the room after he'd been buzzed up was actually a pleasant surprise. She didn't recognise him at all – you tended to see most people around Kirrinfief, at harvest services in the old church, or at the village fête, where her aunt was usually judging the pet show or drawing the tombola. But thank God he didn't look too bad in just a plain black top. She'd worried temporarily if he might turn up in a checked shirt and fleece – pretty common uniform in the Highlands – or, heaven forbid, sportswear. If it had been sportswear, she thought, she could probably just have turned round and texted him that she couldn't make it and pretended not to be there; he didn't know what she looked like either.

'Cormac?'

'Hullo there,' he said in his gentle Highlands accent, very different from the wideboy or posh boy London voices she was used to. It sounded nice. It sounded like home.

＞ ⌒

The girls were sitting round a high table when she got up there, and they all did such an obvious once-over when she arrived it was annoying. But Cormac didn't seem to notice, apart from going slightly pink, but that might just have been the environment. It was loud in there and of course – *of course* – everyone found it very difficult to understand what he was saying whether by design or on purpose, because they found him quaint.

'So you're a *nurse*?' said Portia emphatically, as if she'd never met someone who did such a pedestrian job in her entire life, which in fact was quite likely.

'Aye,' said Cormac. 'I follow up – try and keep people out of hospital. Lot of post-op stuff, wound care, that kind of stuff.'

'Oh, so you're not in a hospital?' said Portia, frowning her perfectly botoxed brow. 'Do you ride around on a little bicycle? How adorable!'

Kalitha, a slender art dealer Larissa had met during a course at the Courtauld, simply glanced him up and down, then turned to Ithica sitting next to her and carried on with the conversation as if he wasn't there, which made Larissa feel an anxious tremor of annoyance and shame. She had thought that this would be nice, or different, but instead they were all being rude and snotty and she was really annoyed that they were theoretically her friends.

Portia turned her attention to the cocktail menu.

'What do you want to drink?' Larissa asked him. Cormac was boggling at the prices, utterly astounded. Cocktails were fifteen pounds! Minimum! Fifteen pounds! He looked up. If he had to get a round in, that would be seventy-five pounds. Getting a round in at Wullie's

140

was twelve pounds. He had the money – he didn't spend much at home and his cottage didn't cost much to rent – and he wasn't tight – he was always the first to put his hand in his pocket. It was just the very idea of it: spending so much on so little seemed to him not so much worrying as totally and utterly immoral. Seventy-five pounds could buy or do so much.

A worse thought stuck him. He was here with many women, which meant as a gentleman he'd normally insist on paying for all of their drinks. If everyone had four cocktails – and oh my God, he had just realised two of them were drinking from a bottle of champagne – he was going to spend as much as a small car.

It's not Larissa's fault, but it wouldn't have occurred to her in a million years what was going through his mind. Money had simply never, ever been remotely an issue to worry about, and the mentality that had to add things up like that had never been a part of her. Plus she'd assumed she'd be getting it anyway; nurses were really super-poor, right? He must know it was her club and her card behind the bar.

'What will you have?'

'I'll … I'll just go to the bar,' said Cormac unhappily, wondering if he could ask for tap water when he got there. Kalitha flicked her perfectly made-up eyes to him.

'Uh, they'll take your order here?' she said as if explaining something to a child, just as an incredibly gorgeous young model-like person in a smart black outfit that patently cost more than anything Cormac himself had ever possessed came up to them, looking at Cormac expectantly.

'Um, pint of 80 Shilling?' said Cormac automatically. He could call his bank and make sure, transfer some money over, probably. Yeah. He'd do that. The crushing thought that these beautiful, groomed creatures might snigger to themselves that he fitted the stereotype of Scottish people being mean was so shaming he wanted to bury himself.

The beautiful model waitress smiled widely.

'I'm so sorry but I don't know what that is?' she said, her voice going up at the end. 'I can ask maybe at the bar?'

'It's a beer.'

'All our beers are imported? We have ...'

And she proceeded to reel off a number of names of things Cormac had never heard of before. Finally, Cormac stopped her just to stop things getting completely out of hand.

'Aye. That one,' he said randomly. The beautiful person smiled.

'Wonderful choice?'

Cormac turned to Larissa but she was emptying the bottle of champagne into a glass, and waving the empty bottle about.

'Keep them coming!'

'Of course!' said the server, and hurried off with another perfect smile.

By the time Cormac had turned back to the group, Kalitha was telling a story about a red carpet that he couldn't really follow but involved lots of squealing, then every so often Larissa or Cags, who seemed slightly kinder than the others, would attempt to bring him in to the conversation by asking him something about Scotland, and he would turn pink and mutter something very unfunny and uninspiring, not feeling like himself at all, and the others would look at him for a second and he could hear Larissa's audible disappointment in him not being a jolly lad or whatever it was she'd had in mind when she started all this.

It was even worse for the fact that Cormac was a perfectly sociable chap, if a little shy. Not the life and soul, maybe, but he was funny and easy-going and the girls usually liked him. Of course Jake would lead the way. Cormac thought how much Jake would be enjoying himself if he were here, telling outrageous stories about people who'd got things stuck up their bums, giving cheeky back-handed compliments to Kalitha and generally being at home everywhere, and he felt completely out of his depth and more and more tongue-tied and awkward than ever. His beer, when it came, was a horrible sweet lager that felt sticky on his teeth, but he drank it determinedly and glanced at his watch so he could work out how soon he could politely leave.

Chapter Eighteen

Jake caught up with Lissa as she left Joan's surgery, exchanging one bundle of notes for another.

'Hi!' he said, and she stared at him as if she couldn't remember who he was (this was not at all the case; she was just still getting used to people recognising her in the street, which never happened in London).

'Oh hello,' she said, flustered. She held her carrier bag closer to herself in case he wanted to see what kind of groceries she had. She'd never realised how exposing it was, living in a very small village. Mrs Murray had already remarked more than once on how many KitKats she seemed to buy at any one period so she was definitely contemplating getting her KitKats online, if she could resist the temptation to buy a box of eighty at a time, which she wasn't sure she could, so that couldn't end anywhere good.

'Jake,' said Jake.

'Yeah ... I know. Ambulance, right?'

He nodded. 'Yup.'

'Busy shift?'

'In fact, no,' he said. 'Young boy fell out of a boat on Loch Ness, but he was fine by the time they picked him up.'

'Does that happen a lot?'

'More than you'd think. We nearly lost a couple o' bairns last year.'

He shivered to think about it.

'Do they get eaten by the monster?'

'Yes,' he said, totally deadpan. 'Monster-related injuries make up about thirty to forty per cent of my job most days. It's okay – we have a venom antidote.'

She smiled for the first time he'd seen, and he saw how it transformed her face beautifully.

'So you know it's the shows?' he said nervously. He wasn't asking her out, obviously. He wasn't asking her out at all – he was just letting her know it was on, which wasn't the same thing at all, nothing like.

He flashed back to the conversation he'd had the previous night with Cormac.

'You should go see her,' Cormac had said. Jake was still a little sore about being cold-shouldered the last time.

'Mebbe,' he'd said.

'I think she's a bit lonely,' said Cormac.

'Oh, do you?! And how do you know?'

'I don't. We exchange medical notes.'

'You're practically having a relationship. I'm surprised your mum hasn't been over.'

'I'm not,' said Cormac.

'Is Emer still in a mood with you?'

'She is.'

'Highland women,' said Jake, not for the first time.

'What . . . what does she look like?' asked Cormac tentatively, not even entirely sure he was asking.

'Oi oi!' said Jake, and Cormac instantly cursed.

'Not like that!' he said quickly. 'It's just a bit weird not to know who's living in your house.'

'Well, get on Facebook then, like normals.'

Cormac screwed up his face. 'I was on it, remember? It was just

144

my mum sending me pictures of armadillos and my old Army pals sharing really, really dodgy stuff. Ugh.'

'Well, then. You'll never know if she's a frog monster or not.'

'Don't say frog monster,' said Cormac. 'Also, is she a frog monster?'

Jake's voice went quiet for a while. Then he started up again, and it had an uncharacteristically dreamy tone to it Cormac hadn't heard before, certainly not when he was talking about Ginty McGhie.

'Well,' Jake said eventually. 'You know Meghan Markle ...?'

'Mmm?'

'Nothing at all like her,' clarified Jake. 'I mean. Not really. I mean. She's curvier, aye, and, well, no, she doesn't look ... But she's got these freckles. And they're ... they're dead cute. And all this hair! She's just got loads and loads of hair and it's all ringletty and it's everywhere and ... anyway ... Anyway. No, I havenae seen her.'

'Jake Inglis! You think she's cute!'

'I do no'.'

'Well. There you go! She's lonely. You can ask her out and thank me later.'

'No!'

'That proves it then,' said Cormac. 'I know how you work. You ask everyone out and run the laws of statistics. If you're not doing it, it's because you're sweet.'

'I don't,' said Jake, although he did and had never seen anything wrong with it. Jake liked woman in the abstract and found something attractive in practically every one he'd ever met. Holding back was very uncharacteristic.

'Well, I'm just glad you're no' harassing her.'

'I don't harass anyone!' protested Jake. 'I'm charming!'

'That is very much a matter of opinion,' said Cormac, although four hours later he would be sitting in an overpriced club full of weird, squawking, beautiful people, wishing he had just a touch of the old Jake charm.

Now, Jake was standing in the middle of the village square, tongue-tied for once in his life.

'The what?' Lissa repeated.

'The shows.'

'Like, waltzers and stuff?' She still looked confused.

'Yeah, and, like, a funhouse and you can win teddy bears on shooting ranges and stuff?'

'Oh, you mean a *fair*?'

'Yeah, that's right,' said Jake. 'There's a fair. And it's mostly run by travellers who do that in the summer but help with the harvest and stuff, so we know them all more or less ... It's grand.'

'Well ... wait, sorry, do I have to work at it?'

'Oh! No. Nobody's fallen off the Ferris wheel for at least a year.'

Lissa wasn't sure whether he was joking.

'I'm kidding. The St John Ambulance do it. No, I was just telling you in case you wanted to go.'

Lissa smiled to herself. She did love going to fairs: the bad boys spinning the waltzers; the clashing scents of popcorn and hot dogs and candy-floss; the sense of danger as night drew in. She used to go with her girlfriends, slipping out of school, turning up their skirts, but hadn't been for a very long time, as if it had been banned, left behind with being grown up and having responsibility, being a health-care professional.

'Um, I'm still here,' said Jake, colouring. He couldn't believe this was going quite as badly as it was. Normally a cheeky wink and a story or two about a particularly daring and possibly slightly exaggerated ambulance call-out and it was a done deal, more or less, or if it wasn't, well, thank you, next, plenty more fish in the sea.

'Thanks for telling me,' said Lissa, slipping out of her reverie. 'Okay, well, good to know it's there.'

Jake put his hand on the back of his neck.

'Actually, I was asking if you wanted to go. With me.'

Lissa's eyebrows shot up. It was the oddest thing – another side effect, she supposed – she hadn't been thinking about boys at all.

Of course, she'd had the same problems dating in London as

every other girl she knew – competing for decent men with approximately infinity other people. And then there was Ezra, of course. The ghoster. She had sent him one short, consoling letter about Kai, hoping against hope he didn't think it was another ploy to get his attention. She hadn't expected to hear back from him, and indeed she hadn't. But to be ghosted had been so painful. The internet was just such a tough place to meet men.

So she was extremely surprised and jolted to be 'asked out' – London men *never* asked you out. You hung with them or you met via the internet. They didn't just walk up to you in broad daylight and . . .

Jake put his hands up as if he was reading her mind. He'd gone puce.

'Sorry!' he said. 'Didn't mean to frighten you! It's all right, don't panic, just a thought, didn't want to trouble you.'

And before she could rearrange her face into something vaguely appropriate, he had gone.

Lissa went back home and called Kim-Ange, who was out with her phone switched off, and of course Lissa couldn't get her on social media any more. Then she pulled up the laptop and realised she'd like to ask Cormac about Jake. But he hadn't sent anything over . . . He was also out, she realised. It was Friday night and everyone was out except her. She wondered where he was. Surrounded by happy people having an absolutely brilliant time, she imagined. While she was just here.

Perhaps she should say yes to Jake.

Chapter Nineteen

Cormac was very much not having a brilliant time. He got up to use the bathroom – nobody really noticed, he thought, although he also wondered if they would all start talking about him as soon as he crossed the room, which of course they did.

He glanced around the large space. Every table was taken up with glamorous people: lipstick shining, hair in bold geometric shapes; tumbling blond or huge afros; incredible fashion and big, coloured glasses. Everyone was laughing and yelling at the top of their voices, or so it seemed. He recognised a few of the faces too: there was someone there who played a doctor in an incredibly popular medical television show that Cormac and Jake watched so they could slag off everything it got wrong about patient care and comment on how they were quite fond of the massive fires and car accidents and extremely not fond of the hard work afterwards to get people from simply not-being-dead to living, functioning humans again.

Well, this was it, he supposed. He wasn't, he thought, suited to being a Londoner after all. He wasn't remotely cool enough, he didn't have any facial hair, he didn't have a bun and his trousers weren't nearly ridiculous enough.

He vowed to use the bathroom – which was pitch-black and covered in tiny spotlights and marble and was stupidly fancy and impractical which more or less summed up everything he was feeling about the night – then make up an excuse and go. He'd have to leave some money at the bar or something, paying with cash which would make him feel stupid and cheap but what choice did he have really, and okay it was humiliating but it wasn't, he told himself, as if he'd ever have to see any of these people again. He had never wanted to be having a quiet pint in Wullie's pub more.

Cormac walked into the darkened lavatories, had a pee by touch mostly, then was just washing his hands when he heard a deep groan.

He stopped. There was nobody else in the bathroom, or at least nobody at the urinals.

The groan came again.

'Uh ... hello?'

Silence. Then a weak moan.

Only one of the toilet cubicles had a closed door. A thought struck Cormac: what if it was people having sex in there? That's what happened at these trendy beautiful places, wasn't it? It was probably two blokes having sex and he was about to make a bad evening a million times worse by interrupting something and having everyone laugh at him for what a rube and how easily shocked he was.

It didn't sound like a sexy groan though. He took a deep breath, finished drying his hands and spoke up one more time:

'Are you okay?'

There was a long pause. Then:

'Heeelllllppp meeee ...'

The voice faded away. If this was a prank, it was a very strange one. But Cormac recognised the tone of voice. It was exactly how people spoke when they came into A&E or in the field or when he had had to free them from cars or from being trapped under walls. He'd heard it a million times.

He ducked into the cubicle next to the closed one and, hoping that expensive places cleaned their bathroom floors more thoroughly than cheap places, put his head down to the floor to look up under the partition.

He got an almighty shock: instead of the pair of feet he'd been expecting, a man's head was lying, inches from his, a pair of wide eyes, blown pupils, staring straight at him. It was so dark in there Cormac used his phone torch to see it clearly – clammy skin and trembling fingers.

'Oh, for fuck's sake,' he said. 'Right. Hold on. Hold on and we'll get you out of there.'

There was no room to crawl under the partition; he scrambled out and kicked the door open with one foot, a move he had practised many times as being an invaluable part of the paramedics' arsenal. He also yelled loudly, although he couldn't imagine anyone being able to hear him over the din of the terrible music and the loud self-aggrandising shouting going on outside.

It was still pitch-dark in the loo though. He dragged the skinny figure through the door and out into a little hallway that led to the toilets. Several beautiful people stared at them suspiciously and stepped over the prone figure, but Cormac wasn't paying any attention; he needed space and room to work.

'Move! MOVE!' he shouted. The man was foaming at the mouth and going into a fit, and Cormac snapped his fingers at the bar staff, who immediately brought him the first aid box.

'Call an ambulance,' he yelled, but several people already had their phones out. Most were calling. One or two were filming, but Cormac couldn't think about that just then.

He put the man in the recovery position, opened his mouth and took off his tie. Then, as the man started fitting in earnest, he cushioned his head and opened his top button.

'You're fine,' he promised. 'You're going to be fine; you're going to be safe. Hang on.'

The man had stopped thrashing but now seemed to be suffocating. He couldn't catch his breath, and turned a horrible shade of blue as his head went back, banging onto the ground. Someone in the room screamed; the music had been turned off

and the beautiful young bar staff were standing around looking panicked.

Cormac immediately started doing mouth-to-mouth on the man,
feeling for a pulse worriedly. He lifted his head briefly.

'Have you got a defibrillator?'

Someone nodded and a yellow box was opened.

'Give it here ... is there a doctor around?'

Of course not, thought Cormac, as he continued to perform CPR.
Real people with real jobs didn't really belong here. He noticed out
of the corner of his eye the man who'd played a doctor on television
approaching.

'You must be joking,' he snarled.

'Well, you see, I have done it a lot and performed it and I feel
quite qualified.'

'You're fine,' said Cormac shortly, and then, relenting.

'Okay, hold down his arms.'

There was no heartbeat at all now. Cormac knelt over his chest
and took the defibrillator.

'Right, when I say clear, leave him go. One, two, three ... clear!'

The man sat back as the body beneath him jolted. Cormac
leaned over, listening for a heartbeat.

'Come on,' he said. 'Come on, wee man. You can do it. Come on.'

He shocked him again, fingers crossed. Honestly, once you got
into this, he knew, as did anyone else who worked in actual medicine rather than TV medicine, that it was over. He had a horrible,
horrible feeling that as well as looking like a tight, tongue-tied
country bumpkin idiot, he was also going to look like a killer or a
lazy and useless nurse according to people who'd only ever watched
resus from the comfort of their own trendy leather sofas, where
everyone had miraculous returns to life.

'Clear! COME ON!' He almost screamed in frustration, leaning
back down to perform mouth-to-mouth, almost yelling into the
man's ears. 'COME ON!'

Suddenly the man's body jolted. Cormac took nothing from this;
aftershocks were incredibly common in the dead. He bent, though,

lowered his head to the man's chest. The relief he felt when he heard, slowly, first one thump then another, was one of the most gushing feelings of his entire life.

'Yes,' he hissed. 'Come on, billy boy. Come on.'

An ambulance crew ran into the room through the now silent crowd, which had parted for them.

'Asystolic?' said the ambulance man, a large, sweet-faced Indian boy.

'Ventricular fibrillation,' said Cormac. The ambulance man nodded and threw him an oxygen mask, which he took gratefully with a thumbs up, placing it over the man's mouth. After several more minutes of working on him, and with both the ambulance crew down, one setting up a drip in situ, they sat back on their haunches as the man, very carefully, opened his eyes.

The three professionals regarded him.

'How you doing?' said Cormac finally.

'You've been taking something naughty, haven't you?' said the ambulance man. 'Come on. Let's go.'

The man, however, once he'd regained consciousness and looked around, realised suddenly where he was.

'Oh *fuck*,' he groaned, raising a shaky hand to wipe the sweat off his forehead. 'Seriously? In front of these tosspots?'

Worse was to come when the man was loaded onto a wheeled stretcher and it became apparent to everyone that he had peed himself on his very expensive suit. He was led out in front of everyone, and covered his eyes with his hands. 'Christ on a bike,' he said mournfully. 'No photos. If anyone tells the *Mail* I will *have* you and don't think I won't.'

'Oh my God, was it a speedball?' came a very loud posh voice from the back. 'Christ, how terribly 1990s.'

The man on the trolley groaned and kept his eyes covered in shame.

Cormac blinked as the ambulance man thanked him and took his name and address. The patient's nose had started to haemorrhage everywhere and a waitress was screaming.

'That's our cue,' said the ambulance man, wheeling him out. 'Will take him for ever to get to sleep, then he'll wake up tomorrow and won't remember a thing about it.'

'Aye,' said Cormac. 'Well, his friends all will.'

The paramedic laughed.

'Yup,' he said. 'Oh well. Cheers – you played a blinder.'

And as they left, the entire room turned round towards Cormac – who was suddenly extremely worried about the state he'd gotten Kim-Ange's jumper into – and to his complete surprise, gave him a round of applause, led by the man who played a doctor on TV.

After that, it was mayhem. People vied to buy him drinks. Kalitha and Caggie were suddenly all over the hero of the hour. Various men came over and announced that they were just about to have done the same thing, or would have done the same thing if he hadn't got there first (this was not, to be fair, an attitude confined to London clubland; it had happened pretty much at every single incident Cormac had ever attended). Finally the manager, an incredibly smartly dressed woman with a brisk manner, took him aside and thanked him from the bottom of her heart for not letting someone die on the floor of their toilets. 'I mean, it's terrible for business,' she said. 'Well, not at first – everyone comes to have a look – rubberneckers – but once that falls off. Well.'

Cormac blinked at this.

'Well, hopefully he'll let you know he's all right.'

'He can't,' said the woman shortly. 'He's barred. Again.'

They had moved from the high table, Cormac noticed, to a booth littered with vodka bottles and champagne. He realised to his shame that the relief that he wasn't going to face the bar bill was absolutely on a par with the idea that he'd saved a man's life.

And then he looked around at the room full of laughing, joking, incredibly beautiful people gossiping and yelling at each other and, well, maybe it wasn't what he was used to, and maybe he felt poor and out of place, but, well, a bit of glamour wasn't the worst thing in the world, was it? Everyone dressed up, trying to impress, to get on and have fun – it might not be real, but there wasn't a lot of fantasy in Cormac's life, or much glitter. He might as well enjoy a bit of it, he thought, even as a stunning brunette puckered very puffed up lips at him and handed him a glass of champagne.

Chapter Twenty

Lissa woke up on Saturday morning remembering she'd agreed to work it to catch up on some appointments she'd missed getting lost from one end of Loch Ness to another.

But she didn't mind, she found. She'd be quite glad of the company. And she didn't feel bad, not really. Not stomach-clenchingly frightened. She watched the lambs jumping about the fields from her bedroom window, clutching a cup of hot tea in her hands. In the woods beside the cottage, she noticed something suddenly, and went outside – at first, she was embarrassed she was wearing her pyjamas, and then it occurred to her, with a sudden burst of freedom, that it didn't matter: nobody could see her on the road! She could wander wherever she liked!

She went inside again to pull a cardie over her old soft tartan bottoms and grey *Friends* top, scraped her wild hair back with a wide band and walked out into the waking morning.

The birdsong struck her first as she opened the back door, the sun illuminating the dew on the grass. It was getting long. She frowned and wondered if she'd have to cut it. She hadn't the faintest idea how one might go about doing that.

Now she was closer to the trees, she could see them better, and she gasped. Suddenly, all at once it seemed that the wood had shimmered and completely changed from having bright green shoots everywhere, to now being completely covered with a sea of bright purple bluebells. The colour was so ridiculous it looked photoshopped. A sea of them; countless thousands running up and over the hill to goodness knows where, for nobody, it seemed, except her.

She knelt and breathed in their delicate heavenly scent. It was extraordinary. She found she didn't even want to cut some for the house; they belonged together, a great, secret sea. She crouched down, still clasping the mug of tea in one hand, and took a dozen photographs, but none of them seemed to capture the thick velvety beauty of the sight, so she put her phone away and simply crouched still. As she did so, she was rewarded with a startle of movement in the distance; the flash of something white which she quickly realised was a tail. A doe was bolting through the forest, followed close behind by the most perfect honeycomb-coloured fawn, its legs impossibly spindly. The speed of them darting through the wood was such that it was as if she'd been visited by a magical creature and Lissa found herself gasping, then shaking her head, amazed at herself. Next thing she knew, she'd be getting wellies.

Lissa took the car, as she had to drive a way out of the village to a house that GPS was absolutely no use for (as far as she could tell, signal burst in and out at unexpected moments). Joan had said something along the lines of, 'the house has its own postcode' which made absolutely no sense to Lissa at all until she'd found the road where it was meant to be, more or less, and driven up and down it several times before she'd realised that the two brick posts that looked abandoned were in fact exactly where she was meant to be.

She drove up the narrow one-track road, marvelling at the idea of it. Vast woodlands petered away either side of the road – bluebells had sprouted here too, a magic carpet, and daffodils burst into view over the crest of a hill. Coming towards the house, she turned the car round the gravel forecourt – there was an empty fountain that looked rather sorely neglected – and stared at something glinting behind the house before finally realising it was the loch itself. Imagine living here! She couldn't.

She went up to the huge old main door and could make out various bangings and some music happening behind it, but nobody appeared to have heard her knock. She hadn't been in the country long enough to realise that she ought to go round the back until a little voice alerted her.

'Are you going to give us jabs?'

A small boy with too long hair was standing on the side by the corner of the house. Next to him was an even smaller boy, with olive skin and very long eyelashes. They were wearing identical short yellow dungarees and yellow T-shirts.

'We're twins,' the boy continued.

'Are you?' said Lissa dubiously. On the other hand, she'd seen lots of unusual things and it was very rude to assume.

'AYE!' shouted the smaller boy. 'We is an aw!'

'Okay then, great!' she said. 'Is your mother around?'

The boys froze suddenly, then they turned as one and marched round the back of the property. Slightly spooked, Lissa followed them.

A very petite dark-haired woman with a friendly face came out of the open kitchen door with a tea towel over her shoulder.

'Hello! I forgot you were coming! Well, I thought you were coming the other day ...'

'Sorry about that,' said Lissa.

'That's okay,' said the woman, smiling. 'I know what it's like when you first get here. Isn't everything huge?'

'I thought Scotland was meant to be a small country.'

'I know ... Shackleton! Get the oven.'

A tall, shambling teenage boy came out with a tray of cooling scones.

'Chill your boots, already done it,' he said.

157

'Excellent,' said the woman, introducing herself as Zoe. 'Want to come in? And have a scone?'

'You're English?' said Lissa, surprised.

'Oh yes! You too! Ha, we're invading the place. Oh God, Mrs Murray will have a fit.'

'Is that the woman who runs the grocery?'

'Don't mind her – her bark is worse than her bite,' said Zoe. 'You could say that about a lot of people round here,' she continued as they passed an older lady who was cleaning boots rather ferociously by the sink.

She put an old-fashioned kettle on the stove, then picked up a list from the messy sideboard. What a comforting room this was, Lissa found herself thinking.

She started unpacking her kit.

'Hari needs his MMR booster, but I don't think Patrick has had his at all.'

Lissa frowned.

'But ... I thought they were twins.'

Zoe yelped with laughter.

'Boys!' she shouted. 'Stop it! Nobody believes you're twins, and you're just confusing people!'

'We are absolutely nearly twins,' said Patrick, and Hari nodded solemnly, pointing at his dungarees as proof.

'Isn't it clear they're not related?' said Zoe, still smiling as she poured out tea.

'I've met mixed-race twins before who looked different from each other,' said Lissa.

'Seriously?'

'Yes, absolutely. Fascinating.'

'She absolutely thinks we're twins, Nanny Seven,' said Patrick.

Zoe rolled her eyes.

'Right,' she said. 'Patrick is five.'

'AND A HALF.'

'Five and a half, and he's Shackleton's little brother ... half-brother. Did Joan not explain this all to you?'

'She just said it was complicated, then went back to reading a book about cow operations.'

'That does sound like Joan,' mused Zoe. 'Okay. She's right – it's complicated. Hari's mine and the rest are Ramsay's. Oh, actually, that's not too complicated when you think about it.'

'Zoe and Ramsay are in love,' said Patrick. 'And that is why we are now absolutely twins.'

'AYE,' said Hari, nodding his head to emphasise the wisdom of Patrick's advice.

Zoe coloured.

'Oh well,' she said. Lissa smiled.

'Did you move all the way up here for a man?'

'Quite the opposite,' said Zoe. 'I moved here to get away from one. Anyway, here we are.'

'Right,' said Lissa. The scones were delicious, but it was time to get moving. She washed her hands carefully in the big old butler's sink, then looked around for a place to line them up.

A thin sallow girl sloped in, looking anxious.

'I hate medical things,' she said.

'You hate everything,' said Shackleton. 'What? Just saying.'

Zoe shot him a look, and put her arms round the girl.

'It's okay,' she said softly. 'I'm right here.'

'I'm just sick of nurses.'

'It'll be quick. But then you'll be safe. I don't want you to catch the measles.'

'Mum didn't either!'

'Of course, she didn't.' Zoe held the girl closer. 'We'll get through this. I'll get some bought cake for later.'

The girl smiled.

'Oi!' said Shackleton. 'What's wrong with my cake?'

'Bought cake! Bought cake!' the little ones were already shouting, clasping hands in delight. Zoe smiled.

'Sorry,' she said. 'It's a bit of a madhouse here.'

It didn't look like a madhouse, Lissa thought. It looked lovely. A fire burned in the big kitchen grate and a large dog was wandering

159

about aimlessly, and there were pictures on the wall and music blaring and a stew on the stove and she couldn't help herself feeling jealous all of a sudden.

'You like it here then?' she said, as Zoe ushered them out of the kitchen to somewhere a little quieter.

'Oh yes,' said Zoe, sounding heartfelt. 'Oh, yes. I really do.'

She saw Lissa's face.

'But it took a while, I promise.'

'I'm only here for a bit. But I like it too!'

'Well, try and enjoy it,' said Zoe, laughing. 'Right, shall we move them somewhere slightly more hygienic than a kitchen with a dog in it and flour everywhere?'

They pushed open the door to a beautiful sitting room lined with books, and Zoe sat all the children on a slippery ottoman.

'Ramsay!' she yelled up the stairway, and just about the tallest man Lissa had ever seen came downstairs and draped his arms over Zoe's shoulders.

'Ah,' he said, looking embarrassed. 'Yes. I've been meaning to . . . yes. Well.'

'Have you got their red books?' asked Lissa.

The very tall man frowned.

'Ah. The thing is . . . I have about ten thousand books, and, well, I'm not . . .'

Lissa produced three new health books from her bag – Hari's was in perfect order – and made Zoe and Ramsay fill them all in, while the children shifted uncomfortably and Patrick attempted to get into a kicking match with Mary, who finally grabbed a book off the shelves and moved to the window seat to ignore him.

'Shall I put both the twins down on the one form?' asked Ramsay wryly as he filled in the forms, and Zoe shot him a look.

'Stop it! You're making everything worse.'

'YES – TWINS,' announced Patrick and the boys started marching around the room singing a loud song as Zoe gave Ramsay an 'I told you so' look.

'Okay, okay,' said Lissa, checking the syringes. 'We're ready.'

Silence fell on the cheery room. Sighing, Shackleton rolled up his sleeve. Everyone watched him as he stoically endured the double injections. Patrick and Hari looked at each other.

'Shackleton's nae greetin',' said Hari in his low growl.

'Shackleton *isn't* greetin',' said Zoe automatically. 'I mean crying. Shackleton isn't crying. Seriously. Your dad isn't going to be able to understand you.'

'Naw, he willnae.'

Patrick had pulled up his T-shirt sleeve and was presenting his arm with the air of a doomed soldier facing the firing squad.

'I will absolutely not cry,' he said, screwing up his little face. Hari watched with interest, then, after it was done, went up and gently wiped away the tear from Patrick's eye. Curiously, he licked it.

'Hari!' yelled Zoe as Lissa reached into her bag and presented Patrick with a sugar-free lollipop.

'Oooh,' said Patrick and Hari's eyes grew wide.

'Oh,' said Shackleton quietly. 'Only, you see, I didn't get a lollipop.'

'You're thirteen!' said Lissa. The child was enormous; he looked old enough to drive a car.

'I didn't realise there was a legal limit for lollipops,' said Shackleton. Lissa smiled, and brought out another one.

'I don't want one,' said Mary loftily.

'Can I have two?' said Shackleton.

'No!' said all the adults in the room simultaneously.

Hari might well have cried, even though he only needed his booster, had not Patrick stood in front of him letting him lick his lollipop as the needle went in. Mary withstood it with barely a flinch, which made Zoe sad at how used the child had been to pain, and she hugged her strongly afterwards. And then they were done.

'Okay,' said Lissa, straightening up. 'There may possibly be a few cold- and flu-like symptoms, but don't worry about them unless they last for more than forty-eight hours.'

Patrick immediately started to cough loudly.

'Or are completely made up.'

'No, no, it's fine,' said Zoe. 'Come on, Patrick, straight to bed with you.'

'Actually, I think I am absolutely fine,' said Patrick, eyes wide.

'It was nice to meet you,' said Lissa a tad wistfully. Obviously, they lived in a big mansion and were terribly busy and everything, but Zoe seemed like the kind of person Lissa would have liked to have had as a friend.

'Thanks!' said Zoe, and Lissa was halfway to the car before she turned round to find Zoe there.

'Sorry,' said Zoe. 'I don't know what I was thinking. Sometimes I still have my London head on, where you never talk to strangers. It's an old habit. Also, young people like you I'm sure wouldn't be remotely interested in hanging out with someone else's billion kids. But listen, would you like coffee sometime? Or we're all going to the shows when they come . . .'

Normally Lissa would have shut down, smiled politely and backed away, desperate not to reveal that she was desperately lonely. But she made a decision as she went to open the car door. To try something new.

'Yes, please,' she said. 'Yeah. I'd really like that.'

And they swapped numbers and as Lissa drove away she found she was smiling and decided, being on a roll, to head into the village square and treat herself to a book.

There were a few people gathered round the book van in the village square and Lissa went up to have a little look. A pretty girl smiled hello as she poked her head round the door. The van was like a little TARDIS, far bigger than it looked from the outside and crammed with every type of book imaginable. It even had, Lissa was amazed to note, a tiny chandelier swinging from the ceiling.

'Hello!' she said. The girl smiled. 'Oh, you're the English girl! Hello again! The locals think we're invading one person at a time.'

'I know, I met Zoe.'

'I'm Nina, by the way, just to remind you. You know, three is definitely enough for a coven,' said Nina. 'It's really going to put the wind up Mrs Murray.'

'Why the influx?'

'Well,' said Nina, smiling quietly to herself. 'The men round here are ... well, some of them.'

Across the square, Wullie and Alasdair, who haunted the pub, were sitting outside on an absolutely ancient bench, enjoying the sunshine, even though they were still wearing their flat caps and ancient overcoats and high tied scarves. They waved to Nina, who waved back cheerfully.

'My investors,' she said, completely bamboozling Lissa. 'So, how are you settling in? Are you going to the shows?'

'That's all anyone talks about,' said Lissa.

'We don't have *so* much going on,' Nina said, looking mildly wistful for a moment. Then her face changed and softened and Lissa followed her gaze and saw a tall sandy-haired man crossing the cobbles with a long stride. In a papoose on his back was a round-eyed baby about six months old, already stretching its arms up in gleeful anticipation of seeing its mother.

'And,' she said, 'the babies up here are *very* ginger!'

She kissed the man and picked up the wriggling infant as his dad unbuckled the sling.

'Hello, captain,' she said, rubbing the baby's tummy. 'How's my best little man?'

'He tried to eat some straw,' reported Lennox.

'Good sign,' said Nina. 'Moving on from dung. Lennox, this is ...'

'Lissa,' said Lissa, putting out her hand.

'Och!' said Lennox. 'You're Cormac!'

'Apparently,' said Lissa. 'Does everyone know each other here?'

Nina and Lennox looked at each other.

'Well, yes,' said Nina. 'That's more or less how it works.'

She kissed the baby, who giggled.

'He's beautiful.'

'Thank you,' said Nina, pleased. 'We like him.'

She blew a raspberry on the happy baby's stomach, and he chortled uncontrollably. 'My mum still can't believe I came back with a ginger baby,' she added.

'God, I can imagine,' said Lissa, then: 'Oh God, I didn't mean it like that!'

The other two just laughed. 'Don't worry about it.'

'How's Cormac getting on down south?' said Lennox. 'He'll hate it.'

'Actually,' said Lissa, who'd woken up to a patently drunken and misspelled email and a picture that was just a scribble. 'He spent last night at a Stockton House and had a brilliant time.'

She had been amazed to find herself jealous. She didn't get invited to many private members' clubs.

'*Cormac?*' said Nina. 'Ha! Gosh, he's changed. Maybe he'll turn into a socialite and he'll never come back and you'll be stuck here!'

Lissa looked out at the sun dappling the cobbles and then back to Nina with her happy baby and suddenly felt rather wistful.

'What's Cormac like?' she asked.

'Haven't you met him? Oh no, I suppose you wouldn't have,' said Nina. 'He's kind. The old ladies love him.'

'What about the young ladies?'

Nina smiled. 'Oh, he's not an alley cat. Not like that Jake.'

Lissa raised her eyebrows.

'Oh, is he?' she said, disappointed.

'Oh no! Did he have a crack at you?'

Lissa shrugged. 'He wanted to take me to the fair.'

Nina grinned.

'That's adorable. Well, he's ... very nice.'

'But a bit of a Jack the Lad.'

'He ... has girlfriends,' said Nina.

'That's okay,' said Lissa. 'I'm not after anything serious. I'm supposed to be chilling out anyway.'

'Well, you've come to the right place,' said Nina. 'But he's perfectly safe to go to the fair with. He's a good bloke. Just not marriage material.'

Right then a woman darted across the square, looking perturbed.

'Lennox!' she yelled. 'Lennox, can you come?'

Lennox looked confused.

'Aye, Carrie, whit is it?'

'It's Marmalade,' she said. 'I can't find him.'

'Carrie!' said Nina reprovingly. 'You can't just ask Lennox every time . . .'

'Aye, I'll have a look,' said Lennox. Nina gave him a look that turned into a kiss. 'You're not the errand boy of the village.'

Lennox rolled his eyes and packed little John back into his backpack.

'Aye, the bairn will like seeing a cat,' he said, as the baby waved his fists in the air. Nina watched him go affectionately and Lissa had the strange sense, as she had experienced a lot recently, of watching other people's happy lives as if from behind a glass or on television, as if taking part in a life that wasn't hers, wasn't a place she could legitimately be in. Why did everyone else seem so sorted and organised (it would have surprised Nina very much to feel that anyone thought this about her; as far as she was concerned they lived on a shoestring, couldn't ever go away because of the farm and she was miles from her family and there were myriad daily ups and downs, just like everyone else in the world. Although, when she got home in the evenings to the farmhouse and the log burner was blazing and John was kicking his little feet in delight on the lambswool rug, smelling of baby oil after his bath, grinning and gurgling up at his besotted father – well, nothing else seemed to matter quite so much).

Would she, Lissa was thinking, would she ever have something so pleasant and so simple? She sighed. Everything like that, all the trappings of a grown-up life – and they had to be nearly the same age – felt so very far away from where she was.

'You seem pretty settled,' she said shyly to Nina, who looked surprised for an instant, then smiled.

'Well . . . it's a pretty nice place to be,' she said and at that moment Lissa could only agree with her.

The next second, there was a terrible screeching of brakes and a yowling sound. Both the woman jumped up, and Lissa dashed out of the van.

165

There in the square was an old battered car and, knocked clean to the side of it, a fat, scruffy-looking orange and brown tabby cat.

Carrie, who had still been nearby, gasped aloud when she saw.

'Marmalade!' she screamed.

'Stay here,' said Nina fiercely, holding the old woman back. 'Can you go?' she said to Lissa. Lissa had absolutely no idea what she could conceivably do with a dead cat but she tentatively wandered over.

An incredibly old woman, who couldn't possibly have seen over the steering wheel, got out of the ancient white car.

'Noooo,' she said. 'Ochh, oh nooooo, is that Carrie's cat?'

'Margaret McLafferty, is that you?' came a loud cracked voice. Nina obviously wasn't having a great deal of luck holding Carrie back.

'Did you just kill my cat?'

'Occchhh noooooo,' said the woman, leaning faintly on the car door. Lissa went up to her.

'Are you all right?' she said. 'Do you need to sit down?'

'Dinnae worry about her!' came the strident voice. 'Save my cat!'

'I'm not . . .'

Lissa went closer. Her heart dropped. The poor creature was in a bad way: one of its ears was ripped half off and its back leg looked as if it was smashed.

The creature eyed her up piteously as Lennox came and stood next to her.

'Aye, that'll be her,' said Lennox shortly. Lissa gave him a look.

'What did you do?'

'Tried to fish her out of a tree. She took fright and bolted.'

'Can you get the vet?' she said.

'No need,' said Lennox. 'There's a shovel in the van.'

'You're kidding!' said Lissa. 'There must be hope.'

She crouched down. The cat yowled and tried, claws out frantically, to back away, but couldn't move because of its shattered leg. The eyes were absolutely panicked. It was heartbreaking to see.

Nina approached.

166

'Vet's over Kinross way,' she said, and Lennox swore. 'Bloody Sebastian. And those bloody horse shows.'

Sebastian was a good vet, but horses were his true love.

'FIX MA CAT!' came the voice again. She still wasn't, Lissa noticed, getting any nearer. Lissa couldn't blame her for not wanting to see it.

'I feel very faint,' said the woman who'd been driving.

'Good!' came the voice. 'Hope you die!'

Lennox glanced at the surgery.

'Where's Joan?'

Lissa winced.

'She said she was going to . . .'

'The horse show,' said Nina. 'Might have known. She'll probably be assisting Sebastian.'

'Christ, if we ever needed her.'

The cat was yowling but it sounded deeper now, and groaning more.

'I could get the spade,' said Lennox helplessly.

'LENNOX, IF YOU KILL MY CAT, I'LL HAVE YOU UP IN A COURT OF LAW,' said Carrie, finally storming over, face alight. 'NO CAT MURDERING ON MY WATCH.'

Lennox's face was a mask of despair.

'You cannae let the wee thing suffer, Carrie. You just cannae do that. It's no' right.'

The baby started crying too, as if to chime in with the miserable atmosphere all around. Nina looked at Lissa enquiringly, who stared back, helpless. She didn't have a clue what to do. Carrie had now burst into noisy sobs.

'SOMEBODY DO SOMETHING! NOT YOU, LENNOX!'

Lissa fumbled in her pocket for the key to the surgery. She couldn't, could she?

It was absurd: there was a world of difference between a boy lying on the ground and an injured cat. They were completely different. But still, somehow she felt something surge within her. She put her sleeves over her hands and attempted to lift the screaming cat up.

'What are you doing?' said Lennox, still outraged that there was an animal in such pain. Lennox was an extremely conscientious and humane farmer, but he was not remotely squeamish. To his mind, to leave an animal in this state was utmost cruelty.

'We can ... get her into Joan's,' stammered Lissa. 'There are supplies there. I could ... I could take a look.'

Lennox looked at her.

'You don't know how to treat a cat,' he said roughly.

'No, but ... I can stop her pain,' said Lissa, and Lennox calmed down a bit.

'How?' he said, taking off his jacket and bundling the poor creature inside it, Carrie hurrying behind them, and Nina rushing in with them too to try and take little John off his dad before the cat scratched out one of his eyes.

'It must be the same weight as a baby,' said Lissa, opening the big manse door, and then the one to the surgery. She pulled out a huge roll of medical paper and moved Joan's files onto the floor, then put the paper over the top of it. Lennox kept the animal covered with his coat, but it had quietened now and was only making the occasional soft whimper, which they both recognised as being distinctly worse. Lissa scrubbed her hands quickly and put a tiny amount of morphine in a syringe, frantically doing arithmetic in her head. It slid in very quickly as she found a tiny vein in the creature's groin, grateful for the amount of times she'd spent taking blood on her various placements.

Then, once the large cat had fallen asleep, she took a look at what they were dealing with.

She palpated the cat's stomach – she knew absolutely nothing about animal biology, but it wasn't firm or feeling like it was filling with blood. Neither was the heartbeat thready, although it was fast – 'Google "cat heartbeat",' she shouted to Nina, who immediately complied.

There was a leg that was patently broken – there was no plaster of Paris on-site, but she could certainly improvise a splint until they could get the cat to a vet.

The most important thing, though, was the shape of Marmalade's face. The skin had been ripped away; you could see sinew and bone underneath, and her ear was hanging off. It was a mess. Lissa looked at it carefully. It reminded her of working A&E, in fact. Underneath the fur, it was just skin and sinew and muscle, after all. Nothing she hadn't seen a million times. She looked at it for a long time.

'What?' said Lennox.

'I reckon ...'

She retrieved the stitching kit.

'Whoa,' said Nina, who had retrieved John, who was now watching the proceedings excitedly. 'Are you really going to stitch up that cat?'

Lennox also looked dubious.

'She's not in pain right now,' said Lissa. 'I mean ... I could have a go ...'

'FIX MY DAMN CAT,' came a voice from outside. 'I'm holding Margaret until the police come! I've just made a citizen's arrest.'

'I'll go calm her down,' said Nina. 'Also, I don't want to watch this; I'll faint and it'll be disgusting. And I'll take the baby outside.'

So Lennox held down the other end of the cat in silence, while Lissa bent to do her work, quickly trying to unravel the ragged ends of severed flesh. It was rather like doing a grisly jigsaw, and Lissa found a certain satisfaction in working away with quick neat stitches, checking the cat's breathing from time to time, and covering each layer in disinfectant powder. Finally, she carefully tried to align the ear correctly. It was always going to be a bit wonky, she figured, but hopefully it would still work.

Once she'd closed the wound, trying to make sure it wasn't pulling in a way that would cause pain, she took a ruler from the stationery drawer and tightly bound the cat's leg to it.

'It's not going to like that,' she observed. 'But it'll last until it gets to the vet hospital. Which is where, by the way?'

'Two hours north,' said Lennox.

'Cor,' said Lissa.

She stroked the cat's head. It was still snoring deeply, out for the count.

'You might just be okay,' she said softly, thinking again of the time when she couldn't make it okay, when she couldn't control it. 'I think you'll be okay.'

Lennox looked at her.

'Well done,' he said. She shrugged, pleased.

'Oh, it's just like being back at A&E,' she said. 'Except furrier . . .'

Suddenly, there was a huge commotion at the door and they both turned around. Nina was walking in with Margaret, who had a black eye.

'What happened?' said Lissa.

'She tried to kill my cat!' shouted the voice from outside.

'I thought you were making a citizen's arrest,' said Lissa crossly, sitting the woman down.

'I was. Police brutality,' came an unapologetic voice, and then Carrie strode in.

'Right,' said Lissa. 'You have to get her to the vet hospital, get her leg set properly.'

Carrie gave the trembling cowering figure of Margaret a contemptuous glance.

'I'll be borrowing your car.'

'You shan't,' said Nina hastily. 'I've got to visit the warehouse anyway. I'll take you in the van.'

Lennox looked surprised at this but didn't say anything as Nina bundled Carrie out and Lissa carefully tended and cleaned Margaret's eye.

'That's quite nasty,' she said. 'Do you want to press charges?'

'Against Carrie? She'd bewitch me and throw me down a well!' said the woman. 'I'm just glad her cat's okay otherwise she might have burnt down my house.'

Lissa stopped.

'There's one more thing,' she said, looking severely at the old woman. Joan had an old-fashioned optician's chart on her far wall. 'Can you read me the bottom line of that chart?'

'Not without my glasses,' said the woman. 'I'm blind as a bat without them.'

'And were you wearing them when you were driving?'

The woman went very quiet.

'If you don't get your eyesight sorted out,' said Lissa gently, because what she was about to say was a complete lie, but she'd used it confidently many, many times before, 'I'll have to report you to the police and the DVLA, otherwise I'll lose my licence to practise.'

'Is that true?' said the woman, looking even more shocked. It had definitely not been her morning.

'It is,' said Lissa. 'And I'll be watching out for you.'

She stood up.

'The swelling should go down – keep this ice pack on it. And I highly recommend going to the bakery and having a cup of sweet tea and a long sit down. Is there anyone who could drive the car home for you?'

'My son,' Margaret said quietly.

'Call him,' said Lissa. 'Seriously. Nobody wants to get the police involved.'

Margaret nodded and left timidly. Lennox looked around the surgery, which looked as if a bomb had hit it, although not necessarily hugely worse than how Joan normally left it.

'Right,' he said. 'I'd better get back. Good work.'

Chapter Twenty-one

After that, although it wasn't of course Lennox who'd told everyone about it, the story got out somehow – and actually it became rather inflated till by the end Lissa had singlehandedly brought a dead cat back to life while fighting off Carrie from performing manslaughter, a fact about Carrie nobody seemed to have the slightest problem believing to be absolutely true. And just like that, it seemed, everyone said hello to Lissa in the morning; people were pleased to see her when she turned up and weren't so quick to take offence if she looked sad or distracted, and she was amazed, truly, that she wasn't anything like as lonely as she'd expected to be.

Plus, Cormac's email made her smile:

> I just want you and everyone else to get this straight: I saved a person and you saved a cat.

That's a cat? Anyway, one: it's entirely debatable that humans are better than cats, and two: whoever saves one life saves the world entire.

Lissa added a tongue-sticking-out emoji.

All anyone in Kirrinfief is talking about is you and that stupid cat and everyone is ignoring my glamorous London heroics.

Sucking face with an overdosing scumbag, you mean?

Well, you brought Carrie's cat back to life. You know that's her familiar? You'll bewitch half the town. You're allowing her to continue her reign of terror. When the crops fail and the cow's milk dries up, you'll change your tune then.

I'll be back in London long before then.

Aye, so you will. I'd forgotten. And I'll be back there, see what's left of my flowers.

There's a lot of those yellow round ones.

Dandelions?

Yes!

You mean weeds?

I like them.

Weeds!

Also, I picked some bluebells I hope that's okay.

It was true. She'd changed her mind; surely nobody would notice a few gone.

Cormac looked out of the window. He loved bluebell season. That heavenly cloud. He didn't want to mention that though for fear of sounding ... well, whatever.

Sure, just write down how many you've picked and we'll tally it up when I'm back.

There was no answer, and Cormac wondered whether he needed to clarify that that was a joke. On the other hand, if she couldn't see it, being told it was a joke probably wouldn't help matters anyway. He waited, refreshing his inbox.

> I think what I'll do is just let you count them when you get back and deduct them from the stocktake you already have?

Cormac smiled as he closed the laptop.

Lissa bit her lip and, for the first time, she realised she wasn't at that precise moment missing London. It wasn't just the daffodils that were coming into season; all sorts of plants and bushes were starting to flower, none of which Lissa knew the names of, and the wildflowers were beginning to tumble and crawl up the sides of the road. It was so fast that there was something new to see every day. And bees! She'd never really seen a bee in the wild before, and there were great fat ones everywhere, butterflies too, orange and black, with eyes on their wings. It was very slightly amazing.

Chapter Twenty-two

Both Cormac and Lissa were rather surprised when they fell out, particularly over someone Lissa had barely met. But Cormac was distracted anyway; he had what Jake would have called his saviour face on.

He'd been wandering home late. He would have found it hard to deny that he rather liked the shiny London streets at night; the neon and lights everywhere, the sense of a lot of people with a lot to do. There was always a palpable prickle of excitement in the air; it was never dull. Cormac saw a chap he'd seen before sitting near the entrance to the nurses' accommodation, over the vent of warm air from a posh office building which, judging by the smell, had a swimming pool in the basement. The man, lolling there, looked about the age of Cormac himself. He felt in his pocket for his wallet. This wasn't right. It was a warm, slightly sticky evening, but even so. Everyone needed a place to lay their head.

He put the money down quietly, trying not to disturb the figure, who was very still, but had their eyes half open.

'Aye, thanks, man,' came a low voice, almost a growl, unmistakably Scottish, and it stretched out a hand. To Cormac's great surprise, there was a badly drawn, pinpricked but nonetheless recognisable tattoo on the bottom of the pale, grubby arm: the clear insignia of his own unit.

'Are you Black Watch?' he asked in amazement.

The dull, lifeless eyes lifted up to him and Cormac caught a strong waft of unwashed body.

'No any more,' said the figure.

'Where did you serve?' said Cormac worriedly, looking at him carefully in case he knew him.

'Fucking … fucking Fadge,' said the man, and Cormac smiled painfully.

'Aye,' said Cormac. 'I was there too. 2014.'

'Fucking … fucking shithole,' said the man.

Checking which way was upwind, Cormac sat down carefully beside the man.

'What happened?'

The man shrugged. He had to be Cormac's age, but he looked far, far older.

'Aye, got stuck in a bit of trouble with the bevvy, aye?'

He looked at Cormac.

'Were you really there, man? Or are you after something?'

Cormac didn't even want to think about what something might mean.

'No, I was there,' he said grimly. 'Did you know that regiment colonel, Spears?'

'Fuck yeah,' said the man, almost breaking into a grin. His mouth was covered in sores. 'That bawbag.'

'I know.'

'Fuck it all,' said the man. 'I lost three mates out there.'

Cormac nodded. He had probably worked on at least one of them.

'What's your name?'

'Robbie.'

'Cormac.'

Robbie offered him a bottle, but Cormac declined, instead offering him the last of the money in his wallet.

'I cannae take your cash,' said the man.

'Always going to help a comrade,' said Cormac. 'Have you got a phone?'

The man laughed.

'Naw.'

'Look. I stay in that building just there. Come find me if you need anything.'

Robbie waved him away.

'Aye, fine, man.'

Cormac couldn't shake the memory, couldn't shake thinking about what had gone on out there, whatever had left Robbie on a pavement, left him treading water in his own life.

Well, *he* wasn't, he told himself hotly. He was doing something now. He was helping out and being useful, wasn't he?

But he was, unusually, very disinclined to lend a friendly ear to Lissa, who was surrounded by people who wanted her to talk about what she'd been through; who would bend anything to help her get better.

Lissa had turned up in good time at the appointment – a post-psych ward discharge, which normally meant a suicide attempt – to be confronted at a beaten-down door of a very small farmhouse by a grubby teenage boy and a large, heavily barking dog with slaver dripping down off his chops, which Lissa didn't like the look of at all.

'Hello!' she said. 'I'm from the hospital.'

'Shut your pus, you mingebag,' was the reply. Lissa blinked.

'Is your mum or dad home? I'm really just here to change your dressings.'

'Feck off, bampot,' came the reply.

Lissa didn't understand any of this, but it didn't sound particularly welcoming.

'Just let me in to have a look,' she said. She noticed he was wearing a large, dirty jumper with long sleeves that he had pulled down over his wrists.

'Get to fud,' he said, turning on his heel in front of the gate. The dog, however, remained rooted to the spot, snarling at her.

'Cormac knows I'm here,' she tried desperately.

'That fannybaws can fuckety bye an' all,' said the boy incomprehensibly, disappearing into the tumbledown old cottage.

Lissa frowned. She was used to drunk or resistant patients, but it was normally only in the heat of the moment. Working in the community, most people were delighted to see her. Someone like – she checked her notes – Cameron would normally be a social work case. On the other hand, someone needed to take a look at his slit wrists, and that someone was her.

She came back a couple of days later but the mother was no help. She refused to open the door, shouting that they were busy. Lissa could hear a lot of yelling and banging around through the door, a TV and radio fighting themselves at top volume and the dog barking its head off, and she heaved a sigh and thought, you know, sometimes there was nothing more you could do: if the state tried to help you and you couldn't take the help, then there was a limit, truly. But the idea of losing another boy scared her rigid, and she was angry that he wouldn't see a woman; only wanted Cormac.

She knew she'd been lulled into a false sense of security: most of the patients she'd met had been lovely, gentle and forever pressing her with food, such as shortbread, home-made bread, cream and once memorably – when she'd confirmed Agnieska from the café's pregnancy – a fresh lobster caught from Loch Ness which she had given to Joan, who had refused to eat it. The lobster was now happily scrappling its way around the surgery fish tank, terrorising the fish.

Lissa was gradually growing used to the warmth of the local

people, so to be confronted like this was terrifying. And, if she was being honest with herself, it was bringing back frightening memories, dialling up her anxiety again. She thought back to what Anita had tried to tell her – to go through the experience again in her head. She hadn't been doing it, and it was showing; a common or garden issue had turned into a large problem in her head.

She sighed.

Cormac,

Hi there. I'm afraid I've had to mark as discharged young Cameron Blaine. He wouldn't open the door on third time of asking; won't respond to treatment requests and is refusing treatment all round. I'm not sure what else to do without breaking and entering the house so I'm going to discharge him and file with social services.

Cormac squinted at it crossly. This was very much not all right. Cameron Blaine had an incredibly difficult background: he'd been excluded from school, his father was in prison and his mother was only not in prison as to save the council a ton of money on trying to rehome all five of the children. The boy desperately needed help and he had ... he'd been doing not too badly. Mostly just hanging out with him. Cormac had got him to wash his car once or twice, overpaid him but tried to make it clear how to do it thoroughly, how you shouldn't figure out how to palm the keys in case you wanted to twoc it later. He'd spoken to Duncan, the amiable local policeman, for whom the Blaine family provided more or less ninety-nine per cent of his active work that wasn't about parking, and they both tried to be casually walking by street corners Cameron was on whenever things looked like they might be getting a bit tasty. Cormac also had an old friend in army recruitment, but he thought that might be a step too far for Cameron, at least at the moment.

It had been a good solid couple of years of work of trying to build up trust, and Lissa was letting it all collapse in two minutes by behaving like exactly the kind of snotty posh woman Cameron had mistrusted all his life. He was angry and emailed back quickly something exactly on those lines, basically instructing her to get back there and get things sorted out.

'He was very grumpy,' she complained to Nina in the van the next day. Nina squinted. 'Cormac MacPherson?' she said. He'd done the health visiting for John when he was tiny and had come in, bounced the tiny creature up and down, dangled him from his fingertips, while she had watched in horror, turned him upside down to glance at his bum and said, 'Yup, perfect bairn, A1,' and got straight up again. Lennox had allowed himself a private grin given how much Nina had fretted about the baby and whether he was all right and if a snuffle meant he was going to die. Lennox knew livestock, and obviously his only son wasn't livestock, but he wasn't exactly not livestock, and Lennox knew something bouncing with glorious health when he saw it.

'I know,' said Lissa crossly. She was more upset than she'd let on; she'd kind of thought they were becoming ... friends didn't seem to quite work. Penpals?

However, she'd made sure every other note she'd sent that day had been entirely professional in possibly quite a passive-aggressive way and he had, equally passive-aggressively, not got back to her at all and left her in quite the temper.

Her face softened, though, as she spied the new Kate Atkinson novel and Nina handed it over.

'Maybe London's affecting Cormac,' said Nina thoughtfully. 'Making him cranky. Is he happy there?'

Lissa looked pensive.

'I don't know,' she said. 'It never occurred to me to ask. I've no idea how he's getting on.'

'Right,' said Nina. 'Well ... maybe you should?'

'Hmm,' said Lissa. 'And what about Cameron Blaine?'

Nina looked around. 'Well,' she said. 'I don't know. I mean, I believe books can fix most things but ...'

She had a sudden thought.

'You could try?'

And she went to the shelf of classics and pulled out *The Catcher in the Rye*.

'Buying him a book?' said Lissa.

'No need to sound so sarcastic.'

'I don't want to buy him a present! I want to clip him round the ear.'

'Tell me you didn't say that to Cormac.'

'No,' said Lissa, looking chastened. 'He's not talking to me now anyway.' She picked up the familiar copy; it was the edition she knew, with the red horse on the cover.

'Do you think? It's ancient now.'

Nina shrugged.

'Does as good a job at reaching adolescent alienation as anything I've ever known.'

'I suppose,' said Lissa. 'Okay, I'll take it. Cormac can pay me back for going above and beyond.'

'Bring it back if he doesn't want it,' said Nina.

'What if he can't read?'

'That too.'

'What if the dog eats it?'

'I think you're procrastinating.'

Lissa thought guiltily of everything she should have been doing, and felt the anxiety surge again.

'Maybe,' she admitted.

'That's okay,' said Nina. 'Most people when they come across the Blaines just turn and run. Procrastination is a step in the right direction.'

But even when she wanted to email Cormac to tell him what she'd done – she'd left a note inside the book, put it on top of the letter box and, she was ashamed to say, run away – she found she didn't because she still hadn't heard from him. And then she was puzzled why she even cared that she hadn't heard from him, and wanted to stop checking her phone, which was annoying because ... well. It was annoying. He was being stubborn and irritating and accusing her of not doing her job, and she was furious.

Cormac was furious. He would have thought that she of all people would understand the vulnerability of damaged young men; she was literally there to try and look after them and make life a bit better. Okay, so they were a bit tasty, but he'd met plenty worse on her beat. He reckoned she thought everyone in the Highlands was just adorable like on a shortbread tin, and everything was gorgeous and perfect. She didn't want anything to cloud her judgement of how beautiful the place was or to spoil her vision of loveliness. It was all about her. But there was poverty and deprivation there as there was anywhere else; sometimes worse due to isolation, stretched services, low wages and bad public transport. She couldn't turn her head away just because it wasn't pretty and she had to realise that. And now Robbie was preying on his mind too.

London annoyed him tonight; it was hot and noisy and he couldn't sleep. He wished he was back at home in the cool breeze of the cottage, the window opened, nothing but the rustle of . . . SHIT! He sat bolt upright in bed.

Chapter Twenty-three

Cormac was still cross with Lissa. He didn't want to email her. And it was late. But he'd forgotten about Ned! How could he? Damn damn damn damn. London had turned his head.

He reached for his laptop and opened it up. Maybe she'd be in bed. Or asleep. And he didn't want to type first – it would look like he'd been apologising.

He looked at his last sent message and winced a little. Maybe it had been a little harsh. But even so, this was serious.

He sat in his T-shirt and boxers on the side of the too-small single bed, rubbing the back of his neck with his large hand, wondering what to do. Finally, he began to type:

Are you up?

Lissa couldn't deny being pleased but was also annoyed that a: she was still up and b: she'd been waiting to hear from him while pretending she wasn't. She typed, rather stiffly:

Can I help you?

> Can you hear anything in the garden?

> What? Why, what is it? Is someone out there?

> No. Yes. No.

Heart beating slightly fearfully, Lissa jumped up. Was it the family she'd seen earlier? Were they going to come round, torch the place or something? She stared out into the garden. She couldn't see anything, but she could hear a rustle. A definite rustle. Her heart started pumping nineteen to the dozen.

> Do I need to call 999?

Cormac stared at the computer in disbelief, starting to laugh.

> God, no. DON'T! It's Neddie. I forgot he comes about this time and I meant to tell you and if you don't feed him he might leave.

> ?????

> In the spring. When he wakes up.

> ????

> He's a hedgehog.

> HEDGEHOG?

> Yes.

> YOU GAVE ME A HEART ATTACK FOR A FRICKING HEDGEHOG!

> He's a very nice hedgehog.

> I DON'T WANT A FRICKING HEDGEHOG!

> I'm not asking you to adopt him. Could you leave a saucer out for him? Water and honey. Not milk – that's a myth.

> You want me to get up right now, go out in the pitch-dark and freezing cold and leave honey for a hedgehog?

> Is that okay? Only if he doesn't find it, he'll go elsewhere and he'll get killed on the road or something.

Lissa looked outside again but couldn't see a thing. There was some rustling. Oh crap, she was going to have to go outside, otherwise she'd be a hedgehog murderer as well as a "bad nurse". She rolled her eyes and went downstairs, squeezing some Huckle honey and water into a little saucer.

The world outside was extraordinary. No cars passed at this time on the little road so there was no manmade light to be seen anywhere except the dim kitchen lamp in the cottage.

An almost full moon shone overhead, making everything bright and clear. The stream rippled, full of gold and silver, and the heavy scent of the bluebells settled over everything. The grass was wet and cold beneath Lissa's feet; it needed cutting but she didn't mind. She stepped forwards carefully into the enchanted midnight garden, not a soul in sight, waited for her eyes to adjust, then knelt down.

She padded as quietly as she could over to the rustling bush, then took out her phone and turned on the torch. And there it was! A tiny flash of two bright eyes, then in a blink the little creature was in a fierce ball.

'It's all right,' she crooned. 'It's okay.'

She switched the torch off immediately; she didn't want to scare him. 'Here.'

She put the saucer down, the moon reflecting straight into the clear ice cool water, then retreated quietly and knelt down by the back door, absolutely freezing, to watch.

After what felt like a long time, when she could make out all the outlines of the bushes and the trees perfectly well, the rustling started up again, and she saw the little shape scamper on tiny feet over to the bowl. It was so cute she nearly made a sound, and she wanted desperately to take a photo but knew she couldn't.

Instead, she simply sat and watched, feeling incredibly privileged as the tiny thing lapped at the saucer happily. She felt as if royalty had come to tea; as if the universe had bestowed upon her a great secret gift.

Euphorically, she stayed completely still until he had had his fill, refilled the saucer, then headed back up to bed, chilled but triumphant.

He's here!

Great!

Why is he called Ned?

187

All hedgehogs are called Ned! Neddie Needles!

His full name is 'Neddie Needles'?

That's what's on his birth certificate.

I've seen worse.

So have I.

How do you know it's the same hedgehog?

I put a splodge of paint on his bristles – did you see it?

Isn't that cruel?

It's a very tiny splodge. Right, I'm going to bed. You can report me to the Royal Society for the Prevention of Paint-Based Hedgehog Cruelty.

There was a pause. Then Cormac wrote:

Sorry for being hard on you about Cameron. I've had a tough day.

No, you were right. I just wasn't expecting it. I bought him a book!

Have you been hanging out with Nina?

Might have.

She thinks that's the answer to everything.

Maybe it is.

If he can read.

I'll pop back in.

Cheers.

Well, goodnight.

Goodnight.

And then a short time later:

189

PART THREE

Chapter One

Ned was gone the next day, but Lissa refilled his saucer anyway. She'd have liked to have taken a picture. On the other hand, she had a drawing. She pushed on through the garden and out into the field behind the house.

Lissa found herself wandering through the waist-high meadowsweet, breathing it in. When it wasn't absolutely hosing it, there was no doubt that the landscape was completely ridiculous. She supposed the rain was what made the green so vivid as to be luminous, and the clumps of wildflowers – and nettles, as she discovered wandering off-piste and being glad she hadn't gone the whole hog and plumped for shorts – so vibrant and full, the bees dancing among the tall purple flowers.

She found another stream nestling through the woods past the bluebells and, worrying slightly as to whether or not she'd be poisoned (she checked for sheep pooing in it: there didn't seem to be many nearby), finally filled her water bottle, the sun was warm on her back, and took a long pull.

The freezing bright freshness of it made her gasp; she could feel it coursing down her throat, so pure and clean and refreshing she felt her eyes dazzle with it, as she straightened up, almost drunk on the frozen light, and found herself face to face with a stag on the opposite bank of the stream.

She blinked and stretched out her phone to take a picture, almost as if it wasn't real until she did . . . but as soon as she moved her arm, to her great regret, the stag turned and bounded away, crackling through the bracken with astonishing speed, until it was gone and she felt like she'd dreamed it.

She carried on, walking almost without direction, off past the village and onto a long road overshadowed with trees. It was further than it looked, and she realised quickly that she was out of condition. She'd just been sitting, she thought to herself. Sitting and fretting and obsessing and fiddling with her phone just to put off . . . well, everything. Looking at pictures of other people's parties. It had been a distraction, but it hadn't helped. Anita was right. Coming off social media was the best thing she'd done.

She hit the roadway eventually, about to turn back when she saw trundling towards her a pale blue van, and recognised Zoe, the woman with all the children driving it, although she was alone for once. She waved, and Zoe immediately pulled over.

'Hello! Want a lift?'

Lissa almost smiled: it felt as if the universe had answered her so quickly.

'Um, yes please. Are you heading to the village?'

'Nina needs to do the banking. Hop in!'

'It's weird to see you by yourself.'

'I know! Having both hands to myself is very strange.'

Lissa pulled herself up into the van's tall carriage. Zoe passed her a bag of tablet.

'What is this stuff?'

'Keeps your energy levels up.'

It was a hard, sugary fudge that, once you were over the insane pitch of sweetness, was incredibly delicious.

'Oh goodness,' said Lissa.

'I know,' said Zoe. 'Shackleton made it. Then I confiscated it in case they all got diabetes.'

Lissa looked at the bag.

'Yes, please eat more,' said Zoe. 'Seriously, it's going to kill me. It's going to kill us all.'

'We should have one more piece each then hurl the rest out of the window,' said Lissa bravely.

'You'd kill the first bird that found it,' said Zoe mournfully. 'Stone dead. No one's body can absorb that much sugar without consequences.'

They both looked at the bag again.

'Perhaps if we just finished it and got it out the way we wouldn't have to think about it again,' said Zoe.

'We could keep some for Nina.'

'She can't have it. It would kill John if he got it through her breast milk.'

Giggling mightily, they put the absolutely delicious vanilla-flavoured lumps of tablet in their mouths to dissolve happily as the van trundled down the country road, not another car in sight, the sun streaming through the open windows, the radio playing a jolly song with fiddles and lyrics Lissa couldn't make out.

Nina was pleased to see them as they turned into the farmyard.

'Watch out for that chicken,' said Zoe to Lissa as she stepped down. A particularly beady-eyed specimen was lurking, stepping from side to side in a corner of the farmyard. 'She's a total nightmare.'

Lissa looked at the chicken, who glanced back at her, then directed her gaze straight back to Zoe. It was almost as if she was looking at Zoe specifically in a threatening fashion, but that couldn't possibly be true.

Anyway, Nina was sitting cheerfully on the steps of the other van and waved them over.

'Kettle's just boiled.'

'Where's John?'

'Out with Lennox,' said Nina, rolling her eyes but looking proud at the time. Her bonny boy and his dad were rarely parted. 'Have a good morning?'

'Yes!' said Zoe. 'Those cuddly Nessies are going like the clappers.'

Nina rolled her eyes again. The tension between her beautifully curated bookshop and Zoe's more touristy shop – Zoe parked up at Loch Ness – was sometimes there, but it didn't matter. They were both making a living and now, sitting out in the sunshine in the shade of the beautiful farmhouse, with three vast mugs of tea, Lissa revelled in their chat, especially as it was about what it was like coming from an English city to such a remote part of the world.

'My mum thought I was coming to the moon,' said Zoe. 'And also that I would be kidnapped by my new employer.'

Nina smiled in response.

'At least you weren't the first English girl ever to set foot here. The silence in Wullie's pub!'

Zoe laughed.

'I think he thought you were going to seduce him.'

'Evil English temptress,' agreed Zoe.

'So what do you think?' said Nina, turning to Lissa. 'Are you going to stay for a bit?'

'I can't,' said Lissa. 'It's just a placement.'

'Why did you choose here?' said Nina curiously. 'I mean, I kind of got stuck ...'

Lissa shrugged.

'The ... I mean, this is where it came up. With Cormac.'

'Good old Cormac,' said Nina. 'I bet he's having an absolute ball down there.'

Lissa wondered what she meant by this but didn't pursue it in case it meant, as she suspected, 'pulling lots of girls', some of whom might even be her friends. Then she thought of her hedgehog picture and smiled, but just as quickly dismissed it. He obviously did that for everyone.

She leant forwards. She was glad she was off social media, but she did miss just having people to chat to. And she felt she ought to be a little brave. After all, they'd all made the move.

'I ... They kind of sent me here to ...'

The other girls went silent, sensing she had something to say.

'I had a rough time in London,' Lissa confessed. 'I was a witness to a hit and run and ... it all got a bit much for me.'

Nobody said anything.

'So. I'm kind of supposedly on a quieter beat for a bit. The NHS equivalent of basket weaving.'

She attempted to smile, but it didn't quite work.

Zoe leaned forwards.

'Was it awful?' she said gently.

Lissa got that horrid about-to-cry feeling again. She couldn't speak, just nodded.

Nina, who was next to her, patted her gently on the hand.

'God, that must be awful. The worst that's ever happened to me was a paper cut.'

Lissa half smiled.

'Is it helping?' said Zoe. 'I wasn't ... I mean, I wasn't anything like traumatised or anything. But I was stressed out and miserable, and coming here ...'

A flock of swallows lifted up from the far field across the road in one great swarm. Lissa watched them go.

'I think so.'

'Hang on,' said Nina, standing up and going inside. She came back with a small book; on the cover was a woman standing.

'Here,' she said. Lissa took it.

'I got two copies by accident,' said Nina. 'You can have it.'

'*The Accidental Tourist*,' read Lissa. 'What's it about?'

'Healing,' said Nina. 'Best book ever written on the subject.'

Lissa looked up at her, touched beyond measure.

'Thank you.'

'You're welcome. Oh!' Her face changed. 'Here they come!'

Lennox was bouncing the baby on his shoulders, heading down for lunch from the fields. In the old days, he'd have taken a lunchbox and thrown a sandwich in his mouth in the barn. Now, he knew there was warm bread in the kitchen from the baker's as well as good cheese and ripe tomatoes and, if he wasn't mistaken, Nina had bought some ironic Enid Blytonesque ginger beer which they were both enjoying entirely unironically. Seeing they had company slightly made him clam up as usual, but the girls talked enough for them all, as they sat out on the first clear, warm day of the year, watching John try to crawl on the rug and the chicken peck sinisterly in the corner of the barn. Lissa clutched her book gift as if it were treasure when she headed off.

'Oh,' said Lennox as she went, 'are you talking to Cormac at all?' Lissa flushed.

'Um . . . only professionally, you know, patient notes and stuff.' Lennox wasn't interested in that.

'Tell him I need harvesters. I'm not kidding. Barn's all set up. Ninety squillion lads in London; they can surely spare a few.'

Lissa blinked, then nodded and carried on her way.

Chapter Two

Cormac headed out, taking Robbie his breakfast. To his surprise, as normally Robbie was unconscious at this time of day, and Cormac would leave it near him, Robbie was actually sitting up, staring into the distance.

'Morning,' said Cormac. Robbie looked at him, and it wasn't the usual unfocused look he had. The sun was out and could just be glimpsed between the walls of the roundabout underpass.

Robbie scratched his head.

'Man,' he said, 'can I ask you something?'

'Sure,' said Cormac.

Robbie looked uncomfortable.

'Can I . . . can I have a shower?'

Cormac thought about it. Sure, nobody was going to mind. The only person he was going to have to deal with was . . .

'Morning,' he said. The grumpy porter looked up and grunted. Then he focused on Robbie, looking disgruntled. There was, undeniably, quite the whiff.

'I brought you this,' said Cormac. 'I just had too many.'

And he handed over a fresh bag of pains au raisins. Being able to go out and buy pretty much whatever you like whenever you felt like it remained quite the novelty to Cormac, and he was enjoying it.

'Try them,' he said. 'I think they're French. They've got custard in them!'

The man sniffed, then without another word, took the bag off Cormac, who quickly shuffled Robbie inside.

Cormac bundled Robbie into the showers with a fresh towel, some of his clothes and instructions to stay in as long as he wanted; the hot water was limitless, even if the tiles were cracked.

Kim-Ange caught him at the basement laundry door and stood there, arms folded.

'Who's that in the shower?'

'A . . . friend,' said Cormac. Kim-Ange beamed.

'A lover?'

'No!'

She frowned at him and he realised he'd got it wrong again. London was teaching him a lot.

'I mean, that would be obviously fine, aye . . .'

Kim-Ange nodded more appreciatively. 'But it isn't . . .?'

'Not on this occasion, no,' said Cormac, feeling increasingly stupid.

'Okay then,' said Kim-Ange. 'So he's a friend of yours?'

Cormac explained. Kim-Ange raised her eyebrows.

'You've let a homeless guy into a nursing accommodation?'

'I thought you were meant to be the tolerant one.'

'Well, have you left your wallet in your bedroom?'

Cormac had of course. He turned round, then turned back.

'I'm sure it's fine.'

'Yes, all right, country bumpkin,' said Kim-Ange.

200

'Oh, for heaven's sake,' said Cormac, as she followed him back upstairs.

The room was empty; the shower too. Cormac called out Robbie's name, but there was no response at all. He'd done a runner, taking Cormac's clean clothes but leaving his dirty ones behind. They were, truly, only fit for the bin.

Cormac clutched for his phone, but it was in his pocket – there was a new message from Lissa, something about Lennox looking for harvesters. Well, he was hardly going to manage that, was he? He scrabbled around the room, trying not to let Kim-Ange see that he was worried, or reveal the huge relief he felt when he saw his wallet, untouched, on the desk, his watch next to it likewise, and he felt both instantly guilty and dreadfully sorry for Robbie. He sat down on the bed, defeated. Kim-Ange made a decision.

'Come for a walk with me,' she said. She was wearing a bright gold sleeveless jacket with a fur trim over her wide back, tight black leggings and high-heeled gold Timberlands, with gold eyeshadow to match. It was a little alarming to the uninitiated.

'What time is it?' said Cormac.

'Going for a walk time,' said Kim-Ange.

Cormac groaned and went over and washed his face in the small sink. 'Are you sure?' he said. 'You don't just want me with you so you can lean on me when your feet get sore in your very stupid shoes?'

They were quite stupid shoes, with a dangerous-looking stiletto heel.

'I do,' said Kim-Ange. 'And bare your teeth if anyone does shouting.'

'Who's going to shout at you?' said Cormac, drying his stubble. 'And even if they do, you wouldn't hear them up there – you're about nine foot tall in those.'

'Catwalk,' said Kim-Ange sagely. 'Come on, we'll go up to Tate Modern. They're all arty up there. I shall be *appreciated*.'

She smiled at him. 'Well done for this morning. Risky, but you pulled it off.'

Cormac didn't feel much better though.

Although once they got outside into what Cormac considered to be a terrifying heatwave and everyone else thought was a perfectly normal day, he felt that something had changed. At first, when he'd gone into clothes shops or walked through Soho, marvelling at the looks, the fashion, the different types of people – male, female and everything in between – he'd found it embarrassing. Why would anyone dress like that? Why would people want to stand out and have everyone stare at them, giggling and pointing? Now, as he started to get more used to the ins and outs of the inner city, he'd realised something that would have completely surprised him: he liked it.

He liked the individuality of people's dressing. He liked the effort that went into having silver hair, or wearing a wig, or something incredibly uncomfortable, just so that everyone else didn't have to look at the same boring jeans and fleeces all day.

He also had a theory: in Scotland, the colours and the world around you changed daily, hourly even – the pink of the blossom bursting; the gold of the daffodils; the deep greens of the grass after the rain; the soft lavender of the heather on the hillsides; bright yellow fields of rape; fresh white lambs dotting the place like clouds; sunsets that stretched uninterrupted for miles.

Here it was grey pavement, grey buildings, grey pavement, brown buildings everywhere you went. Always the same, never changing. Harsh electric lights burning yellow, over and over again. You could barely see the sky from the street; couldn't see anything bursting into life and colour, changing day by day. Nothing changed. Everything was at the same temperature; everything was built upon, and anything that wasn't had a crane sitting on top of it.

So people dressing colourfully – wearing yellow spectacles or bright turquoise suits or pointy red shoes – were all adding to the brick urban landscape, giving you something beautiful and interesting to look at because, in Cormac's mind, they were so unlucky as to be trapped somewhere they couldn't look at the sea and the trees and the sky.

They walked up along the embankment of the vast sludge-covered river. It being the weekend, the pavements were completely thronged with crowds – families; people on bicycles and scooters; ridiculous grown men with funny beards; brightly coloured groups of young Italians with vast rucksacks; self-satisfied people stepping out of the curious Globe theatre – so that it was a squeeze past the Oxo Tower. There were just so many people. How, thought Cormac, did you ever get used to it? He understood completely now why you couldn't say hello to passers-by; couldn't even make eye contact. It would be impossible and exhausting. And, as he got carried along by the throng, he found himself thinking, You know, if anyone was looking at me, they wouldn't necessarily think that I came from a tiny village or that I'd never spent time in the city before. They would see me walk and not think anything of it; think I'd lived like this all my life. And he found, to his surprise that he rather liked that sensation.

'We're going to look at some art,' announced Kim-Ange.

'I don't know anything about art,' said Cormac.

'You doodle all day long!!'

'That's different. And modern art is weird. It looks like a kid did it.'

'What an original and valuable insight,' said Kim Ange. 'You're in the middle of one of the best centres for art in the world and all you want to do is sit in steak house windows in Leicester Square.'

Cormac wished he'd never told her that.

'Shut up.'

'No, you shut up! You might learn something!'

Cormac trailed after her like a reluctant child as they entered a huge factory-shaped building with high brown chimneys right on the riverbank. There was a set of low, wide glass doors along the back end, and small children with scooters and tricycles were gleefully careering about the open space.

Inside, away from the sunlight, it was gloomy and cool. The sloping concrete floor opened on to a vast underground chamber filled with odd shapes and sizes. Cormac folded his arms and announced that he couldn't tell a piece of sculpture from the sign telling you where to go to the toilets, but Kim-Ange oohed and aahed while Cormac nodded patiently and wondered if there was a fast food restaurant nearby – he was fifty miles from the nearest McDonald's in Kirrinfief and he found it something of a treat as it reminded him of birthdays when he was a child when the entire family would make a special trip, and also Jake had been bugging him to find out what KFC tasted like.

'Come look at this,' said Kim-Ange, recognising a bored person when she saw one. 'These are cool. It's a guy who went mad. And he painted pictures of his madness. And they're the best insights into trauma I think we have.'

Cormac was expecting something weird and surreal; melting clocks maybe.

He wasn't expecting what he saw. The upper galleries were dimly lit, practically dark, and he found himself in a small room shaped like a pentagon with vast canvases hanging on each felt-covered wall. The effect was close and claustrophobic.

The first thing he noticed was that there was nothing on them. No shapes or drawings of anything at all – just great blocks of pure colour looming above him. What on earth was this? What a complete waste of his time. He didn't understand modern art, and that was that. Kim-Ange, meanwhile, was off to the side staring, utterly rapt.

He peered closer, then took a step back so he could take in the whole of the canvas in one go. It was three blocks of colour but it could – did, in fact – look like the ground, the sea, and the sky. The sky section was a deep ominous rust colour, like dried blood or the warning of something ominous; the blue section below was battered and rough, as if the sky was upsetting the sea, because something terrible was coming; and the earth was brown and dry, as if everything was hopeless. It was unutterably bleak and extraordinarily beautiful. How? Cormac thought. It was just some paint on a wall but they filled him with deep and heavy emotions.

'Oh my God,' he said finally.

'I know,' said Kim-Ange, who had a look of fervent reverence on her face, as if having a religious experience. 'Aren't they amazing?'

Cormac looked at another one. Here there was a diseased yellow; the colour itself, the very pigment like a howl of disgust and misery. It had the ability to spear his mood, get right to the heart of him. He felt the artist was crying out personally for help, straight to him.

'Who *is* this artist?'

'Mark,' said Kim-Ange, respectfully. 'Mark Rothko.'

'Is he still alive? What happened to him?'

Kim-Ange looked and Cormac immediately knew the answer.

'Suicide,' he said. 'It's written there.'

'Plain as day,' said Kim-Ange in an uncharacteristically grim tone.

Suddenly Cormac found himself thinking – of Robbie, yes, but also of Lissa. Is this how she had felt? Why she'd had to move?

'Amazing,' he said, gazing at them.

And they passed through halls and rooms of modernism; of the world sliced up and twisted round.

'Why did they start doing this?' he said.

'Why do you think?' said Kim-Ange, pointing out the Braques. 'Look when it all started: a hundred years ago.'

Cormac blinked.

'After the First World War.'

'After the war,' nodded Kim-Ange. 'When the world got ripped apart. After Hiroshima, it got torn up again. You couldn't look at life the way people had looked at it before.'

Now Cormac couldn't see enough of it. He wandered through the galleries of Picassos, Dalís, mouth open.

'They're all soldiers.'

'We're all soldiers,' observed Kim-Ange, eventually pulling him away. 'Art is amazing. *And* you get a slice of cake at the end of it. Shall we?'

And Cormac was just about to enthusiastically agree, and concede that, okay, London maybe *did* have a bit more to offer than he'd originally thought . . . but his phone buzzed, and he took it out and stared at it disconsolately, reading the message.

'Oh bugger,' he said.

Chapter Three

'Why didn't you call me?' he almost yelled down the phone.

'It's just a broken wrist,' said his mother, equally crossly. 'I called a taxi – honestly, don't worry about it.'

'What were you doing?'

'I was on the trapeze.'

'Mu-um.'

'My stupid bicycle. How's London?'

'So who set it for you?'

'Some nine-year-old up at the hospital.'

'I'll pop up,' said Cormac.

'You won't "pop up",' said Bridie. 'I am perfectly fine and Nadia is coming over.'

Nadia lived in Inverness with Lewis, the middle son.

Cormac sighed.

'I can get a flight.'

'You can do nothing of the sort! You've got a job to do. I am totally fine.'

Cormac took stock. After his father had died, his mother's default was "totally fine", and she took any insinuation to the contrary as a total insult.

'Okay,' he said. 'Well, at least there'll be someone to check it for you. I wouldn't have been allowed.'

'It's fine!'

'I mean, I would anyway ...'

'It's fine! I'm busy anyway.'

'Which wrist is it?'

'My right,' admitted Bridie.

'Mum!' tutted Cormac. 'It's okay, I'm going to get the new girl who's standing in for me to pop in.'

'I've seen her,' said Bridie. 'She has hair all over the place.'

'So I hear,' said Cormac.

'And she's a bit stand-offish.'

'You think everyone who doesn't come from Kirrinfief is stand-offish! Remember what you said about that woman in the book van.'

'Aye, she's all right, Nina.'

'She is!' said Cormac. 'So is Lissa. I'm pretty sure.'

'Mmhmm,' said Bridie. Which is how Cormac found himself writing a note on Monday morning asking, as politely as he knew how, if Lissa could possibly go and visit his mother.

Lissa was curious; she couldn't help it. Cormac sent her stupid little pictures, but he didn't give that much away. Not that she'd been thinking about him, but you had to figure, given she was living in his house. She couldn't help but be a little curious. Couldn't help being slightly aware, even in the tidy cottage, of the smell of someone else's aftershave, shampoo, pillowcases. She hadn't snooped. But she'd considered it.

She picked up the notes from Joan, although there was nothing in them – a sixty-four-year-old woman in tremendous health with a snapped wrist from falling off her bicycle – and went round, faintly nervous.

The woman didn't answer the bell of the small, neat Victorian stone house with an arched porch and pretty pathway, and Lissa eventually found herself pootling down the little close at the side until she got into the immaculate back garden, which was filled with neat rows of daffodils, bluebells and rhododendron bushes in a tight line, and grass so immaculate it looked like someone had trimmed it with nail scissors. The woman was trying to weed with one hand, the other in a sling, and it looked like she would topple over any moment.

'Um, hello?' said Lissa, trying not to startle her. Mrs MacPherson stood up with a start.

'Hello?'

'I'm Lissa Westcott . . . the nurse practitioner liaison? I just came to check up on you.'

The short woman with steely grey hair cut close to her head – no room for vanity here – looked at her beadily.

'Yes, I ken who you are. You're doing my son's job. Why are you here?'

'Well . . . because it's procedure?'

'It's a broken wrist! Have you come round to give me a lollipop?'

'No. Although if you'd like one . . .'

'Or perhaps I count as geriatric now and you're here to move me into a home where you cannae have a hot bath for health and safety reasons?'

Lissa shook her head.

'Cormac asked me to come take a look,' she said honestly. 'He's just worried about you.'

'So he sent a *spy*?'

Nonetheless, Bridie bustled her inside through a small set of French doors built into the back of the house. After a moment or two, Lissa started to follow her.

'Beautiful garden,' said Lissa.

'Is this truly the best use of NHS resources?' grumbled Bridie. Lissa could see it was an effort for her to fill the kettle.

Once the kettle was on, she looked around. There were pictures of little boys everywhere – she hadn't known he had brothers. It was impossible to tell which one was Cormac from the three sandy heads and toothless grins and Lissa was suddenly too shy to ask. She did feel like she was spying, but not on Bridie.

'So can you wiggle your fingers for me?' she said, taking Bridie's hand once she'd made them both tea. 'And put some pressure on my hand here ... and here ... good. Good.'

She moved her head closer in the embarrassing bit where she had to sniff the bandage for evidence of rot or bad skin healing, without looking like that was what she was doing.

'Are you *sniffing* me?' said Bridie rather crossly.

'So is Cormac enjoying himself in London then?' asked Lissa quickly.

Bridie shrugged. 'I dinnae ken. Is he staying in your hoose?'

'Well, my digs,' said Lissa. 'It's a nurses' halls really. Nothing like as nice as his place.'

'Nurses' halls. I'm so proud,' said Bridie drily. Lissa caught sight of a photo of a handsome man wearing a smart Army uniform, including an elaborate hat that came over his chin, with a younger Bridie and a stooped man either side.

'Is this him?'

'Naw,' said Bridie, her voice softening a little. 'That's Rawdon.'

'He's in the Army?'

'So was Cormac once. Now he's busy living in nurses' halls, apparently.'

Her voice sounded raw.

'He didn't like it?' ventured Lissa.

'Not everyone can cut the Army,' said Bridie sharply. 'He's just like his faither. Anyway.' She changed the subject sharply. 'Here it is. It's a broken wrist. Well done. Can you tick your ninety-five file boxes, give me some nonsense survey and be on your way, lass? I'm busy.'

She didn't to Lissa's practised eye look remotely busy. The house was immaculate.

'Is anyone helping you out?'

'Aye,' said Bridie. 'This is Kirrinfief. We help each other oot. Dinnae worry about me. I ken you English types don't really believe in friendship, but we do round these parts.'

'All right,' said Lissa, knowing when she was beaten. 'Okay, I'll tell Cormac you're fine.'

Bridie sniffed. 'Well, make sure you don't interrupt him being too busy in the nurses' halls, filling in all those forms.'

Lissa blinked. She glanced out of the window into Bridie's spectacular garden, where a pair of starlings were pecking on the lawn. Then she got up.

'There is nothing wrong with you – you're healing fine,' she said. 'Do you want me to tell Cormac I'm popping in every day and then not come?'

Bridie smiled.

'That would be perfect.'

In a funny way, although she had learned nothing about him, Lissa was actually quite happy. It was quite easy, when you were having a difficult time, to think of everyone else's lives as absolutely perfect and straightforward. This was why coming off Instagram had been, on balance, quite a good idea. So although she felt slightly sorry for Cormac having a grumpy mother – she could empathise: her own mother had had pretty high expectations of her too – she also felt a little comforted.

And so she wrote to Cormac:

She's fine. Big Army fan.

She is.

There was nothing more. So she typed:

Were you in the Army for long?

Eight years.

211

That is a long time! Why did you leave?

Why did you leave A&E?

How did you know I was in A&E?

Kim-Ange told me.

That's very unfair.

You went to my mum's house!

You asked me to!

This was straying into the realms of a very personal conversation, and Lissa was suddenly worried that she'd gone too far. She was, after all, sitting in his house. It wasn't really fair; it was just a professional swap.

She changed the subject, anxious not to offend him.

How were the Lindells?

Cormac mentally groaned, although at least he was on safer ground. He did feel uncomfortable, wondering what his mother had told Lissa; what she told everyone else in the village, in fact. She didn't know what he'd seen, what it was like out there. Neither did Lissa, or Emer. Nobody did.

He wrenched his memory back to his unpleasant afternoon.

212

It was horrible to see.

I know.

The oddest thing was that Cormac had just been thinking how surprised he had been by the city; how it hadn't at all been what he was expecting. From the papers, you'd think it was all pollution and crime, but instead he found himself daily impressed by the contrasts. There were the layers of history, from the Roman walls in the City to the modern-day mudlarks down by the Thames with their metal detectors, searching for ancient coins and treasure from the two thousand years' worth of boats that had travelled up and down the river. And from the shining international glass towers to the beautifully preserved old Georgian buildings – such as those of the neighbourhood he was in then – of weavers and artisans past. Walking there, he had passed an ancient building where they made up coats of arms for the great merchant companies of the cities; then, being characteristically early, he had taken a detour via the extraordinary inns of Chancery, with their fountains and gardens and mysterious shops selling wigs and pens, and signposts to the 'yeoman's office'. Cormac had never been academic, but even he was quietly taken aback to walk past the red brick of Middle Temple Hall and read a small plaque modestly mentioning that Shakespeare's *Twelfth Night* had first been performed within its walls. He had then passed the famous circular church of the Knights Templars, with its grey stone effigies laid to rest.

It was a completely different world from any he had ever known; he felt there was a surprise, in London, behind every corner; a sense too of the huge weight of history, commerce and grandeur that made it easy – perhaps even necessary – for them to send a bunch of young lads from small towns far, far away from Westminster to fight and die in a distant desert.

And so he was in a thoughtful frame of mind when he reached his next appointment, and what happened next did not alter it.

The house itself was utterly beautiful: down a quiet residential street tucked away, where the great steel towers met the Georgian byways of Shoreditch. It had big, flat-fronted windows, and neat potted plants of lavender and small orange trees by the window and brightly polished panes of ancient glass in freshly painted pale green windowpanes. It was all immaculately restored, and Cormac could only wonder about the amount of money invested in such a project. He'd double-checked the address, but no, it was here, all right.

A stunning woman answered the door; she had tanned skin and blonde hair tumbling over a pretty, long dress. It was a sunny day, and the yellow light pooling into the lane made her appear to glow.

'You're from the hospital?'

Cormac showed his badge.

'Not the social?'

The way she said 'the social' sounded odd with her posh accent; it wasn't, in his experience, the kind of thing women who looked like that and lived in multi-million-pound houses normally said. They normally never met with social services at all.

'Just the health worker,' he said, almost adding 'ma'am' to it, her tone was so imperious. She sighed.

'I'm sure you feed back to your spy network,' she said. Cormac wrinkled his brow and tried to imagine what that might be like.

'Sorry,' he said. 'Is this a bad time?'

She shrugged in bad grace and let him in.

The interior of the house was even more beautiful, architecturally designed, full of light and slick lines. Expensive-looking art books were piled up heavily on the tables; abstract pictures hung on the walls. Cormac eyed them with a newly found interest.

It was a haven. It looked like a magazine shoot. Inside the

vast light-filled kitchen, which had been extended back over the glorious garden, were folding doors which today were flung open, meaning the indoors and outdoors mingled, and you could hear birds squawking and bees buzzing – the first time, Cormac realised with a start, that he'd heard these things since he'd left Kirrinfief. A tall, incredibly handsome man wearing tortoiseshell glasses and a perfectly ironed linen shirt was making a green juice in a blender. He turned it off and gave a distant smile to Cormac. The pair of them were so tall and beautiful they could be in an advert, or identical twins.

'Right,' said Cormac. 'So . . . the patient?'

The woman rolled her eyes.

'She's *fine*.'

The woman led him upstairs, past more pictures and bookshelves, expensive lighting and polished wood and the scent of posh candles. They continued to a second-floor bedroom, a beautiful, hand-painted room full of friezes of flowers and fairies dancing, a soft pale carpet on the floor and a huge armchair. The room was stuffed full of books and toys, with a large doll's house propped underneath the window. It was a dream for a little girl.

Lying there on the bed was a pitiable figure.

Soaked in sweat, bright red in the face, was a little girl of around eight or nine. She was completely covered in red dots. Cormac looked at her, telling himself not to let the horror show in his face. A Filipina woman was sitting by her head, squeezing a rag in iced water and placing it over the child's forehead.

He moved over.

'Hello . . . Titania,' he said, worried he'd pronounced it wrongly. 'Hello. I'm Cormac. I'm a nurse and I'm here to see how you're getting on.'

In response, the child burst into tears. Cormac carefully took her temperature, then looked at the mother.

'Have you been giving her the ibuprofen?' he said as gently as he could.

215

'No!' said the woman. 'She's my child! I think I know what she needs! I'm treating her homoeopathically!'

'I think that can be very useful,' said Cormac, who thought nothing of the kind. 'When given in conjunction with other medicines. When it comes to beating back a fever, ibuprofen can really help.'

'Well, you would say that,' hissed the woman. 'You're part of Big Pharma.'

Cormac wished that, if he were, Big Pharma would top up his salary once in a while. The woman's calm, beautiful expression had gone; she now looked tight-faced and pinched.

'Are you giving her plenty of fluids?'

'Yes!' said the woman triumphantly. 'This is Kona Nigari.' She held up a fantastically complicated-looking bottle. 'It's collected from a Hawaiian spring and is the purest in the world. We get it flown in specially. There's nothing we wouldn't do for our precious Titania.'

She smiled beatifically at the child without actually touching her.

Cormac wiped the girl's forehead with a cloth, propping her up a little.

'You're going to be fine,' he said to the child, who was moaning. 'It's just not very nice for a little while. But soon you'll be able to watch CBeebies again.'

'Actually, we consider screen rays dangerous for children?' said the mother in a sharp voice. 'We don't believe in them.'

Cormac was reasonably sure he'd seen the husband on his phone downstairs but didn't mention it. Instead, he made notes on the form, saw that Titania's temperature was down a little and that she was probably on the mend. But seeing a child suffer for no reason was almost more than he could bear.

And afterwards, he couldn't help asking (it was his duty, after all), 'When she's well, will you consider vaccinating against other diseases?'

'Well, she can't get measles again?' said the mother as if he, Cormac, was being quite the idiot.

'No,' said Cormac. 'But you would maybe want to consider rubella?'

'But God knows what the government puts in vaccinations!' she said, almost screaming. 'Have you ever seen an autistic child?'

Cormac, of course, had seen many.

'If you think I'd subject my perfect daughter to something the government – the *government* – thinks is okay, you have another think coming.'

Her face was now bright red and Cormac didn't think she was anything like as beautiful as he had done when they'd first met.

'It can protect other people who can't be vaccinated,' he said gently. The woman stared at him.

'You've been totally brainwashed,' she said quietly. The child moaned on the bed. Cormac held up his hands.

'I think Titania needs rest. She's going to be fine.'

'Of course she is!' said the woman. 'She's being treated. Naturally. By me!'

And the great city had looked a little meaner to Cormac as he'd headed back home.

> For no stupid reason! For some stupid woman who thinks she knows better than hundreds of years of medical science! Stupid spoiled spoiled spoiled cow.

Then, ten seconds later, he realised.

> Shit! This is our official NHS account!

> I know!

> Shit! Can you delete that? Please? Quickly?!

> It's NHS IT. They can't tell the arse codes from their elbow codes!

> I know. But!

> I know.

And that was how they swapped telephone numbers and moved on to text messaging.

Chapter Four

Jake finally plucked up the courage, much to the disappointment – and rather unkind remarks, if we're being honest, by Ginty McGhie at the hairdresser's, who also might have mentioned in passing that if that new nurse thought that she, Ginty McGhie, was going to do her hair for the big night she had another think coming – to ask Lissa to the farmer's dance that took place before the fair arrived.

It was a big affair round their neck of the woods, and with the typical Highlands imbalance of men and women, it wasn't like Ginty McGhie hadn't already been asked four or five times already by shy, sturdy, red-cheeked young men, but that didn't matter – she wasn't the least interested in them, and very interested in flashing dark-eyed Jake Inglis and the excellent time they'd had last summer, and he seemed to have time for no one these days but that exotic-looking incomer, which was men for you.

In general, Ginty's clientele agreed with her (it is wise, incidentally, if you live in a very small village, not to get on the wrong side of its only hairdresser). Lissa to them still seemed a little strange and stand-offish, always looking as if she was in a hurry to get places, dashing here and there. That was English folk for you. And now (once Jake had, while slightly drunk in the pub, revealed his intentions to ask her to the dance) here she was, waltzing off with the most eligible man in the village, now that Cormac MacPherson was down south too. Talk about having your cake and eating it.

Then Jake had asked Cormac for Lissa's number and Cormac had found himself feeling slightly awkward about passing it on.

Jake asked me for your number.

I know.

I was going to ask you if it was okay to give it to him.

Of course.

Of course? thought Cormac.

But Mrs Murray and some very angry hairdresser told me he was going to ask me out anyway. The hairdresser is quite scary.

She is. Are you going to go?

Cormac loved the farmer's dance. He thought back ruefully to the previous year where he'd drunk a load of cider and let Emer do what she'd been pretty clear she'd wanted to do for some months, given how often she happened to be walking past the cottage in full make-up. He wasn't God's gift, Cormac would be the first to admit, but when girls liked him, they *really* liked him.

I don't know. Should I?

> You should. It's at Lennox's farm, they always put a good spread on. And what else are you doing for fun?

> Is this the bit where you show off about going to that private members' club again?

In fact, Larissa had texted him but Cormac had pretended he hadn't seen it. It wasn't really his scene. He didn't tell Lissa that though.

> Well, maybe you should up your game then.

> What game?

> The 'who's having the best secondment?' game.

> That's not a game!

> That's exactly what someone losing a game would say.

Lissa looked at the screen, slightly annoyed and amused. A tiny bit of her was, she thought, possibly – just a tiny bit, not really – hoping he might be jealous.

> All right. I will go to your stupid dance. What should I wear?

Piss off! And that looks nothing like me!

I'm relieved to hear that.

And what's the music going to be like? All fiddle-dee-dee twiddly-dee 'I would walk five hundred miles' stuff?

Cormac didn't answer and Lissa wondered if she'd offended him. She absolutely had.

After Cormac didn't reply, Lissa glanced around the room and noticed something she hadn't noticed before: a small stereo system, exactly the kind of thing that a well-meaning but otherwise utterly clueless auntie would buy you for your fourteenth birthday. She had the exact same make and model, but it was in the attic at her mum's house. Next to Cormac's, however, was a line of CDs. Nothing as cool as vinyl; she thought of her London hipster mates with their vintage record players and independent record shop habit. Who still bought CDs? She leafed through them. Runrig, Orange Juice, Deacon Blue, Biffy Clyro, Del Amitri, Belle & Sebastian. Then she pulled out one with a picture of two identical men wearing glasses and playing the guitar on the cover. Ah, she thought to herself.

> Can I play some of your music?

> It's a bit 'twiddly-dee' for you , isn't it?

She *had* offended him! Oh no! Boys and their music. She would hardly be offended if he didn't like, for example, her mum's calypso music (this was a total lie; she would have been completely offended).

> Maybe I'll give it a shot.

> Don't put yourself out.

Lissa smiled to herself. For a moment, she found herself thinking that maybe she could tease him later when she saw him ... And then she remembered that he was in London and she was here and this was a professional work placement, and she rolled her eyes to herself and went to look at her very limited wardrobe.

➤ ➤

Jake was incredibly pleased that Lissa was coming out with him, even if it did mean bad haircuts for the rest of his life. And Cormac was good enough, listening to Jake's boasting, not to mention that he had had a little something to do with it. And he didn't mention to Jake, or even to himself, how much in fact he maybe would have liked to have been there too.

Tentatively, Lissa texted Zoe. It was really awkward, trying to make a new friend. She felt like she was asking out a boy aged fourteen, and more or less expected not to hear from her. Instead,

Zoe immediately texted her back and said why didn't she come and get dressed up at the house. Ramsay could drive them there, seeing as he wasn't going, as the male to female ratio was already hopelessly skewed, which meant he wouldn't get five minutes with his girlfriend without her being asked to dance all the time, plus he had a deep and abiding horror of having to stand around in front of everyone from the village who would undoubtedly have much to gossip either to or about him. Also, he had to bend over so far to hear anyone it gave him a sore back and the only person he liked to dance with was Zoe because she was so little he could pick her up and stick her legs around his waist, then carry her straight home, something which he assumed would be rather frowned upon by other people. He smiled, though, looking at his happy busy girlfriend, always keen to welcome new people into her life; his opposite, in fact, which was probably why he loved her so much.

Chapter Five

'Where is your *happy face*?' demanded Kim-Ange loudly as she ran into Cormac that evening in the old battered lift.

'Ach,' said Cormac. 'It's the village dance coming up. Was just thinking about it.'

'Ha! God, I can't imagine Lissa going to something like that.'

'She is going!' said Cormac. 'I made her!'

'Seriously? *Lissa?*'

'Yes.'

'At a *village dance*?'

Kim-Ange burst out into a peal of loud laughter.

'It's no' that weird," said Cormac.

Kim-Ange shook her head. 'I know. It's just . . . until she's had a few, Lissa's not much of a dancer. She's far too shy.'

Cormac blinked at this. It hadn't occurred to him that Lissa might be shy. She didn't seem so to him. Of course, they'd never been face to face though.

They made their way through the dingy common room. Kim-Ange looked around it.

'Well,' she said. 'Why don't we have a village dance?'

Cormac gave her some side-eye.

'We could have it here! They let people use it if you book it. Get some music and you can teach people to dance. Sell tickets. They can set up a bar.'

'Who'd come to a ceilidh in a nurses' halls?'

'Every drunk Scotsman in London! And there are a *lot* of them.'

Cormac thought about it.

'I suppose I could design a poster.'

'Give me some,' said Kim-Ange. 'I'll take them up to the hospital.'

The response was absolutely extraordinary and immediate, partly because on the whole, when Kim-Ange suggested you do something, it was normally easier just to do it. They sold out all their tickets immediately and Cormac had enough money to hire a small ceilidh band with a caller to tell people what to do, and to stock the small bar with additional Tunnock's Teacakes and Caramel Wafers.

Kim-Ange took over the décor and, amazingly, with a few metres of tartan cloth and ribbon and a vast amount of Ikea tealights, she transformed the scuffed hall and battered old tables into something rather magical. From seven p.m., hordes began pouring in. Cormac had absolutely no idea there were so many Scots in London. Although most of them were from Glasgow and Edinburgh, he still found it comforting to be surrounded by familiar voices again as well as red hair, freckles, loud laughter and the sound of people calling each other tubes and bawbags.

But there were also all the nurses who lived there, who came from everywhere – all over the world. One after another they came up to him, giggling and pleased, often telling him what their local dances were like.

The band set up in the corner, and the caller was excellent, marshalling her forces extremely effectively, which meant that the Scots – who had been taught the dances at school and knew them back to fronts – and the girls from the halls could partner up extremely well. The lights flashed as Nadeeka, from Sri Lanka, bounded round the eightsome reel, her small hands in the great meaty paws of Tam Lickwood, one of the hospital porters, a proud Govan man. There were consultant surgeons from the hospital, thin, austere men who'd learned their trade in the chill sea winds of Aberdeen and St Andrews; a young radiographer from Elgin who'd brought his entire team; a clique of Glaswegian nurses who'd trained and moved to London together, who gathered and fussed round Cormac like he was a new puppy – something, he felt very strongly, must be of enormous comfort to their patients; and a girl called Yasmin, or Yazzie, whom he'd noticed in the halls who now seemed clamped to his side whenever he needed a partner.

Kim-Ange wore a yellow dress in Buchanan tartan, a pattern so loud that many was the Buchanan descendant who had arrived in Scotland to track down their ancestors and, after shown their family stripe, turned away in defeat. She had also tied large bows of the same material into her hair, which meant wherever Cormac was in the room, he could usually spot her, enthusiastically twirling in the arms of a faintly concerned-looking porter called Piotr; she was clearly having an absolute whale of a time. He smiled to himself and agreed to make up the third member of a Dashing White Sergeant team with Chi-Li, who lived down the corridor, and to whom he had never so much as nodded to before but now, wearing a bright red dress with a tartan trim, he thought she looked glorious and danced beautifully on tiny feet. He did, in fact, survey the entire scene with some satisfaction, and quickly sketched it in his head to send to . . . Ha, that was odd. Why was he thinking of Lissa right then? He wondered how she was getting on at her dance.

Chapter Six

Lissa was sitting absolutely flat on her arse, her skirt splayed around her hips, howling with laughter. She hadn't realised, to be fair, quite how formidably strong the elderflower wine was – it tasted like cordial – despite Zoe giving her a few worried glances.

It had been so very long since she'd been able to cut loose. And it was, the tiny insects in the air notwithstanding, the most utterly beautiful evening. Lissa couldn't believe how light it was, was convinced it couldn't be past six p.m., even as the clock ticked on deep into the night.

The whole village was there in a flood of different colours and kilts, everyone cheerful and laughing. Many was the night they had had to hold the ceilidh in Lennox's barn, and dash about in the mud when there was absolutely nothing to be done about that except to deal with the fact that you were going to get very muddy indeed.

But on a night like tonight, the heavy sun hung in the sky like syrup, slowly and patiently lowering itself, the midges buzzed and hummed imperceptibly, the fiddles played wilder and the grass came to your ankles while the elderflower wine tasted like nectar and could persuade even a nervous, slightly uptight Londoner – as Lissa was explaining to all and sundry – to dance.

On the straw in front of the barn, she could see Joan hoofing merrily up and down with Sebastian the vet (who in real life was her everyday nemesis, as she was constantly second-guessing his diagnoses and sending his clients crazy), galloping the pair of them to the same reel that was taking place in slightly more cramped conditions five hundred miles to the south.

The contrast was stark. Down there, different people from different backgrounds were taking a shot and throwing themselves into things and having a laugh. Up here, it was a deadly serious business, like people playing sport. The fiddles played fast and clean; there was no caller, just a brief announcement – 'Flying Scotsman!' 'Cumberland Square Eight!' – and then people would immediately dissolve partnerships or join up with others, pulling the awkward-looking teenagers off the walls they were leaning against. And Lissa had danced every one.

Lennox had stridden up, little John on his shoulders, and was watching cheerfully, leaning on a barn gate – he wasn't much of a dancer – and Zoe had introduced Lissa to her friends Agnieska and Murdo. But Lissa, emboldened by the music, wanted to dance everything. It was just fun in of and for itself – not showing off, not spending a lot of money (it was five pounds entrance and a pound a glass), not wearing clothes they couldn't afford that would get returned in the morning, not queuing for hip restaurants in the rain to be jostled into a tiny space in return for handing over vast amounts of money for bao. Yes, people were taking photos, but only snaps in which they were laughing, not repeated instances of themselves making puffy-lipped pouts for Instagram, or insisting on taking the same picture one hundred times. They didn't have time for that; they were too busy having fun, in the hazy, dripping golden light, with a drum, a fiddle and a big double bass.

And then Jake approached. He was wearing an open-necked white shirt made of heavy cotton, and a pale green and grey kilt, his shadow passing over the grass. Lissa wished more than anything else that Kim-Ange was there; she would have fainted clean away. Obviously, it was just totally normal around here but it was pretty hot stuff regardless.

'Stop there,' said Lissa, smiling and taking out her phone. 'I want a pic. You look like you're in *Outlander*.'

Jake smiled bashfully but in fact was pleased and secretly felt like cheering. He spotted the empty glass of elderflower wine by her side. He should probably warn her a bit about that.

'Okay,' said Lissa. 'I'll send it.'

'Don't you want to be in it?' said Jake. 'Hey, hi, Ginty, can you take a picture of us?'

Ginty scowled, but stepped forward nonetheless. She wanted to take an unflattering picture of Lissa, but Lissa was so happy and, for once, carefree and utterly amazed at just how free she felt, she couldn't stop grinning, and the sun shone through her light floral dress and Jake leaned in and just ever so gently put his arm round her to touch her opposite elbow, and he was grinning too, and Ginty could have hurled the phone back at the pair of them.

'Ooh!' said Lissa, and she sent it immediately to Kim-Ange.

'Aw, look at this,' said Kim-Ange, who was hot and sweaty from all the dancing. She passed her phone over to Cormac. She had absolutely no idea he'd never seen a picture of Lissa before. Taking pictures of everyone and everything was one of the cornerstones of Kim-Ange's life.

He saw the shot and winced. He'd been right about the curly hair.

Well. Good for Jake. They looked incredibly happy.

'That's the first time I've ever seen her,' he said.

Kim-Ange looked at him crossly.

'You don't follow her on Insta? Although her Insta *is* very boring,' said Kim-Ange, whose Insta was not in the slightest bit boring.

'Ach, I don't really go in for that stuff,' said Cormac shyly.

'You're sleeping in her bed!'

'I know,' said Cormac, still staring. Her smile beamed, the sun shining straight in her face, her eyes shut. The photo faded from Kim-Ange's phone and he handed it back, somewhat reluctantly.

He had kind of known what she looked like from what Jake said. But from her missives – her slightly short, occasionally sarcastic emails – he'd been expecting someone a little . . . more uptight.

The girl in the picture. She was radiant.

'She looks happy,' said Kim-Ange. 'Good. It's been a while.'

'Yeah,' said Cormac. 'Good.'

And they tried to take one together to send back but Kim-Ange wasn't happy with the angle, and insisted on nine more, and then Cormac got called away to pay the bar staff, and it never happened after all.

Chapter Seven

Lissa fell, got up, danced and constantly felt she was absolutely fine because it was still light outside, even as everybody else started to drift off. She wanted to dance on and on. The relief of it all was quite something.

Finally, there was a massive circular 'Auld lang syne' and when the music stopped, you could feel, at last, the chill of the spring night come on them, and Lissa found herself shivering. Jake immediately took one of the blankets off the hay bales and put it round her shoulders. She smiled at him gratefully.

'Thanks,' she said. She looked around. The previously shy teenagers were now snogging their heads off by the side of the barn. Cars had vanished from the fields, and the lowing of cows, disturbed, reached them across the distant fields.

'Walk you home?' said Jake, handing her a large glass of water that she downed in one.

'Oh thanks,' she said. 'I needed that.'

'Fierce stuff, the elderflower,' said Jake.

'Uh-huh,' said Lissa as she put her foot into a massive muddy rut on the road and nearly stumbled over. Jake put out his arm to steady her and, once he had done so, left it there.

'So,' he said. 'You had fun.'

Lissa's tongue felt thick in her mouth, the way you are when you're trying to explain something but can't quite remember how, but somehow feel that regardless, it's still very important to get over what you mean. In other words, she was a little drunk. Pinpricks of stars were appearing overhead.

'I *did*,' she said. 'I did, you know. And for the first time . . . for the first time . . .' She heaved a breath. 'I wasn't . . . It was like I was just feeling lighter. Just living in the moment. Not anxious, not scared every second of the day. Not terrified for whether I was safe.'

'Is that because you were pished up though?' said Jake with a smile.

'Yes . . . *No!*' said Lissa emphatically. 'It's because when you're dancing you can't really do anything else. Not when you're trying to remember the steps and how it goes.'

Jake kindly did not mention that not one single time had Lissa managed to remember the steps and how it went.

'You just have to get on with it. And then you manage it, and it's fun and it's just different to everything, and everything else falls away, and all you're doing is dancing.'

She attempted a pirouette in the middle of the road. Jake steadied her again.

'Oh! Sorry!' she said, realising she was blundering.

'But,' she went on, 'it's been so hard . . .'

'Cormac said,' said Jake and Lissa blinked, suddenly realising she wanted to tell Cormac; wanted to tell him she wasn't feeling so cranky any more or so annoyed with everything. She picked up her phone but when she had to shut one eye to read anything off it, she put it away.

'So,' she said as they reached the doorway of the little cottage, the roses starting to bud in the beds alongside it. 'Thank you. That's what I wanted to say. Thank you.'

She looked up at him, but Jake could see her mind was elsewhere. And she was definitely rather on the squiffy side. It absolutely wasn't, he thought, the moment to try and kiss her.

Even though her eyes were sparkling, her smile wide. She'd regret it tomorrow, he thought. And he wanted to see her tomorrow, and after that if he could.

'Drink some water,' he told her, taking back the blanket. He could drop it in in the morning. 'Lots of water. Take some aspirin.'

It was true – just in that moment, there had been, Lissa had felt, a tiny bit of magic in the air; a definite sense that she might say, Screw it. Give me a little bit. Give me a little bit back of being young.

Give me back my fearless side that violence has stolen away. Give me some carelessness, where I am not worried and scared and trying to please people.

Give me tonight, with a handsome man in a kilt by my side, and a heavy warmth and a short night and a pair of fiddles and a glass of sweet elderflower wine, and let me dance.

Jake saw it in her eyes. But he knew – or suspected at least – that anyone would do; that her wild mood was dangerous.

And, he had to admit it to himself, he liked her. He really liked her. He didn't want her to wake up, head pounding, full of regret, too embarrassed to see him again after a night's wild fancy.

'Go to bed,' he said. 'Let's have coffee in the week.'

She smiled flirtatiously at him, and he turned away quickly before he changed his mind and followed her into the house – Cormac's house, he reminded himself.

Ah well, thought Lissa, trying to brush her teeth and making a bit of a meal of it. If she'd lost her ability to pull, that was one thing. But still . . . She drank a pint of water; the freezing freshness of Scottish water never failed to make her gasp and splutter. Still. It had been good. It was a small country dance in a barn in a tiny village clinging to the edge of a loch. To Lissa, it had been everything.

Five hundred miles south, Cormac finished tidying up the common room, its plain walls looking duller than ever as the ribbon and candles came down. Countless people besieged him to tell him what a

234

great night they'd had, invited him for a drink, or to go on up to their rooms in the case of a particularly jovial bunch of Spanish nurses, all of them raving beauties out of their scrubs, or Yazzie who'd been constantly trying to catch his eye.

He smiled blankly at them all, then went upstairs and fell asleep with the sound of the drums beating in his ears and the faint outline of the photograph – he tried drawing it, but could make no fist of it – in his head.

There was a shy knock on the door. He blearily opened it to Yazzie and he felt suddenly lost and empty and sad and homesick and confused, and he let her in.

Chapter Eight

Cormac couldn't believe how hot it was. It was ridiculous; worse than Spain apparently. Practically as bad as . . . Well, he wasn't going to think about his old job. But he disliked the heat; didn't trust it. And London felt oddly feral when it got hot. The bins stank; the people were out in the streets more; you felt how crowded the city was, how constantly everyone managed to bubble along but that sometimes it felt precariously close to boiling over. Cars with windows open blasted out incredibly loud music with rumbling bass lines you could hear coming a mile away. Groups of young people sat and drank pints on the pavements outside the bars, looking for a space even when there wasn't anywhere to sit and getting sometimes aggressive, yelling at the passing cars, who circled, shouting out at the girls.

It was oppressive. Cormac had never known a summer like it. There was no air conditioning in the nurses' halls so he slept with the windows open, which meant all night he could hear police sirens screaming and helicopters going and voices and music, and smell drifting barbecues. How, he wondered, could people live like this all the time, piled on top of one another, without going mad? He was naturally calm but this was making him enervated yet wound up. His patients were fretful, full of complaints about the hospital and their injuries and illnesses. For the housebound, it was unpleasant being in stuffy rooms in stuffy houses, dreaming of fresh air that was nowhere to be found. He tried to be particularly kind; not to get upset when the tar was practically melting on the roads or when drivers were screaming at each other, confronting each other in jams and accidents, the frustration never far away.

For the first time, Cormac felt homesick and less interested in shaking up all the new experiences London had to offer him even though he felt completely nonchalant now, strolling down the South Bank and crossing Tower Bridge.

He didn't see Robbie, although he looked for him every day, for another week, and then he recognised his old trainers, sitting in one of the underpasses.

'Hey,' he said.

'Hey, yersel',' said Robbie.

'How's it going?'

Cormac couldn't help thinking of Robbie leaving his wallet. Of how difficult it must be for someone with nothing not to have taken it. But even to imply that would have been so awful.

Robbie shrugged.

'Listen,' said Cormac. He'd been wondering about something but needed to ask Lennox. It might be worth a shot. It wasn't like Lennox wasn't used to all sorts coming along to help with the harvest. 'If I knew of a job, would you be interested?'

Robbie shrugged.

'I've got a record,' he said. Then he glanced up at Cormac, his eyes wild and haunted. 'No' for anything bad! Just a bit o' street drinking and that . . .' He tailed off. 'Nothing bad; you can check.'

Cormac believed him.

'It's hard work. Just harvest. But there's a bed, and three meals a day.'

'I'd like to work hard again,' mumbled Robbie.

'Let me have a word,' said Cormac.

Back at the nurses' home, It didn't help that Yazzie, while

237

absolutely delightful, was proving slightly difficult to avoid seeing as they lived in the same building, and much as he was generally pleased to see her it did seem to be mounting into something he didn't quite have the full inclination for so he was relieved when she went on nights.

Jake, uncharacteristically, was furious when he heard about this.

'What?' said Cormac. 'I thought you'd be thrilled I'd kind of started seeing someone.'

'No,' said Jake. 'You do this all the time! You're out do-gooding.' (Cormac had told him about Robbie.) 'And you use that as an excuse so you don't make any effort and some girl moves on you and you just go for it because you are lazy as shit and then they get upset. You should see Emer mumping about the village.'

'Um,' said Cormac, surprised he was getting a telling-off from Jake of all people.

'Well, I'm not thrilled,' said Jake. 'There are lovely women out there in the world ... lots of them nurses ...' His voice took on a slightly dreamy turn. ' ... and all they want to do is good in the world and help others but it doesn't mean they block out other people ... and they deserve someone who is absolutely crazy about them.'

Cormac paused.

'Who are we talking about here exactly?' he asked. It wasn't like Jake to be quite so romantic.

'No one,' said Jake sullenly. 'I'm just saying. If you want her, you should treat her right and if you don't, you should let her go politely. It's not fair.'

'Yeah,' said Cormac. 'Also, can you tell me how much ransom money you want for holding Jake?'

'I'm just saying!' said Jake.

'Jake, if I want disapproval, I can call my mother.'

'And you need to call your mother. I saw her the other day.'

'I do call her! All the time! She says she's too busy and then makes sarcastic remarks!'

'She's an old lady with her hand in a sling,' said Jake.

Cormac sighed. Outside, the sun was beating through the windows and his little room was uncomfortably hot.

'Do you think I should come back? It's the Fordell Fair this weekend.'

'No!' said Jake quickly. 'No, it's fine.'

'Jake,' said Cormac, unable to keep the smile out of his voice. 'Is there someone doing my job and living in my house who is in fact herself a nurse that you might be rather fond of in a very un-Jake-like fashion and you really don't want me around?'

'You could not,' said Jake stiffly, 'be further from the truth.'

But Cormac was still chuckling by the time they rang off, and rather cheered. Though Jake, irritatingly, was right about Yazzie, and Cormac vowed to do better.

➤ ➤

Lennox had a certain amount of tolerance for wounded birds, and though he was worried about the drinking, he'd agreed to give Robbie a trial. Cormac walked him to Victoria bus station, having bought him new clothes from Primark, a toothbrush and a wash cloth, then could do nothing but wish him his best.

'*Nemo me impune lacessit*,' he said as Robbie turned to go.

'Black laddies,' said Robbie in return. Then, falteringly: 'I'll try.'

'They're good people,' said Cormac. 'Go well.'

Chapter Nine

Nina called Lissa, and they went together.

'If you could just check him over,' Nina said. 'He's going to live out in the barn . . .'

'If he's an alcoholic, he shouldn't be coming off drink right away,' said Lissa. 'That could be worse. I'll check him over, sure.'

She tried to make her voice sound neutral.

'So, this is a friend of Cormac's?'

'I think so.'

The coach steamed up to the little stand at Inverness bus station, and a few road-crumpled people got off. The girls were both a little nervous; Nina had left John behind at the farm. She smiled.

'The last time I was here, I was picking up Zoe and Hari.'

'Really? What was she like?'

'Very, very dirty,' said Nina, grinning. 'Gosh, I thought it was going to be a disaster. She was just so miserable.'

Privately, Lissa thought Zoe was one of the happiest-looking people she'd ever met. But even she had turned up battered and bruised by life.

'Maybe Kirrinfief is magic,' said Lissa, which was precisely the wrong thing to say to a dreamy bookworm like Nina, who immediately got a distant expression and started talking about Brigadoon.

Robbie was the last passenger to get off, everyone else swallowed up in a mass of happy families welcoming home students or grannies who'd been on a trip to the Big Smoke. Robbie emerged, barely looking up, as if he never expected to be greeted anywhere; his few belongings were in an Army-issue canvas bag.

'Uh, hello,' said Nina. Lissa was looking at him curiously. Was this what Cormac was like? Shaggy round the edges, covered in home-made tattoos; an old soldier by any measure.

Robbie didn't look frightening, though, or violent. His eyes were haunted, and he looked very, very tired.

'Did you sleep on the coach?' asked Nina gently, and he shook his head. They led him to the book bus out the front. He looked at it enquiringly, but didn't say anything.

'Things been tough?' said Lissa, and he nodded sadly and she looked at him and suddenly, piercingly felt simultaneously ashamed at her own trauma and more determined to push through it. Because when you couldn't, it could consume you. She was lucky; she had a loving family, friends and a job that had given her an amazing opportunity to start over. Robbie had been unlucky. But maybe Scotland gave everyone a second chance.

'Let's get you back and checked over.'

➻ ⤙

Robbie was quiet as a lamb as Lissa examined him in the room next to the barn after he'd washed up. He had scabies, but that would clear up with Permethrin. He'd shaved his own head, which would probably help with the lice, and his skin wasn't as yellow as she'd feared; hopefully he wouldn't present with liver complaints, but it was too early to tell. Then they discussed withdrawal and alcohol management.

She had done this many, many times working in A&E. Sometimes, though, she felt that it might work. Robbie might be one of the lucky ones. She directed him to the nearest group, gave him every leaflet Joan had and added him to be checked up on by her, twice a week.

'And now,' she said with a slight smile, 'I think they probably have work for you to do.'

Lennox had already arrived at the doorway, little John in his papoose on his back as usual, carrying two trowels in his pockets and two cups of tea in his hands.

'Three sugars,' he grunted. 'We've got a few poison berries on the upper field to get rid of. The buggers eat 'em, then we're really in trouble. You up for it?'

Robbie's face, however, had completely changed when he saw the baby.

'Aye, look at yon bairn,' he said, a half-smile indicating his rotten teeth, and Lissa made a mental note to get him on a dentist's list. Little John beamed and waved in response.

'Oh, he is bonny,' said Robbie, moving closer. He put out a yellowing finger, and John grabbed it tightly, grinning at the game.

Then Robbie nodded.

'Aye,' he said, and followed Lennox out into the sunny farmyard, scattering chickens as they went. Lissa watched them both go, and crossed her fingers.

~ ~

Still very thoughtful, Lissa went back to the cottage. She had an hour before her next appointment. Looking for something to listen to while she made lunch, she pulled out Cormac's CDs and, smiling when she remembered how cross he'd been, slid in the Proclaimers.

She had been expecting the bouncy song she half-remembered. Instead, a slow old piano was starting a waltz. A soft, lamenting voice started to sing, joined by another.

'*My heart was broken . . . my heart was broken . . .*'

Then it simply repeated:

'*Sorrow. Sorrow. Sorrow. Sorrow.*'

Lissa turned round, frozen. It sounded ... It sounded exactly like someone voicing what she'd been feeling for so long.

'My tears are drying ... my tears are drying ...'

By the time she got to the bursting, heartfelt, hopeful chorus, she was an absolute wreck. It felt as if, in some odd way, the song was a tiny key, unlocking something very important.

Lunch forgotten, she listened to it over and over again. Then she texted Cormac.

> I might have been wrong about that band you like.

The response came back, quick as a wink:

> Aye. You were.

Chapter Ten

'You won't believe this!' Kim-Ange was gasping down the phone to Lissa, who was simultaneously warming herself in front of the smouldering peat fire, having woken up to a cool foggy morning. She couldn't believe Kim-Ange was actually boiling hot when they inhabited the same land mass. They were busy being jealous of each other's weather. Kim-Ange did not take to the heat well; it played havoc with her make-up regime, which was prolonged and highly technical.

'You'd know if you were still on Instagram and Facebook.'

'I explained,' said Lissa patiently. She had felt more at peace since she'd closed her social media, and was amazed at how pleasurable a novel and hot bath could be. Plus she could always rely on Kim-Ange to let her know what was really happening. Like now in fact.

'Well, Yazzie's been all over it. Him. It! After he had a man in too!'

'What are you talking about?'

'Your Scottish boy!'

'He's not "my Scottish boy",' said Lissa, feeling slightly uncomfortable. 'I've never even met him. I don't even know what he looks like.'

'You can see half his arse on Yazzie's Instagram. I think she took the picture while he was asleep,' said Kim-Ange musingly.

'Well, that doesn't sound very nice ... What, they're going out together?'

'Well, she hasn't changed her Facebook status ... and he doesn't have one so ...'

'Not even to "It's complicated"?'

'Nope.'

Lissa was annoyed at the fact that she felt slightly relieved.

'Maybe it's just a casual thing.'

Still, she was disappointed in him. She hadn't thought of him as a player like that. Mind you, wasn't that the point about players? They were really sweet and fun – that's why they reeled you in every time.

But she'd definitely thought he was different.

'Yazzie *is* a filthy mare.' Kim-Ange was still talking. 'Of course, I approve of that.'

'And gorgeous,' said Lissa.

'What do you care?' said Kim-Ange. 'Haven't you got a date?'

Lissa thought of cute Jake.

'I do,' she said, smiling wryly.

'Well then.'

'What about you?'

'Yes!' said Kim-Ange. 'See, this is a lot of news. I like catching up like this.'

'It's almost as good as having you here,' said Lissa. 'Not quite though.'

'Well, spray a shitload of Jo Malone perfume around and it will almost be the same.'

'Almost too much.'

'What?'

'Not at all too much! Who is your date with?'

'Piotr.'

Lissa had to think for a minute. It wasn't just nurses in the accommodation; it was more a general housing back-up facility for

245

anyone who had to work at the hospital and couldn't quite manage on the wages the hospital was prepared to pay.

'Piotr Porter? Amazing!'

It was indeed the diminutive porter Kim-Ange had spent the evening dancing with at the ceilidh, who was completely overwhelmed by her.

'Is he nice?'

'I don't care,' said Kim-Ange. 'There are no men in this town and I haven't had a date in eight months. As long as he doesn't eat weasels, I'm probably going to let him get to second base.'

'What if he licks weasels?'

'First base.'

Lissa smiled.

'I just can't believe we've all got dates!'

'I know,' said Kim-Ange. 'Skype me later and I'll tell you why you're dressed all wrong.'

>- -<

Cormac sent over the last of the week's notes to Lissa and couldn't stop himself from adding at the bottom, seemingly innocently, 'Going to Fordell Fair?'

Lissa saw the line in the email and smiled, then frowned. Word got around. She took another bite of her russet apple.

> Maybe. What about you? Busy, I believe?

Cormac squinted at the message. Oh, obviously she'd heard. Kim-Ange would have been all over it. It felt very odd; were they . . . were they *friends* now?

Throwing the core of the russet he was eating into the bin, he typed:

> Oi!

246

There you go, all *EastEnders* again. Where are you going?

Some hot new restaurant.

You'll be queueing for four hours and it'll be full of snotty types and all anyone does is take photographs of the food and the plates will be too small and you won't get enough to eat and it will be filthy expensive.

Well, you might throw up on the big dipper.

Shan't! *And* Kim-Ange has a date! It must be summer.

So we all have dates.

Cormac grabbed another apple from the bag.

Good!

Good!

Lissa decided on another apple, and bit into it, trying not to betray how cross she was, and then she went out to feed Ned.

Chapter Eleven

The fog rose on the little town of Kirrinfief that Saturday and they had by noon one of those days in the Highlands known as 'you should have been here last week'. It is a fact, sad but true – though please don't ever let it put you off visiting our beautiful country; we will be so happy to see you, I promise – and a fairly hard-wired one at that, that if you want to plan a visit to Scotland, or go to a wedding or a barbecue there, the mere planning is seen as an act of hubris that upsets the weather gods. Lugh, he of the one eye and the ability to summon storms, will be displeased and at the very least there will be light drizzle and ominous grey skies, and if you are in a place that has a beautiful view you will have to put up with people telling you there is a beautiful view, because you will not be able to see it.

But take Scotland by surprise and you might just get a day when the sun warms every nook and cranny, but the breeze gently pootling over a loch as calm as glass will keep you from getting too hot, and the stillness of the air means the cries of the many birds can be heard more loudly than ever, as well as the lightly crashing hooves of the deer in the forest.

The sky is a freshly washed blue; the green of the meadows far greener than anything you would expect to find without a heavy filter on it; fat bees buzz merrily among the meadowsweet and long grass; the evenings last for ever. And Lissa Westcott is going to the fair.

In London, Yazzie had persuaded Cormac to come out with him to a new restaurant and he has said yes because he didn't know what else to do and Kim-Ange was mysteriously unavailable. Kim-Ange was going to the Polish club with Piotr who was both excited and slightly concerned about it.

And five hundred miles away, Lissa was in a blue dress which for once she was wearing without a coat or a cardigan. It was a plain dress but it suited her, and she had left off the make-up apart from a little bit of pink lipstick, and her hair was bouncing down her back and she felt not ... not fine exactly. But, as Kim-Ange gave her the thumbs up from the laptop in the corner of the room and she reminded herself again and again, It's only Jake, it's only Jake, she could be feeling worse.

They were all of them out in the warm of a British evening as beautiful as they come, hundreds of miles apart, but each with the same combination of butterflies and cheerfulness and a slight aura of dread and a consideration of just cancelling the entire thing and never mentioning it again, running away to sea to be a sailor which characterises the process of dating. But they were all young(ish) and it was a lovely evening, and there was potential magic in the air, so you couldn't be too worried for them, not really. Tonight, even for Lissa, the bad things felt a little further away, protected in the magical sweetness of the air, a summer's caress, a new pair of boots, the scent of candy-floss on the air and of expectation, possibilities, aftershave and checking wristwatches and best earrings and chewing gum.

Chapter Twelve

The fair was easy to smell along the old farm track. The normal scents of pine and bracken in the air, with an undertone of cow that at first Lissa had noticed but now rather liked, had been overtaken by smells that were familiar and strange all at once; the fairground mix of candy-floss, popcorn, diesel and dirty old engines.

Lissa remembered her mother hurrying her past a fair in London, refusing to let her go, completely uninterested in the entire affair. Lissa hadn't wanted to catch the eye of the rougher girls in case they teased her later (which they did anyway, calling her stuck up which it was hard to disagree with because her mother was so very insistent about these things that that's exactly how she appeared).

And then, another time, when she was a little older, she did exactly what her mother was so scared she would: pretended she was going round to someone's house to study whereupon the two of them both slipped out to 'the library' and rushed down to the common, pooling their money which left them with just enough to share candy-floss and have one ride. The scrawny boy on the waltzers had a tooth missing, but to them that made him look even more exotic, like a pirate. He came and hung off the back of their car as they screamed their heads off. The evening was dark and the music was incredibly loud and as Lissa spun round and round, her neck hurting from the pressure, she couldn't remember feeling more alive, more naughty.

Of course, one of the girls from school saw them and, even though she was friendly enough, word got around and someone's mum ran into her mum at Sainsbury's and the worst came to the worst and she was grounded for a solid month.

It had been so worth it though.

Jake was standing there, wearing an open-necked blue shirt that suited his hair. He'd had it trimmed, Lissa noticed, for the occasion. It looked ridiculously sharp and contoured and gelled and she wasn't crazy about it (fearing retributive ear-cutting, Jake had gone into the nearest town, forty miles away, and had got it done by somebody who hadn't known him his entire life).

He grinned at her nervously. She looked lovely, her curls bouncing behind her. And the smile he never normally saw in the daytime appeared, shy, tentative.

They awkwardly attempted a social kiss, which went a little wrong. Jake would normally have taken her hand but, suddenly shy, didn't. Instead, he gallantly offered her his arm, and she took it, also rather shyly.

'Okay,' he said. 'So what do you want to do first? What's your favourite thing?'

'I don't know,' said Lissa. 'I've never been to a fair properly before. Except the waltzers. I like the waltzers.'

'You've never been?' He was incredulous. 'Were you brought up in a cupboard under the stairs?'

'No,' said Lissa.

He stopped himself suddenly.

'Sorry, is it . . . like a culture thing?'

Lissa gave him a sideways glance.

251

'How would that work then?'

'I don't know!' said Jake, lifting his hands in horror in case he'd said the wrong thing.

'No,' said Lissa slowly. 'We have funfairs in London. My mum just didn't really approve.'

'Because . . .?'

Lissa thought about it.

'Oh . . . I suppose she was a bit of a snob.'

This was such an out of character thing to say that Lissa lifted her hand to her mouth. 'Oh my God,' she said. 'I can't believe I just said that about my mum. She's amazing, really inspirational character, very . . . all of that.'

Jake smiled.

'She sounds . . . terrifying. And amazing, obviously,' he added hastily, horrified at how he was doing.

Lissa smiled again.

'Oh God.' She swallowed. 'Okay. She is both of those things.'

She wondered suddenly. Why hadn't she confided more in her mum? Would she even have needed to come here? Would her mum have been disappointed?

She thought of Cormac too, and his mother, fussing him about. It was odd, sometimes, just a little. The strange things they had in common.

'Well then,' said Jake after a long pause, trying to get her attention. 'Where shall we start? I really need to win you a large soft toy.'

'I don't need one of those.'

'You don't need one,' said Jake who had, truth be told, been practising, 'but I think you should have one. To make up for all the ones you missed when you were a child.'

And he bought her a large candy-floss, which immediately stuck in her hair, and they both laughed, as it was just as sticky and ridiculous a concept as a foodstuff as Lissa remembered from nearly half a lifetime ago, and was also potentially going to make a terrible mess of her hair but she found she didn't care. She wondered briefly if she didn't care because she was so relaxed, or because she genuinely

252

wasn't that fussed about the guy she was with, but soon told herself to stop bothering and just enjoy herself. And she did.

They passed Ramsay and Zoe with their clutch of children, the two little boys wearing identical Spider-Man costumes, holding hands and looking terrified.

'What about the ghost train?' Zoe was saying and the taller of the small children replied, 'We absolutely do not want to meet any more ghosts, Nanny Seven,' the littler was shaking his head in terror, and Zoe said, 'What do you mean "more" ghosts?' rather nervously and Patrick and Hari just looked at one another.

'Hello, you two,' said Zoe. Lissa felt odd to hear them referred to as a couple.

'Hello,' she said, smiling.

'LOLLIPOPS!' hollered Patrick. 'You're the lady with all the lollipops. And jags. And lollipops.'

He narrowed his eyes as if trying to work out whether seeing her was a good or bad thing.

'I don't have any lollipops. Or jags,' said Lissa reassuringly. 'Are you having a good time at the fair?'

Patrick and Hari shook their heads firmly.

'They won't go on anything,' said Zoe in despair. 'They think this entire fair is a plot to kill them.'

'Mary said so!' said Patrick.

'Oh, Mary,' said Ramsay, holding the girl.

'Well, at least it's cheap,' Zoe agreed vigorously.

'Ah disnae want to die,' said the tiniest of the children.

'You're not going to die!'

A large ride that tipped people upside down about forty metres in the air suddenly did just that and a huge amount of screaming rent the air. Both the lads looked absolutely petrified.

'Perhaps the spinning teacups,' grimaced Zoe, marching them off.

'HOT TEA ABSOLUTELY NO THANK YOU' was the last thing Lissa heard of Patrick as the oddly shaped family vanished into the crowd.

'They probably will die now,' predicted Jake. 'Just to be ironic.'

'Did you bring your med case?'

'I am technically off duty,' said Jake. 'So don't let me go too near the St John Ambulance tent. They are all madly in love with me.'

'That's very cocky,' said Lissa, but she had to eat her words when they passed the tent, Jake notably skulking, only for a large older lady to come fluttering out. She had very small feet in very high-heeled shoes given the ground was still pretty muddy.

'THERE'S MY FAVOURITE AMBULANCE MAN!' she trilled. Other women in the more familiar green outfits poked their heads out of the tent. One appeared to be busy attempting to cut candy-floss out of a small child's hair; another was comforting a child sobbing its heart out.

'What's the matter?' said Lissa instantly.

'Och,' said the woman thoughtfully. 'I'm no' sure if the ghost train is getting scarier or bairns are getting more scared.'

'The world is getting scarier,' surmised Lissa. 'We probably don't need ghost trains too.'

'AYE,' said the wee lad whose shoulders were shaking.

Meanwhile, Jake had been bustled away and fed.

'You know this lad. Always ready to help out,' said the first women, handing him a plate piled high with sandwiches and choc-olate biscuits.

'Well, it's his job,' said Lissa, watching him, amused.

'Here you go, Jakie, tea just how you like it,' said another one, piling sugar into a large enamel mug. He looked at Lissa, rather shamefaced.

'Would *you* like a sandwich?' said one of the women, not in a par-ticularly friendly way. 'Only they're really just for the volunteers.'

'I'm fine without a sandwich, thank you,' smiled Lissa. 'That's okay, Jake, you eat your fill.'

Chapter Thirteen

Cormac popped next door in response to a loud banging on the thin wall. It was definitely a summonsing banging.

Kim-Ange was standing with her hand behind her shoulder, waving uselessly.

'Can you zip me up?' she said. She was wearing a bright purple chiffon dress with a chain belt around her waist. Cormac stood behind her as she looked at herself in the mirror. Her purple eye-shadow matched exactly, as did her high velvet boots.

'Well?' she said, turning round nervously.

'You look beautiful,' said Cormac, and he meant it. 'Knock him dead.'

'Not literally, like, by accident or anything?' Kim-Ange sounded uncharacteristically worried.

'No,' said Cormac. 'By being your gorgeous self.'

And she was about to say something sarcastic, but instead grabbed her purple clutch bag, kissed him on the cheek and left.

'You didn't wish me luck with my date!' shouted Cormac behind her.

'No, I didn't,' said Kim-Ange, whose opinion of Yazzie was unsisterly, but it was too late, as Yazzie was already standing there, her large eyes looking at Kim-Ange tremulously. Kim-Ange decided, again uncharacteristically, to suddenly take the stairs.

There is something about standing in a very long queue that is not conducive to a good date, however beautiful Yazzie looked – which she did, in a long orange dress that perfectly set off her dark braids and huge dark eyes.

London was still ridiculously climate-change hot and people were walking about in shorts, red-faced, with a vaguely suppressed aura of threat in the air. They walked past the skateboarders under the Royal Festival Hall, shouting while entrancing children, cheek by jowl with expensively dressed older people on their way to concerts and the theatre. There were frozen-still mimes standing in the middle of the street, balancing on poles and getting in the way; art for sale, hawkers, jugglers, people yelling and handing out leaflets, book sales and the whole noisy cacophony of life, the smog hanging above the water and the great towers of the east taking on a pink tinge in the early evening.

The air smelled of food vans and garbage and fuel and Cormac felt stuffy and hot in his best checked shirt which had made Kim-Ange pretend to vomit but then decide was good enough after all. No designer borrowing tonight, he noticed.

Yazzie was chatting about someone she'd seen on her ward rounds and he listened cheerfully enough, but distractedly, as they dodged and wove around the hundreds of other people on the narrow bridge that cut its way up to Charing Cross station, next to thundering trains on the track beside them, above grey water filled with pleasure boats and dredgers, those odd flat structures covered in cement, and an RNLI station. The clouds seemed to seal the heat in to the ground. Cormac accidentally bumped into one group of tourists, fell back and jostled a large man who looked furious with him and swore under his breath.

His new-found fondness for the big city was muted tonight. He was thinking about how the fair was always such a fun time. He'd normally go a couple of times. Jake would get in with the St John Ambulance ladies who got free passes to everything but never wanted to use them – it was obviously a scam; they should have gone to a much more deserving cause, but Jake had the gift of the gab and that was that.

He hoped Jake would be nice to Lissa. It would be cool there tonight. Bright as well; you wouldn't get a whiff of sunset till well after ten p.m. There'd be a breeze probably; the right kind of evening for just a shirt and a jumper and being totally comfortable wherever you were, with a freshness and the sweet smell of the last of the bluebells on the air, as well as the gorse, warmed by the sun through the day ... he could almost feel it. And smell the candy-floss ... when you couldn't be happier ...

'So, anyway, we drained about a litre of bile from his abdomen,' Yazzie was saying. Cormac blinked.

'Is that right?' he said.

She looked worried.

'Sorry, is that gross? Before dinner?'

'Naw, naw, not at all,' said Cormac.

In fact, it wasn't before dinner at all. Lissa had been right they'd have to queue. What she hadn't been correct about was it certainly wasn't an hour. It was at least ninety minutes.

Something happened in the queue. Looking around, Cormac could see most people on their phones; some had been left to hold places while their presumably more popular mates whooped it up in a local bar somewhere. There were couples tight in conversation, as if they were as happy to be in a queue together as they would be anywhere else, and groups of friends were doing that noisy slightly nervous loud thing groups do at the beginning of a night out, before they've all managed to have a drink and settle down, were whooping at each other and shouting performatively and welcoming more and more members to their group until Cormac started to doubt whether he and Yazzie were ever going to make it at all.

'What do they sell here?' he said, realising that actually both of

257

them just loitering on the pavement were finding the conversation a little slow and stilted; that, even before they knew each other, they kind of looked like one of those couples with absolutely nothing to say to one another, once she'd told him about that drained cyst.

'Buns,' said Yazzie, pointing to the menu in the window.

'Buns?' Cormac screwed up his face. He didn't want a bun; he was starving.

'Bao,' said Yazzie. 'They're like Korean street food. They're filled with meat and stuff.'

'Meat buns,' said Cormac. They had already been there for forty-five minutes. His shirt was sticking to his back and his neck felt grimy simply from standing on a narrow pavement with cabs and trucks squeezing past him every second.

'Apparently they're amazing,' said Yazzie sullenly, because she had bought a new orange dress for this and told all her mates about how she'd managed to pull that hot Scottish NPL they all liked, and now she was standing on a pavement with a guy who looked like he'd rather be on the moon than here.

If it was warm in Kirrinfief, there was a little hidden bay down by the loch where you couldn't drive, only walk, and they would light a fire there and as long as you took all your rubbish away, the polis (Duncan from Hart's Farm; they'd all been to school together) would turn a blind eye to it, and they'd light the bonfire and drink cider and watch the sky barely darken as the hour neared midnight, and they could play their music as loud as they wanted as nobody was anywhere near to hear them, not for miles, and they watched the stars pop out, one by one, never too bright, for the night wasn't long enough for them to shine; the north of the planet had tilted too far on its axis.

Stars were for a different season, and this was the season of light. Someone would sometimes bring a guitar and everyone else would groan and throw stones and call them a James Blunt fud, but even so, if the gentle chords of 'Caledonia' or 'Sunshine on Leith' started up, well, it wouldn't really be possible not to sing along to that, would it, as the moon reflected on the calm waters of the loch and its endless rippling glory, with the dark shapes of the mountains on the other side, and as soon as the sun was sunk, it felt as if the lightest rays of the dawn were just appearing once more.

They had been such happy nights. Cormac found himself wondering if that's where Jake would take Lissa, and whether she'd like it. Just a bonfire, some cider, a bit of music, some hamburgers and marshmallows. Nothing fancy. Occasionally a soft toy someone had won at the fair which would get to sit on a proper throne made of sticks, after the year Gordon Lowrie had thrown one in the fire as a guy and the nylon had sparked and melted horribly and the plastic eyes had dropped down the edge of the pink bear and all the girls had screamed and got upset with them. After that, stuffed animals had pride of place.

He smiled to himself. Yazzie cleared her throat crossly.

'Ach. Where were we?' he said, looking up. The queue hadn't moved at all.

'Meat buns,' she said.

Chapter Fourteen

Meanwhile, three miles across town, two people had amazingly found a very quiet space.

Piotr had arrived in London with absolutely no money whatsoever; nothing more than the bus fare to Victoria station. He had spent the first six months, when he couldn't afford even to eke out a beer at the Polish Centre, walking for miles round and round the huge, terrifying, expensive city, along unfamiliar pavements with foreign signs and extraordinary monuments and strange things. So he was taking Kim-Ange to somewhere he really liked because you could only be a tourist for so long before you started getting deeper and deeper into what was around you, and one of his endless Sunday drizzly walks had taken him to this enchanted spot. Piotr thought she might like it, and he was right, she did.

Buried deep in Holland Gardens, well off the main thoroughfares and hard to find unless you already knew it was there, was the Kyoto Garden, its colours burnished and bright in the West London evening, full of exotic plants and knotted trees and streams with little bridges. There was nobody there but a pair of cranes nested at the water's edge, just below the waterfall. It was breathtakingly lovely.

Piotr opened the rucksack he had been clunking all the way from the tube station, and pulled out one large bottle of brown beer, one smaller one of vodka, a large bag of dumplings one of his substitute aunties at the Polish Centre had rustled up for him, a box of sushi just in case and a large bar of Dairy Milk. Kim-Ange grinned widely and grabbed the vodka and the chocolate.

'Normally,' she said, looking around at the tranquil site, the water trickling down through the curves of the beautifully made little streams with wooden bridges, smooth rocks and carp, 'I hate picnics. But I might make an exception for you.'

And some time later, Piotr was sitting giving bits of dumpling to the fish until Kim-Ange made him stop and they found their two hands together, and their heads even closer and suddenly, as the fish bubbled in the water and the waterfall tinkled overhead and there was a faint rustling of perfectly manicured fronds, but nobody else at all, they kissed and even if there was a whole London, a whole seven million people around them, they were not aware of another soul.

Strolling back to the tube station, giggly, tripping over their feet, clutching hands, Kim-Ange whispered something into his ear. Piotr shook his head.

'To me, you are only yourself,' he said stoutly, for his diminutive figure, narrow hips and small height belied a man with the heart of a lion.

'Only yourself.'

Chapter Fifteen

Lissa supposed people liked fairground rides for the same reason they liked scary films: the freedom of knowing that you felt a little scared but you were actually incredibly safe.

But these rides – these were more than watching a horrible film. It was stupid, and she felt she was making up for being a kid, but it was the wind in her hair and, in fact, the view you got, even when the ride only paused for a little bit at the very top, that was like a double-edged sword while everybody else was screaming their heads off with delight or horror.

She, by contrast, wanted to try and hold the sight in her head; it was the best view she had had of the absolute vastness of the loch. It seemed to go on for ever, and even though the day was still bright, the centre of it was pitch-dark. No wonder, she thought, they believed there was a monster in there. It was magical. She almost forgot to scream as they plummeted like a stone until it looked like they would hit the ground – just in time they brushed past it and were on the rise again and the view rose up like a magnificent carpet, and she could see further and further as she turned her head: the rolling roofs of the little cobbled village, undulating over the fell; the neat layout of the fields stretching ahead; the long line of the railway with a dark red train hurtling down its tracks; the great body of water. She felt like she could touch the clouds. She wanted to stay up there for ever.

Jake thought he'd have to put his arm round her – it was, he was finding, a very intense ride indeed, particularly when you'd just eaten three egg rolls and four Penguins, as pressed upon him by the good ladies of the St John Ambulance. He felt distinctly queasy and wished the damn thing would stop. He shut his eyes to make it pass.

Lissa, meanwhile, wasn't in the least bit nervous and couldn't have enjoyed it more. The ride had made her feel as high as the mountain tops and as close to the birds that circled in the updraughts. She sighed with something perilously close to happiness.

'That was amazing,' she said, when they finally got unclipped and rejoined the music and flashing lights and commotion of the fair at ground level. 'I'd be happy just to be up there all the time!'

Jake couldn't answer; he was very busy simply trying not to throw up as he wiped the sweat off his brow.

'Are you okay?' said Lissa. He nodded, wishing he could sit down.

'Do you need . . .?' Lissa smiled. 'Do we need to go back to the St John's tent?'

The thought of more egg rolls was simply too much for Jake. He held up a finger and charged off into the woods.

Lissa, surprised, laughed softly to herself. Then she glanced at her phone out of habit rather than thinking anyone would be in touch. She wasn't missing Instagram and Facebook, not much. But she would have liked to have posted the view. It was quite something.

There was nothing for her, of course, except a little dot on her WhatsApp. She opened it. It was a picture of three white spherical things, hard to make out.

'Meat buns,' she read. 'Ninety-minute wait. Excellent!'

She put her phone back, smiling. Well. Someone was having a good date, she supposed.

Cormac couldn't help it. He was distracted, and that wasn't fair. Ironically, of course, it was Jake who had told him all along: don't be distracted; stop just falling into things; think about the person you're with.

He looked up at Yazzie, who smiled back at him nervously, aware this wasn't going very well. She'd started on a long story about the worst wound she'd ever seen which, on balance, she really wished she hadn't, especially as she had to shout above the insane noise levels in the bar. They were crammed into a tiny corner space. At least, she thought, the food was delicious – and it truly was. Cormac had never tasted anything like it; every herb and flavour was superbly delineated, tasting fresh and light, so that was something.

'This is amazing,' he said. Then he found his thoughts, once again, straying north and wondering if the hot dog stall was there and if Lissa was enjoying herself. He resisted the urge to check his phone; this was awful. He was behaving like some kind of bounder.

'So, wounds, huh?' he found himself saying as Yazzie picked unhappily at the wonderful food.

'Did you always want to be a nurse?' she asked him.

Cormac half smiled to himself.

'Ach, not quite,' he said. 'Everyone in my family joined the Army. So I joined up too. Became a medic.'

'Ooh,' said Yazzie. 'That's interesting.'

Cormac shrugged.

'A bit too interesting at times,' he said.

'Did you get shot at?'

Cormac blinked. This was ridiculous. He found suddenly that he almost answered the question, and then reined it back. But why . . . why? Why did he suddenly feel almost ready to tell someone . . . but then had held back?

It was the newness, he decided. Everything being new. He could see for the first time the benefits of the big city; shaking off who you were, where you were from and what you came with – the baggage. That you were free to start over, to ditch everything. To feel lighter. He shrugged. The people in the queue were doing exactly as they had done – staring ferociously at those who had already managed to sit and get fed – he felt the weight of their hungry eyes on him.

'Nah, it was fine,' he said briefly. 'Shall we head?'

That was the problem with the food: it had come served in little wicker baskets, each perfect boxes of steaming heaven, but they had come quickly, and they'd eaten them even faster, and now the waitress was eyeing them up and making it very clear that if they were sitting and not actually stuffing their faces, they were costing her money, and would they mind terribly moving straightaway?

Cormac paid the eye-watering bill and they hadn't even got up from their seats before the next couple of hipsters were on top of them, photographing and uploading selfies to Instagram before they'd even sat down.

It was still light when they hit the noisy streets.

'We could go somewhere else?' said Yazzie, but neither of them knew where to go, and all the bars and pubs were stuffed to the gills, spilling their clients out onto the pavement. A warm Saturday evening in central London was not in any way conducive to quiet chatting. Even if he could think of anything he wanted to say to her.

In the end, they gave up and walked home in silence, Yazzie growing increasingly irritated and very ready to go back and complain to all her friends about how that Scottish boy might be hot, but oh my God, he was the most boring man in the universe and a total waste of time.

She wouldn't sleep with him again, she vowed to herself. This was going nowhere, and she wanted a boyfriend, not someone who lived on the next floor with benefits.

On the other hand, the sleeping with bit had been pretty good. Better than pretty good.

No. Definitely not.

'Um, I'm not sure where …' said Cormac, looking at a street spilling over with young Londoners on a night out.

'Actually,' said Yazzie. 'I'm working tomorrow; I'd better get an early night.'

It was irritatingly insulting how quickly he agreed with her.

Chapter Sixteen

Jake came out of the bushes looking slightly greenish, but more or less recovered.

'Gum?' he offered, but Lissa smiled and politely refused. They walked on in silence. Lissa wanted another shot on the rides, but she felt under the circumstances it wouldn't be very tactful.

Instead, Jake insisted on going to a ridiculous shooting arcade and attempting to hit enough travelling ducks with a toy rifle to win her a huge tiger, despite her protesting she really didn't want a huge tiger and probably wouldn't have anywhere to put it. They couldn't agree on that, and hitting the ducks also proved – particularly if you were feeling a little wobbly to begin with – rather more difficult than Jake had anticipated, and he kept missing. Unfortunately, once he'd started, he was not the type of man who, like Cormac, would simply have raised his hands and laughed about it. Instead, he gave the carnie more and more money while Lissa stood at the side, faintly embarrassed, and Jake's ears got redder and redder and the anger made him even shakier on the trigger and the entire thing went from fun to awkward rather quickly, particularly when small groups of boys appeared from nowhere to laugh at him.

'Aye, gies it another one, mister! You're a really good protector of ducks, aye!' shouted one.

'Aye, he's one of those environmentalists,' said another. 'Protecting species everywhere.'

Jake cursed at them and looked ready to lose his cool altogether until at last, after paying out far more than the cheap nylon toy could possibly have cost in the first place, he retrieved the white tiger and handed it over, looking bashful.

'Well,' said Lissa, trying not to smile too much in case it looked like she were laughing at him. 'Thank you, I suppose.'

'So listen,' said Jake, stuttering slightly. 'There's a wee barbecue happening down by the loch – you fancy it? There's a nice bonfire and that . . . um . . . music, I think . . .'

Just then, Ginty and her friends appeared out of nowhere. Lissa still had absolutely no idea who she was. She was looking really impressive, that much was clearly true, in a pair of skin-tight black leggings, enormous wedge heels, a cropped off-the-shoulder pink top that showed off her nice round belly and vast bosoms, and more hair than Lissa had ever seen on a human person. It tumbled down her back in great blonde waves, all the way to her bottom. There seemed to be no end to it; it looked like at least four people's hair. Along with the breasts (natural) and lips (much less so), in the normally dressed-down life of the village and the beginning chill of even the sunniest of Highland evenings, she stood out like a rare orchid. It wasn't a look Lissa could have ever worn herself, but she couldn't help but be impressed at the commitment it took. Ginty's huge pneumatic lips were polished to a high sheen; her eyebrows were perfectly shaded brown geometric shapes that looked carved into her forehead; her hair was absolutely everywhere.

'Hi, Jake,' she said seductively, tossing her hair over her shoulders. Lissa smiled. She clearly expected Jake's tongue to unravel like a cartoon fox.

Jake, meanwhile, had been having a profoundly disappointing evening. By now, in his personal schedule, Lissa should have been incredibly impressed by how he knew everyone, and terrified on the very high ride and he'd have had to comfort her with an arm round her. She should also have thrown her arms around his neck when he'd easily won her the biggest toy in the fair and, well, it was a pretty short trip from there back home, he reckoned. But it was worse than that. His entire gift of the gab had deserted him. He'd always found it easy to chat to women; they always liked him. He had treated it like a game, and it had worked.

Lissa hadn't felt like a game, and that had made it completely impossible. He couldn't think straight. And now Ginty McGhie was throwing another spanner in the works.

'Hi, Ginty,' he said in a resigned tone of voice.

'Who's this?' said Ginty as if she didn't know.

'Oh, you know ... this is Lissa? She's doing Cormac's job?'

'Where are you from?' said Ginty.

'London,' said Lissa putting her hand out. The other girls looked at that and sniggered.

'No, I mean, where are you really from?' said Ginty.

'London,' said Lissa shortly, bristling. The evening, which had started so promisingly, had taken on a sour turn. The brightly painted machines and stalls of the fair suddenly looked tawdry, chipped under the bright lights; grubby and cheap.

'Mm,' said Ginty, undaunted. She liked to think of herself as someone who was straight with others and told them what they thought of them to their faces. Not everyone saw this as quite as much of a virtue as she did.

'So, Jake, are you coming down to the bonfire again? Everyone's going.'

Too late, Jake remembered that the previous year he had spent the evening of the fair – several evenings, in fact; it wasn't as if there was so much entertainment came to Kirrinfief that anyone only went once – down in the sand dunes, rather close to Ginty. Extremely close actually.

'Um ...'

'What's the matter, didn't have a good time last year? Don't you remember?'

269

Ginty was pouting now. She turned to Lissa. 'Jake and I have always been ... friends ...'

The other girls sniggered.

'They've lit the bonfire,' Ginty went on. She bit her lip seductively. 'It's pretty hot down there.'

Jake was absolutely scarlet.

'Do you know?' said Lissa. 'I'm feeling pretty tired.'

'I'll take you home?' said Jake desperately.

'But you'll miss it!' said Ginty.

Lissa looked up.

'You know what,' she said. 'It's okay. You go.'

Chapter Seventeen

The music of the fair faded as Lissa made her way along the still light road, stopping to watch a baby rabbit make a desperate plunge across it in front of her. She smiled, then pulled out her phone. Then put it away again. He was on a date. With Yazzie. She shouldn't be even thinking about him. This was ridiculous. It was just that she didn't know him, that was all. And she was in a strange place and dealing with a lot of crap in her life, and of course she'd glommed on to the nearest person who seemed okay and not a terrible loser. She knew nothing about him, not really, didn't have a clue even what he looked like. It was a fantasy in her head, that was all, and to start talking to him at ten p.m. on a Saturday night was . . . Well. It was ridiculous. A conversation that had begun about someone else's snake.

She stared at the phone. To her amazement, she had a text message.

> Hey?

She picked it up with fumbling fingers.

> Hey.

Cormac had been staring out over the lights of London. He was amazed how electrified he was to hear from her. He'd texted Lennox too – they'd picked up Robbie, who had apparently gone to work with gusto. Fingers crossed it would last. The news had made him feel happy and anxious all at once, and he wanted to talk to someone about it.

Someone specific, he realised.

> You still out?

> Nearly home.

Cormac felt a huge gush of relief. This was ridiculous. He didn't even know this girl. But somehow he'd found that she was the one he wanted to talk to.

> You?

> I'm back too. It's hot out there.

> But what about the delicious meat buns?

> It turns out I'm quite quick at eating meat buns.

Lissa felt her heart beating faster as she reached the little cottage. She went into the back garden to try and take a picture of Ned, but he hadn't appeared. She continued anyway:

> So what's on your mind?

A bit of her, the tiniest bit, thought she should call him. But somehow, in the absolutely stillness and quiet of the night, it seemed strange; such a boundary-crosser. She was too nervous. This was safe, and she needed to feel safe.

> You know when you were at that accident?

Yeah.

> How did you feel?

You sound like my therapist! *Shit*, I need to skype with my therapist.

> Had you forgotten?

Yes!

> I wonder if that's a sign.

Of me being a coward, probably.

> Of you getting better, maybe.

Lissa looked around the garden, the evening scents of the cooling grass hanging heavy in the still air. It was lovely, even if it was getting horribly overgrown. The stream tinkled prettily.

This place is quite special.

It is. So is London.

Is this about meat buns again?

Yeah probably.

Anyway, why are you asking?

I just . . . I think. It might be a bit the same as the Army.

Lissa didn't say anything, just sat and waited; the little glowing phone in her hand was the centre of her world right then. And Cormac poured it all out, typing as if his life depended on it, his spelling all over the place. Telling her about the hideous injuries, the pointless pain, the children caught in the crossfire, the waste of all of it. How he couldn't sleep, couldn't stop worrying about it. How he had come home, and his mother was ashamed of him, and he felt like a coward for leaving his comrades. She read it all, patiently and carefully. And at the end of it, she typed just two words.

I know.

And she signed it off with a kiss. Cormac held his phone close to his chest as, five hundred miles away, Lissa was doing exactly the same thing, as if they were holding each other's hearts in their hands.

Chapter Eighteen

Oh, the luxury, the rare luxury, of waking on a sunny Sunday morning with nothing to do and someone else to think about.

Once upon a time, this would have made Lissa panic. She would have felt lonely and worried that she was living in the centre of the greatest city in the world and not making the most of it. She would have been entirely concerned that she was wasting time; desperately checking her Insta in case her friends had been up to something fun that she would have wanted to go to; pinging her mates immediately to see if anyone was up to anything, while trying not to look too needy; worrying if her mother was coming in to visit, as she would want to complain about her hair or her living conditions or darling, why didn't she just look at these brochures for research chemistry, she'd been so *good* at chemistry at school and there were all sorts of interesting careers that could spin off it now, it wasn't just in labs, you know, you could travel all over the world . . .

But there was something about living in Kirrinfief that had changed all that, she could tell. Something about being perfectly content with your own company – you had to be in a region the size of London but with eight thousand people living in it instead of eight million. If you wanted company, you could simply wander into the village and someone you knew would come along immediately. You could head down to the fair, or the pub and find yourself caught up in whatever came along. If there was anything to do – a fiddle band playing, a community play, Nina running a book reading – everybody went automatically. And if there wasn't, you stayed in and suited yourself. In the middle of nowhere, she found, she didn't feel lonely at all. She was so far removed from everything she couldn't possibly be worried about missing anything. And what was she missing anyway?

Nonetheless, she thought, stretching luxuriously, the sun making panes on the duvet, she would potter into town, buy something nice and actually cook for herself; pick up some eggs from Lennox's farm, which were very fine things indeed; buy a book from Nina to sit and read in the sun; maybe see what Zoe was up to. Zoe always seemed happy to have her around, even if there was never a moment when she didn't have about five people climbing all over her. She didn't seem to mind a bit. Lissa occasionally wondered if she didn't actually bother counting up however many people were in her kitchen at any one time. Then tonight she'd open a bottle of wine and call Kim-Ange and see how her date had gone and they could laugh about hers being a bit of a disaster, which would help, and maybe – *maybe* – she would tell her about her and Cormac. But tell her what, truly? That they messaged a lot? Kim-Ange had met plenty of men who were happy to chat online but when it came to meeting, everything changed. In the cold light of day, it could just be anyone offloading.

She walked across the quiet kitchen that she had grown to love in its understated way, boiled the kettle and was briefly startled by the rattle of the postman at the front door. Little arrived for Cormac except bills and circulars. She needed to send him his statements on actually. She smiled to herself. The post office was open until lunchtime, so she would go and do that. She liked the women who worked there, and they also sold incredible cheese and local bacon on the side (nobody in the Highlands had only one job really) so

276

that would give her a little purpose to her morning, which would somehow allow her to spend the entire afternoon lazing around, having completed her purpose. And maybe, she thought. Maybe... *maybe* ... talking to Cormac.

She picked up the letters. Two political leaflets for parties she'd never heard of, one in a language she couldn't read and then, to her great surprise, a letter to her. It was in a white envelope, her name and address typed, with a redirect stuck over it in Kim-Ange's flamboyant handwriting. She frowned. There was a crown printed on the envelope, and suddenly she realised what it was.

She put it down on the table incredibly quickly, as if it were hot, and stared at it.

The Crown Prosecution Service.

Instantly, she could feel her every muscle tighten; her fingers curled too. Her throat felt like it was closing over. She was suddenly gasping for breath. Every ridiculous claim she'd made the night before about feeling better, about getting over things – they were all nonsense.

No, no, she kept telling herself. No. She stumbled towards the door, opened it wide and drew in as many deep breaths as she could. The fresh, bright air stung her lungs as she told herself to calm down. Calm down. The road was empty and she stumbled across it to the copse of trees on the opposite side.

Feeling faintly ridiculous, she held on to one of the trees, and it seemed to sooth her. The deep heavy scent of the bark and the sap, and the overwhelmingly neon greenness of the new leaves filled her senses; the shade and the height of the great oak made her feel strangely safe. She leant against it, hands on her knees, and took great deep breaths, her back against the trunk, she felt her heart rate gradually return to normal. She had known this was coming, of course she had. She always did. Anita had told her about it, over and over again, but she had been too resistant. Classic health professional: terrible patient.

But she had been stupid and arrogant and frustrated at having to pay attention, to think about the thing she didn't want to think about – and now she couldn't cope with this, not at all. She had thought she was getting better, had genuinely truly believed it. But now she felt back at square one.

Cormac?

Yes?

I got the letter from court. I have to testify.

Cormac couldn't help it; his heart started to beat a little faster.

You're coming to London?

I have to go to court.

When?

Next week.

What's going to happen?

I have to stand up and . . . go through it again.

That will be okay, won't it? Help put it to rest? Isn't that what you're meant to be doing?

I'll have to see his mother. I'll have to see the man who did it, and what if I can't remember his face?

He's not going to get off. He's not going to come after you.

His friends might.

She felt her breathing rise again, felt the panic rise.

I think you'll feel sorry for him more than anything else.

I don't know what I'll feel.

There'll be a lawyer with you.

Oh God

Honestly, don't panic. I promise. You got this.

How do you know? You haven't met me. I might be completely useless.

Not according to my sources.

279

She half smiled at that.

Have *you* been in a court case?

There was a long pause.

Yes.

What was it?

Friendly fire.

Lissa blinked.

Did you shoot someone?

No. It was a friend of mine. A translator, working with us. Out with his friends. Some of the squaddies got a little ... well ...

He got shot?

Everyone got shot.

He deleted that last message but it was somehow worse after the fact that he'd done so. It made it clear that it had had a big impact on him. Which it had.

Lissa looked at her phone for a long time. Finally, she put together a row of screwy-face emojis and typed:

What are we like?

Cormac looked up at the grey river and smiled to himself. Suddenly, in the midst of eight million people, he felt incredibly close to someone very, very far away.

He turned back to his phone.

> Eejits.

Lissa smiled to herself and wrote back:

> Eediats.

And that was the moment Cormac nearly called her. He almost pressed the button. But what if he called her and she didn't pick up? What would he do then? What if he broke the connection and ruined everything? He thought of Jake telling him that he didn't behave well with women. He thought too of Jake, who thought he was dating her. Oh lord. Well. He put his phone back in his pocket so he wasn't tempted.

He was so tempted.

Lissa stared at the screen. Maybe he would just call? Throw caution to the wind? Call and talk and tell her everything? She wondered if he sounded like Jake, with that melodious Highlands accent. Maybe deeper; Jake said he was taller than him. She sighed to herself. This was ridiculous. She was building it into something it really wasn't. The wind rustled through the trees.

But just connecting had worked, somehow. He had calmed her down, made her feel better. She straightened up again, looked around her. The birds were calling, high up in the fresh air. Their days, she supposed, were all the same. The world was awake around her.

And it wasn't going anywhere. The trees had been here for hundreds of years. The wood had been standing through wars and great changes, but had never been uprooted. The foxes and deer lived their lives; the trout still jumped in the stream; the seals would still flap along the lochside.

For the first time, Lissa started to wonder. Could she build a life here? Not with Cormac of course – that was ridiculous! They hadn't even met; she didn't even know what he looked like; of course he wasn't going to like her, how could he? It was an absurd crush, that was all; a good distraction from the anxiety and the pain. Plus she had his job.

But even without that … might this be a place for her? She thought of Nina's friendly face behind the piles of books she organised so beautifully. She had found a home here. And Zoe too, even if she was trailed by what looked like six or seven children at all times and, if Lissa's professional opinion was not mistaken, what looked like another one on the way.

They had found a place here. Could she?

She got up slowly. She would read the letter. She would read it, and she would face up to it and then, when the secondment was over, then she would see.

She glanced sadly once more at the phone. She missed him already.

Just as she crossed the threshold, it pinged. She grabbed it delightedly. Was it him?

It was:

> So …

Cormac had thought about things. He'd heard from Jake about Ginty McGhie, which was patently terrible news for Jake, who was stuck somewhere with a terrible headache and deep regrets.

And he'd thought about everything. About everything he'd learned in London, where people were bold, not shy; where people came to get what they wanted, to try everything and anything out there. He knew he'd been lazy in relationships; had always preferred to think of humanity in the abstract, rather than people in particular. He wanted to change that. Starting now.

> Wanna meet in London then?

Chapter Nineteen

The letter had been short and straightforward, with a date a week hence and a time she was due at Southwark Crown Court then. It warned her that the timings might be off and that she may have to wait, and there was a form for expenses.

The lawyer, Roisin, had rung her just as she was trying to pluck up the courage to ring them, and had talked her through what had happened. She would be allowed the opportunity to read the statement she'd given at the police station first time round to refresh her memory for the small details, then Roisin would walk her through the event on the stand.

Then the defence lawyer would ask her a few questions, but honestly, said Roisin, you're a noble, trustworthy health-care worker who happened to be walking past and did their absolute best to save the life of a child. They'd have a devil of a job making you look bad in front of a jury and I would be very, very surprised if they bothered to try. They'll probably get you off the stand as soon as possible. All you're doing is confirming the line-up, people you've already picked out.

'What if I can't remember their faces?'

'I'll ask you if you recognise the person driving the car. If you do, say yes.'

'But what if I don't . . .?'

'Alyssa,' said Roisin. 'Don't panic. It's okay to be nervous. He'll be in a suit, but it's the same person. The police had to pull him out of his car, remember? When it was surrounded by the lads from the estate?'

' . . .okay,' said Lissa, swallowing hard.

'Who are also on the CCTV that is going to be played to the jury.'

'Can I watch that?'

'Nope. I'm just saying. Don't worry about it.'

Lissa sighed.

'It's all right,' said the lawyer. 'You're going to be fine. Honest. And you'll be back in London. Enjoy that, surely!'

Lissa bit her lip. She couldn't help it but she did have a tiny thing to look forward to. A tiny green shoot. She'd teased Cormac: he'd suggested going to Borough Market, which made him *such* a Londoner, she'd said. It was an incredibly expensive, very chichi food market just on the south bank by London Bridge station, which sold all manner of exotic and organic foods at incredible prices.

But it was still a lovely place to roam around, smelling the cheeses and the coffee beans, the beautiful cakes that were practically works of art and the unidentifiable (certainly to Cormac) spiky fruits. It was an oasis of beauty in the big granite city and Cormac had liked it straightaway; it was so different to the very solid, decent farmers market in Kirrinfief where you could buy the freshest local brown hens' eggs with great big melting yolks, half a dozen for a pound. Here you could buy a single ostrich egg for seven pounds. At the Kirrinfief farmers' market, you could buy punnet after punnet of fresh strawberries, huge, some a little battered, from the fields all around them for miles and miles. Here you could buy six perfect strawberries curated in an artisanal punnet and they would cost almost a pound each.

But Cormac still liked it. It reminded him a little of home and he respected people who took their food seriously, even if he had been slightly taken aback when asked to pay eight pounds for a toasted cheese sandwich.

And it was a five-minute walk away from the court. Her stomach fizzed.

Lissa had told herself not to get carried away, not to build it up too much. She had failed miserably.

'You look very distracted,' said old Joe Cahill the previous Thursday. Seeing as she was checking his foot operation post-wound care, and seeing as, distractingly, he had a set of the most gnarled and twisted hobbit feet toenails she'd ever seen, it wasn't, Lissa thought, coming back to herself, the worst place to lose her concentration.

She straightened up.

'Your wound is fine, Mr Cahill,' she said. 'But did they not tell you to cut those nails?'

'Aye, they did, aye,' he said mournfully. Then he looked down at his expansive stomach.

'Och, it's no' that easy, no,' he said with a sigh.

'Did they not get someone to do it there?'

'Aye, they tried but they couldnae work it with the scissors, eh.'

It was true: they looked like sheep's horns.

'Let me have a shot,' said Lissa. 'You'll never get walking with those on.'

But Joe had been quite right; there was absolutely no shifting them. Outside, a brief shower had made everything sparkle and bounce in the light. She could see the sheep nudging their way around the luminous green field. Suddenly she had an idea.

'I'm just going to see if Joan's about,' she said.

Joan did in fact happen to be in the general area (which she gauged as being within fifteen miles) and came over immediately, happy at the suggestion.

'I wondered,' said Lissa, 'if you knew if there was a technique that they used on, like, boy sheep and stuff.'

'Boy sheep?' said Joan, her lip curling.

'Um, yes,' said Lissa.

'I'm not sure we're going to make a country girl out of you. But your thinking isn't bad. Joe!'

'Whit?'

'Stop eating pies; this is ridiculous.'

She prodded at his round stomach.

'Actually, I was taught not to fat-shame patients,' said Lissa quietly, feeling Joan had been unkind.

'More's the pity!' boomed Joan. 'Come on, Joe.'

'I do like a pie,' said Joe.

'You can have a pie! Just don't have all the pies!'

'Um,' said Lissa.

'Okay,' said Joan. 'Where's your hacksaw?'

'His what?'

'It's a small saw people use for cutting things,' said Joan.

'No, I thought you would have some animal thing . . . some technique they use on animal's horns.'

'I do! It's called a hacksaw.'

'There's one through in the lean-to,' said Joe.

The lean-to was a ramshackle space utterly filled with junk and tomato plants.

'If he can get around, he can tidy up,' muttered Joan. 'You did the right thing to call me in.'

She peered at Lissa over her spectacles.

'Just as you're getting the hang of it, you'll be heading back, eh?'

Lissa shrugged.

'The court case is soon.'

'Yes, I saw on the roster.'

There was a pause as they rummaged through a large pile of seed catalogues, a lot of ancient copies of *Farmers Weekly* and a medium-sized stuffed owl.

'I never thought you'd manage up here,' said Joan finally. 'With your London ways. But I think you've done rather well. I think people are finally taking to you.'

Lissa blinked. 'Except Ginty.'

'Yes, except Ginty. She hates you. I heard all about it last time I was in.'

'Oh good.'

'I wouldn't worry about it. Everyone feels sorry for whoever is in Ginty's firing line. That poor Jake ... Aha!'

Triumphantly, she pulled a small hacksaw from the bottom of a teetering mass of unpleasant soil samples.

Lissa followed her back into the bedroom.

'I feel like I'm taking off someone's fingers for frost-bite! Again!'

Lissa checked to see if she was kidding, but she didn't appear to be.

'Right, Joe, feet up. Lissa, you hold him.'

Lissa took one ankle at a time. It was a ridiculous business, but Joan worked quickly and carefully, sawing through the vast twirly nails, then Lissa neatly clipped what was left over and swept them up with a brush and pan.

Joe couldn't stop staring at his toes.

'Well,' he said. Then he walked a few paces, and then a few more.

'Well,' he said again, scratching his head as if he couldn't quite believe it. 'That is quite something. That is really quite something.' His eyes lit up. 'I feel like I could—'

'Do *not* dance,' said Joan quickly. 'You still have a foot injury.'

'Och, just a jig ...'

'No dancing. For a week. Then, dance a lot. It'll help. And *no more pies*!'

'Aye,' said Joe. 'But noo I can dance, I dinnae need pies.'

He did an experimental twiddle.

'I am warning you!' said Joan. 'No dancing. Some mild tidying up I would absolutely suggest to you.'

'I need to find my dancing shoes,' agreed Joe.

'Fine.'

'Thanks, lass,' he said, looking at Lissa. 'This was your idea. You know, for a Sassenach, you're no' that bad.'

～ ╭

The sun was still high in the sky as they left, and the sheep pootled around, completely disinterested in them as they headed towards their respective cars. It was a glorious evening though; the breeze ruffled Lissa's hair. Joan marched straight to her car, the dogs as usual going bananas in the back.

'Um,' said Lissa just as she was about to get in. 'Just . . . just . . . when Cormac comes back . . . just . . . do you think . . .? Do you think there might be another opening here? For another person? I mean, I'm qualified for community nursing too.'

Joan frowned. 'Oh, I don't think so, dear. We're a shrinking region; there just aren't enough people here to support two NPLs. But there's loads of places in the Highlands that would snap you up . . . and I'd write you a good reference.'

'Okay. Right. Thanks,' said Lissa. But she didn't want anywhere in the Highlands. She wanted here.

Well, it was worth asking. Maybe getting back to London would make her feel more homesick; she'd always assumed that she would be. Once she saw all her friends and got back into her commute and with her life there . . . Feeling lonely among crowds; making herself busy because somehow not being busy was associated with failure; cramming her calendar full of events she didn't really want to do, because she lived in London and how else was she supposed to manage?

No more wandering down into the village on a morning where you could see the changes from the day before; the new colours and flowers pouring out of the sides of the roads; the trees getting thicker every day; the loch mist burning off before she'd had her second cup of coffee.

And the noisy quiet of the countryside – the birds and the occasional growl in the forests; the sound of the wind in the fireplace and the sweet smell of burning whisky wood – couldn't really compare to pigeons eating old McDonald's leftovers; they didn't have quite the appeal of the herons that took off from the very tip of the loch like ballerinas.

Well. There was a lot happening. A lot coming up. She should just get through it a bit at a time.

Chapter Twenty

Lissa looked around the little cottage. It was as if, she realised, she'd never lived there at all now that she'd neatly packed her black carry-on case and emptied out the jam-jars full of wilting wildflowers.

Why, she found herself wondering , had she not put up a picture? Set the books up on shelves rather than scattering them underneath her bed? The cottage was beautiful, and she could have made it even lovelier. She must have been in such a bad state when she arrived.

Especially now that she knew that Cormac wouldn't mind. She thought about him briefly, imagined him walking in – in her head, he was alternately very tall and very short and stocky; sometimes he had a beard and then he really didn't. Nurses never had beards anyway in case they had to do mouth to mouth. Also, if he'd been in the Army . . .

But she did— This was ridiculous of course. He hadn't mentioned Yazzie again; he might even be still seeing her anyway. And she hoped he hadn't discussed her with Jake. They wouldn't, surely? They were Highlands blokes – surely they'd just be discussing who'd won at the shinty.

She realised she'd actually had the conscious thought 'who won at the shinty'. God, she had changed.

When she got back from London, she vowed, she would make it beautiful for the time she had left in the Scottish summer, when it never got dark and the air softened. She was so looking forward to it, although she reminded herself to bring a super-strength midge spray back with her. They must sell something in London for people going en route to the tropics. Something must kill those pesky mites.

She couldn't help it though. Imagining. What it would be like if he walked through the door and grabbed her and . . .?

She was being ridiculous, she realised. But also, it was good; good that she was thinking about a chap again. It had been so very long. Since her mind hadn't felt closed, confused and frightened all the time. Even her ability to daydream, to fantasise, seemed to have been turned off by the anxiety; the luxury of even believing in a brighter future for herself. That had been lost; now it seemed to have been found. Even if, of course, it was nonsense.

Still. They were meeting. After the trial. Better than that: he had promised to take her out to lunch. She hadn't (and she felt guilty about it) even told her mum or Kim-Ange about it, even though she knew they were both longing to see her. This was bad but it was going to be such an awful day, and only the thought of Cormac was keeping her hanging on.

Her Skype bonged, and she groaned.

━ ⌒

Anita was fully dressed and had two suitcases by the side of her kitchen table.

'Is this a bad time?' said Lissa, not wanting to point out that Anita had called her.

'Hff,' said Anita, glancing nervously at a pile of paperwork on the kitchen table. 'Apparently I'm passport monitor and it's making me very nervous.'

'Perhaps try some deep breathing exercises,' said Lissa, then immediately felt bad. 'Sorry, I'm sorry.'

But Anita was looking around anxiously.

'Where is that sodding cat?' she was saying to herself. Just at that exact moment, a cat shot past the screen so fast it was just a blur, pursued by two rampaging children.

'Not on the road! Not on the road!'

Lissa found herself thinking about Zoe and Nina: baby John pottering about the farmyard with his dad; Zoe's little tribe cavorting about the fields. Anita obviously lived in a nice terrace house in South London; it was probably worth more than the entire village up here. But as the children pelted around the expensive kitchen, it couldn't help crossing Lissa's mind to wonder if it was worth it. How much it must cost to pay the mortgage; how hard it must be to raise children you couldn't let out on their own.

'Honestly I can ...'

'No, you have these sessions paid for and I need to complete them before you go.' She looked crestfallen. 'Sorry they've been a little rushed ...'

'It doesn't look easy, your job,' said Lissa mildly.

'I know,' said Anita, as heavy little shoes pattered overhead. 'I'm sorry ...'

Lissa shook her head.

'Actually,' she said. 'Turning off my social media ... it really helped.'

'Did it?' Anita brightened.

'Yup. And so did you telling me to go over it in my head.'

'Did you?'

'No, but I thought the idea was solid. So ...'

Outside Anita's door, a taxi honked its horn and her face fell.

'Tell me quickly,' said Lissa.

'It's quite strong,' said Anita.

'I don't care. Call it efficient and I'll give you a good feedback form.'

'That would be good,' said Anita, looking stressed.

There was a pause.

'Okay,' she said, then took a deep breath. 'If you don't go over

292

this, right now, out loud, whether to me or somebody else, this is your last chance. Tomorrow you'll be in the witness box. And the perpetrator is going to be staring straight at you. Possibly his mates will be there. Staring at you. Threatening you. I'm not trying to scare you, Lissa. But what if you freeze? Clam up?'

'Oh, actually this is quite harsh,' said Lissa. The honking grew louder. Anita paused.

'I won't freeze,' said Lissa suddenly.

'You might.'

Lissa blinked back tears. Suddenly the day outside the window didn't look soft and welcoming: it looked ominous and oppressive.

'And I have to warn you: you could cause a mistrial. Or let the offender go free. If you can't explain clearly what you saw.'

Lissa could barely speak; the lump in her throat was huge.

Upstairs, Anita's children were yelling their heads off. Anita leaned forward.

'Lissa. I have black sons. One day you might too. The streets of the city have to be safe for them. You know that. You know that, right?'

And her voice was intense and serious and not at all distracted. All Lissa could do was back away from her gaze, nodding slowly. The taxi honked for the last time and Anita straightened up.

'And now I have to go,' she said, and Lissa simply nodded.

There was another honking sound, and Lissa belatedly realised it was her own cab. Her heart was racing. She knew Anita was right. She knew. But suddenly it seemed harder than ever.

Chapter Twenty-one

> I won't know what you look like.

Lissa was messaging Cormac in her anxiety. They hadn't been communicating beyond the professional in the last week, mostly because both of them, without mentioning it, were extremely nervous. Lissa nearly wrote 'It's a blind date' but managed to delete it just in time because it wasn't a date – it was a meeting with someone she had been doing a job-swap with – and was professional if anything. Even though they had already discussed dates they'd had with other people. So. The fact that she hadn't mentioned it to Kim-Ange had ... nothing to do with anything.

Cormac also hadn't mentioned their meeting to Kim-Ange. She would just make a big deal out of it. She and Piotr were madly in love and snogging up a storm at breakfast time every day and frankly making everyone a tiny bit sick, and nothing would make her happier to think of the two of them ... going for lunch, no more no less, he told himself, nonetheless ironing his best shirt, a yellow check.

He glanced at her message, and sent:

I'll recognise *you*. You'll be the one loudly complaining about diabetic prescribing.

It just makes everything else *more difficult*.

And Cormac smiled at the bugbear that always amused him.

Roisin had told Lissa to look sensible in court, so she pulled her hair back into a tight bun that made her look more professional than the curls everywhere did, and put on a sleek houndstooth check skirt suit which she never really got a chance to wear. Paired with a blouse and some smart earrings her mother had sent her (as well as the suit), she looked surprisingly professional, particularly after having spent the last two months either in uniform or wrapped up in woolly jumpers and thick tights, even through the Highlands spring.

She took her overnight bag as she was coming back on the night train, which she was rather excited about; it stopped just up the road and was patently the best way to get there, even if it was expensive.

All she had to get through was the trial.

Her heart was beating hard all the way to the airport. Being in Scotland had felt safe; protected; away from everyone else. Not having to face what had happened. There weren't any teen gangs in Kirrinfief, at least not that she'd heard of. Children ran around practically free range, something that had surprised her when she'd first noticed it, but then realised that everyone knew everyone in their small corner of the world; their children were everyone's children. It was nice to see children playing in the streets and down on the little shore and not have to worry about them.

As the little twin prop plane burred its way down the length of the country, Lissa looked at the patchwork fields through the window, unable to concentrate on the book Zoe had pressed on her, worrying more and more about coming face to face with Kai's family again. Would they be mad at her? Would questions be asked about that dreadful night at the hospital? No complaints had ever been filed; nothing had happened to her except the secondment, and that hadn't ended up feeling like a punishment at all.

Maybe, she thought, it would be straightforward. Would take two minutes. And there would be ... the Loch Ness monster. She bit her lip. It was nice of him, that was all. And no doubt he wanted to cast an eye over the person who'd been sleeping in his spare room, would be trying to work out whether she'd killed all his plants or broken his fridge or not. At least he probably knew she hadn't exactly been having wild parties.

Then another two weeks to pack up and then ...

Well. She'd think about the future when she had to. She had had a little fantasy, it was true. Of possibly renting out the guest room, if he was keen; just imagine living somewhere you could afford to have a spare room on an NHS salary. It still beggared belief. Of finding a job nearby. Maybe not what she was doing, but there must be something. Of, dare she say it, escaping once and for all. The pressure and the racing and the craziness of the city. Just turning her back on it. Leaving the fancy restaurants and the high heels and the hot new things to other people. People who got more out of it than she did. People who wouldn't be constantly worried every time they heard an ambulance whoop or sirens go off or a helicopter pass overhead.

She blinked. She had barely slept and the drone of the engines was making her want to drop off, but every time she came close to doing so (and everyone else was comfortably snoozing), she remembered, yet again, what the day was for, and bolted back upright again.

Southwark Crown Court was a squat brown ugly eighties building put up by someone who had obviously taken their inspiration from an out-of-town supermarket. It was faceless and bureaucratic; neither terrifyingly grand nor trying to be welcoming. It simply was. Lissa supposed in some way that that was the point.

It was boiling. A damp, oppressive heat. Lissa couldn't remember the last time she'd been so hot. She was wearing far too many clothes, it was ridiculous. She pulled off her large coat and jammed it on top of her wheelie bag, making it unwieldy and hard to get past the crowds on the tubes. She'd forgotten about those too. So many people! How did anyone get anywhere? And could she really have forgotten about this in such a short space of time? She felt herself begin to sweat. This was the last thing she needed, looking damp and flustered.

Roisin, short, business-like and dressed in a smart black suit and heels that looked absolute torture to march about in all day, met her at the side entrance. People were milling around and Lissa was anxious, concerned about seeing the boy's mother again; jerking back, again and again, to the memory of everything that had happened before.

She looked around nervously. How would the families of the defendant be? Angry? frustrated? Violent?

Instead, she saw a mixed line-up of smartly dressed solicitors and barristers hurrying in and out of entrances; clerks with huge bundles of papers and files, sometimes rolling them along in carry cases; and other people, some dowdily dressed, smoking patiently by the bins or sitting staring into space. It did not feel like a cheerful place, and nor was it meant to.

'You'll be fine,' said Roisin, sitting her down in the witness waiting room after they got buzzed in. It was completely plain and bare, and the coffee, in a thin white plastic cup, was absolutely disgusting. Lissa kept forgetting and taking automatic sips of it.

She read over her statement again. It was just as she recalled and she felt her heart begin to thump. The day, the person she'd been visiting. Seeing the boys in the walkway. Hearing their banter. Then the flash, the hideous flash of the phone, glinting in the sun; the crunching of bones; the squelching of flesh.

The rush. The ambulance. The sitting. The begging. The bargaining. The faces.

She started to cry.

'You'll be fine,' said Roisin again, glancing at her watch. 'Come on! You've been a big tough A&E nurse! You're used to all sorts! How come this one is bothering you?'

She remembered the boy's soft face lying on the hard pavement.

'It just does,' she said.

'Well. Distract yourself,' said Roisin. 'How's country life treating you?'

At this, Lissa felt herself turned pink.

'It's all right,' she said.

'Seriously? Lots of cows to talk to?'

'Yup,' said Lissa. 'Lots of cows.'

'Isn't it freezing? I couldn't handle the weather.'

'It's fresh,' said Lissa. 'I quite like it. It's better than ...'

She indicated out of the tiny window where the heat shimmers came off the pavement and the scent of bins rose into the stuffy air, smoke everywhere.

'Well,' said Lissa. 'I quite like it.'

Roisin sniffed and Lissa bent again to the black and white sheet of paper.

Chapter Twenty-two

Cormac woke early that morning, the room stuffy already, excited about something before he remembered exactly what it was. He sat up, grinning to himself. Then he stopped and felt worried instead. Today was the day. He was going to meet Lissa.

He told himself to stop being daft. He was a grown man, and he felt like a teenager on a first date. Getting overexcited was only going to lead to disappointment. Plus she was stressed out and worried anyway; the last thing she'd be thinking about was him. But he could be there for her, take her to lunch – he was proud of discovering somewhere lovely to take her – listen to her, get to know her. That was all. Yes.

He still couldn't keep that infernal smile off his face as he got into the shower, and as he pondered the new slightly flowery shirt Kim-Ange had persuaded him to buy. It wasn't his style at all, and had been to his mind hideously expensive, but Kim-Ange had been extremely persuasive on the issue and sure enough, nobody had pointed and laughed when he'd worn it to the pub for half an hour just to give it a run out.

The way he was thinking about Lissa though ... nothing Emer or Yazzie had ever come close to. No. He was being ridiculous. Overthinking everything.

But it was the first time in such a long time that he'd just felt so . . . so alive.

He thought back to Robbie. He'd better call Lennox and see how he was doing, although so far no news felt like good news. And Lissa would be seeing him of course . . .

Don't go overboard, he told himself. But she was in for such a tough day. Testifying in court. Reliving that awful time. I mean, he had to play it cool.

Or, he also found himself thinking, he could turn up early, go support her in court. It wasn't right she had to be in court by herself. He could just say hi, just let her know that he was there for her. Would that be weird?

It was a glorious day out there. Perhaps he would take a stroll – just a casual stroll – in his new shirt, along the South Bank, a place he had come to . . . well. It wasn't Scotland. But it definitely had *something*. So. He could take a stroll. Get a lovely cup of coffee that took someone quite a while to make and grind beans and stuff and, well . . . he could see where the day took him.

The curvaceous woman and the tightly pulled back hair barely gave the man in the flowery shirt who held the door open for her a second glance as she marched towards it, head down, anxious beyond belief about what was coming.

Cormac didn't notice the woman either; he had meant to look around for someone who might be Lissa, but his phone had rung just as he was walking in. He recognised the number and picked it up, grimacing.

'Hi!' came the English-sounding voice. 'Is that the lifesaver?'

Cormac frowned.

'Larissa, hi.'

'Hi! Listen, darling, beautiful day – we've got lunch booked on the roof of Coq d'Argent. It's beautiful and you'll be able to save anyone that falls off it. See you there, yah?'

Cormac passed the door to the girl behind him, who took it with muted thanks and dived past the annoying man walking too slowly in a flowery shirt.

'I'm a bit busy today,' he said quite happily.

'Oh, don't worry about that, darling – we'll be there all afternoon. Ciao!'

But Cormac's thoughts were still on a laughing girl with tumbling curls, plus he had realised to his slight annoyance that he was miles too early – bursting, truly, from turning up, too excited and over the top – and was contemplating going back out again to find another coffee, but then he'd have had far too much caffeine and that really wasn't an ideal situation for meeting someone in either so he decided to go fill up his water bottle from somewhere and sit on the front and stare out at the passing boats and, hopefully, calm the crap down before he ruined everything.

Chapter Twenty-three

Roisin passed over the piece of paper.

'Are you ready? You do know this is a murder trial?'

'Why isn't it manslaughter?' said Lissa.

'Because we have evidence the defendant thought Kai was a gang member from a rival group, even though he wasn't. It was mistaken identity, but we're fairly clear it was deliberate. Kai was the youngest of the friends; he was only fifteen. They thought he was a runner. He wasn't. The driver never meant to get caught, but he did mean to do it.'

Lissa thought again of the car speeding up. Speeding up. This was worse: it had not been a hideous accident, but a deliberate attempt to extinguish a young life. The wrong life. It was almost unbearable.

Lissa took a deep breath and bent her head to the paper. The words swam in front of her eyes.

... I saw the car swing round the corner and mount the kerb ...

She saw the boy again, his phone glinting as it was thrown up, and fell, thrown up and fell, spinning in the sunlight.

... and when I got to him ...

She remembered the trickle of blood dripping from the side of his mouth; the shouts and yells of the rest of them chasing the car down; the cries and the shrieking of brakes and the drip drip drip of the blood.

Blindly, panicking, unable to breathe, her heart trying to burst out of her chest, she stood up, leaving everything behind her, and ran out of the room.

Chapter Twenty-four

Cormac wandered back into the courthouse, figuring he needed to use the bathroom and surely the case would be starting soon. He was still annoyed at how restless he felt. When someone pushed past him . . .

It was a flash, nothing more, he didn't catch sight of the person . . .

At first, he dismissed what he glimpsed because he knew she had curly hair, that was what he pictured, then it struck him, as the figure dashed past in a blur, ringlets bouncing out of their tight band, that after all she might well be here by now, and by the time his heart had suddenly dialled up to a hundred miles an hour and he'd turned around, there was a loud bang, and he realised that the figure had disappeared into the disabled toilet and locked the door behind them.

Ah. Now here was a thing. Lurking around the loo was . . . Cormac tried to think of a worse possible way to meet Lissa for the first time – if it even was her; it might just have been his mind playing tricks. How would he even know?

The corridor was empty and he backed away carefully, concerned at the loudness of the bang she (if it was her) had made and the speed she'd been running. Whoever it was, they were clearly upset.

He was about to take out his phone and text her, then he put it away again. If it wasn't her, it would be very weird. If it was, saying 'Have you locked yourself in the toilet right now?' was hardly going to come over well.

He was turning to go over to the courtroom, check if he could see her there, when he heard a noise coming from the door. Just a sob. The tiniest little sob.

Cormac stopped in his tracks. Whether it was her or whether it wasn't ... someone was really upset. And it just wasn't in him not to pay attention to that.

He went over to the door and knocked gently.

Lissa froze. She had tried to keep quiet, but it was almost impossible; the lump in her throat was overwhelming. Oh God. She couldn't believe it. Someone needed to come in. She was gasping for breath, didn't know what to do. She tried to calm herself down.

'Um ...' Cormac listened. He could hear heavy breaths. If she was genuinely having a panic attack, adding an extra stressor by identifying himself was probably the worst thing he could do. If it even was her.

Lissa put her hands on her knees, tried to suck in some air.

'Just a minute,' she managed weakly.

She straightened up slowly, trying to breathe properly. She didn't recognise her own face in the mirror. She was being ridiculous. This was nuts. She had to go and do this. She had to ... she had to ...

She felt the tears welling up again.

'Are you all right?' came a soft voice.

She froze. She hadn't thought even so far ahead, just knew she had to escape that airless little room; the words in front of her; the memories.

But time was moving on; they were going to call the case. There was a whole roomful of people waiting for justice; waiting for her to help Kai. She had to be there. But she couldn't.

There was a silence. Cormac cursed to himself. He couldn't believe he'd spoken. Now what kind of trouble was he in?

If he said who he was, she might get really upset or take umbrage or it might be just incredibly weird.

If he didn't and she found out later, that would be awful too. But he couldn't run away. She needed help. He knew she did. He couldn't leave.

That was when Cormac MacPherson, in a split-second, made possibly the most ridiculous decision of his entire life.

'Yeah awright, luv, tell me what's up, duck.'

He winced at himself. He sounded more Welsh than Cockney, probably. Or just downright insane.

Lissa squinted. The voice – she couldn't tell where it was from – sounded kind. She threw more water on her face, trying to make her heart stop racing. But she couldn't stay like this, she couldn't.

Snuffling slightly, she moved a little closer to the door, tried to catch her breath.

'I have to ... I have to testify.'

On the other side of the door, Cormac blinked. He wished he could go inside, hold her, tell her everything was going to be all right.

But he didn't know this person. He didn't know her at all. Instead, he found himself saying, 'Oh yeah. Innit?'

Then wincing all the more, Lissa replied: 'I ... It should be straightforward. Just ... just say what happened.'

'Yeah, that sounds awright.'

'And ... I'm just so scared.'

'Wot 'appened then?' said Cormac. 'Tell me ... duck.' He wasn't at all sure about duck. 'Weren't rude or nuffin'?'

Lissa slumped to sit down on her bag, her back to the door. Cormac sat down too, his back on the other side, separating them only by a few centimetres of wood.

'Oh ... no,' she said, half smiling. 'No, "nuffin' rude".'

She squeezed her eyes together. A kind stranger on the other side of the door ...

'Sorry, do you really need the bathroom?' she said, suddenly gripped by the worry that it might be an actual wheelchair user outside.

'You're awright, luv,' said Cormac, begging himself to stop talking. There was a pause. And somehow, Lissa found her heart rate slowing a little as everything went quiet.

'I just have to tell them . . .' Lissa began. Cormac pressed his head against the door to hear her better. 'I just have to say . . . that I saw the boys. Talking, and laughing. And then I saw the car. And the man in the car. And I saw him hit the boys. That's it. That's all I have to say. That's all . . .'

Her voice caught as she saw once again the phone whipping through the air; heard the hideous clunk of Kai's head on the concrete.

'Yeah,' said Cormac. 'You can do that.'

'I saw . . . I saw the car come round,' said Lissa again, her voice still wavering. 'I saw it come round too fast. I saw the colour of it. I saw it.'

'Yeah,' said Cormac, more encouraging now.

'I saw it hit . . . I saw it hit the boys. I saw it. I *saw* him. I saw him hit the boy, and Kai . . . Kai's . . . the boy's . . . Kai's phone. Went up. In the air. I saw it. And he went up, he was thrown up and . . . and he killed him. I saw it. I did. I saw it. I was there.'

' . . .?'

'SCUSE ME.'

Cormac blinked, the spell broken, and looked up. A large girl with a lot of straw-coloured blonde hair and a crop top that seemed slightly unusual in a court situation was glaring at him.

'Need to use this loo.'

She didn't seem obviously disabled but Cormac knew better than to judge that. On the other side of the door, Lissa had gone totally silent, just, Cormac thought, as she needed to speak up.

'There's someone in,' said Cormac. 'Is it urgent?'

'Fuck off,' said the girl.

There was a slightly awkward standoff. Cormac stood up carefully.

'Could you just give us a minute?'

'No,' said the girl. 'I'm gluten-intolerant?'

'Oh,' mumbled Cormac. 'Oh, okay, I see ...'

On the other side of the door, Lissa struggled to hear what was going on outside. She had been so caught up in the moment. She stood up and threw some more water on her face.

Oddly, she felt better. She'd said it. Aloud. She'd said it; seen it in her head as she spoke aloud.

Even talking to a stranger – or perhaps exactly because she *had* been talking to a stranger. It had let her say the words out loud, the words she needed to say; to prepare to point the finger she needed to point, to get justice for the Mitchells; to see justice be done without letting anyone down.

She decided to open the door, thank the odd chap who'd been there, start to move back ... Roisin must be wondering where she was; she'd left her phone on the table. And her bag. She couldn't decide if your handbag would be safer in a crown court or much less safe.

She took a deep breath and moved towards the door. Which was the precise second the fire alarm went off.

Chapter Twenty-five

WEEEEEEEEEE!

The round girl eyed Cormac crossly.

'Did you just set the *fire alarm* on me?' she said, looking murderous.

'What? No!' said Cormac in consternation. If Lissa burst out now ... well, awkward didn't quite cover it ...

There was a vast, pummelling noise full of shouting barrelling down the corridor and as Cormac stepped towards it, he realised what he was looking at.

The hallway was full of fighters – gang members – the boys who were there as witnesses, and the huge and intimidating family of the defendant himself.

The court was specially set up to avoid this kind of thing happening; to keep families and gangs apart.

Cormac didn't know what had broken down today, but something obviously had.

The woman waiting for the bathroom turned around.

'Oh for fuck's sake,' she yelled. 'I told you all to stay in your rooms!'

Ah, well, that explained a lot, thought Cormac, as the melee bowled ever closer, and a high-pitched squeal burst from someone. Cormac didn't hesitate: he headed straight towards the trouble.

Chapter Twenty-six

Violence had burst out in the constrained space of the corridor: a mass of youths against a family of mixed ages and sizes, many blond. Screams and curses filled the air. Cormac saw one boy unleash a huge fist and start punching a man full in the face, not immediately pulling back his hand or breaking his fingers, which was unusual. He obviously had boxing experience. The smaller and older man beneath him was cowering, his nose squashed to a pulp. As the huge boy raised his fist again, Cormac jumped on him from behind, took his arm and tried to twist it upwards in a restraining position.

'Come on, lad,' he said in as reasonable a tone as he could manage. 'Settle down.'

There was considerable swearing from all sides at this. Someone glanced Cormac with a blow on the ear but he didn't let go of his grip on this chap who was far too big for him. Terrible tragedies were caused by young men who didn't know their own strength; who didn't know they could fell a man or break a neck with one punch. They could spend the rest of their lives in jail for one fatal, white-hot moment. The man on the other side of him, with the jelly nose, was whimpering and trembling and didn't seem able to move at all. Cormac had seen a million fights in the Army and in hospitals. They were always like this, never like the movies: slightly pathetic, very noisy and completely confusing for everyone involved.

'Come on!' he said, as the big youth spun around trying to dislodge him, and one of his other mates grabbed Cormac's ear even harder, which, ridiculous though it was, also hurt like hell.

'GERROFF!' shouted Cormac in what would have surprised him to learn was an exceptional London cabbie accent.

They stumbled backwards, hitting the wall, and Cormac was about to give up, hissing at the man in front to move out the bloody way before he got punched again, when the worst thing happened.

Chapter Twenty-seven

Lissa unlocked the door, and as soon as she did, the other woman pushed her way in and locked it behind them both.

'It's kicked off,' she said.

The two women in the loo looked at each other rather awkwardly as the shouting and fighting continued beyond the bathroom door.

'Weird sort of panic room,' said Lissa in a wavery voice, attempting to break the ice.

The fire alarm was still going off, but nobody was moving. Lissa assumed, correctly, that someone had set it off on purpose to get everyone out in the corridors. Certainly, you couldn't smell anything. The woman had her phone out and was tutting loudly.

'Sorry,' said Lissa. 'Did you really need to use the loo? I can stand in the corner if you like.'

'You don't look very disabled,' said the woman crossly.

'I know,' said Lissa. 'I'm sorry about that. I was having a panic attack. I know that doesn't count.'

The woman shrugged.

'Oh. Well. Maybe that should count.'

'Not if other people need it.'

'I'm gluten-intolerant.'

'Oh!' said Lissa. 'Oh well, I *am* sorry to hear that . . .'

Their voices tailed off.

'Why were you panicking?' said the other woman eventually, giving up tapping on her phone.

'I . . . I'm meant to be giving evidence. It's scary to think about it,' said Lissa. She couldn't believe she'd even managed to say that out loud. 'I never used to be frightened about stuff. Then I saw a horrible accident and it really knocked me over.'

She paused. This was . . . this was exactly what Anita had told her to do. Talk about it, over and over. Relive it till she couldn't be scared of it any more. That guy too.

'The guy outside . . . the guy I was talking to. He said I should just talk about it.'

'He's probably right,' said the woman. 'Mind you, he went off to have a fight, so God knows.'

'I know . . . Bit weird taking advice from a bloke on the other side of a toilet door.'

'Take it where you can get it, I say,' said the woman, looking at her face in the mirror and adjusting her carefully painted-on eyebrows. 'I have some advice for you. If you're meant to be sitting with five lads in a jury situation, don't go to the toilet.'

It took Lissa a minute.

'Oh God,' she said. 'Is this . . .?'

The woman looked at her.

'Sssh,' she said. 'I'm a youth worker, yes. But I really did have to go.'

Her brow furrowed.

'Not so much now.'

'I mean, please do . . .'

'I can't now; I'm too uptight.'

The alarm stopped going off.

'Phew,' said Lissa, feeling oddly better now she was comforting somebody else. 'How about now, without the alarm?'

'Nope,' said the woman. 'Still not feeling it. It's like all the pee

313

has hopped back up me.' She frowned. 'This is going to do nothing for my gluten intolerance.'

'Well, no,' said Lissa truthfully.

They both approached the door. The noise seemed to have died down.

'Do you think it's safe?' said Lissa.

'Well, either that or they're just a pile of corpses out there,' said the woman. 'I'm joking! I'm joking! Wish me luck!' She paused. 'And listen. I know they sound rowdy. But they're just lads. Tell the truth and shame the devil, and it'll all be fine.'

'That's what toilet guy said,' said Lissa.

'Well then.'

And they smiled tentatively at each other, and Lissa turned the handle on the door.

Chapter Twenty-eight

'But I was just passing by!' said Cormac uselessly as the two policemen marched him into the van.

'That is what they all say,' said a slim, bespectacled police officer with a wispy moustache.

'I know!' said Cormac. 'But I'm a medical professional.'

'And I am the uncle of a monkey,' said the policeman, unnecessarily, Cormac thought. The local copper in Kirrinfief knew every single person in the village and spent a lot of time posing with tourists and trying to stop toddlers escaping from the nursery.

There was a paddy wagon ahead. Surely not, thought Cormac. This was a joke. But there it was. He was being arrested, as was everybody else.

He remembered back a few short hours when he had woken up with the sun on his face, full of happiness and feeling like singing out loud. What a wonderful day he had planned. Surprising Lissa at the courthouse and seeing her lovely face beam the same smile on him as he'd seen in the photo . . .

Rather than of course what had actually happened, when he'd ended up kneeling down in a dirty corridor doing a fake accent while she sobbed uncontrollably. Not exactly what he'd had in mind.

Oh, and now he had handcuffs on.

It struck him that this wasn't remotely funny, and also that he should probably let her know that he wasn't coming for lunch. He scrabbled around in his back pocket for his phone, which promptly fell on the floor.

'I'll have that,' said the young officer, taking it peremptorily and putting it in a bag.

'What! I need to call someone!'

'You'll get your call at the station. Until then, all phones are confiscated.'

There were general growls of annoyance all round. Cormac blinked. If he had only one call ... could he call someone he'd never met to come bail him out? That really was an almost worse introduction to someone than meeting them for the first time when they were collapsed sobbing on a dirty bathroom floor. Oh God.

'Seriously, I'm not involved!' said Cormac in desperation.

'This is why we had to pull you off someone in an affray,' said the constable. 'Okay. Got it.'

Cormac winced. This could be bad.

And who the hell was he going to call?

Chapter Twenty-nine

Once order had been more or less restored, Lissa crept back to the witness room. Roisin was waiting for her, arms folded.

'Well, you're here now,' she sniffed.

'Sorry,' said Lissa.

'I'm sympathetic,' said Roisin, sounding anything but, 'but you're lucky it got delayed. We can't do this without you. You're the only witness who wasn't involved!'

'I know,' said Lissa, breathing deeply. 'But I think ... I think I'm all right.'

'Good,' said Roisin as a number flashed up on the wall. 'Okay, that's us. Let's go.'

The courtroom – a windowless room with a stained, cheap carpet and pinboard walls, that smelled of stale coffee and dusty lighting – was not remotely impressive. The judge sat looking half asleep, not a flicker of interest on her face, as Lissa entered.

The big group of Kai's friends had all gone, likewise the family of the defendant. He stood, defiant in a cheap suit and a razor-sharp haircut, swaggering in the dock facing the judge's podium. The room was filled with computer screens. A stern-looking lawyer was sitting behind him, scribbling. There was also a hodgepodge line-up of people sitting expectantly to the side which Lissa realised of course would be the jury.

'Lissa Westcott called to the stand,' said a bored-sounding woman on the side.

Lissa took a deep breath. She wished, suddenly, that she'd asked her mum to be here – or even, she thought suddenly, Cormac. He would have come. Still, she would see him after-wards. All she had to do was go through with this and ... She checked her mobile phone. She hadn't heard from him, but that was okay. She'd message him when they were out and then – well, she'd probably better redo her make-up and Christ, her hair. But then ...

'Phone off!' hissed a court clerk and she immediately passed it on to Roisin.

But she still held on to the idea as she walked slowly up the stained carpet towards the chair with the microphone, where she swore an oath, her hand a little shaky on the faded bible they offered her. Just think of what happens next, she told herself. Just think about what happens next.

'Can you tell us what happened on the fourth of March of this year?' said the busy-looking woman.

And slowly, haltingly, Lissa told the story all the way through, even though the man with the razor-cut blond hair stared at her, slowly and menacingly, as if he could beam malevolence and fury towards her, while she avoided his gaze; even when Roisin asked her very clearly in her experience did the car slow down or speed up as it turned the corner. She answered slowly so she could not be misunderstood by the jury, the judge or anyone else.

'Yes. He sped up.'

'And can you see the driver in this courtroom?'

'Yes. He's over there in the box.'

The man hissed at her, actually hissed, and was immediately

318

disciplined by the police officer standing to his left. Lissa was suddenly very relieved none of his family were in the room to see her.

'You're sure?'

'I'm sure.'

'But the car was going quickly,' said the defence lawyer, when it came time for questions. 'You can't have got more than a glimpse.'

'He stared straight at me,' said Lissa. 'I remember everything about it. I'm a trained A&E nurse. We see a lot of potentially dangerous situations. Sir, he grimaced at me. Just like that. It was him. He drove round the corner, he sped up and he drove straight towards ... Kai. He knocked his phone out of Kai's hand, then Kai went straight up in the air and landed on the concrete. Then he sped off.' She took a deep breath. 'That's what happened.'

The defence lawyer looked at her. A young nurse, calm, clearly telling the truth, who had absolutely no reason to lie and absolutely no reason to be here except for justice. He could sense the waves off the jury of how much they approved of her. He looked at Lissa one last time, looked at the jury, cast his client a slightly apologetic shrug and stood back.

'No further questions.'

Chapter Thirty

Leaving the courtroom, unable to quite believe she was free, Lissa walked slowly down the aisle. At the end she caught sight of a face she recognised. Quickly and without ceremony, Mrs Mitchell, Kai's mother, nodded briskly.

Lissa felt chastened, but relieved; glad that she had managed to do what she needed to do, and overwhelmingly guilty because she was feeling happy now that she was in a position to get on with her life. And Mrs Mitchell never, ever could. She gave a half-smile of apology and regret, but she had to leave, and the court had to carry on with its work, as human misery spilled out from courtroom after courtroom, in town after town.

It felt like a breath of liberty as Lissa pushed through the doors of the sour-smelling court, the security guards wired and buzzy after the fight that morning, everyone twitchy and tired and stressed.

The sunshine hit her full in the face, dazzling her. She had headed back inside – into the shared ladies bathrooms this time – to reapply a whole face of make-up, and curled her eyelashes right out, something she almost never did. Her eyebrows were a mess, as she did not trust Ginty with them, but she'd done the best she could, adding a pretty, rose-coloured lipstick to her lips and a little blush to her cheeks, and letting down her hair, then laughed at herself for being so over the top. Then she squirted on some more perfume just in case.

Still nothing on her phone from Cormac. She frowned. Well, it wasn't far to Borough. Maybe he thought court would run later. She'd been surprised herself how quick it had been in the end. She'd been a good witness, Roisin had told her, which had felt so good.

Or perhaps he'd be waiting there ... sitting in the sun. She reminded herself that he might be five foot tall and three foot wide, then wondered how much that would really, *really* matter, as to much as how much she looked forward to talking to him; how his messages were the highlight of her day.

And so she practically bounced along the South Bank, cutting through side streets to avoid the crowds, walking straight past the police station Cormac was currently being held in.

Chapter Thirty-one

Cormac sat in the holding cell with two other kids from the court-house, both of them cursing and swearing.

'We were just there to support Kai,' complained one, whose name was Fred. 'Just to show him he isn't forgotten.'

'By kicking the lumps out of some guy?' said Cormac. 'Come on, lads. You must know that isn't helpful.'

'Are you Scottish?' said one of them. 'I thought Scotch folk *loved* kicking lumps out of people.'

'He was doing a good job with Big Al,' pointed out the other boy, who presumably had a name that wasn't Nobbo, but Nobbo seemed to do.

'So you were,' said Fred.

'I was trying to stop him accidentally really hurting someone. And ending up in prison,' said Cormac.

'We're in prison now,' said Fred.

'I realise that,' said Cormac.

Borough Market was absolutely heaving in the summer sun. Every stall was rammed. And Lissa didn't know who she was looking for. She looked around. What kind of thing would Cormac like? She didn't even know that, she realised. She knew so little about him.

Finally, right at the back, she spied an empty table at a little tapas hole-in-the-wall. That looked absolutely perfect. She slipped into it, smiling at the man serving, who showed her to it with a wave of her hand.

'For one?'

'Two,' said Lissa, beaming nervously. 'I'm waiting for someone.'

The man smiled.

'Lovely. Can I bring you a negroni?'

Lissa looked around, still feeling excited and nervous and so pleased with the fact that she'd managed to do the right thing. It wouldn't bring Kai back, but she'd been able to look Mrs Mitchell in the eye as she'd left.

'Yes please!' she said. Then she took a picture of the bar sign and texted it to Cormac.

She also sent Anita a Skype message to say she had done it and thank you: the woman had been right all along. Anita responded by sending her a picture of an ice cream cone and Lissa smiled to herself.

꒷ ꒦

Lissa finished her drink and immediately declined another, the idea of being drunk when Cormac arrived too hideous to contemplate. She considered a coffee, then worried her breath would smell, and settled for a fizzy water. The waiter looked a tiny bit concerned. A cloud passed across the sun.

She thought whenever Ezra hadn't been in the mood to see her, he'd just not answer any of her messages or texts. It happened to Kim-Ange all the time when she met guys and then they got cold feet. Ghosting was awful.

But that wasn't going to happen here. Not with Cormac. He'd asked her to lunch after all. They'd arranged to meet.

Although they hadn't booked anywhere specific, had they? They hadn't actually said, 'this restaurant in this place'. Just Borough Market. It was fairly non-specific, after all, when you thought about it.

She shook herself. Come on. She was catastrophising, over-thinking, everything a therapist would say was unhelpful. She'd got through one thing today. She was going to manage. She was.

She tried not to drink all her water too quickly. Her battery was running a little low. Still no message.

Chapter Thirty-two

'So you came to meet some bird,' said Fred scornfully, 'that you've never even met.'

They had been in the cell together for some time and were trading stories.

'Yeah,' said Cormac.

'What if she's, like, a fuckbeast?' said Nobbo.

'I'm sure she's not a fuckbeast,' said Cormac carefully.

'Well, did she send you pictures? Of her tits and that?'

'No, of course not! Women don't do that.'

'Fuckbeasts don't.'

'Could you stop using that term? It's really unpleasant.'

Fred sniffed a bunch of catarrh up his nose with one finger closing a nostril and hoiked it into the seatless metal toilet at the side of the room. Cormac didn't necessarily feel this was an improvement. He paced up and down, feeling worse and worse – she must be there, or had she left by now? Stormed off, furious with him? Maybe she'd never speak to him again. Maybe that was his chance and he'd muffed it. After all there was only another couple of weeks to go . . .

And he'd be back home which was . . . well, it was fine of course.

But the cottage could feel a little empty on those long, dark evenings that came in the winter time.

'MacPherson?' came the guard at the door, unlocking it. 'You can make your phone call now.'

'Are you charging me?'

'We're going to have a word, so hold your horses.'

'He was just pulling off Big Al!' shouted Fred, and Nobbo agreed vociferously, while laughing like an eighteen-year-old at the same time.

Cormac sighed as he followed the officer down the hallway. Who on earth was he going to call?

Chapter Thirty-three

Kim-Ange shook her phone crossly.

'Oh for goodness' sake!'

There was a blubbering noise.

'Stop crying,' she said as Lissa tried and failed to stop crying down the telephone.

'Come home immediately. You know, I didn't have him pegged as a wasteman. Mind you, he treated Yazzie pretty shabbily. And I never saw his "friend" again.'

'I mean ... I keep thinking, maybe he's here, but nearly everyone's gone and all the stalls are closed up and the vans have driven off and I've drunk a litre of mineral water ...'

'Well, that's good,' said Kim-Ange encouragingly.

'So I keep thinking I'll miss him every time I go to the toilet and ...'

'Are you freaking out?'

'It's been a very long day.'

'Take deep breaths.'

'I've been trying that. The waiter is looking at me funny. He was friendly three hours ago.'

'Don't tell me you waited for him for three hours!'

There was a pause.

'I can't not tell you that.'

'Would Beyoncé wait for Jay-Z for three hours?'

'No,' said Lissa in a quiet voice. 'Although Kim probably has to wait for Kanye for three hours all the time.'

'Three hours?!' said Kim-Ange again.

'I ... I really thought I liked him,' said Lissa.

Kim-Ange bit her lip.

'Come over,' she said. Then: 'Hang on, let me just make sure he's not here.'

'Oh God,' said Lissa. Then, more hopefully, as if the thought had just occurred to her: 'Maybe he's fallen asleep or something, just lost track of time!'

Kim-Ange couldn't bear to hear the forced casualness in her voice.

'Mm, give me a minute.'

She banged loudly on her side of the wall, their normal method of communication.

'Nope,' she said finally. 'That always works. He's not here. You're safe – come over.'

Lissa felt her heart plunge. That was her last hope. Well, that or him being wounded with something painful but not aesthetically disfiguring in hospital somewhere where she could tenderly nurse him back to health, but she didn't really want to say that one out loud.

'But then he'll find me sitting there when he gets back like some kind of mega stalker! He's already in hiding from me!'

Kim-Ange sighed.

'I am taking you to the gin bar. That is the only way out of this situation.'

'Can we talk about him?'

'No. Just gin.'

'Can I cry a little bit?'

'Gin only.'

'Engaged,' said Cormac ruefully, hanging up the phone. Kim-Ange would almost certainly be talking to her parents again, something which took place, on and off, quite a lot of the day.

'Mmmm,' said the policeman, uninterested. Cormac was still worried about whether or not they were going to charge him.

'Want a solicitor?'

On a list of things Cormac wanted, a solicitor was so far from being something he wanted he nearly cried. Instead he said clearly, no, he didn't, and hoped he'd made the right decision.

The interview room was horrible, small, with a tiny cracked reinforced glass window set high above their heads and a revolting stale odour made no better by the heat of the day. What was lovely outside in London was very muggy and unpleasant in a basement near the River Thames. Feet were just visible above his head, walking back and forth in freedom. He watched them pass, feeling defeated, which he imagined was the point of the place, after all.

$$\rightthreetimes \quad \curvearrowright$$

'I was trying to stop the big lad hurting anyone,' said Cormac for the fourth time to the two police officers opposite them. 'I was using Army defence methods to restrain him, nothing more. They went slightly wrong,' he continued. 'But you know the trouble these big lads get themselves into. We were already there because of a horrible accident. Really wasn't in the mood for another one.' He sniffed. 'Also, sorry to point this out but we were in a courtroom facility crawling with police officers and security guards. Why was I the only person in there trying to sort something out to stop them killing each other?'

The police officers looked at each other for a moment.

'Okay,' said the policeman finally. 'Well. Big Al said to say thanks. He could have killed that guy and he'd feel very bad about that.'

He was reading from a piece of paper.

'He's pleaded guilty to affray. Shouldn't get him into too much trouble – slap on the wrist if he's lucky.'

'Anger management? He needs it.'

'I hope so,' said the female officer. 'Perhaps a medical professional could write a letter of recommendation.'

'Happy to,' said Cormac.

They all looked at each other. Cormac tried desperately not to glance at the clock.

'Ex-Army, huh?' said the police officer, checking the files on her computer. 'Says here you served in Fadge?'

Cormac nodded.

'But you've never been in trouble?' She smiled, rather wryly. 'My brother was out there.' She gave him a shrewd look. 'He found it quite tricky coming home.'

Cormac found himself swallowing suddenly.

'Yes, ma'am,' he said in a quiet tone of voice.

'But you're doing well.'

'Apart from being in prison,' said Cormac, thinking of everything that had happened, everything he'd learned and seen in the last few months. 'I'd say ... nae bad.'

The officer stood up.

'Right. Off you go. Stay out of trouble.'

Cormac chanced his arm.

'They're just lads, you know. And they've been through a lot.'

'They have,' said the woman. 'So have a lot of people who don't start punch-ups in public places.'

'They started ...'

Cormac realised quickly he was going to get himself into trouble again as a frown crossed the other officer's face. He stood up fast.

'Thank you so much.'

➤ ➤

The sarcastic police officer looked practically disappointed to see Cormac ready to walk out.

'Leaving so soon?' he said.

'Aye,' said Cormac. He was handed back an envelope containing his wallet, watch and phone. The battery was completely drained. Shit. He winced when he saw it. Then he realised he didn't have a lot of time to lose. The other lads had already been released; he was the last one.

'Good luck with the fuckbeast!' shouted Nobbo as Cormac ran out of the police station at top speed. They had found a pub next door to the police station, which seemed to Cormac unwise to say the very least, but he didn't have time to do much other than wave quickly.

Chapter Thirty-four

'I have been ghosted,' said Kim-Ange dramatically – she had quickly put on a large black fascinator to chime with the sombre feel of the occasion, 'twenty-seven times. It has been terrible every single one of those times.'

'Perhaps he's dead,' said Lissa hopefully. Kim-Ange had bought four massive balloons full of a gin concoction to save time, and she was drinking from them, Lissa realised, rather like she'd drink beer, just because the glass was so big. This was unwise. On the other hand, screw absolutely everything.

'TO DEATH,' said Kim-Ange, and they chinked glasses. Lissa sighed.

'Was he really tiny though? Did he look like a mole? Did his nose come straight out of his neck?'

Kim-Ange sighed. Shook her head.

'I had no idea you liked him so much.'

'Neither did I!' burst out Lissa. 'Until I literally found myself *right here*, saying this. I think I just . . . I needed a little crush.'

'Are you sure it isn't his house you like?'

'I *do* like his house,' said Lissa, thinking of the cosy fire and the little wooden staircase.

'That's what you've done,' said Kim-Ange comfortingly. 'Projected the idea of home ownership onto some bloke. It's the idea of owning your own house you are in love with.'

'Maybe,' said Lissa a little dreamily. 'So, he's a wasteman then?'

'He has,' said Kim-Ange, crossing her fingers to try and save her friend from more pain, 'seven toes on each foot and ears bigger than his head. He comes up to my waist and sheds hair like a pony. And, oh my God, the smell.'

'Really?' said Lissa, approaching the bottom of the vast glass. The house didn't smell at all. Nice, if anything; that scent of almond shampoo, the same type she'd started using.

'Yup,' said Kim-Ange. 'Lucky escape if you ask me. Another?'

Chapter Thirty-five

'Kim-Ange?!'

But nobody was answering the door. Cormac slumped in the door frame, sweating. He had run all the way there, and even though it was later, the heat was still dense and humid, unpleasant, as if all the buildings were holding it in, storing it all day like a battery only to give it back during the evening. Cars had honked and people had yelled as he tore past, his lungs ragged with what felt absurdly like freedom. She had to be at the nurses' halls, she had to be. Where else would she go but to see her best friend? There were a million places she could go of course, but he couldn't think of that right now; only that she'd be there.

He had charged through Borough Market, but the stalls were closed and the bars full of couples and groups and as if she'd have waited all day; it wasn't even possibly or remotely likely. Nobody noticed him as he ran past, tension on his face, except for one waiter, clocking on to his second shift, who looked at him as he tore through and wondered . . . just wondered . . . and hoped it would be okay for the sweet girl with the sad face.

And here he was. Stav the doorman had smiled happily at him – it had taken a quarter of a year but Cormac had worn him down eventually with a very expensive pain au raisin habit – as he'd hopped up, sweaty and dishevelled, checked his own room then banged on Kim-Ange's door, even thinking he really ought to take a shower but unable to wait, completely unable to wait even one second more to see her.

Yazzie walked past.

'Hey!' said Cormac. She sniffed loudly at him, which he found slightly puzzling as he had absolutely no idea she was annoyed with him. 'Have you seen Kim-Ange?'

'She's got a boyfriend,' said Yazzie pointedly.

Cormac blinked.

'Aye, I know that ... I just wondered if you'd seen her.'

'You look filthy and awful,' pointed out Yazzie.

'Thanks,' said Cormac.

'Just call her,' said Yazzie.

'Could you? I'm out of charge,' said Cormac. 'Please? *Please!* Tell her if she's with Lissa I can explain ... please? Tell her I'll call.'

'Sure,' said Yazzie, walking off and pretending to put her phone to her ear.

He glanced at his watch. Shit! It was after eight o'clock already. The train left at nine. Euston station was half an hour away.

Chapter Thirty-six

'Did you call your mum?' said Kim-Ange, pouring Lissa into a taxi. 'Don't call her now, I mean. Just ... call her.'

'I didn't tell anyone I was coming today,' said Lissa. 'Because I didn't know if I could manage it ... and because I wanted ... I wanted to spend it with ...'

Lissa's lip was wobbling. Kim-Ange leant into the cab and gave her a big full-body hug.

'Don't worry about it,' she said. 'You did the right thing. Go back to Scotland, pack up and I'll see you back here in a couple of weeks. Don't worry about that wasteman. I will make his life absolute hell.'

'Don't put prawns in the curtains, because when I come back they will still be my curtains,' said Lissa.

'Okay.'

Lissa checked her phone again.

'PUT YOUR PHONE DOWN! You know you *will* hear from him. Tomorrow, with some bullshit excuse,' said Kim Ange fussily. 'Then it'll all pick up again: the flirting and the little jokes and everything until it comes time to meet again and then the same thing will happen. Trust me. I know men.'

'I know,' said Lissa.

'Is she going to spew in my cab, love?' said the taxi driver.

'NO!' they both said together.

'Give me the phone,' said Kim-Ange. 'Come on, hand it over. You're pissed and in possession of a phone: it's a deadly weapon.'

Lissa sighed. Kim-Ange grabbed it and hit a few buttons. She'd done this before.

'I've blocked his number. Stop any recriminatory texts.'

'I've got his number at home.'

'Yes, but that will be the morning and then you can *think about what you're doing*. In between sending me a thank you bouquet.'

The meter ticked on.

'Don't . . . don't lose the messages,' mumbled Lissa.

'Messages are saved, but you can't send any more and neither can he, if he sends you one – which he WON'T,' said Kim-Ange. 'You wouldn't get it anyway. At least, not till you sober up.'

'Thanks,' said Lissa, flinging her arms around her again. 'You're a great friend.'

'I am,' said Kim-Ange grimly. 'Now I am going back to set fire to his bed.'

'It's *my* bed!'

'Oh yes. I'll think of something.'

It felt suddenly unbearably unfair to Lissa that Kim-Ange was going back to Cormac and she wasn't.

'Maybe he is dead,' she said. 'Saving a bunch of children from a burning orphanage. Even then I still hate him.'

'In you go,' said Kim-Ange, slamming the door behind her as the cab shot off into the night.

Chapter Thirty-seven

There are several ways of getting from the South Bank to Euston in half an hour: Thameslink, the Northern line, the number 63 bus, a black cab which will do puzzling things around Bedford Square – but if you are in a tearing hurry and, frankly, a bit of a panic, you could always try running it. I wouldn't, personally. But then it very much depends whether or not you are thinking straight.

Cormac wasn't thinking straight at all.

But as he flew down the stairs and out into the humid night, hit the great river and charged along it, he felt better running, more free than jiggering about in a cab stuck in heavy traffic or a tube inching forwards. He couldn't have borne it.

To his surprise, he realised he knew where he was going. Across the bridge at Embankment, diving across Trafalgar Square and into Covent Garden, passing hordes of Lycra-clad tourists looking confused and buskers looking tired, cutting through towards Bloomsbury with its pretty red mansions and well-trimmed squares. He felt the ground under his feet and realised at last the pull of the city – that it could be your city, that it was expensive, yes, and grubby and strange, but you could belong too once you knew how to skirt the crowds, find your corner; then you could experience the whole world on your doorstep.

And even as he ran, Cormac couldn't help but feel a little comforted. He crashed across Tottenham Court Road, avoided the sofa shops and grabbed little alleyways he thought would get him through. He passed the big hospital and emerged, panting, utterly exhausted yet somehow exhilarated too, along the great throbbing gristly artery of the Euston Road. This was Lissa's great city, and she got closer to him with every step as he pounded up the road, black and filthy with traffic, Euston station squat and grim across. Not all of London was beautiful. He glanced at his watch. Ten to nine. At home it would have been bright daylight still; here the streetlights were coming on.

He couldn't cross the road. Six thundering lanes of traffic were roaring without a break. He hopped from foot to foot at the traffic lights. Stop. STOP!

Chapter Thirty-eight

There was something almost motherly in the way the attendant on the sleeper train greeted Lissa and, worn out as she was, she almost started to cry.

'Have you had a nice day, hen?' said the woman. The accent was familiar to Lissa, and she bit her lip.

'Mm,' she said as her name was ticked off on a list and she found her way to her own tiny bedroom on the train.

She sighed happily as she opened the door. A bed was made up with a fresh white duvet and white sheets, two pillows and a tartan blanket. There was a sink at one end, and a shelf for her clothes and a bottle of water and it felt at that moment like the ultimate in luxury. A place to shut herself in, lock the world out and lick her wounds.

The window showed the dank black interior of Euston station. She didn't want to see it. She pulled down the shutters and opened her bag to finally – *finally* – get into her pyjamas and forget about today altogether.

'I'm afraid you need a ticket, son,' said the woman on the reception desk at the train, now looking not quite as nicely at the large, rather sweaty figure in front of her.

'Where can I get one?!'

'From the booking office . . . if it's still open.'

Cormac looked back in dismay. The booking office was miles away. They both looked at the clock. It was four minutes to nine.

'Am I going to make it?' he said.

The woman looked sad.

'You can get the 23.50 to Edinburgh,' she said brightly. 'That'll be fine.'

'If I was going to Edinburgh that would be fine!' said Cormac in anguish. If he didn't get on that train, that would be it – it would be over. She'd never trust him again.

'It's nice,' said the woman. He gave her a level glance. The train started to make noises, the engines huffing up.

He screwed up his eyes.

'Is there . . .? Someone I really need to see is on this train. Can you call her for me?'

The woman protectively hid her clipboard with her hand.

'What if you're a murderer?'

'Okay,' said Cormac desperately. Doors were slamming up and down the train now and a guard was raising a whistle to his lips.

'Can I . . . can I just run up and down the train and see if I can see her?'

'Am I going to let you, a murderer, run up and down the train and peer in everybody's windows?'

'Pleeeease! This is someone . . . this is someone really important to me. Please. *Please!*'

The woman looked at him sadly.

'I cannae,' said the woman. 'Health and safety. We've had a lot of training.'

'Me too,' said Cormac ruefully.

'*Peeep!*' blew the whistle.

Lissa stood up and leaned her head against the window of the little cabin, peering out into the world of the sooty, fluorescent station beyond, with its smell of fast food, the shouts of cheery or drunken commuters. When had London started to feel so strange?

She gazed out. Funny, it was almost as if it were calling her name. But as she strained her ears to hear, there was another sharp blow on the whistle, and the train began smoothly to chug its way out of the great, black, dirty station.

Chapter Thirty-nine

'That,' said the train guard, covering her ears, 'is quite the shout you've got there.'

And she lightly stepped onto the guard platform as Cormac, throat ragged, cried out 'LISSSAAA!' one last time to no avail. As the train took off, he tried to run alongside it, even as security hailed him, and he stopped, put his hands on his knees, utterly out of breath, utterly defeated.

Empty, exhausted, feeling foolish and simply ridiculous for having pinned so many hopes and dreams on that day, Lissa sank down on the bed, feeling the soothing motion of the train beneath her. She glanced at her phone . . . No, no, no. Of course.

She had been so stupid. Well. This was modern life, she supposed. She sank back against the pillows. No way was she going to sleep. She was going to lie awake in a frenzy of embarrassment and recrimination all night, then she'd have to get straight back to work the next day, which was why she'd bought a sleeper ticket in the first place.

She turned her head into the pillow. Well, tomorrow was another day, she supposed. But somehow – and having her phone off definitely helped – the slightly jolting motion of the train, the fresh white linen, the sheer exhaustion and, let us be honest, the several gins somehow worked their magic and, within moments, Lissa was utterly and completely asleep.

Outside in the streets of London, it was dark, and the corner pubs were starting to take a more aggressive tone. There was distant shouting and omnipresent sirens, and a helicopter somewhere overhead. Cormac again had the faint, tense feeling that there were too many people, all hot and drunk and angry, in too small a space. King's Cross was absolutely heaving, its restaurants and piazzas overspilling with people.

It crossed his mind – it absolutely crossed his mind – that Larissa would still be in her fancy restaurant with her fancy mates. That he could at least sit and lick his wounds surrounded by sympathetic company.

But it was strange: those girls didn't appeal to him. Not at all. Not Larissa; not Yazzie. Nobody did. Nobody except the person who probably thought he'd dropped her. After all, who these days didn't have their phone? Who would ever believe it? Only a very stupid person, and he knew she wasn't that.

Cormac turned blindly south again. Retracing the steps he had run with so much hope in his heart was bitter and exhausting. A group of cabaret performers shouted at him as he accidentally trod on the tail of someone's feather boa, and he recoiled and apologised. A drunk heckled him from the street and, instead of stopping, he passed on by, head down. Stop trying to care for everyone and just care for one person, he thought to himself bitterly. Well, look how brilliantly that had turned out.

It seemed so far now, through endless paved roads, past endless taxis at endless junctions, their yellow lights glinting into the distance. He considered taking one, but there was no benefit to arriving home any earlier, was there? Even if he plugged his phone in straightaway, by the time it charged she'd be over the border, cursing him for ever. And 'I was in prison' wasn't exactly the excuse he'd been hoping to give.

He sighed as he passed the police station for what he hoped would be the last time ever. The lads were still, to his utter amazement, at the pub next door where, he was astounded to see, the coppers were now drinking as well; everyone seemed very merry. A mass cheer greeted him as he stumbled past.

'Did you find her? The fuckbeast?' shouted Nobbo. One glance from Cormac convinced him otherwise.

'Awwww,' said the group in chorus.

'What's this?' said the sarcastic copper, and to Cormac's horrified amazement, they immediately started telling him the entire story, while someone fetched Cormac a pint, which he declined in favour of a very large glass of water. The absolute last thing he needed was to get maudlin.

As the story unrolled, the sarcastic copper screwed up his face.

'He's never even *seen* her?'

'Naw, mate!'

'That's nuts!' He pulled out his phone.

'What's her name? She's got to be on Instagram.'

But he found nothing.

'Look for her on the police database,' said his colleague.

'Do *not* do that!' said Cormac.

'Well, you tried, you failed,' said Fred. 'Might as well just hang out with the rest of us ...'

'No!' said the sarcastic policeman. 'If you want her, go get her! That's what I had to do with Gus!'

'Where did Gus go?' said his colleague.

'Um ... West London,' said the policeman, and everyone gave a sharp intake of breath.

'Well, I tried that,' said Cormac. 'Didn't quite work.'

'Hang on!' said Fred, possibly somewhat over-refreshed.

'Where is Scotland anyway? If you drove, would you get there faster?'

'Where is *Scotland*?'

'Focus on the question, mate, not your national pride.'

Cormac glanced at his watch. 'Well. Maybe. But I haven't got a car.'

'We've got a car!'

The policemen immediately looked up.

'You have?'

'It's insured!' said Fred instantly. The others nodded.

'I won't be on your insurance,' said Cormac. 'And youse are all too pished up to drive.'

'Yeah, we are,' said Fred thoughtfully. 'But the insurance covers everyone.'

'Otherwise we can't afford it,' piped up Nobbo. 'We had to pool it between everyone.'

'You have a shared communal car?' said Cormac.

'Rotas are a nightmare,' said Fred.

'I'm going to run the plates,' said the sarcastic police officer.

'Leave 'em,' said the other copper. 'You're off duty, Nish. Just leave it. For once.'

'Okay,' said Nish.

'You're a great copper. You just need to know when to relax. Switch off. Do a bit of self-care.'

'You're right.'

'Just ... do your job. Don't let it consume you.'

'Thanks, Harry.'

'Don't mention it,' said Harry, looking sadly at Nish's wedding ring.

The lads were getting up.

'Okay, let's go,' said Fred.

'You're not coming,' said Cormac.

'Course we are! It's our car!'

'Also, we're not doing anything else,' said Nobbo, a little sadly.

'ROADTRIP! ROADTRIP!'

Cormac looked at them for a second, about to say don't be ridiculous, everyone had to go home to bed and work to go to. Except they didn't, did they?

'ROADTRIP! ROADTRIP!'

Then he thought about Lissa. And then unexpectedly he had another thought.

He took out his phone, remembered it was dead, then reminded himself to text Lennox as soon as it was charged that he *might* have solved his harvest crisis.

Chapter Forty

Unsurprisingly, the boys bantered and chugged beer and yelled and tried to honk the horn for at least all the way to Birmingham. He'd explained there might be jobs up there for them, and they'd agreed to check them out instantly. Whether they'd feel the same in the morning was another story, of course.

Then, like the lads they all still were, they fell asleep, snoring loudly on the back seat, Fred beside him.

Cormac had managed to plug his phone into the charger in the car – at last – and watched it anxiously as it pinged into life. There were messages up till about four o'clock, jolly at first, then increasingly curt (from Lissa and, in fact, Larissa too), but they stopped abruptly (this was when Kim-Ange had got hold of the phone). Nothing recriminatory; nothing drunken or angry.

This was the worst thing of all. If there had been upset texts, he could have convinced himself there was still a chance that she cared for him; that this had meant something to her too, not just been some stupid fantasy he'd concocted in his head.

He couldn't help it. He pulled over onto the hard shoulder and texted her. Just a simple 'Hey'.

It pinged back immediately. Number blocked. His stomach plummeted.

He was, he realised, exactly halfway between London and Scotland. Two hundred and fifty miles to go. Before he could fall down at her door. Or not.

He could turn around, work out his half of the exchange and never see her, only talk briefly about the cases. They never had to meet at all. He could go back; professional relations would be resumed. She'd succeeded in what she had to do and given her evidence. Everything would go back to normal as if it had never happened.

Lissa woke suddenly on the train, not sure why. At first, she was completely disorientated, couldn't remember where she was. Then she went to the window. They were flying through moonlit valleys and dales, not yet in Scotland but somewhere in the heart of the UK, between two worlds. London and Scotland. She sighed. That was what it felt like to be in different places at once. Her heart in Scotland but her life ... well. Her life was in London. She knew that now. She could thank Cormac for that, she supposed. Whoever the hell he had turned out to be in the end.

Cormac's phone pinged. He leapt on it, his heart beating, pulling over to do so safely.

> Up for baby. Good news; desperate need.

His heart sank. It was Lennox, expecting him to be turning up with lads who would work for a bit.

Maybe he could drop them off and turn around. Have a quick nap and head back.

Nobbo snorted in the back, turned over. Cormac thought of them all, young lads, nothing to do, hanging about on street corners, starting fights. How much they might change; how much they were capable of. He already knew how well Robbie had settled in, and he had been in a much darker place.

He stared at his phone again. She'd blocked him. Maybe Kim-Ange had dissed him – he hadn't even though of that. Told Lissa what a rube he was, how many mistakes he'd made. Maybe they'd laughed themselves silly at the narrow escape she'd had. Oh God.

He took a deep breath. Turned the key in the ignition.

He drove on.

It was strange; he didn't feel tired. Even though it was the early hours of the morning, he felt strangely alive, crossing the fells through the beautiful Lake District; climbing higher and higher through Cumbria till he finally crossed the border, and on and on they went, through a blissfully snoozing Glasgow and up, north, ever north, across the Campsie Fells, and now when he opened the window the air was fresh and freezing and clouds passed across the moon as the stars began to vanish, one by one and at first it was the faintest passing of black to navy and navy to blue and a very thin line at the horizon to his right, promised a new day.

Chapter Forty-one

It was just after six when Cormac reached Lennox's farm, but everyone was up already, Lennox beaming broadly when he met the lads stumbling out of the car, blinking and rubbing their eyes, some of them already regretting their drunken plans from the night before. Nina had got up too and prepared a large breakfast for the incomers.

The train didn't arrive till seven. Cormac was edgy and itchy and couldn't put his phone away, which Nina noticed.

'Can I use your shower?' he asked awkwardly.

'Why don't you go to your own lovely house and use your own lovely shower, Cormac MacPherson?' she said.

'Because ... there's a girl in it,' he said.

'Oh, she's lovely, Lissa,' said Nina. 'I'm sure she wouldn't mind.'

Cormac turned bright scarlet and tried to answer, but couldn't. Nina gave him a very shrewd look.

'Here, I'll get you a towel,' she said, John on her hip as she went towards the airing cupboard. 'You can borrow a shirt of Lennox's too, if you're desperate.'

'Uh, thanks,' said Cormac.

'If you see her,' said Nina, bustling off, 'tell her I've got that copy of *Daddy-Long-Legs* in I ordered for her. Actually here, take it yourself.'

And she went back downstairs to pour thick cream and honey on the porridge and brew fresh coffee for the new batch of harvest boys.

Cormac followed her outside.

'Actually, I might just … head back to London,' he said, head down. Nina looked at him, frowning.

'Why?'

'Um, long story. But I need to get packed up down there. Head back here. Just … tie up some loose ends.'

'Are you okay?'

Cormac shrugged.

'Ach. There was a girl. It didn't work out.'

Nina smiled sympathetically.

'English girls,' she said. 'We're terribly tricky.'

'I might as well go back and get it sorted out. Plus I think the lads share that car with about twenty other people. Don't want to get anyone into trouble.'

'Are you sure you don't want to sleep?'

'Neh, can't really miss a shift. I'll be fine.'

'Okay then,' said Nina. 'See you next week.'

He paused.

'I don't think the streets of London really are paved with gold.'

Nina looked around the bustling farmyard. In the corner, a quiet Robbie was sitting on the ground, crawling up to little John and pretending to be a bear while John cackled hysterically. Robbie had adjusted to the quiet of the farm so quickly, Nina hadn't seen him take a drink since he got there. He ate with the other labourers every night, kept himself to himself, but the relief in his face was obvious, and Nina always dug him up an extra slice of bacon from somewhere. Little John adored him; he was the only person who could make Robbie smile, and he crawled around after him half the day. If it hadn't been ridiculous, Nina would have thought he understood that he was needed.

At a long table set up in the barn, the London lads were nervously joshing with one another, showing off, talking about who had the biggest muscles for working in the fields while eating vast second helpings of porridge and thick cut bread and marmalade, and surreptitiously texting their mums to let them know they were all right.

'Oh, I don't know,' said Nina.

Chapter Forty-two

The long rambling bus had toured the hills at dawn, and Lissa felt it was very unfair, listening to the elderly couple behind her who were clearly having a massive argument, but because it was in Gaelic, it sounded completely beautiful to her ears.

Scotland was doing this on purpose: ray after ray of sun was breaking through the morning cloud, revealing fields so green they could have been made of neon; nearly grown lambs were tearing about in joy; towering peaks overhead sheltered little stone villages huddled around market squares in their lee. The air had a catch of cold early morning mist in it; you could feel it in your throat, but also you could smell and feel a warm day ahead, when the scent would rise off the heather, and your hands would trace the high, high tops of the wildflowers, intertwined everywhere with butter-flies and bees.

Still groggy – as well as suffering from the after-effects of the gin; the shock of the change between grimy Euston and here was like jet lag too – Lissa stared out of the window, her chin on her hand. What a privilege it had been in the end, she supposed. To get to come here. It was annoying in a way that the HR people and the therapist and her friends had all been right. It had done her good.

Okay, she didn't get everything . . . but that had been a silly fantasy. It shouldn't – it mustn't – define her stay, define her or take away what she had gained from this amazing country.

She stepped out into the early pink morning. Kirrinfief was still quiet apart from old Mrs Whirter, trundling up with her trolley to hit the newsagent first. She waved to Lissa and, completely ignoring the fact that the girl obviously just wanted to go home, looked exhausted and was carrying an overnight bag, immediately jumped into the bunion conversation again.

Three months ago, Lissa would have given a half-smile and hurried on. This morning, she put her bag down and let the whole story – involving evil daughters-in-law and, for some reason, an Irn Bru margarita – unfold, before promising to squeeze in an extra appointment and pop in later once she'd got herself squared up. Mrs Whirter smiled broadly and said that wouldn't be necessary, a chat with Lissa was a tonic in itself and wasn't it a terrible shame she had to leave?

Fortunately, her eyes weren't quite good enough these days to see the rapid tears forming in Lissa's.

The road to the little cottage was wildly overgrown, the hedgerows riotous and crazy with the never-ending sun and rain, sun and rain. Lissa took in their morning scent as the sun began to slowly rise, lifting the mists off the loch. The birds sounded in the trees, and barely a car passed to disturb them, or her thoughts, as she trundled her case behind her.

The little house looked sweeter than ever to her as she slipped up to the doorway and put the big old key in the lock. For the oddest moment as she turned it, she wondered . . . no, of course not. She was being ridiculous. And the kitchen was just as she had left it – was it really only twenty-four hours ago? That was ridiculous. But yes. Twenty-four hours before; one cup and one plate all by themselves neatly on the drying rack as proof.

Nothing had moved; nobody had been there. It was just her, alone, again. Her phone pinged. She couldn't help grabbing at it. Her mum.

She smiled. 'I'll call you later,' she texted, and made a promise to herself to do so. She should bring her mum up here, Kim-Ange too. Everyone should get a chance to enjoy it before she had to leave.

Lissa left her bag as it stood, went to the sink and threw that icy water on her face, then drank a large glassful of it. Okay. She was straight back to work today, due at surgery in half an hour. Time to wrap things up. She could send . . . well, a formal email to Cormac, she supposed. Signing off on all the patients so that ideally they could slip seamlessly back into their own lives, pretending nothing had happened, pretending she hadn't changed . . . and one day, far in the future, Scotland would be just a distant dream, a memory that she told her children about; in some far distant future, where she had a place of her own, and a partner and a grown-up life. 'Once upon a time,' she would say, 'I visited a magical land . . .'

She stopped suddenly, her heart in her throat. She was standing in front of the large window at the back of the kitchen, and out in the garden, there was a dark shape.

She took in a deep breath, fighting her panic response. This was Scotland, for God's sake, not central London. The biggest crime here was someone crashing into the bus shelter when they'd had a few.

She took another deep breath, then glanced around for something to use as a weapon. Perhaps someone had thought the house was empty or abandoned.

The dark shape was on the lawn, crouching. She stepped forwards, then turned around, looking for a knife. She could only find a bread knife. She wasn't sure how effective that would be, but she took it anyway, then found herself ducking and crawling to the door at the back of the house. The figure was stock-still. Was it staring at the house? Had it seen her?

Heart palpitating, she stood by the back door, closed her eyes, took another deep breath, remembered that she was meant to be a braver person these days, whether it felt like it or not, and flung open the door.

Chapter Forty-three

'He— Hello?'

Her voice was trembly and weak. The figure didn't move. Lissa edged forward a little bit, then a little bit more. It was like a statue.

She moved cautiously to the end of the garden.

'Hello?'

It was a man she had never seen before, fast asleep, curled up with a hedgehog in his lap.

Cormac had thought he would just pop in, grab a change of clothes, feed Ned and go again. He knew what time the train got in; then she would have to get the bus, so he wouldn't be disturbing her. He toyed with leaving a letter saying 'sorry' but figured it might be creepy and decided against it. He had let himself get completely out of control: it was a silly crush and there was no point pushing it any further.

The sun was streaming in the garden and he realised, as he fed Ned little grubs with his hands, suddenly just how exhausted he was from driving all night.

The hedgehog snuffled as Cormac slumped down onto the stone by the undergrowth, steadily warmed by the sun. He would get up and head in just a minute ... but it was so soothing simply being home. Just to breathe the air of his homeland, just to let all the stress and pressure of the city rush out and fade away ...

He didn't look at all as she'd expected.

But the hair was the same as he'd drawn in the pcitures: curly, overgrown, a little unruly. And it would take quite a burglar to fall asleep in a garden not their own.

Apart from that, he was much larger than she'd imagined: not fat, but solid; broad-shouldered, heavy-legged – more like a squaddie or a rugby player than came across when he wrote. She couldn't see his eyes but dark lashes left a shadow on ruddy cheeks, and there was bristle on his strong chin. He really wasn't at all like she'd conjured in her head. But ... but there was something in the large bulk of his shoulders, the careless tangle of hair and the wide mouth which looked as if it would laugh easily.

She couldn't stop staring. He was breathing easily, the little hedgehog snuffled in his lap, entirely comfortable in his presence. What on earth was he doing here?

He never knew what woke him. One minute he'd been to see Ned; the next, the sun was beaming straight into his eyes, and standing over him, her face hidden by the sun ... All he could see was a full head of bouncing curls. He squinted upwards, confused. Was he asleep? Dreaming? Where was he? What was happening?

Suddenly:

'YOW!'

He jumped up. He had somehow woken Ned, who had responded in the only way he knew how, and now he had a big jab in his hand.

Lissa couldn't help it. She completely dissolved in giggles; Ned was still hanging onto his hand for dear life, his tiny paws scrabbling in the air.

Cormac would have sorted it but he was transfixed by the laughing, sun-touched face, the exact face he'd seen in the photo; in his dreams. Lissa jumped forwards with her coat and scooped up the tiny creature, crooning, 'It's okay, you're all right, you're all right, little one' in a softer voice than the one he'd heard yesterday through the door.

He was about to say something but suddenly it struck him that the words 'you're all right, little one' were somehow so much what he'd wanted to hear for so long, and suddenly, for a moment, he couldn't quite say anything at all.

Lissa, heart pounding took a step forward, and gently helped the hedgehog down, whereupon it instantly scurried away.

'Are you okay?' she said as Cormac clutched his hand, a very confused look on his face. Not taking his eyes off her, he raised his hand to his face. It was bleeding very slightly. They carried on, just staring at one another, Lissa feeling her heart beating in agony, in the dancing, buzzing, swishing noise of the garden.

Slowly, infinitely slowly, a smile began to spread across his face. It transformed it completely. Lissa still hadn't taken her eyes off him.

'Well,' he said in the soft Highlands accent she had dreamed of. 'Well noo. I don't suppose you ken anybody in the medical line?'

Chapter Forty-four

Work was still out there but, after calling in to London, Cormac made up a plan to divvy up the calls so they could finish by lunchtime and spend the rest of the day together.

Lissa flew through her rounds, bestowing huge smiles on everyone. Cormac, of course, took far longer, as he was corralled by every single person he met and forced to repeat more or less everything he'd done down south while also listening to them telling him how they didn't trust that London, and how nothing good ever came out of it, until he found himself getting more and more defensive of his adopted city. Plus, he had to pop in and see his mum, and was touched by how delighted she was to see him. Breaking her wrist, he realised suddenly, had made her more vulnerable that he'd realised, and he gave her a huge hug, as she told him how the strange new nurse hadn't been as bad as she'd expected for an English.

They met up back at the surgery. Cormac watched Lissa crossing the market square. Without even thinking about it, he put his hand out, and she took it. It was the strangest thing; he had barely had to apologise; had barely had to explain himself at all. Which was a relief, as he decided to keep the bathroom encounter to himself. Just for now. There'd be time for all that.

The dogs set up a melee of barking as they arrived and Joan let them out so they were both pawed half to death.

'Oh, good, good,' she said, noticing immediately. 'Always good to mate outside the pack.'

Lissa and Cormac were both so startled, they laughed in surprise.

'Anyway, also good – I have a puppy going spare soon. You two can have it.'

'Um, we've literally just met,' said Lissa. Joan waved her away.

'Are you telling me I don't know anything about the natural world? Oh! Speaking of which . . .' She peered at Lissa. 'You know I said there were no nursing jobs?'

Lissa stared at her.

'Wait, you asked?' said Cormac, beside himself.

'No!' said Lissa. 'Well. Maybe. Just an enquiry. Um. I wanted a puppy.'

'How much midwifery experience have you had? Ever since you English started invading, there's babies all over the place. They're hiring a community midwife.'

'Oh,' said Lissa, her face falling. 'That's not what I am.'

'You could manage, couldn't you? Also, there's occasional lambing. It doesn't say that on the ad; I'm just telling you that there is round here.'

Lissa shrugged. 'Not really.'

Cormac looked thoughtful.

'Well,' he said. 'There's something I wanted to talk to you about. There's an outreach project in London . . . helping people on the street. They're looking for part-time. It would mean I'd be looking for a job-share.'

'I don't understand.'

'You do a bit here; I do a bit there and a bit here . . . I don't know – do we have to work out the details right now?'

'You're kidding,' said Lissa. 'Oh my God, I could kiss you.'

Cormac blushed.

'Would it be a wee bit forward to invite you into my hoose?'

'I'll have to go with you anyway,' said Lissa. 'I don't know how to unblock your number from my phone.'

'Good,' said Cormac. 'You'll just have to stay very, very close by.'

Both of them were trembling as they stood in the little cottage room in front of the fire, which Cormac admired, making Lissa feel rather proud. It was so exciting; so frightening and strange all at once. He put some music on and moved a little closer to where she was standing at the sink, filling the kettle for tea. Lissa didn't want any tea – she just didn't know what to do with herself. They talked about Carrie's cat, who was back behaving as if nothing had ever happened and strolling across roads at will, and young Cameron, who had joined the local football team. Mostly to terrorise opposing players, but it was a step in the right direction.

He moved closer behind her. 'Is this okay?' he said in a very soft voice, and she nodded without quite being able to turn round.

'Normally this should be late and at night and we should be very drunk,' complained Lissa. 'That's the English way. *And* the Scottish way, I have observed.'

Cormac smiled and moved even closer. She could feel him towering over her, smell the almond shampoo. He took his left hand, put it round her waist. She stood stock-still and, very gently, he bent his shaggy head and kissed her lightly on the nape of her neck.

'See, this way,' he said gruffly, 'you still don't need to see me.'

Lissa grinned then and turned round.

'Maybe I want to do that,' she said, reaching up on tiptoes.

'Braw,' he said, and the fresh clear Scottish water ran up and over the top of the kettle, and neither of them noticed at all, and soon the Proclaimers were singing to an empty room.

Chapter Forty-five

Two months later

There had been a short violent rainstorm the night before, but by the time the train got in the next morning, the world was bright again, shining in the wet. Lissa had warned Mrs Mitchell to wear a coat when the woman stepped off the bus into the September glow in a brand-new Arctic level North Face jacket. They were both there to meet her, holding their hands out to her, their faces grave.

She pulled up to the little row of houses just beside the town square, the little quiet row of cottages.

'Are you ready?' Lissa said, Jake helping her down.

Word had got around in Kirrinfief, as it so often did, and there was quite the crowd who happened to be passing.

Lissa rang the bell and Mr Coudrie opened it, more people spilling out either side.

The house's inhabitants and Mrs Mitchell stood, staring at each other curiously and respectfully.

'I . . . I don't know what to say,' said Gregor finally.

'I understand,' said Mrs Mitchell without smiling.

He was about to invite her in when, suddenly, there was a whirl of noise and movement, and Islay burst out of the house onto the pavement. She was wearing a new dress, bought in honour of the occasion, and had a ribbon in her hair, delighted there were so many people about and in the mood to show off. Her parents still couldn't get used to the fact that she could work off her natural energy without them being terrified.

She stopped suddenly when she saw Mrs Mitchell though, who had made a small sound.

'Do you want to come inside?' said Gregor. More people were crowding round now. Mrs Mitchell didn't even hear him. Lissa steadied her with her arm.

'This is . . .?' she asked in just above a whisper. Lissa nodded.

'I'm Islay!' said Islay cheerfully.

Mrs Mitchell looked at her for a long moment, tears rolling down her face.

'Can I . . .?' she said suddenly, looking at Islay's parents.

'Do you mind, Islay?' said Gregor, realising instantly what she was asking. Islay, who had been well briefed by Cormac, opened her arms wide.

Mrs Mitchell took one tottering step forward, then another. Then she quietly leant her head forward and pressed it against the little girl's chest, and held it there, Islay for once standing still, so she could hear her son's heart beating, beating, beating.

The street turned silent, and when Mrs Mitchell straightened up again, tears in her eyes, Islay grinning her usual toothy grin, Islay's mother walked up to her.

'I am your child's mother now,' she said calmly. 'And you are Islay's. Your child is my child. And my child is yours.'

Mrs Mitchell nodded, and together they disappeared into the house. And Cormac and Lissa squeezed their hands together, hard.

Acknowledgements

It is incredibly useful for a writer for her two best friends from school to be a doctor and a lawyer, and I unabashedly hit them up for free help on this book (although all errors or simple fiction smoothing – few thing come to court as quickly as they do here, alas – are of course mine).

So huge thanks – and love, as always – to Karen Murphy, FRCS, and Alison Woodall, BA (Hons) Law.

Also Muriel Gray for plant help, Claire and Fredi Melo for helping me out with the Albanian – *faleminderit!* – and Rona Monroe, my secret Fairy Plot Godmother.

Huge thanks to Jo Unwin, Maddie West, Lucy Malagoni, Milly Reilly, Donna Greaves, Joanna Kramer, Charlie King (NICE BABY YOU GOT THERE), David Shelley, Stephanie Melrose, Gemma Shelley and all at Little, Brown; Deborah Schneider, Rachel Kahan, Dan Mallory, Alexander Cochran, Jake Smith-Bosanquet and Kate Burton.

And finally, as they deserve top billing: I am so thrilled we were allowed to use not only 'I'm Gonna Be (500 Miles)', but also lines from 'Sunshine on Leith' thanks to one of the best bands in the known universe, the Proclaimers, and the best management in the business, Braw Management.

Massive thanks are due to Sandra McKay and the estimable Kenny MacDonald as well as Sarah Sharp at Warner Chappell Music and of course the amazing brothers themselves. If they're not a band you're familiar with, you're in for such a treat. I apologise once more for the shocking illustration.

Read on for an exclusive
sneak peek at Jenny's
heart-stopping new novel

Sunrise
by the Sea

Chapter One

The sun had been out earlier that day, and the family had all gone out to play.

If you were to glance at the family, you probably wouldn't notice anything strange at first.

It would probably make you smile to realise that the children were twins, and that they each took after a parent so convincingly – the boy his father's double, with a shock of unruly blond hair and a wide smiling face; the little girl more cautious-looking, with freckles and her mother's strawberry-blonde hair and pale skin.

Look closer and you would also see something flapping around them, and assume there was something wrong with your vision, because what on *earth* was a puffin doing there?

Avery and Daisy had come tumbling down the lighthouse stairs in their usual noisy way.

For the first year or two of their lives, the stairgate had never been opened and had basically confined the children to the barracks of the sunny ground-floor kitchen, because Polly Miller, née

Waterford, was terrified of them tumbling down the lighthouse's circular staircases and cracking their heads open. It was an even stupider idea to live in a lighthouse than it had been before the children, love it as they may.

But her hopes of keeping them safe were completely thwarted when, around eighteenth months or so, she looked away for two seconds then turned back to see Avery holding up the bolt while Daisy turned it, and Neil (the puffin) standing on the gate, almost as if it was his idea. He certainly fluttered up the stairs guiltily as soon as Polly caught them. The days of the stairgate were numbered. She remembered it as if it were yesterday.

'Now,' she had said patiently, as she had a million times before, pulling them on to her lap on the squishy threadbare sofa, the blond head so like Huckle's; Daisy so like her, 'we don't go upstairs.'

'Ustairs,' repeated Avery. Daisy nodded. 'Ustairs . . . NO?'

Huckle had come in for lunch then, and grinned, as the twins scrambled down and hurtled across the flagstone floor shouting 'DADA!'

'Are you teaching them that going upstairs is the most exciting thing in the world again?'

'They opened the stairgate. Working as a team.'

Huckle hoisted the two little people up, one arm each.

'Oh, you are brilliant,' he said, as they giggled, and he nuzzled them both.

'It is *not* brilliant,' said Polly. 'They start scrambling up there and someone is going to fall and kill themselves.'

'I thought that's why we had two,' said Huckle, heading towards the stove.

Now, four years on, they had indeed both tumbled down several times, seemingly without injury, and retained the same basic gang set-up – boy, girl, puffin – that took getting into mischief to new levels all the time.

'I always thought Neil would have been jealous of the babies,' Polly was saying now, as they watched the three of them trying to play swingball – Neil hovering, then flying up when the ball came round – while she and Huckle sat out in preciously warm spring sunshine.

The lawn streamed down towards the rocks, and normally it was too windy to sit out there, but there was a spot, just behind a low wall, where the wind was blocked and you could lie down and feel the sun on your face and just for a moment everything would be warm and lovely. Unfortunately it also blocked Polly's views of the twins, so it necessitated bobbing up and down every couple of minutes like a meerkat, and steeling yourself against the wind.

'Neil was unbelievably jealous of the babies!' said Huckle, astonished she'd forgotten. 'You were in a milk coma. A nuclear bomb could have gone off and you wouldn't have noticed unless a piece of dust had gotten on the babies. What do you think all those marks are on the cradles?'

'I thought they were just features.'

'Peck marks!'

'Oh goodness. Bad bird.'

'He's a terrible bird,' said Huckle with equanimity. 'Almost like you shouldn't keep wild sea birds in captivity in the first place.'

'You shouldn't,' agreed Polly. 'He keeps me.'

When Polly had first moved to Mount Polbearne, alone and nervous years ago, following the collapse of her business and engagement, in short order, a baby puffling had crashed into the bakery one night. After nursing his broken wing back to health, she had tried to release him back into the wild, but he hadn't taken. Neil had decided that living with a baker was infinitely preferable to diving into the cold sea every day to find fish, and Huckle was inclined to agree with him.

They both watched Neil sweep around the children.

'I mean, he *could*—' Huckle started.

'Neil can't babysit!' said Polly sternly.

'I know, I know,' said Huckle. 'I just thought it might be a nice night to sit out at Andy's' – Andy ran the local pub and a superb chippy – 'or even go up to the posh place and have a glass of wine. Without some small monsters wriggling all over it.'

'We could call Kerensa,' suggested Polly, meaning Reuben's wife, their rich friends who lived on the mainland.

'I'm not in a Reuben-handling mood,' said Huckle. 'Plus . . . Lowin.'

Even though the twins were miles off, they bounced over.

'ARE WE GOING TO LOWIN'S?'

Lowin, Reuben and Kerensa's son, who was now almost eight years old, was the hero of the twins' lives, living as he did in a huge Tony Stark mansion with every computer game and every piece of Playmobil ever made. Lowin, for his part, tolerated the children more or less, as long as they did everything he said in every game and obeyed his every whim, just like the paid staff did. Daisy and Avery were his very willing slaves and were quite happy to go along with whatever Lowin's newest phase was. Normally it was fine when it was an Avengers obsession phase, or a racing cars obsession phase. But Lowin's latest obsessive phase was snakes, and despite Kerensa's promises, Polly was never 100 per cent certain Reuben wasn't about to buy him a huge boa constrictor and just let him wear it everywhere like a scarf until it ate Neil.

'Not today.'

The twins' faces looked downcast.

'But he's getting a huge slide shaped like a snake! The biggest ever!'

'That sounds dangerous,' said Polly, getting up. 'Okay. It's just leftover chicken.'

'That's all right,' said Huckle, who was about to hit the road again, repping his honey business. Times had been tough – there had been floods all over the West Country and a lot of business were finding it difficult to keep going but he was doing his best. 'It's good to have home-cooked food. It's going to be nothing but restaurants and hotel food for a fortnight.'

'Say that like you're sad about it,' pleaded Polly.

'I am!' said Huckle. And then, more seriously, grabbing her hand. 'You know I am.'

'I wish I was going off to stay in hotels.'

'It's not the Ritz! It's a Travelodge off the A40!'

'I know. But anywhere is the Ritz with you.'

They shared a kiss. He hated going away. But he had to. They had enough trouble keeping their heads above water as it was.

'Think of the windows,' he said.

'I know, I know.'

If they could replace the lighthouse's ancient rattly single-paned glass with English Heritage-approved double glazing, the difference it would make in the quality of both of their lives would be immeasurable. No more icy plunges down the circular staircase; no more painful hauling themselves out of bed.

Although, who knew? The house might never be warm to other people's standards – Polly's mother's, for example, or Kerensa's, or, well, anyone's, really. But to the four of them – the children had never known anything else – it was just perfect. Huckle had put an old TV in the master bedroom, and through the cosy nights of winter all four of them curled up with the electric blanket on, Neil hopping on the nightstand, watching *Moana*, and it was, windows or not, as happy a place as Polly could possibly imagine.

And now spring was coming! And if Huckle made enough this year they were going to get windows *and* a new boiler, so there was very little to complain about, thought Polly, as she headed back into the kitchen, listening to the merry voices of the twins demanding that their father became a tiger MEEJETLY which he obligingly did, growling so fiercely that Polly wondered if Avery would get upset. Daisy would dry his tears if he did.

She added barley and vegetables to the chicken stock she had boiled up from the roast, happily looking forward to when Huckle would be home for the summer, and the tourists would start to arrive for the season and they would be cheerfully flat out. She couldn't wait to feel the sun warm on her face again, not the endless winter storms that had seemed to arrive every single weekend.

For months the rain had thrown itself against the windows and the house was full of wet wellingtons and the children got cranky when she couldn't get them out enough, the pleasure of building dens indoors and helping Mama bake having grown stale. The storms had been getting worse – climate change, she knew – and the winters were getting harder.

'What's up when I'm away?' Huckle asked now, following her in while simultaneously half-listening to Avery talk about how Lowin was getting the biggest snake in the world for his birthday.

'Usual,' said Polly. 'Oh no, I forgot! Reuben's waifs and strays are arriving!'

Chapter Two

At that moment, over in Exeter on the mainland, one of Reuben's waifs and strays had no idea that was what she was about to become.

Caius – 'pronounced "keys"', as he liked to tell people snottily when they attempted it for the first time, unless they by some chance got it right, in which case he would say, 'It's "ky-us", actually?' – was banging heavily on his flatmate's bedroom door, but to no avail.

'Marisa!'

It was, fair enough, hard to hear over the racket.

Caius theoretically liked having lots of friends who were DJs, or said they were, but then he made the mistake of asking them to come and play at his parties and it was horrendous and they all squabbled with each other over how expensive their headphones were, and mixed up their stupid boxes and vied to play very obscure stuff, and frankly, it was a racket.

If he'd cared about his neighbours he would have factored that in too, but, being rich and good-looking, Caius so rarely met people that didn't like him that he often found it hard to imagine what that might be like.

The flat was absolutely heaving, mostly with people he knew, kind of, some he didn't, but they were good-looking and appeared well-off, so that was fine too.

But he needed the little room his parents had insisted he let out – something to do with 'learning how to take responsibility' or 'managing efficiently'; it had been hard to tell, he had been on the worst comedown while they'd been talking to him and he still had his earpods in so it could have been anything.

'Marisa,' he yelled again, as loud as he could. He winced. Caius didn't really like shouting; he liked drawling or, even better, not saying anything at all and merely waving a hand at waiters bringing him things.

'Marisa! Come on, it's a party! Can't you make us some canapés?'

Still no reply. He pouted. She must have heard him by now.

Marisa used to be fun. Well, not *fun*, exactly, she had a real job and went to bed at a reasonable hour. But she cooked and smiled and was funny and he quite liked someone kind of looking after him.

Then she'd gone all quiet and sort of vanished and he knew she'd told him why, some family shiz, but he kept forgetting, and it was really terribly tiresome.

'Marisa! People want to use this room! For coats!'

'And also sex and taking drugs,' said one of a trio of people in black eyeliner appearing behind him, the other two vigorously agreeing.

'No! Totally none of those things, just probably coats!' said Caius. He frowned. 'You know there's tequila out here, right? There's tequila out here and none in where you are, which means I don't understand you *at all*.'

Well, they agreed about one thing, thought Marisa. Because she didn't understand herself either.

Chapter Three

Inside her little box room – like many of these expensive new builds in Exeter, the main room was flashy and showy with a big glass wall and a balcony, but the smaller bedrooms were done on the cheap – Marisa Rossi sat on the end of her bed, knees up to her chin, headphones on, the clatter beyond the door more or less white noise.

Another party. Another night when the rest of the world was out and about, having fun.

Everyone else seemed fine. Everyone else always seemed fine.

And, in the scheme of things, losing a grandparent was hardly heartbreaking loss. A lot of people lose grandparents. Everyone, when you think about it.

And they all still seemed able to go to parties. Everyone but her.

But somehow, she could only think of her *nonno*, Carlo: her kind, funny grandfather in Imperia, Italy, descended from generations of shipbuilders – a tradition that had only stopped with her mother, Lucia, who had left for the UK to find a better life, and married a man from Livorno, just down the road. Marisa's father couldn't bear the cold and the rain and left England- and Lucia alone, with Marisa and her brother, Gino. Marisa tried not to take it personally.

But her grandfather had stepped into the breach, and then some. Her fondest memories were golden: holidays spent in Italy; long days on the hot windy shores of Imperia, as the great big industrial ships rolled past; late dreamy evenings at restaurants as she ate spaghetti vongole and fell asleep under the table as the adults talked and laughed long into the night; cool hands rubbing in cream to sunburned shoulders; ice creams as big as a beach ball; stones underfoot as you ran into the water; the pungent scent of the exhausts of the Vespas of the young men gunning around the town, a contrast with the smartly uniformed *navale* stationed there; the long rolling rhythms of Italian summers.

Abandoned in her teens for holidays with her British friends on cheap packages in the Balearics, drinking shots and laughing uproariously, they sometimes, in her memory, felt like a dream; snatches of an older language tugging somewhere at the fraying edges of her brain, another person, happy and free, in big fussy-bowed dresses her grandmother – who was as stiff as her grandfather was loving – liked to buy her, and which she adored and her mother thought were absolutely awful.

Then life interfered, took her to college and on to Exeter and a job she used to love – being a registrar for the council. Births, marriages and deaths, it required a combination of a love for and interest in people, with a fairly meticulous approach to record-keeping, and nice handwriting. Marisa was not a show-offy type of person at all, but she was incredibly proud of her handwriting.

Then Carlo had died.

'There's no rhyme nor reason,' her nice but very harassed GP had told her, when she explained the insomnia, the constant crying and, increasingly difficult for work, her encroaching fear of leaving the house and speaking to people, that seemed to get worse every day. 'Grief affects everyone differently. It seems to me you have an anxiety disorder, shading into agoraphobia. I would suggest the best course is antidepressants.'

'My grandfather died!' Marisa had said. 'I'm sad! I'm not "depressed"! This is normal.'

'I'm just saying that they would almost certainly help.'

'But then ...'

Marisa fell silent.

'What if I don't even miss him any more? What if I don't feel anything?'

The GP, too, fell silent, wanting to be reassuring; unable to mislead.

'The wait for counselling is very long,' she said, finally.

'Put me on it,' said Marisa. 'Please. Please.'

'Okay,' said the GP.

'Why?' said Marisa. 'Why am I the only person who can't get on with their life?'

The nice GP shook her head sadly.

'It only looks that way,' she said. 'Don't be fooled for a moment.'

She hadn't been able to make it in time. He'd been out pruning in the garden, in the big black hat he wore all the time, probably, and had collapsed. No time to call, no time to say goodbye to the most important man in her life.

People saying he wouldn't have known a thing about it, that it was better that way, did not, in Marisa's opinion, know what the hell they were talking about. Did they seriously think he wouldn't have wanted to say goodbye to the family he loved so much: her mother Lucia, her sister Ann Angela (actually Anna Angelica but quite the mouthful by anyone's standards), the boys, and ... well, her?

Somehow, she found the funeral, which she had to dash to, even more difficult. Her *nonna*, or grandmother, garbed in black, was cross and busy in the kitchen, insisting on cooking for thousands and refusing, in Marisa's eyes, to face up to what was happening at all. And there was so many people – cousins, family, friends, bloody butcher and baker and candlestick maker – talking about how much they'd loved him (and, by inference, how much he had loved them in return), that the entire noisy family felt overwhelming on that wet October Italian day, and there was so much shouting and noise and Marisa, who had always been quiet, had retreated further into her shell, worrying that, after all, the love she had felt from her grandfather had meant little, amid the clamour. He had been quiet too. She yearned for his big hand in her smaller one; couldn't believe that she would never feel it again. But everyone else's grief had felt louder, more pressing. And so she had taken hers home, let it sit, forming inside her, more and more layers building up, cementing it in place, holding her down like a ball and chain, and as the months had passed she'd found it increasingly difficult to leave the house at all.

'Do you think you need your aura cleansed?' Caius had said, and she had given him a look, but Caius was one of those people who could never notice when he was being annoying, and probably wouldn't believe you if you'd told him. He'd been sent from the US to do a very expensive course in something or other near some uncle, but Marisa hadn't seen him go once.

'You just need to come out and get pissed up, durr, obviously,' said her best friend Olive, but she somehow couldn't face doing that either.

She pretended she had evenings out planned with work colleagues, which was a complete lie, but the other lie would be to pretend she had a date, which she didn't, or she could be honest and say she was occasionally seeing Mahmoud again, but they all hated his guts for being a lazy cadging loser (albeit a very, *very* handsome, fit, lazy cadging loser) so she didn't want to say that either. Aged twenty-nine, Marisa's romantic history was ... not patchy exactly. But being an introvert meant that often she hadn't quite managed to pluck up the courage to tell people she didn't like them that much, and things could bumble along, or she would lack the courage to make it clear to people she did like that she liked them, and they'd pass her by. When Olive had fancied Keegan, for example, she'd stuck on her false eyelashes and her push-up bra and simply turned up everywhere he was. And now they had bought a flat together and were planning on a baby and Marisa was delighted for them, of course she was, but the world was easier, she felt, on the confident Olives than on the shyer girls. Also, Olive pointed out that Mahmoud treated her like a doormat and the fact that that was completely true didn't make her feel any better.

Anyway, because she didn't like going over to his any more to watch him play computer games – Mahmoud was generally too lazy or a bit stoned to come over – that didn't matter, and gradually, she'd found, as she sat and read over old letters from her grandfather or dug up old photographs of an evening, that it was just easier not to go out, much easier.

She told herself she'd do it tomorrow, or maybe the weekend.

And she volunteered for more and more of the admin work that didn't mean having to go into the office. Nazreen, her boss, was puzzled – Marisa had always been so good at facing customers – not an extrovert, but calm and reassuring in her dealings with everyone. Now, though, she had become so terribly timid. Facing the public was so much the fun of their job, always had been. But although she couldn't understand it, Nazreen was too busy to question what was going on. Marisa was still as efficient as ever and she let it go.

Oddly, Caius was the one who didn't give up.

'Have you done your ten thousand steps? You know you could probably do with a mantra.'

'No thanks.'

'MDMA?'

'No!'

'Okay! Hey, what should we have for dinner?'

He looked at her imploringly. When Marisa had moved in he had been pleased: she was nice, tidy, pretty but not his type (which was unusual, as the people who were Caius' type was just about every-body), and best of all, she cooked. Caius didn't eat very much – you didn't stay model thin and cool if you did – but when he did, he liked it to be the very best.

And now, all of that had gone. She looked tired and sad and miserable and there was never any food. This wasn't fun in the slightest.

Inside, Marisa was gripped with fear. What was happening to her? She wasn't crazy, was she?

She just ... didn't like going out any more. The world seemed scarier. Nobody would mind if she just stayed in, would they? She wasn't bothering anyone. Just keeping nice and quiet in the back ...

And then sometimes at night she would wake up breathless, and panicking, and think to herself, *My life is going by*, and find it hard to breathe, and think that she must, she must do something, and would go and pour a bath so hot she could barely sit in it, the water fierce against her skin, driving away her thoughts in a cloud of steam, staring out at the dark, thinking, *Is this it now?*

Christmas had made everything notably worse. Lucia had wanted a big family get-together to remember her grandfather, and the thought of it had made Marisa a bit panicky. In the end, she hadn't been able to go; to face everyone again, cheery and loud and getting on with their lives.

She'd tried looking for other things to do, and making excuses, but Lucia was having none of it, and in the end there had been a horrible bust-up on the family whatsapp. Her brother Gino had phoned, then Lucia had, in dramatic tears calling her selfish, and gradually they had ended up in one of those heated family rows. Usually when this happened someone would eventually have to get up and make a cup of tea and, at the end of an excruciating amount of time would have to shout, 'Anyone else want one?', and after that everything would be mended. But this time, not being in physical proximity to each other, that hadn't happened. And so nothing got mended. It had shocked both Marisa and her mother, Marisa thought. Lucia was used to Marisa being a quiet, acquiescent little mouse and now she'd made a stand.

Even though, Marisa knew deep down, the stand was no good for her. She should have been with her family.

But guilt added a new layer of calcification to the stone inside her that was dragging her down and keeping her in; layer upon layer of sadness and grief and worry that was growing too large for her to do anything at all.

She had spent Christmas inside, on her own, fielding increasingly nasty texts from her mother, not so subtly implying she was doing it for attention. She'd gone to working full time from home. Her appointment with the NHS therapist still hadn't come up. And, three months on, things were looking worse, not better.

The morning after the party, Caius came to a decision that was going to make things worse still.

~ DREAM WITH ~

JENNY COLGAN

Keep in touch with Jenny and her readers:

 JennyColganBooks @jennycolgan

 JennyColganBooks

Check out Jenny's website and sign up to her newsletter for all the latest book news plus mouth-watering recipes.

www.jennycolgan.com

LOVE TO READ?

Join **The Little Book Café** for competitions, sneak peeks and more.

 TheLittleBookCafe @littlebookcafe